Praise for
CHILD OF FIRE
The first book in the
Twenty Palaces series

"Excellent reading . . . has a lot of things I love in a book: a truly dark and sinister world, delicious tension and suspense, violence so gritty you'll get something in your eye just reading it, and a gorgeously flawed protagonist. Take this one to the checkout counter. Seriously."
—JIM BUTCHER

"A fast-moving, entertaining story, with an interesting take on magic and its consequences, not to mention tantalizing glimpses of a clearly well realized backstory."
—Booklist

"An engaging mash-up, a fantasy noir written from the unlikely perspective of a hired goon . . . This supernatural thriller is perfect for fans of Jim Butcher's The Dresden Files, or anyone who enjoys rough, two-fisted tales of magic and mayhem."

D0963045

The Twenty Palaces Series
by Harry Connolly

CHILD OF FIRE
GAME OF CAGES

GAME OF CAGES

OF

A TWENTY PALACES NOVEL

HARRY CONNOLLY

BALLANTINE BOOKS • NEW YORK

A Del Rey Mass Market Original

Copyright © 2010 by Harry Connolly
Excerpt from a forthcoming novel by Harry Connolly copyright © 2010 by Harry Connolly

Published in the United States by Del Rey, an imprint of The Random House Publishing Group, a division of Random House, Inc., New York.

DEL REY is a registered trademark and the Del Rey colophon is a trademark of Random House, Inc.

This book contains an excerpt from a forthcoming novel by Harry Connolly. This excerpt has been set for this edition only and may not reflect the final content of the forthcoming edition.

ISBN 978-0-345-50890-4

Printed in the United States of America

www.delreybooks.com

9 8 7 6 5 4 3 2 1

For MaryAnn

CHAPTER ONE

It was three days before Christmas, and I was not in prison. I couldn't understand why I was free. I hadn't hidden my face during the job in Hammer Bay. I hadn't used a fake name. I honestly hadn't expected to survive.

I had, though. The list of crimes I'd committed there included breaking and entering, arson, assault, and murder. And what could I have said in my defense? That the people I'd killed really deserved it?

Washington State executes criminals by lethal injection, and for that first night in my own bed, I imagined I was lying on a prison cot in a room with a glass wall, a needle in my arm.

That hadn't happened. Instead, I'd met with an attorney the society hired, kept my mouth shut, stood in at least a dozen lineups, and waited for the fingerprint and DNA analysis to come back. When it did, they let me go. Maybe I'd only dreamed about the people I'd killed.

So, months later, I was wearing my white supermarket polo shirt, stocking an endcap with gift cards for other stores. It was nearly nine at night, and I had just started my shift. I liked the late shift. It gave me something to do when the restlessness became hard to take.

At the front of the store, a woman was questioning the manager, Harvey. He gestured toward me. At first I figured her for another detective. Even though the last press release about me stated I'd been the victim of identity theft and the police were searching for other suspects, detectives still dropped by my work and home at random times to take another run at me. They weren't fooled. They knew.

But she didn't have a cop's body language. She wore casual gray office clothes and sensible work shoes, an outfit so ordinary I barely noticed it. She walked briskly toward me, clutching a huge bag. Harvey followed.

She was tall and broad in the hips, and had long, delicate hands, large eyes, and a pointed chin. Her skin color showed that she had both black and white parentage, which in this country made her black. "You're Ray Lilly, aren't you?" she asked.

"Who's asking?"

"My name is Catherine Little. I'm a friend of your mother's."

That hit me like a punch in the gut. The last time I saw my mother, I was fourteen years old and headed into juvie. She was not someone I thought about. Ever. "Who are you again?"

"I'm Catherine. I work with your mother. I'm a friend of hers. She asked me to contact you."

"Where is she?" I peered through the glass doors into the parking lot, but it was pitch-dark outside.

"Okay. This is the hard part. Your mom's in the hospital. She's had some . . . issues the last few days. She asked for you."

I laid my hand on the gift cards on the cart beside me. They toppled over, ruining the neat little stacks I'd been working with. I began to tidy them absentmindedly. "When?"

Catherine laid her hand on my elbow. "Right now," she said. "It has to be right now."

Something about the way she said that was off. I looked at her again. There was a look of urgency on her face, but there was something else there, too. Something calculated.

This woman didn't know my mother. I knew it then as clearly as if she was wearing a sandwich-board sign that read I AM LYING TO YOU.

Her expression changed. My face must have given me away, because she didn't look quite so sympathetic now, but her expression was still urgent. "We have to hurry," she said.

Harvey laid his hand on my shoulder like a friendly uncle. "Ray, go get your coat. I'll clock you out."

I told Catherine I'd meet her out front and went into the break room. She had to be with the Twenty Palace Society; there was no one else who would want me. I had been dreading the day they would contact me again. Dreading it and wishing for it.

I grabbed my flannel jacket and hurried outside without speaking to or looking at anyone. I could feel my co-workers watching me. Just the thought of talking to Harvey—or anyone else—about my mom, even if it was a bullshit cover story, made me want to quit on the spot.

Catherine waited behind the wheel of an Acura sedan, one of the most stolen cars in the country. I sat in the passenger seat and buckled up. She had a sweet GPS setup and some electronic equipment I didn't recognize. I squinted at a narrow slot with a number pad on the side—I could have sworn it was a tiny fax machine. While I had been living the straight life, cars had moved on and left me behind. She pulled into the street.

"I'm sorry," she said. "That really hit you hard, didn't it? They told me to contact you that way. I didn't realize . . . Sorry." She seemed sincere if a little standoffish.

"Who's 'they'?" I asked, just to be sure. "Who are you?"

"My name is Catherine. Really. 'They' are the Twenty Palace Society. We have an emergency and I need help. You're the only other member in this part of the country at the moment."

My scalp tingled. It was true.

Part of me was furious that they'd dangled my mother in front of me like bait, but at the same time I wanted to lunge across the hand brake and hug her.

Finally. Finally! The society had come for me. It was like a jolt to the base of my spine. *Finally, something worth living for*.

"Are you okay?" she asked warily.

"I'm okay." I did my best to keep my voice neutral, but I didn't succeed all that well. Christ, she'd even said I was a *member* of the society. I belonged. "We need to go by my place."

There were no tattoos peeking from the cuffs of her sleeves and the collar of her shirt. She had no sigils on her clothes or the interior of the car. No visible magic. She might have had something hidden, of course. I was tempted to rummage through her pockets to search for spells.

She drove to my place without asking for my address. My hand was trembling and I gripped my leg to hide the adrenaline rush. I'd thought about the society often over the last seven months. Aside from a visit from an old guy with a brush mustache who'd debriefed me about Hammer Bay, I'd heard nothing from them. I hadn't even gotten a call from Annalise letting me know how she was. I had been telling myself I wanted to be cut loose. I had been telling myself I wanted to be forgotten.

But now they had come for me again and every traffic light and Christmas decoration seemed saturated with color. In fact, all my senses seemed to have been turned up to ten. I felt alive again, and I was grateful for it.

At my aunt's house, I had Catherine drive around to the back. I climbed the stairs to my mother-in-law apartment above the garage and let myself in. I went to the bookshelf and pulled a slip of paper from between two yard-sale hardcovers. It had been covered on both sides with mailing tape and had laminate over that. A sigil had been drawn on one side.

My ghost knife. It was the only spell I had, except for the protective tattoos on my chest and forearms. They didn't count, though; the ghost knife was a spell I'd created myself, and I could feel it as if it was a part of me.

I slipped it into my jacket pocket and looked around. What else did I need? I had my wallet and keys and even, for the first time in my life, a credit card. Should I pack clean underwear and a change of clothes?

Catherine honked. No time for that, I guess. I rushed into the bathroom and grabbed my toothbrush. Then I wrote a quick note to my aunt to tell her I'd be gone for a while and please don't worry. Catherine honked again before I was done. I carried the note down the stairs and annoyed Catherine further by running toward the back door of the house. I stuck the note on the back-side of the wreath on the screen door, rattling it in the frame.

The inner door suddenly swung inward. Aunt Theresa was there, looking up at me. "Ray?" She wore a knit cap over her wispy gray hair and a bright red-and-green scarf around her neck. Cold, she was always cold. It was one of the many things about her that made me worry.

"Oh! I thought this was movie night. I was leaving you a note." She must have come to see who was honking.

She popped open the screen door and took the note with fingers bent sideways from arthritis. "Movie night is tomorrow, dear." She opened the note and read it. The note didn't mention my mother—it was Catherine's cover story, not mine, and I wasn't going to lie to my aunt about her little sister.

I glanced at the room behind her, expecting to see

Uncle Karl in his badge and blue uniform, scowling at me. He wasn't there.

Aunt Theresa looked up me. "Will you be back for Christmas?"

The way she said it startled me. Of course I had gifts to give her and Karl, but I hadn't expected her to care if I . . . I felt like an idiot.

"I hope so," I said, and meant it.

She shuffled forward and hugged me. I hugged her back. She knew a little about what I did. Not about the society itself, and not enough to get into trouble, but enough to worry. "Be careful."

We let go. I backed down the stairs and hurried to Catherine's car. I should have said something reassuring to her, but it was too late now. Time to go.

I climbed into the Acura and belted up. My adrenaline was high, and I couldn't help but smile. Catherine didn't like that smile. "Do you have everything now?"

The ghost knife in my pocket felt like a live wire. "Yep."

She rumbled through the alley and pulled into the street. I thought it would be best to let her tell me what was going on when she was ready, but after driving in silence for four blocks, I couldn't hold back.

"What's the emergency?"

"Well . . ." she said, then fell silent while she negotiated a busy intersection. Her body language had changed again—she was irritated. I wasn't sure why; didn't it make sense for me to stop at home before I went on a job?

"Well," she said again, "earlier today we found out there's going to be an auction. Tonight. In fact, it might be taking place right now, although I hope not. I went an hour out of my way to pick you up, so you better be worth it."

This was a sudden change in tone. I wondered where it had come from. "I'll do my best," I said, but that made her scowl and blow air out of her nose. "What's being auctioned?"

"A predator."

That was the answer I didn't want to hear. Predators were weird supernatural creatures out of the Empty Spaces. I'd seen two so far, along with the pile of corpses they left behind. "Do you know what kind?"

"What kind?" She seemed to think this was an idiotic question, but I had no idea why. "No. I don't know what kind."

"Okay." I was careful not to snap at her.

"Who are you?" she asked. She looked me up and down. I didn't feel a lot of friendliness coming from her.

"I'm Ray Lilly," I answered, keeping my tone neutral. "Remember? You just pulled me out of work."

"I know your name," she said, leaving out the word *dumbass* but implying it anyway. "What were you doing at that supermarket? What are you doing in that apartment?"

"Working. Living."

"That's not cover for a mission? Okay. What I want to know is who you are in the society. Because you are definitely not a peer. Are you an apprentice? An ally?"

"I'm not any of those things," I said. "I'm Annalise Powliss's wooden man."

She exhaled sharply, then laughed to herself a little. "For God's sake," she said, then fell silent. After a few seconds more, she pulled into a Pizza Hut parking lot. She didn't turn off the engine. "All right," she said, and I could tell by her tone that I wouldn't like what she was about to say. "Somebody fucked up. You shouldn't be here, not with me, and I shouldn't have been sent a fucking hour out of my way to pick up a fucking wooden man, not on a supposedly emergency job. What's the point in having you along? I don't need you and I don't want you. Hell, I don't even like looking at you, knowing what you are.

"So here's the deal: you keep quiet and do what I say, or you get out right now. I have a long night's work ahead of me, and I don't need you getting in my way. So, which is it going to be? Because if following orders is going to be too much for you, you need to be out of my car and have yourself a nice day."

She stared at me, waiting for a response. It had been a while since anyone had spoken to me like that. If Catherine had been a guy . . .

Not that using my fists had ever turned out well for me. Old habits don't just die hard, they make living hard, too. "You must be part of the diplomatic wing of the society."

She sat back, rolled her eyes, and sighed. "What the hell did I do to deserve this?"

"I'll tell you what you did," I answered. "You talked to me like I ran over your dog. Whatever your problem is, it has nothing to do with me."

"Oh no?" She turned the key, shutting off the engine. "Bad enough to have a peer or an ally along. Then I would spend all my time praying the collateral damage doesn't hit me. But every wooden man I've ever met was either a stone-skulled thug, terminally ill, or a terminally ill stone-skulled thug." She made sure to look me straight in the eye as she said it. She had guts. I would have liked her if she wasn't so obnoxious. "Which are you?"

"Well, I'm not terminally ill."

She frowned. I'd lived down to her expectations. "Well, that's just dandy."

"If you order me to get out of your car," I said, "I'll hop out right here. I'm not going to ride with someone who doesn't want me. But that's the only way I'm getting out. When the friendly guy from the society turns up to debrief me, I'm not going to tell him I *chose* not to go. Understand?"

She turned away from me. The society had kept me out of jail, somehow. I had no idea what would happen if I refused to take a job. Would they kill me? Would they lift whatever spell kept the cops off my front door? I had exactly one person handy who I could ask, and she was trying to kick me out of her car.

Pizza-delivery guys carried red cases across the lot. They didn't seem happy about the way we were parked. I wondered how much they made a month.

"All right then," Catherine said. "We go on the job, and you take your orders from me."

"That ain't going to happen, either," I told her. As Annalise's wooden man, I went when she said *go* and I did when she said *do,* but that didn't mean I was going to take orders from everyone in the society. Not unless Annalise told me to. "If you have a good idea, I'll be happy to go along with it. If not, then not. That's the only deal you're going to get. If that's not good enough, *you* can explain why you gave the boot to the guy the society sent you an hour out of your way to pick up."

She chewed on that for a while, then pulled into the street and drove onto the ramp to the highway. We weren't talking, apparently, but I could bear it. At least she didn't want to kill me.

We drove to 520 and headed east toward the Cascades. Two hours and several increasingly narrow roads later, we turned off just before we came to a pass. We drove north for a short while, following a winding two-lane highway through the mountains.

It occurred to me that Catherine might have a report or a file about the job we were on. I asked, but she shook her head. Either she didn't have one, or she wasn't sharing. They came to the same thing for me.

We changed roads a couple of more times, weaving and winding through the Cascade foothills. We didn't play music. Catherine was a very good driver, although I doubted most people would recognize it; she had complete control of the car, held the same steady speed, and had excellent lane discipline. Nothing flashy, but she knew what she was doing. I wondered how much time she spent behind the wheel every day.

We skirted a small town, passing along a road in the hillside above it. It was late, but Christmas lights still burned in the town below. It felt strange to be traveling several hundred feet above a star, but I was probably just tired.

I didn't see the name of the town and realized I had no idea where we were. It didn't matter. By my watch, it was just past eleven. The road and rain forest looked fake in the headlights, like a TV show. I felt adrift in the darkness.

We curved south and quickly came upon a high black iron fence on one side of the road. Catherine pulled to the shoulder and checked her GPS against a slip of paper in her pocket. "This is it. The gate should be up ahead."

"I can cut through the fence," I told her. The long drive had eased tensions between us. "We could hide the car and sneak onto the property."

"That would take too long. The driveway from the gate to the house stretches three miles, and the terrain would be difficult. There's also a second road off the grounds that heads east-northeast toward town and a whole twisty mess of access roads and horse trails, otherwise I'd suggest we hide outside the gate and snap photos of drivers and license plates of everyone who leaves. We're going to have to risk driving it."

I nodded and kept quiet. After a few minutes we came to the gate. Catherine drove by, slowing slightly to allow us to look up the driveway. I didn't see any cars or guards, but a heavy chain held the two halves of the gate together.

She drove down the road a ways, turned off her headlights, then did a quick three-point turn. We approached the gate from the other side and stopped at the entrance. "I have a bolt cutter in the back," she said, reaching for the door.

"We don't need it," I said. I opened the passenger door and closed it as quietly as I could. The *chunk* sound it made was loud in the thin mountain air.

If there was an alarm system on the gate, it was hidden. There were no wires, electric trips, or warning signs. I took the ghost knife from my pocket. Holding it felt like holding my own hand.

I approached the chain snaked through the gate and laid the laminated edge of the ghost knife against it. *It cuts ghosts, magic, and dead things.* With a quick flick of my wrist, I slid the sheet of paper through the steel, slicing it in half.

Metal rods extended through the bottom of the gate into a hole in the asphalt. I cut those as well.

The chain came off in two pieces. They had been wrapped around the gate but not locked together. I hadn't needed the ghost knife at all.

I pushed the left gate open, making enough room for the Acura. No klaxons went off, no lights flashed, no Dobermans charged out of the darkness at me.

We drove up the driveway with our lights off. It was a winding road, dipping and curving around gullies and rock faces. I was glad Catherine had shot down my idea of crossing the estate on foot—it would have taken hours.

It occurred to me that, if the society wanted to get rid of me, this was the way to do it. Send a woman to pick me up. Dress her in bland, nondescript clothes. Drive all the way into the mountains. If this estate belonged to Annalise or one of the other peers, no one would ever find me.

I shook that off. A peer could just as easily throttle me

in my bed and burn down my apartment. Or pull my head off with their bare hands. They didn't need to be clever.

Catherine and I gasped at the same time as a curve in the road revealed a pair of headlights shining from around the next bend. She braked gently. I laid my hand on the door handle in case I needed to bolt from the car.

"Don't," Catherine said. The headlights were not moving toward us. In fact, they weren't moving at all. We backed up a few yards and turned down an access road I hadn't noticed. The tires crunched on downed branches and muddy gravel. She drove twenty yards, then shut off the engine. Once the sun rose, anyone on the drive above would be able to spot the car, but I hoped we would be gone by then.

We shut the doors as quietly as we could. Catherine changed from her office shoes into hiking boots and slung a pack over her shoulder, then followed me back to the driveway. My own black leather low-tops slipped in the mud.

Once back at the driveway, Catherine laid a long pine branch across the shoulder. She then placed a pinecone in the center of the asphalt.

With the access road to the car marked, we crept along the shoulder, staying just inside the line of trees. I heard the wind blowing above me, but I was sheltered down in the hills. Unfortunately, we were heading up. My jacket was too thin for December in the mountains, but I'd be okay if I kept dry.

I reached the edge of the curve. A BMW sat on the shoulder of the road, grille facing me, but the headlights were off. The lights actually came from a second vehicle: a panel truck on its side, the windshield cracked and the low beams shining into the trees across the road. The truck was lit by the headlights of a third car that I couldn't see from where I stood. I watched for a minute or so, waiting for the drivers to show up. They didn't.

Catherine crept up beside me and peered around the trunk of a tree. I wished I knew the hand signals TV commandos use. I leaned close to her and whispered: "Let me check it out. If no one shoots me, you follow."

The reflected headlights illuminated Catherine's face clearly. I saw her nod gratefully.

I rubbed the tattoos Annalise had put on my chest and forearms, but I couldn't feel anything. That was how they worked: where the marks covered my skin I was numb, but those marks could bounce bullets.

It wasn't much. My neck, my face and head, my back, my legs, and a couple of other places I didn't like to think about were not bulletproof, but it was more than most people had.

I darted from one tree to the next. The headlights lit the accident scene pretty well, but anyone who might be standing guard was well hidden. Or there was nothing to guard. To hell with this. I climbed down the embankment and walked along the shoulder.

The BMW was an xDrive 50i in a lovely burgundy. An X6. It was also empty. The license plate holder showed it belonged to a "luxury" rental agency. Out of habit, I checked the ignition. No keys. The driver's door was unlocked, though. I had always liked stealing BMWs. They were fun to drive and valuable enough to ship out of the country. That wasn't my life anymore, of course.

I jogged toward the toppled panel truck. I was too close to creep around in shadows, and it would have looked suspicious if I'd tried. Instead, I strode directly through the headlights, trying to make my body language say *I am a Good Samaritan.*

The truck was lying on the passenger side, with the

cab partly blocking the driveway. The mud beside it was smeared with footprints.

Standing by the roof, I pulled myself up and peered into the open driver's window. There was blood on the steering wheel and a bloody handprint on the side of the door.

Then I noticed the front driver's-side tire. It was dead flat, and there was a finger-poke hole in the metal rim.

A skid mark stretched from the middle of the road to just a few feet away. Uphill was a long, gentle slope, very unlike the terrain we'd passed on the estate so far. The trees were scant on that part of the hill, and at the far top I could see the lights of a house.

I walked around the front. There were no dents in the grille, so it was clear there'd been no collision. At the bottom of the truck, I could feel the drive train still giving off heat. Gas dripped out of a small rupture in the plastic gas tank.

Catherine jogged up beside me. "This accident just happened," I said.

"Did you notice the color on the roof?" she asked.

I followed her around the truck. Now that she'd told me it was there, I saw it immediately—there was a dark circle just under two feet in diameter on the part of the roof next to the ground. I knelt close to it. The blue paint of the truck was nearly black there, although it was difficult to judge color accurately in the moonlight.

Was this circle fresh paint? I picked up a stick and poked it.

"Don't—" Catherine said, but she was too late. One tap against the circle caused the whole area to crumble to dust, leaving a hole in the roof.

I jumped back, careful not to get any dust on me. "Holy shit," Catherine said. "What did that?"

"I was going to ask you," I said.

She took a flashlight from her bag and shined it down onto the pile of dust. It looked like fine metal filings. She turned the beam of light into the truck. "I can't tell what I'm seeing in there."

I walked to the back. The third car parked behind it wasn't a BMW. Something about it caught my attention, but the headlights were bright and I was too focused on the truck to think about it. The truck's double doors were unlatched. One door hung across the opening. Half of a bakery logo was visible on it. The other door lay open on the uneven ground. It would have been convenient if the headlights of the third car had lit the interior of the truck, but it had been parked at the wrong angle for that.

Catherine joined me but kept well back from the open door. She knelt and shined her flashlight into the darkness of the truck. Right beside the opening was a car battery. Beyond that, I couldn't see much detail.

I didn't see or hear anything moving inside. I stepped onto the open door. It groaned and bent under my weight. I knelt below the other door, not wanting to touch it in case it made more noise, and I crawled inside.

Catherine followed. Her flashlight illuminated the contents well enough. Beside me was the car battery. Only one lead was still attached.

At the far end of the truck bed was a Plexiglas cube, three feet on each side. It was still bolted to the floor, which meant it was now midway up the side of the tipped-over truck. There was a broken battery mount on it, and each corner of the cube had a floodlight aimed toward its center. With the battery broken off, presumably by the accident, the lights had gone out.

"What the hell is this?" Catherine asked. Her voice echoed off the metal panels.

"A cage," I said. I remembered something Annalise had once told me: *Predators like to be summoned, but they hate to be held in place.* I moved closer to it. There was a discolored hole on the "roof" of the cage.

"Don't touch that, please," Catherine said. "I have to

breathe the air in here, and I don't want a lot of plastic dust floating around."

"Good idea."

"It looks like we're too late," she added. "It looks like the owner of this truck won the auction, then had an accident while they were driving away. The battery mount broke, the lights went off, and whatever was inside escaped. Seem right to you?"

"Sure, except about the accident. That left front tire was shot out. You can see the bullet hole on the metal rim."

She nodded. I had the impression I'd passed the first IQ test. "Okay. If the gunfire has already started, then we should gather up what information we have and get out of here. But what do you think about these discolored holes?"

"I think I don't want to get in this predator's way."

She handed me the flashlight, then stepped outside. I could hear her texting someone, probably reporting to the society.

I shone the light around the enclosure. There were small stones at the front of the truck bed. I got down close and saw they weren't stones at all. I picked one up. It was half a dog biscuit.

I climbed out of the truck just as Catherine shut off her phone. "Well?"

"They'll be on their way as quickly as they can. It'll take hours, though. Probably not until tomorrow night or later. Did you find anything?"

"Just this." I held up the biscuit. She frowned at it.

"Weird. Do you think they fed a dog to the predator?"

"What are the odds that this predator eats doggy treats?"

She gave me a look that told me I'd failed my second test. She held out her hand and I gave her the flashlight. As she stooped below the hanging door to enter the truck again, she said: "No offense, but I'm going to check your work. I'm the investigator here."

She was? That was useful information. I'd never met a society investigator before, but I knew they were supposed to look into suspicious situations, file a report, and get out. It was up to the peers—and their wooden men—to do the fighting.

She was inside the truck for just a minute or two, but it seemed much longer. Someone was going to catch us here if we didn't move on soon.

I looked at the third vehicle and stopped short. No wonder it had caught my attention: it was a Maybach Landaulet, roof closed, naturally. Christ. Someone was rolling in the cash.

Finally, Catherine climbed out of the truck. "I have an idea," she said. She walked around the truck to the hole in the roof, then began searching the muddy slope. "Look."

She pointed to an indentation in the mud. It was perfectly round and flat, as if someone had tamped down the earth with a big soup can. There was another nearby farther up the slope, then another and another. They were spaced out like footprints, and there seemed to be a lot of them.

"Are there two predators?" I asked.

"Either that, or it had more than two legs. And look at this." She shone the flashlight onto a separate set of tracks, this time made by men's dress shoes. They headed up the small rise and over it, the men chasing the escaped predator.

"Which way do we go?" I asked. "Do we follow the tracks or continue toward the house?" I nodded up the slope at the house lights.

"Can the spell you used to cut the chain out front kill a predator?" she asked, her tone making it clear she didn't have that sort of weapon.

"It has in the past," I admitted. To push away the

memories that statement churned up, I kept talking.
"Whether it will work on this one or not, I don't know. I
don't even know what we're facing."

"Neither do I," she said.

We trudged through the mud after the footprints. At
the top of the rise we saw a long, even, tree-lined slope
headed downward. And four bodies.

CHAPTER TWO

"Oh, shit," Catherine said as she backed away. I moved toward the dead men, more out of a sense of duty than common sense. Apparently, searching the dead wasn't part of an investigator's job.

The three men whose faces I could see—one was face-down in the mud—were Asian, and they were all dressed very well. They wore wool three-quarter-length coats and dark suits. One suit had pinstripes, which was a stylish touch. Their hair was neatly cut, and they were all closely shaved.

The nearest man had been shot in the side of the head from very close range. Two others farther down the slope had been shot in the chest; they lay on their backs, Glocks in their hands. The fourth man, the one lying facedown, had at least eleven exit wounds in his back and one in his neck. He also held a gun, but the slide was back. His gun was empty.

There was a little white mark on the side of his face. I crouched down to look at it more closely. It actually looked like the end of a mark, as though someone had rubbed bleach on his face with the pad of a thumb. It ran from his temple down toward his cheek; the rest, however much there was, was covered by mud. I could have seen more if I'd wanted to move the body, but I didn't.

He had a wallet bulging in his back pocket. It ruined the line of his suit, so I pulled it out for him and opened it up. It contained American greenbacks along with a number of foreign bills. There was an identity card, but it was written in some kind of kanji and I couldn't read it. The picture showed a very serious Asian man with a crooked nose but no white mark.

Damn. Seeing him with his eyes open, even if it was only on a driver's license or whatever, gave me a chill. Images swirled in my mind—food, laughter, booze pukes, fucking, boredom in line at the bank—all the memories I imagined would make up his life, all reduced to this lump of dead meat on a muddy hillside.

Catherine was watching me. I held the wallet open to her. "Can you read Japanese, or Thai, or whatever?"

She shook her head and folded her arms across her chest. I closed the wallet and slid it back into the man's pocket. I didn't take the money, not even the U.S. bills. I wasn't going to pick a dead man's pocket in front of Catherine.

"Who shot them?" she asked.

"I think they shot each other," I answered. "I'm no TV detective, but this dude was shot at close range, and . . ." I opened the first man's coat. His weapon was still in the holster. "Yeah, he didn't even get a chance to draw his gun. Those two were shot from farther away, and they have their guns in their hands.

"And this bastard is lying here with an empty weapon and a good dozen bullet holes in him. Are there more footprints going down the hill?"

Catherine went around the bodies. The starlight was pretty dim, but our eyes had adjusted. "Yes," she said. "But there are fewer of them."

"I think Mr. White Smudge here shot the others. The ones who killed him probably stood around *what-the-hell*-ing for a while, then took off after the predator."

"Wouldn't they want to carry their friends back to the car? Or call the cops?"

I shook my head. These guys had expensive suits and

identical weapons. I figured them for somebody's hired muscle—a crew. I'd been part of a crew once. We'd done everything together, but we hadn't been friends. Not really.

I looked at Catherine. "Do you want to turn around?"

"Let's keep going," she said. "We decided to chase the predator, and this doesn't really change things, does it?" Her arms were still crossed. I didn't suggest she take one of the dead men's guns. Her body language made it clear what she thought of the idea. Besides, it hadn't done them much good. She glanced at White Smudge as though trying to figure out what had turned him on his buddies. Then she looked away.

We followed the footprints down the hill, through a stand of trees into a meadow. Some of the bark was scorched black as though from a fire. The damage looked months old, though, and the forest was rebounding.

The weird soup-can footprints didn't pass through any of the trees. At least, there were no dark circles on the trunks. I wondered why the predator didn't take shortcuts through them. Were they too thick? Too alive? Something else? I had no idea.

"Look at this," Catherine said.

The soup-can footprints headed straight across open ground, then clustered together as though the creature had turned to face its pursuers. Then the trail split apart.

One set of prints continued ahead down to the meadow. Another went to the right. A third led off to the left. The shoe prints also split up to follow the three separate trails.

"It's not cloning itself, is it?" I asked. Catherine shrugged.

I followed the trail of prints to the right. After about five feet, they vanished.

Catherine waved to me. "The prints stop here," she said. She was standing about ten feet away on the trail that led to the left. A quick check showed the same thing on the center trail. After about five feet, it vanished.

The shoe prints milled around, then split up and led away in those three different directions. What the hell was going on?

"Maybe it cloned itself and flew away," Catherine said.

I felt goose bumps run down my neck. The night sky above me was empty, as far as I could see. It gave me the willies to think that the predator might have been above us all along.

"What do you think?" she asked.

"I think I don't want this thing to swoop down on me."

"I meant what do you think we should do next."

Was this another test? I looked around. By the starlight, I could see trees, underbrush, uneven ground, and far, far down the slope ahead I saw a single burning bluish streetlight. I reminded myself that I was here with an investigator. A peer would have hunted the predator to kill it—a single predator on the loose could, in the long run, lead to the extinction of life on this planet. Investigators, though, collected information for the peers.

Who would be getting here soon. I hoped.

"Well," I said, shrugging, "there's nothing to be learned wandering around out here. And I definitely don't want to come up on those gunmen by accident. I say we should check out the house."

She half smiled, then led the way back up the slope. For a brief moment I thought the four dead men were gone, having been carried off into the night sky by whatever we were following, or even worse, having gotten up and shambled off. Then I saw that they were just a little farther away than I'd thought.

No one had come to check on the cars. Catherine didn't want to drive her Acura any closer to the house, and I agreed. A strange car pulling up at this time of night would attract the worst sort of attention.

Catherine insisted we hike along the driveway rather than take the direct route across the estate, and after a half mile I was glad of it. The slope was not as smooth as it had appeared. We kept to the shoulder, watching ahead and behind for headlights. We were ready to dive into the trees at the first sign of a car, but none came.

We rounded a curve in the road and saw the house up close.

I'd certainly seen bigger. In L.A., all you have to do is drive along a freeway and look up; huge houses are scattered on the hillsides. But this house was huge and isolated and completely out of place. It was three stories tall, with a high, slanted roof and tall, narrow, arched windows like a church. It had chimneys like a porcupine had quills, and I couldn't imagine the kind of person who would look around at this isolated patch of rain forest and decide it was the place to build a mansion.

There was a garland in the front windows and nets of tiny multicolored lights draped over the bushes along the front. Someone had made the effort.

We ducked off the road into the trees, pushing our way through scattered blackberry bushes and scraggly ferns.

The grounds around the front had been cleared, and the road had been widened into a little parking lot with a wide section at the end, probably to give delivery trucks room to turn around. At the moment, the lot was filled with cars, all pointed toward the gate. I saw another BMW to match the one by the truck, a pair of black Yukons, a black Mercedes, and finally a Passat, of all things. At the far end of the lot the asphalt narrowed again into a path leading to a multicar garage.

I stared at the cars, searching for movement or a human shape inside. The X6 had to-go coffee lids on the dash, and the Yukons had bright red-and-white cards in the front windows, but otherwise they were empty.

I moved close to Catherine. "Do we circle around?"

"To where?" She pointed toward the near side of the house, where there were twenty-five yards of lawn separating the tree line from the building. There appeared to be even more space around back. "Do you see any people?"

"Yeah." I pointed toward the door, where a man in a heavy wool coat and a furry Russian hat stood just out of the porch light. I thought he was dressed too warmly for the weather, but I'd been jogging up a long hill and he'd been standing around. Still, bulky coats made me nervous.

"Crap." Catherine pulled me back from the edge of the hill to a stand of trees. When we were out of sight, she let go of me quickly, as if she was afraid I'd take it as a gesture of friendship. "We need photos of the license plates."

"What if they're all rentals, like the one down the hill?"

"I still want them," she said. "But what's more, I don't want to kill anyone. Not everyone we meet is going to be part of some plot to bring predators here to eat our spleens, and I would like to kill as few of them as possible. Can we agree on that?"

I stared at her. Had the society told her what I'd done? I felt a sudden flush of shame, but not for the people I'd killed. I hadn't killed any innocent bystanders. At least, I didn't think I had. Annalise may not have cared about collateral damage, but I had been more careful.

But I still felt ashamed, because I knew the society was, at the core, vigilantes. I believed they had good reason for doing what they did, but their day-to-day work was finding people and killing them.

And not only had I taken part, I'd been eager to drop everything to come on this job, eager for the adrenaline rush, and I couldn't honestly say I didn't know what we'd be doing.

And I liked Catherine. Her heart and her head were in the right place, and if she was a little weird and distant with me, well, she was right to be.

"Agreed," I said. Standing still in this wind was giving me chills. "Around the side?"

"Not this side," she said. "I'd rather enter from the garage, in case there are more plates to photograph there."

We circled around the property. The ground near the garage was thick with trees and brambles, which gave us more cover but also slowed us down. And we made more noise than I would have liked. There didn't seem to be anyone to notice.

We moved toward the side of the garage. There were no footprints in the mud. There was a single window in the wall, but it was dark. I hoped no one was inside, watching us approach.

The backyard was even larger and more open than the front. The ground still sloped upward, but it was mostly a gentle rise. A bungalow sat well away from the house, in the middle of the meadow. Heavy black power lines ran out to it from the main building.

A guesthouse for a home this large? Maybe there was no such thing as "big enough" for some people.

I led the way toward the back door of the garage. More than one trail of footprints went back and forth from the house, so I couldn't tell if someone was inside. Fair enough. I turned the knob and pulled the door open.

Very little light shone through the dirty windows, leaving the inside nearly pitch-black. Catherine handed me her flashlight, and I flicked it on. There were four cars parked here, all packed close. Right beside me was a fifteen-year-old Civic hatchback. Next to that was a white Audi SUV, a Q7, with tinted windows, then a long black Fleetwood—maybe a '54, but I'm not an expert on vintage cars. Beyond that was a modern sedan, but all I could see was the line of the roof and back windshield. Huh. Maybe the Civic belonged to a servant.

Catherine took a camera from her bag. She focused on the license plate of the Civic. A little orange light illuminated the back bumper, and she snapped a photo. The flash lit up the room.

I moved away from her, wishing she had waited—maybe the windows had curtains I could draw or something. I understood her urgency, though. The predator, whatever it was, was on the loose.

She went around the car to snap a photo of the front plate, too. I walked to the far end of the room. The sedan was a BMW 745i. All of the cars were empty, thank God. There were garden tools along the walls and ladders, canoes, and ski equipment up in the rafters.

Meanwhile, Catherine snapped the front and back plates of the Audi. I crouched beside the BMW to cut the fuel lines. If we had to run, it would be a huge help if the cars were disabled.

The back door clicked open. I dropped to the floor.

"Um, excuse me?" a man said. His voice was high-pitched and gentle. "Who is in here?"

"Nothing's getting stolen!" Catherine said, taking an angry tone. The change in her personality was startling. "I just have a job to do, so you go ahead and go back where you came from." She sounded so offended that I half expected him to apologize, but he didn't.

"Ma'am, I have to ask you to look at my hands."

Catherine's voice became low. "You put that gun away."

"Ma'am," he said, his voice just as gentle, "I purchased this weapon not knowing whether I would have the chance to use it. Frankly, I find the prospect thrilling."

"Now, you just wait a minute . . ." Catherine sounded less sure of herself.

I lifted myself off the floor and shifted position, peering

under the fender. All I could see of him was a pair of khaki pant legs tucked into rubber boots. This guy wasn't with the Asian men we'd found out on the hill-side, not in that footwear.

"I will not wait," he said. His voice was still high and soft, but there was a breath of excitement in it. "If you don't do exactly as I say, I will shoot you right now. Then I will drag your body into the woods. No one on the premises will care except me, and I will only feel the secret satisfaction of knowing exactly what I am capable of."

"Whoa, now," Catherine said. "I'm unarmed! The *Times* sent me."

"Put the camera down," the man said. I heard something being set gently on the trunk of the car. "Turn around."

It wasn't doing any good to look at this guy's shoes. I kept my feet in place to avoid scuffling against the concrete floor and walked my hands backward until I was in a crouch. I peeked through the windows of the BMW and the Cadillac. Catherine was moving very slowly. Behind her, I saw a man in an orange parka so thick it looked like it had been inflated.

I took out my ghost knife and held it across my body like a Frisbee. "I'm a journalist," Catherine said. "That's all. No need to freak out. I'm just a woman doing a job."

The man leaned her against the back of the SUV the way a cop would, but he didn't make her spread her stance. He stepped forward and patted her down, moving behind the blind spot by the Cadillac's back window.

Then I heard the unmistakable sound of a pair of hand-cuffs.

"You're not putting those on me," Catherine said, her voice rising in panic.

"Stay calm," the man whispered.

"You're not putting those on me!"

I had to step in whether I was ready or not. I stood.

The man in the orange coat started to turn toward me as I threw my ghost knife. He raised his pistol. At the last moment, the ghost knife swerved into it, cutting through the metal and the gunman's hand.

He gasped and staggered against the wall. Tools rattled as he bumped into them. The pieces of the gun fell to the floor. I *reached* for the ghost knife again, calling it back to me. It flew into my hand as I came around the back of the BMW. Before I could get there, Catherine spun and hit him with an elbow just below his ear.

The man staggered but didn't fall. I hissed at Catherine to make her stop. She did. A moment later I was beside the man, examining his hand. As usual, there were no cuts or blood—the ghost knife hadn't cut him physically.

"I'm sorry," he said. His high, soft voice was full of regret. "Holding that weapon—I should never have let that power go to my head. How awful for you, ma'am."

Good. The ghost knife had done its job. All his hostility and willpower had been cut out of him. The effect was only temporary, but there was a lot I didn't know about it—such as whether a beating would bring him back to himself.

"I'm tremendously sorry," he said again.

Catherine looked at me in disbelief. She shifted her stance, bumping something metal with her foot. I shined the flashlight on it, confirming that it was half of the gun. It looked like an old .45. She stared at it, then back at me. Guess she had never seen a ghost knife at work before.

"You can make it right," I told the man. "Start by lying down and spreading your arms. And tell me your name."

"Okay," he said as he did it. He didn't even sound afraid. Only contrite. "My name is Mr. Alex."

I searched him. His wallet gave his full name as Horace Alex and listed an address in New York State. He was a long way from home. He had keys to a rental car, house keys, a small backup gun, a fat Swiss Army knife, a cellphone, a little paperback book written by some-body named Zola, a spare clip for his .45, and a pack of gum. I dropped all of it into a plastic bucket.

He wasn't local, and he certainly wasn't working for the man with the Maybach. Now it was time to find out who he was.

"What are you doing here, Horace?" Damn if I was going to call this guy *Mr.* anything.

"I saw the camera flash and came to investigate."

"Why are you here, though, so far from home?"

"Several of the Fellows put together a kitty for the auction, but it wasn't enough." The way he said *Fellows* made it sound like a title, not a group of friends. "The bidding topped forty-two million very quickly, and we were left behind."

Catherine leaned down toward him. "What were you bidding on?" Her manner had changed again. Her voice was low and friendly, and her body language mirrored Horace's. She had become a different person.

"Some sort of creature from the Deeps. Only Profes-sor Solorov was allowed to go up the hill to see it."

"The professor's full name?"

"Elisabeta Solorov."

"What about the other bidders?" Her voice was soft; it invited answers.

"I'm sorry, but there were no introductions, formal or otherwise. There was a Chinese fellow who spoke Can-tonese. He won the auction and left a short while ago. There was also a fat, scruffy-looking Silicon Valley man who looked completely out of place. Finally, there was an extremely unpleasant old man who spoke German. That's all I know about them."

"Why didn't you leave when the auction winner left?" I asked.

"The rules state he gets a two-hour head start, then the rest of us can go."

"Does anyone know you've come in here?"

"No."

Catherine wasn't finished with him. "Did you hear anything about the creature? Was it big, small, furry, scaly?"

"I'm sorry," he said. "Professor Solorov will certainly tell us about it privately, but we haven't had a private moment yet."

"Fair enough. How many people are inside?"

Horace turned thoughtful. "Each bidder was supposed to come with no more than five people, but our party consisted of seven. Several Fellows refused to contribute to the kitty if they couldn't come along. I thought it was bad form to bring so many, but the gentleman from Hong Kong brought twelve. The German brought only two employees, and the fat Californian brought a single bodyguard. The hostess has only one servant that I saw and, of course, the handler. Plus the hired security men in those brown uniforms."

Catherine and I looked at each other. We hadn't seen any security. If we didn't count uniformed guards or the winning bidder, there were fourteen people, with the possibility of more servants. Great. I didn't care how big the house was, that was too many people for us to go wandering around the grounds. Someone was bound to look out a window and spot us.

I picked up the handcuffs. Catherine put her hand near my elbow but didn't touch me. "How did you find out about this auction?"

"Professor Solorov met with a man while she was in Los Angeles. Not the fat Silicon Valley person. He told her about the auction, and she brought the news to us. We were very excited. Forty-two million dollars is a lot of money for our group. Too bad it wasn't enough."

"What group?" Catherine asked.

"We call each other 'Fellows' but don't have a name,"

Horace answered. "We don't even have a charter. We're a social group with a common interest."

"Interest in what?" Catherine asked before I could jump in with the most likely guess.

"Magic."

That would have been my guess. Before I could respond, Catherine asked another question. "Do you have spell books? Artifacts?"

She was deliberately blocking my questions. What the hell. She was the investigator. I backed off to let her do her thing.

"No," Horace answered. "None. All we ever do is read magic theory and case reports. None of us have seen a creature of the Deeps, and we certainly haven't done any magic."

"Theory? What books?"

Horace began to recite a long list of titles. I couldn't follow them, but Catherine seemed intensely interested. She had her cellphone in hand. She was probably recording him. "There are some others I'm forgetting," he finally said.

Catherine asked where the books were kept, and he gave an address in a town I hadn't heard of. Then, at her request, he listed the other Fellows. They were just names to me, and I couldn't remember them.

When that was over, I looked at Catherine to see if she was finished. She only shrugged. "Okay, Horace," I said. "On your feet." I lifted him and handcuffed him behind his back.

The rear door of the Caddy was unlocked, and the seat was spacious. I loaded Horace inside, then emptied his backup revolver and tossed it into the nose of a canoe in the rafters. I slid the tip of the ghost knife through his ankle and told him to get some sleep. He thanked me and closed his eyes.

When I turned away from him, Catherine was standing very close. "What do you have there?"

I slipped the ghost knife into my pocket. "A spell."

"It made him answer all our questions. He didn't hesitate at all."

"Yeah," I said. "He also didn't want to kill us anymore."

She laughed a little. "That's a good thing, too. Okay. I think you should give that to me." She held out her hand.

"Um, what?"

"That spell. You should give it to me and show me how it works. I'm the investigator here, and that thing could really help me with my job."

"This is my spell," I said. "I cast it."

"I understand." She didn't pull back her open palm. "But you can see that this would be for the best."

I was surprised that she would even ask this of me. "It's my spell," I said again with more emphasis. "I cast it myself. It's pretty much a part of me. You might as well ask for my thumb."

"Oh." She let her hand fall to her side. "Is that how it is?"

"Yeah. You didn't know?"

"I'm just an investigator. People with spells don't usually explain anything to me."

"Let me explain this much, then: I can feel this spell like it's a part of my body. I don't know how to explain it better, but it feels like it's alive. And it's mine."

I could see that she had more questions, but all she said was "Thank you."

"Did you get all that," I asked, "with the list of books and people?"

When she answered, her voice was low. "Yes, but we don't need it. The society has a mole in their group. That's how we knew about the auction. I was just testing him to see how compliant your little spell made him."

Sure, now that she knew she couldn't have it, it was a *little spell*. "How do we find this mole? Maybe he can give us better information."

"He's not here, unfortunately. Not only did he give us this information at the last possible minute, he's gone into hiding. Probably ice fishing in Canada or something."

"So, this group without a name—"

"The Fellowship."

"Okay. This Fellowship: What do we do about them?" I wasn't sure whether the society wanted to dig into their secrets or if they wanted us to keep our hands off in case we flushed out their rat.

"Just don't kill them all," she said, her voice tight. Apparently, that was all she had to say.

She finished photographing the license plates, then we followed the path Horace had made in the mud to the house.

Catherine pulled herself up and peeped into a window. "Empty," she said. "Let's go."

She hurried to the back door. I saw a keypad on the wall and a sign announcing which security company would send a car if the alarm went off. Luckily, Horace had propped the door open with a hand truck.

She went inside and I followed. I didn't like it, but I followed. The oppressive warmth and bright lights made me feel like I'd been captured already.

"This way," Catherine said. She moved the hand truck quietly against the wall.

She led me through a mudroom into the kitchen. We passed a gas grill, a fridge that had a door larger than my bed, and a long stainless steel counter.

"There." Catherine hurried into the pantry and began inspecting aprons hanging from hooks. When she reached a white, double-breasted jacket, she yanked it down and held it against my chest. "Put this on. It'll let you get close enough to these guys to do your mind-control thing."

I stripped off my jacket and gave it to her. "It's not mind control, you know. All it does is make them sorta docile. They get all apologetic if they've been trying to kill me, but that's it."

"What if they're not trying to kill you?" She grabbed a tray off a metal rack and placed a plate on it. "What if you just need information from them?"

"I tried that," I answered. "But only once. I didn't like the results."

I pulled on the white jacket. It was too small; my wrists and shirttails stuck out. She picked up a silver tray, and then we heard footsteps. I slapped the light switch off, and Catherine swung the pantry door until it was just open a crack. She peeked through the opening, and I joined her.

At first we could only see an empty kitchen. We heard a rattling doorknob and a woman cursing under her breath, then she hurried into view. She was at least seventy, hollow-looking, with long, stringy hair. Her nightgown was dingy and speckled with food. It looked like she hadn't bathed in a long time.

Heavier footsteps followed her. She grabbed a ladle and held it in both hands. I didn't think she had the strength to hurt a squirrel, but she looked enthusiastic. "Keep away!" she said. Her voice had an air of lost authority.

Then the man she was warning off stepped into view. He was about thirty-five, with the pouchy face of a hard drinker. He wore sloppy nurse whites and had just enough muscle to push around old women.

"Regina," he said with warning in his voice, "you know better than this."

"You keep away," Regina said, her voice high. "You're fired!"

"Regina, if you come peacefully—"

She swung the ladle, hitting him on the fat part of his shoulder. The blow didn't have enough force to dent a stick of cold butter, but the nurse bared his teeth. "How many times do I have to teach you this lesson?" He snatched the ladle out of her hand and tossed it clattering into the sink. Regina cowered, but he wasn't in a merciful mood. He grabbed her wrist and pinched the skin of her upper arm viciously. Regina's face contorted with pain, her mouth making a silent *oh oh oh* as she tried to slump away from him toward the floor.

Cold revulsion flooded through me and rekindled a fire that I'd been lacking for months.

Catherine must have sensed something because she held her hand in front of me, trying to keep me in hiding. Unfortunately, I wasn't made for investigating.

I pulled a skillet off a hook, not caring how much sound it made, and stepped forward. Catherine backed away from the door and let me pull it wide. She knew there was nothing to be gained by scuffling with me.

When the nurse noticed me, his smugness turned into astonishment. I charged at him. He shouted "Hey!" An instant later I was on him. He threw his hands up and flinched, but it was all instinct. Instead of swinging the skillet in a wide arc, which probably would have killed him, I jabbed with it, angling it between his elbows. It struck the side of his jaw.

He tumbled backward onto the floor. He was out like a light, and I felt no satisfaction in it.

Regina was still crouched beside the sink. I offered her my hand, and she looked at it as if it might burn her. She stood without my help.

More footsteps came toward us.

I offered her the skillet, and her eyes lit up. She took it gratefully. I put my finger to my lips and slipped back into the pantry.

Catherine had taken up a position behind the door. I left the door open just enough to peek out at Regina.

I heard people rush into the room. Regina raised the skillet over her head. "Don't come any closer!"

"It is all right, ma'am," I heard a woman say. "There is no need to be violent." I liked the careful way she pronounced every word.

Regina glared. "What have you done with Armand?"

"Not a thing, ma'am, I assure you," Well-Spoken Woman answered.

"Madam," a man's voice said. "May I approach this man? I fear he might be dead." He had a Russian accent.

"I hope he is dead." Regina still held the skillet high, but she was getting tired. A hiking boot and a gray pant leg entered my field of vision, but I didn't widen the opening to get a better look. "I hope he's as dead as a . . . as a . . ." She sighed and let the skillet fall against her shoulder. It was late and she was tired. "He always did things to hurt me."

"I'm sorry for that, ma'am," Well-Spoken said. "And who are you, if I may ask?"

Regina straightened up. "This is my house."

Someone else rushed in with the clicking footsteps of high heels. "Aunt Reggie, what have you done?" another woman asked. She had a high, harried voice and a slight southern drawl.

"I stood up for myself," the old woman said harshly.

"Oh, God, is he dead?"

"No," the man said. "He is unconscious and possibly has a broken jaw. He should be taken to a hospital."

"The two-hour grace period has not yet ended," Well-Spoken said.

A woman stepped into view and took the skillet from

Regina without kindness or cruelty. She was nearly thirty, with an orange tanning-booth tan. She wore a green suit with touches of gold at the lapels and cuffs. Something about her put me off. "She's right," she said. She was the one with the drawl. "It'll be another half hour before anyone can leave. We have to give Mr. Yin's truck the head start we promised."

They don't know. They don't know that, just a mile away, the truck was on its side and the predator was on the loose.

The gray pant leg and shoe moved out of my field of vision. "And if he dies?" Mr. Accent asked.

"Then his family will sue us." The niece turned to Regina. "Aunt Reggie, let's get back to your room. Please. I don't have time for this right now."

"What about Armand?" Regina asked as she let herself be led away. "What do all these people have to do with Armand? I want to see him! Why won't you let me see him?"

Her voice receded, and a man I hadn't heard before said something in a language I couldn't identify. His voice was harsh and low.

"There's no need to be rude," Well-Spoken said. "But I agree. The old woman can also identify us to the police."

The harsh voice spoke again. Was it German? The woman answered in the same language.

The Russian man cleared his throat. "I do not like the idea of killing a sick old woman. If it is necessary, of course I will do it, but she is very like my own grandmother. Why would we need to kill anyone? There is nothing illegal here."

The harsh voice answered with a short remark.

"I agree." Well-Spoken was still cool and relaxed. "It is one thing for us to know what was sold here, but the woman could raise an outcry, especially if she regained

part of her fortune. I would hate to attract the wrong
kind of attention."

The harsh voice again. Well-Spoken answered him:
"Perhaps not, but they could harm *us*."

"We would also prefer not to attract the wrong kind
of attention," the Russian said. "But I still do not like
the idea of murder."

"Security has been inadequate from the moment we
arrived," she said, ignoring the man's comment. "For
instance, there is also the problem of Mr. Kripke."

"Yes," the Russian said. "He and the group he repre-
sents are not discreet."

The German man spoke. The woman sighed and
answered: "I'm afraid I must say the same. Unfortunately, I must leave soon to meet Mr. Yin. Neither of us
can linger long enough to take care of him." I wished
one of them would step into my line of sight, narrow as
it was. I wanted a good look at anyone who talked that
casually about murder.

The Russian sighed. "We will do it. No one will find
the body. But in exchange, we spare the old woman.
This is America—no one will listen to her."

"Acceptable," Well-Spoken said. A pale man in a long
scarlet ski jacket arrived. He was as tall and crook-
necked as a stork. I figured him for one of Horace's Fellows. He lifted the nurse's legs. Unseen hands helped
him carry the man away.

Then a man stepped into my view. He wore heavy
canvas pants with a leather jacket. His hair was blond
and wispy and his skin pale. He had the face of a man
who'd taken a lot of beatings and the expression of one
who'd given out even more.

But that wasn't what made me catch my breath. He
had tattoos just like mine on his hands, neck, and even
his face. I could see that they went up his sleeve, down

his collar, and under his hairline. He didn't look like part of—what had Well-Spoken called him?—Yin's crew of pin-striped gunmen. But who was he with? Was he the German voice, working for the "extremely unpleasant old man"? Kripke's bodyguard turned traitor to his boss? Or was he one of the Fellows? I hoped he was part of the Twenty Palace Society. Or even—what had Catherine said?—an ally. I didn't like the look of him and didn't want him as an enemy.

He stared at the pantry door, his expression alert and calm. I knew he wouldn't be able to see me—the room was too dark and the gap too small—but then it occurred to me that I was assuming he had everyday human eyes. If one of those marks gave him X-ray vision or something, I was in for a fight.

Someone's cell began playing Mozart. I heard Well-Spoken answer it in a language I didn't recognize. Some kind of Chinese, maybe? Horace had said Mr. Yin spoke Cantonese, so maybe that was it. After a delay, she said: "My employer wants me to speak with our hostess. If you'll excuse me."

I heard her walk away. The tattooed man walked away too. I waited, listening to the silence. Tattoo hadn't acted as though he'd seen me, but maybe he had a great poker face. Maybe he was going to another room to get a shotgun.

Catherine came toward me, her eyes widened as if to ask *Are they gone?*

"I guess so," I said. No one heard me. No one shouted *Hey* again. I opened the pantry door on the empty kitchen.

Catherine slapped my shoulder. It wasn't a playful tap, but it wasn't meant to hurt, either. "Dumbass," she said. She kept her voice low. "You nearly got us killed for that old woman."

"Maybe so."

"Definitely so. I understand the impulse, boy, but bigger things are at stake here."

I didn't like being called *boy*, and I didn't need to be reminded of the stakes, but there was no edge to be gained squabbling over it.

Catherine wanted me to eavesdrop on Well-Spoken Woman's conversation with the host while she got into position to take photos of the bidders as they left. We agreed to meet in an hour at her car. If one of us didn't make the meeting, we would meet at nine A.M. in the parking lot of the post office in the town below. My flannel jacket didn't go with the white servant's coat, so Catherine promised to bring it to the car.

"Don't get killed" was the last thing she said before she left.

CHAPTER THREE

I had NO idea where Well-Spoken was going, but I knew how to follow voices. I picked up the silver tray and left the kitchen.

The halls had dark paneling and were hung with landscapes of sunny places thousands of miles away. The floor was hardwood with a strip of burgundy carpet down the center. The carpet had been plush once but had been worn thin down the middle and dotted with faint brown stains.

I walked quietly but not sneakily. I still had the too-small servant's jacket on. It would probably fool anyone who didn't actually live or work here, and I hoped that was good enough. I held the tray in front of me to hide my shirttails.

Well-Spoken Woman and the Russian had talked about *attracting the wrong kind of attention,* and I knew they were talking about me. They wanted a predator; the Twenty Palace Society kills people who have predators.

And while I'd killed people, I'd always known who I was killing and why they deserved it. I tried to picture myself kicking open the pantry door and shotgunning those strangers, but I couldn't. That wasn't me.

The corridor ended at a T intersection, and as I approached, a small group of people walked by. The man in front was the tall man with the stork neck who'd carried the nurse by the legs. Behind him was a blond woman of about fifty with salon hair and makeup. Two more men walked at the rear. Both were balding, one short and skinny, the other short and fat. Both had big square glasses and porn-star mustaches.

The men were dressed like Horace—they had ugly winter coats and cheap boots. Stork Neck was wearing rubber galoshes, and between the three of them, their haircuts couldn't have cost more than fifteen bucks.

The woman was different. She wore a stylish brown leather coat that reached to mid-thigh. Her boots were also leather and trimmed with fur. In the seconds I had to look at her, she gave the impression of being very carefully put together, very exacting and self-aware. She drew my attention the way the men with her did not.

Was this Well-Spoken Woman? The three men were obviously Fellows, but—

The woman and the two mustache guys glanced at me. They saw my servant's jacket and looked away. I was invisible. I was help.

When I reached the intersection, I had the choice of turning right and following them or turning left toward the direction they'd come from. To the left was a pair of heavy doors, both shut tight. I didn't know what was behind them. I turned right.

Ahead of me, Stork Neck's party turned left. I hustled after them and peeked around the corner just in time to see them file into a room.

I walked to the door. The woman was speaking, and her voice was deeper than the one I'd eavesdropped on from behind the pantry door. She wasn't Well-Spoken Woman after all. "It's a surprisingly small library," she said. She had an accent like a Kennedy.

A man's thin, nasal voice answered: "But the quality is excellent, if you are interested in road building, Bigfoot, or Ayn Rand. Otherwise—"

"Now," the woman said.

I heard the rustle of clothing and peeked around the edge of the door. The woman stepped backward, allowing the Mustaches to pull sawed-off double-barreled shotguns from under their puffy coats. They pointed them at two men seated in the corner. One was a pudgy young guy with Larry Fine hair, and the other was a huge-bellied biker in riding leathers.

The biker looked startled, then let his hand creep toward the waistband of his pants. Something he saw in the expressions of the Mustaches changed his mind. Stork Neck came up behind him and patted him down.

From my position, I couldn't see Larry Fine's expression. "What the hell are you doing?" he said.

Fat Mustache answered him: "The other bidders here have asked us to kill you both." He was the Russian-speaker. I'd followed the wrong party.

"You can't do that!" Larry Fine blurted out.

"Of course I can," the woman answered. Her voice was mild. Stork Neck removed a little revolver from the biker's belt. "However, I'm tempted to let you live, if you cooperate."

I crossed the doorway to have a better view. No one saw me. They were all paying very close attention to one another. Larry Fine had a look of blustering outrage, as though he had been told he couldn't have nutmeg in his latte. "This doesn't even make sense—"

"Don't be dense, Mr. Kripke. You did not come here to purchase this creature. You don't have the cash to bid or the resources to hold it."

"I didn't expect the price to start so—"

"Shut up," she said. Her tone wasn't harsh or angry, but he did it. "You came here to gather information for your little electronic circle of friends. You plan to put our names and descriptions into your database. Don't bother to deny it."

His mouth worked while he decided whether to take

her advice. "You're wrong and you're right. I would have bought the creature if the price hadn't been so high, just like you. I'm also planning to make a record of everything I've seen, Professor Solorov, also just like you." Kripke had an edge of contempt in his voice, as though he didn't think they had the guts to kill him.

Biker looked uncomfortable and edged away from Kripke. I could tell he took the threat seriously, and so did I.

The ghost knife was still in my pocket, but I couldn't use it. Both Mustaches had their backs to me, and I couldn't see their guns. My spell would pretty much hit whatever I wanted it to, but I couldn't hit what I couldn't see. I also expected them to have backup weapons. Horace did.

I could have targeted the men rather than the weapons, of course, but I couldn't hit all of them together. Someone would have time to squeeze a trigger, and I wasn't protected well enough to survive a shotgun blast.

"Perhaps we will," Solorov answered. I wondered if she said *we* when her gunmen weren't around. "But there are crucial differences. First, we know everyone we will share this information with personally. Second, we brought more guns. You." She spoke to Biker for the first time. "You're his friend, correct? He didn't hire you as a bodyguard; he asked you to come along, right?"

"Right," Biker answered. His voice was hoarse.

"We thought so," she said. "We're going to split you up, but we're willing to spare your lives if you *both* cooperate."

Kripke let out a dismissive puff of air. "I wouldn't join your group if you—"

"I didn't say you could *join* us," Solorov said sharply. "You can *work* for us. I know someone has been feeding you information—recent information. If you share it with us—all of it—and if you report to your group in exactly the manner I indicate, you and your friend may survive."

Kripke looked over at Biker. The look on his friend's face drained all the insolence out of him. He nodded.

"You're lucky, Mr. Kripke, although I doubt you have the wit to see it. If Mr. Yin had been asked to get rid of you, two of his men would have walked in here, shot you both, and left you dead on the floor. And that crotchety German bastard would have cut you open and *eaten you*. At least I—and the rest of the Fellows, of course—have given you a chance to live and be useful."

Stork Neck and Skinny Mustache waved at Biker. He stood. They were leaving.

I slid away from the door as quietly as I could. There was one other door in the hall, but it was locked. The rattle of the latch sounded as loud as an alarm bell. I hustled away, holding the tray in my left hand.

The corridor ended at a door with a dead bolt. I didn't bother to rattle the knob. To my right was another mudroom and a door into the backyard. To my left was a flight of stairs. I walked up the steps.

The library door clicked shut. At the top of the first landing, I heard Biker's hoarse voice say: "You guys don't have to kill me, you know."

"We know." I didn't recognize that voice.

"You . . . you wouldn't really do it, though, right?" I could hear the question in Biker's voice: *Are these guys really killers?* "Have you ever done this before?"

"I wanted a monster," a new voice said. It sounded high and thin, as though the speaker was under terrible strain. "I came here to get a monster, but we weren't fucking rich enough. Do you know how long I . . ." He let that sentence trail off as though he was swallowing all his disappointment and resentment. I wouldn't want to be on the ugly end of his gun.

"We won't do anything we don't have to do," the first man said calmly.

They went outside. I climbed the second flight and came to a huge back window. Through the drapes, I saw Stork Neck and Skinny Mustache lead Biker toward the woods, away from the garage.

According to Horace, the guesthouse was where the predator had been kept. That was my next stop.

There was a muffled *chunk* of a slamming car door. I crossed toward the front of the house. The nearest door was unlocked and the room inside was filled with furniture covered with white sheets, just like in the movies. The musty smell made me wrinkle my nose.

More heavy drapes hung over the windows at the front of the house. Each window was taller than my apartment. I pulled the drape open a crack. The X6 backed up, trying to make its way through the crowded lot. When it was as close to the door as it was going to get, the guy in the furry Russian hat climbed out of the driver's seat and hustled around the front. He opened the back door like a chauffeur.

A small woman slipped into the backseat. From above I didn't have the best view of her, but I saw that her very dark hair was parted severely down the middle and curled into a librarian's bun. She had a dark complexion and wore a gray suit.

The chauffeur closed her door, got behind the wheel, and sped off. If she was leaving before the others, she worked for Mr. Yin, which meant she was the Well-Spoken Woman who was so casual about asking other people to kill for her. I hoped Catherine was in position to snap a photo.

I mentally ran through the list of bidders Horace had given us: Yin's people were all out on the hillside hunting for the predator. I hadn't seen Yin himself, only his gunman and Well-Spoken Woman, who was his representative.

Kripke and his biker bodyguard were accounted for and not doing very well. I'd seen Professor Solorov and about half of her mismatched, badly dressed Fellows; on their own, they didn't impress, but their guns were dangerous enough.

And there was Tattoo, who had to be the German with the harsh voice. I didn't like the look of him, especially since Horace had said he was one of the "old man's" people. The professor had said the old man would have eaten Kripke, and based on previous experience, I knew there was a good chance she meant it literally. I didn't want to meet that old man.

That meant I'd had at least a glimpse of each of the four groups of bidders. Hopefully, what I'd learned would be useful to the society.

I went back into the hall and heard the faint jabbering of a radio. I peered into the darkness and noticed a tiny sliver of light shining from under a door. I had a hunch I knew who was behind that door, and if I was right, the guesthouse could wait.

"I can hear you out there!" Regina shouted. "You can't fool these old ears."

Fair enough. I opened the door and went inside.

The bright light hit half a second before the smell. Who ever brought Regina up here hadn't expected her to sleep. Maybe they didn't care. Three halogen lamps filled the room with an acid-yellow light—there was no way to nod off in here without a blindfold.

The room also stank of unwashed bedpans, sweat, and neglect. My initial impulse was to flee back into the musty shadows of the hall.

"I know," Regina said. I guess I wouldn't have made much of a poker player in that moment. She switched off a small transistor radio on the bed beside her. Her niece had buckled her left wrist to a bolt in the frame. She was still wearing the dirty nightgown, and I wished she would pull it down over the black-and-blue patches on her legs. They gave me goose bumps. "It sickens me, too. Just be glad you don't have to live this way."

"I am. My name is Ray."

"I'm Regina Wilbur. When I was a girl, my father would have had you thrown out of this house for introducing yourself to me. You'd have left with a muddy boot print on your derrière."

"Things have changed," I said, for lack of anything more profound to offer.

She rattled the short chain on her restraint. "So they have. What have you done with Armand?"

"I'm sorry, but I don't know who that is," I said, hoping it would prompt her to explain.

Instead, she sighed bitterly and looked around the room. "This house was mine once. My father built it with timber money. My husband built four more just like it all over the country, and one in the Italian Alps, too. He took my father's fortune and doubled it five times. Trucking lines, at the beginning, then tires and road building. He was a bastard, but most are. At least he had the decency to die young.

"But now Stephanie has taken it all, and the little bitch didn't even have the good manners to wait until I had dirt over my face. She's going to sell it, just like the ones in Carolina and Maine, so she can live in *California*." She said that word with special distaste. "All auctioned off! All the history here. All the gifts from politicians and people desperate to do business. Even from enemies who wanted my blessing . . ."

Her voice trailed off and she stared across the room. Her eyes were like dark river stones. The whole situation made me uneasy.

She seemed to have forgotten me. To prompt her, I said: "Was Armand one of those gifts?"

"Yes," she said, savoring the word like it was candy.

"He was a gift from one of the most powerful and dangerous men in the world, Nelson Taber Stroud. Dead now, of course. He and I clashed over all sorts of garbage over the years, especially mining rights, but that changed once Armand arrived. Nothing else mattered after that. Armand was *everything*."

What is he? I wanted to ask. That seemed too direct. Regina may have been in a bad spot, but she was still sharp. And she hadn't asked for my help, hadn't even hinted that she wanted it. She was either tough as hell or completely crazy.

"It sounds like you loved him very much."

"You bet I did. I made sure Ursula kept his cage clean and stayed with him in his house. He was *loved*, and I made sure he knew it."

She looked at a nightstand loaded with pictures in silver frames. I circled the bed toward it. I had to move in front of a window, but the glass was so dirty that I wasn't worried about being spotted. The closest picture, though still out of her reach, was of a much younger Regina holding a Scottish terrier to her face. The dog wore a diamond necklace. "Is this Armand?"

She twisted her mouth in disgust. "That's the first Armand. Give me that."

I handed the picture to her. She snatched it with her free hand and flung it across the room. It smashed against a radiator with a noise I thought the whole house could hear.

Damn. Now I understood why it had been out of her reach. I slid my hand into my pocket next to my ghost knife, just in case someone came to investigate.

"That's what I think of that," she said with finality. She turned back to the other pictures.

Regina was much older in these. Every picture showed her crouching beside an empty Plexiglas cage similar to the one in the wrecked truck, only much larger. Flood lamps lit the interior, and the cage was spiderwebbed with electrical wiring.

But all I could see inside the cage was a blurry blue smear. Whatever it was, I couldn't make it out.

I looked at the other pictures. There were at least a dozen, all showing Regina posing with the empty cage. Her hair was longer in some pictures than in others, but she had the same creepy, ecstatic smile in each. Something about them bothered me, though. The smile was the same, but the expression was not. It seemed that the longer her hair was, the more ferocious her eyes became.

I studied the background of the images. They had been taken indoors; there was a couch, a ski jacket, and skis against the wall in one photo, a tiny stove in another. The space looked pretty cramped, and I guessed it was the guesthouse out back.

One picture showed a different woman who didn't smile at all, but her face glowed with smug contentment. She was younger than Regina—maybe in her early fifties—with a pale, stolid look about her. Her eyes had the same fierce glint as Regina's.

"I can't see Armand. Was he in the cage when this was taken?"

"We didn't *cage* him," she snapped, forgetting that she'd already told me she kept his cage clean. "We kept him safe. But yes, he was there when we took those. He doesn't turn up on film. He isn't a regular animal, you know. He's special."

Now we were getting to it. "How is he special?"

"He is *beautiful*!" she cried. "He's the most beautiful thing on God's green earth. His eyes are like the stars of the Milky Way, and he's as delicate as thistledown. He's the only dog of his kind in the world. A sapphire dog, Stroud called him. He's as beautiful as a dream at twilight. Like holding the sky in your arms."

I wondered how she could hold the sky in her arms

while it was inside a plastic cage, but it didn't seem polite to argue. "That's a pretty way to describe him."

She waved my comment away. "I didn't write it. Some college professor did. I held a poetry contest years back to find someone to capture Armand's *essence,* if you know what I mean. The winner had retired up here from some southern university to start a winery, and he won the cash prize hands down. Then I invited him to the house.

"He didn't think much of writing a poem about some rich broad's dog until he met Armand, of course. Then he fell in love, just like anyone would. He spent six months here, sleeping on a cot, watching Armand—staring at him. What I said before is all I remember of the poem he wrote. You'd think it was sap if you'd never *seen.*"

Her tone had changed. Something told me I should probe further. "What happened?"

"He refused to *leave,*" she answered, her mouth twisting with anger. "He even told me that he loved Armand more than I did. That I wasn't 'sensitive' enough to appreciate him. Ursula had to taser him to keep him from breaching the cage. Hah! I appreciated Armand enough to take care of that old fool."

The way she said that gave me a chill. "What did you do?"

She bared her teeth. "I . . ." Then she stopped. It was pretty clear that she'd been about to confess to a crime. "Well, I paid him off," she said, in the least convincing way possible. "Also, I had the sheriff run him out of town. Out of the country, actually. He'd committed a crime against me, stolen books out of my library, if you have to pry. I warned him that I was going to call the police the next day, and he was gone before morning. To Canada, maybe. Or Fiji. That's all and nothing more."

She lifted her nose and looked away from me. Most people are terrible liars, but she was the worst I'd ever met. She could contradict herself all in one breath. "I'm not a cop," I said. "I'm not going to arrest you. You killed him, didn't you?"

"Yes," she said, smiling at me with open contempt. "Yes, of course I did. I knifed him and pulled him out into the woods on a big old sled all by myself." She looked at me as if she might like to cut me open and gulp down my heart. "And I'll do the same to anyone who tries to come between me and my Armand."

"Is that right?"

"It is. It's very right. And don't lie to me—I'm not fooled by that big silver tray and that tiny jacket. I know you're one of the people that bitch brought here to buy him. Stephanie doesn't understand. She's never been close enough to really see, to really *feel it*. But if I thought you had my Armand, I'd cut your pathetic little johnny off and stuff it down your throat until you choked on it!"

I nodded. I had gotten the message. Of course, if she found out what I really wanted to do to her pet, she'd come apart at the seams. The bidders only wanted to buy him.

The urge to throttle the miserable life out of her made my hands shake. I went into the hall, closed the door, and walked away. It wasn't my place to put people out of their misery or dish out punishment for old crimes. I wasn't pure as snow myself. Besides, no matter what she'd done, I didn't want to see the expression she'd made when the nurse had pinched her.

I went back to the stairs. Voices echoed up from the bottom floor, so I went farther down the hall to a narrow set of steps at the end. I paused at the top, but the only sound I could hear was a TV announcer droning away. I crept down.

There was a short hallway at the bottom of the stairs that led to an exterior door. There were also three interior doors, one of which was open. The announcer's voice and a flickering TV light came from there.

I looked around, wondering how I was going to pass that open door without alerting whoever was inside.

An old woman in a maid's uniform stepped into the doorway and stared at me. She glanced at my white jacket with contempt; she wasn't fooled for a second.

While I considered what I should do, she rolled her eyes and shut the door. Apparently, she wasn't being paid to be security.

I walked to the exterior door. There was a dead-bolt key on a hook by the door, but I left it. As long as I had my ghost knife, I didn't need keys. I set the tray against the wall and went outside. After the musty warmth of the house, the cold made my skin feel tight on my face and hands.

The cottage sat at the top of the bare slope. When I crossed to it, I would be in full view of anyone looking out of a back window. I wished I had some cloud cover to darken the lawn; the thick black power line that ran from the house to the guesthouse cast a moon shadow on the lawn.

I jogged across the damp crabgrass. *He's the only dog of his kind in the world,* Regina had said. *A sapphire dog.* I wondered if she was being literal or if that was more rotten poetry. I still imagined something with wings.

Maybe it was a bad idea to imagine anything. Whether it had wings, was shaped like a dog, or was just a blue smear of light, I was going to have to destroy it. If I could. Better to keep an open mind.

A stairway of mortared stone led up the muddy slope. I jogged up. The cottage faced away from the main house, and all but one of the ground-floor windows were shuttered. I peeked inside. A desk lamp shone onto scattered papers and a closed laptop, but the room beyond was dark. I circled around.

There was a huge metal tank and a generator against the building. I rapped on the tank. It was nearly full. Regina had enough fuel to run that generator for weeks.

The front of the cottage was pretty much what illustrated fairy-tale books had taught me to expect. There was a heavy wooden door with an even heavier lintel. On either side was a window split into four panes with a window box underneath. At the far side of the building, I saw the front of a parked ATV.

By the floodlight above the door, I saw muddy footprints smeared on the stone walkway leading to the door. I knocked, then knocked again. No answer.

The door was locked. I slid the ghost knife between the door and the jamb, then put it into my back pocket. The door creaked open.

"Hello?" I called. The room was silent. I reached for a light switch, then stopped myself.

A ceramic tile hung on the wall just above the switch. It was about the size of my palm, and it was painted white with an emerald-green squiggle on it.

Out of habit, I glanced down at my hand. The squiggle didn't look exactly like the marks on me, but it was similar enough to make me nervous. I took out my ghost knife again and sliced through the tile.

It split in two, but even before it fell, the broken squiggle released a jet of black steam and iron-gray sparks. I jumped out of the doorway to avoid the spray.

A magic sigil can throw off a lot of energy when it's been destroyed.

After it died down, I stepped back into the room. Whatever that spell had been created to do, it was just a mess on the floor now. I flicked on the light.

The cottage was a single room with very little furniture. A narrow bed was set into the back corner with a small dresser beside it. Next to that was a narrow desk with a lamp still burning, and beside that was the tiny stove from Regina's photo. The shelf above the stove was filled with can after can of Dinty Moore beef stew.

I saw no TV, no stereo, no bookshelves, and no Charlie Brown Christmas tree strung with lights. There was one thing in here to occupy a person's attention.

A large Plexiglas cage was set into a recess in the floor. It was larger than the one in the truck, maybe five feet on each side. It, too, had powerful floodlights at four corners, all aimed inward. Tiny electric fans were set on opposite sides of the cage, one to blow in, I guessed, and one to blow out. The black electrical wires powering them were strung all around the Plexi and held in place with peeling yellowed tape. There was also a plastic hatch along one side with an additional light shining through it.

Hanging from the ceiling was a smaller Plexiglas cube that could be fitted to the hatch. I guessed it was a holding tank so the main cage could be cleaned.

But there was nothing in the cage that needed cleaning—no bowls, blankets, litter boxes, or squeak toys. There hadn't been any of that packed in the truck, either.

A rocking chair was set at the edge of the recessed section of floor. I imagined Regina sitting and staring into the cage.

The door banged open behind me. I spun. A woman was silhouetted by the floodlight. She was almost six feet tall, broad in the shoulders and hips and dressed head to toe in white ski gear. Her plump face was pale and puffy. It was Ursula.

I felt the edge of the ghost knife in my pocket. "Don't move!" she shouted with an accent I couldn't place. She extended her arm, and I realized she was holding a gun.

It was a Colt .45, very old, very intimidating, and very aimed at my head. Someone who knew more about guns would have aimed it at my chest, where I had protective tattoos. I didn't have any protection on my face.

"Put that away," I said, sounding much more calm than I felt. "I've come to offer you a job."

"Hands up!" she barked. "Take your hand out of your pocket slowly. It should be empty, or I will shoot. Yes?" Her accent was northern European—Swedish maybe. I left my ghost knife in my pocket and showed her my empty hands.

"How did you get in here without . . . ?" She glanced back at the wall and saw that the tile was gone. She didn't think to look on the floor. "Who are you?"

"You should hear me out, and quickly. I'm not kidding about that job."

"I think you are kidding. Even if you were not, I would never work for a man dressed as kitchen help. Besides, I already have a job. I will be traveling with Armand early tomorrow, and I do not have time to waste."

I smiled. "Armand isn't going to Hong Kong with Yin."

She smirked at me. "Do you know something I don't?"

"Everyone knows something you don't. Why don't you close that door? This jacket isn't worth a damn."

I held open the servant's jacket so she could see I was unarmed, then stripped it off and tossed it onto the top of the plastic cage. She stared at me in shock. Apparently, touching the cage was Just Not Done.

She entered and pulled the door shut. The latch didn't engage because I had cut it off. "This is my home," she said.

I felt a twinge of guilt at that. I had done a lot of rotten things and I'd broken my share of laws, but I didn't like scaring women. Not that she looked scared.

Too late now. "I'm sorry for barging in, Ursula," I said, trying to keep any genuine regret out of my voice. I didn't think she'd trust a sympathetic face. "I had to see this setup for myself. It's not much, is it?"

"What is it that you know that I do not?"

"That Asian fellow offered you a job, correct? To keep caring for Armand?"

She nodded. "Of course. I have cared for him for years. I am the expert."

"Well, he doesn't have Armand anymore."

Her expression didn't change. "What do you mean? Who has him, you?"

"No one has him, as of an hour ago. He's running loose on the mountainside."

Her expression still hadn't changed. I didn't like the way she was looking at me. It reminded me too much of Regina's flinty stare. "Why should I believe you?"

"Because I'm here." I sat in the rocking chair and didn't let my smile fade. "I wanted to see whether he came back here. This is his home, isn't it?"

"It has been for twenty-two years." Both of us stared into the empty cage.

"Do you think he will come back here eventually? His home doesn't look very comfortable."

"He does not need comfort. He is not like other kinds of dog. At first, we gave him chew toys and soft blankets, but he never bothered with them. He never ate, either. Never drank water. I'm not even sure he ever breathed . . ." Her voice trailed off. I wanted to keep her going.

"Never ate?" I prompted. "What kind of dog is he?"

"He is not a dog, of course. Not a real one. He is a spirit. We fed him with our love. That was all he needed."

We heard a pair of gunshots. They were far away, faintly echoing off the mountainsides. Maybe Biker wasn't going home after all.

"My God!" Ursula said. "Are they hunting him?"

"No one is going to shoot him, not when he is worth so much," I said. "It was probably—"

She turned toward me and raised the Colt. I threw myself and the rocking chair to the side as the gun went off. I rolled onto the floor, wondering if she'd hit me.

The ghost knife was already in my hand. I threw it.

The gun went off again, splintering the wooden floor. A moment later, the ghost knife sliced through the Colt's barrel and hammer. Then the spell passed through Ursula's shoulder.

Her ski jacket split open, but I knew the flesh beneath would be unmarked. The top of the pistol fell to the side, and the spring in the magazine flung the remaining rounds into the air. I *reached* for the ghost knife, and it returned to me, passing through Ursula's stomach.

She stared in amazement at the weapon in her hand. I relaxed a bit and checked myself for bullet wounds—I'd heard people could be shot but not feel it. I didn't find any blood. She'd missed. A little shiver ran through me; I'd been lucky.

I kicked the rocking chair away and felt it wobble. The gun or the fall had broken it. I rolled onto my knees.

The floorboards shifted. On impulse, I raised my arm just as Ursula body-slammed into me. I heard an electric crackle, then felt a sharp, burning pain on my biceps.

My whole body jolted as an electric current ran through me, making all my muscles fire at once. We hit the floor together, and the impact broke the connection. I twisted, reached up with my other arm, and caught her wrist.

She'd burned me with a stun gun, and if I hadn't raised my arm, she would have zapped me in the eyes.

Her face was close. Her teeth bared, her eyes wide with a killing urge. Damn. The ghost knife had passed through her. Twice. Why hadn't it worked?

I tried to push her off me, but she was too big and too strong. She raised herself up and put her whole weight behind the stun gun, forcing it toward my face.

I didn't have the strength to hold her off with just my left hand, and my right was numb and weak from the shock. She grinned at me, and I could see triumph in that smile.

I forced the stun gun to the side and heard it crack against the floor by my head. Ursula cried out and dropped it. I twisted against her, letting her body weight roll over me. She fell onto the broken rocking chair and hissed in pain.

I tried to get out from under her, but she lunged toward me, mouth gaping. I leaned away as she snapped at me, her teeth clamping down on my collar inches from my throat.

To hell with this. I put my knees against her hip and kicked. She fell back and I rolled away onto my feet.

Ursula grabbed the stun gun and lunged at me, arm extended. She was a big woman, but she was slow. I caught her wrist and pulled her toward me, knocking her flat on her stomach. I pinned her elbow and quickly knelt on her shoulder. Now she was the one without leverage.

"Damn," I said. "You're a pain in the ass." I wrenched the stun gun out of her hand. One of the metal leads was broken. I doubted it still worked. "Hold still, or I'll use this on you."

She didn't. The thick ski jacket made it tough to control her. If she didn't settle down, I was going to have to either let her go or hurt her. I laid the stun gun against the back of her neck and shouted at her to be still.

She answered in her native language, whatever it was. I couldn't understand, but I knew she wasn't asking how I take my tea. I tossed the broken stun gun away.

The ghost knife was nearby. I could feel it. I *reached* for it and it flew into my hand.

Ursula grunted from the effort of trying to throw me off. In a few moments she would have her knees under her and I'd have another fight on my hands.

I slid the ghost knife through the back of her head. She didn't react at all. The spell was supposed to "cut ghosts, magic, and dead things"; it could destroy the glyphs that sustained spells, cut through inanimate objects, and damage people's "ghosts." I didn't know exactly what that meant, but everyone else I had cut with it had stopped trying to kill me. Why didn't it work on Ursula? Did she not have a "ghost," whatever that was?

Ursula nearly bucked me off. She was still cursing at me, and I had no way to control her except by throwing punches.

I wasn't going to do that. I had fought in the street for the Twenty Palace Society. I had broken into homes and burned them to the ground. I had shot men in cold blood. But I wasn't ready to punch this woman.

She kept thrashing. "Let me go," she said, her voice vicious with rage. "I have to check on Armand."

"No one is going to hurt Armand, not if he's worth so much."

She kept fighting me. I wasn't getting through.

I was going about this all wrong. I leaned close to her and spoke quietly. "This isn't his home, is it? If it was, he'd have come back here as soon as he was free." She stopped struggling, although her breathing was still harsh. "I came here to see if he'd return to the people who loved him. But he won't, will he?"

A low moan escaped her throat. I kept talking. "You love him, I know you do. But now that he has his freedom, he's never coming back. He doesn't want to be your prisoner anymore. All these years you've kept him trapped in this little room, giving him your love, and now you know what he's always wanted."

She made a terrible, heartrending sound. It was the sound a mother might make over a dying child. I let her buck me off.

We both scrambled to our feet. She looked at me, her

eyes brimming with tears. Then she looked at the Plexiglas cage, turned, and ran out the door.

I looked around one more time. The place made my skin crawl. I'd spent time in prison, but this disturbed me in ways I wasn't ready to think about.

I heard Ursula shouting outside. I hurried to the window. She was lumbering toward the house, screaming and pointing back to the cottage. Back to me.

CHAPTER FOUR

Damn. I raced out the door. The tree line wasn't far, but I didn't want to run into the woods. Not when Catherine's car was in the other direction.

The ATV had a key in it. I grabbed a bungee cord from behind the seat and strapped the handlebars down. Then I started it up and sent it on its way.

As I came around the edge of the cottage, Ursula ran through the servant's entrance of the house and slammed the door behind her.

I sprinted down the hill toward the house. I had nearly reached the doorway, still stupidly planning to follow her inside, when the back light turned on. She had roused the house faster than I expected.

The corner of the building was just a few yards to my right. I ran around it and ducked out of sight, staying in the muddy tracks Biker and his two killers had made.

The only tool I had was my ghost knife, but I was pretty sure I could crack a steering column with it. Unfortunately, the cars in the garage were on the other side of the house. Horace had distracted me before I could disable them, but I couldn't get to them right now. I could have gone around the front, but if the guard at the main entrance had been replaced, that wouldn't turn out well.

I peeked around the corner. Six Fellows streamed through the back door, each carrying a shotgun. They fanned out across the yard, one particularly fat one moving toward me. Dammit. The ATV had overturned on a tree root across the yard; hadn't they noticed it?

I leaned away from the corner of the house. The tree line was not close enough for me to risk it, especially considering how much noise I'd make in the undergrowth. I'd end up like Biker, a rotting corpse with a bullet in my back. But there was a basement window at my feet. I dropped to my knees in the freezing mud and cut through the latch. The window opened toward me, but the gap was too narrow for me to fit through. The man with the shotgun would come around the corner at any moment. I cut both hinges and slid through the opening, pulling the frame in after me.

The basement was pitch-dark, except for the yard light shining through the narrow windows along the ceiling. I landed on something flat and solid. It didn't tip over and crash onto the floor. I pressed the window frame in place—it was upside down and didn't fit properly, but I tried to hold it absolutely still.

The fat man in the parka walked in front of the window. His puffy face was already red from the cold, but something in the way he scanned back and forth made me wary. He was calmer than the others. More in control.

Luckily, he was looking toward the trees opposite the house, not at his feet.

My ghost knife was in my back pocket, but I wasn't sure it would work on him any better than it had on Ursula. Was it running out of power, or did she have a protection spell? My ghost knife didn't *feel* any weaker, and it had cut the window readily enough.

Someone shouted, "There!" and the fat man trotted back toward the others. I blew out a long, relieved breath and fitted the window, carefully squeezing it into the jamb. A strong wind would knock it out again, but I planned to be long gone by then.

I climbed down to the floor. The low dresser I'd been crouching on had a white cloth draped over it. Each window was about ten feet from the next one, and by their faint rectangles I could see the shape of the room. It was obviously the size of the house above, but the weird silhouettes and broken shadows showed me it was full of clutter.

My eyes were not accustomed to the darkness, so I moved slowly, my hands guiding me around chair legs, discarded bicycles, and other junk I couldn't identify by touch alone.

At first I intended to go to the front of the building to steal a car, but I heard shouting from the back of the house and moved toward it.

The window closest to the back entrance was blocked by a tangle of what appeared to be broken garden equipment, but the next one over had two steamer trunks stacked beneath it, along with a pile of lacy dresses. I climbed onto them, probably ruining them with my muddy clothes, and peeked out the window.

There were shoes just a few feet from me. One pair were green Chuck Taylors, soaked through by the mud. Beside those was a pair of hiking boots fresh from the sporting goods store. The third pair was the professor's fur-trimmed leather boots. The man in the Chucks fidgeted back and forth but let himself be hemmed in by the other two. It was Kripke. It had to be.

Beyond them, I saw the two Mustaches marching across the open meadow toward the ATV. A third man was with them. He had a lean, hollow look and was dressed completely in cold-weather bicycling gear. He was another Fellow, I was sure. No one else would dress so badly.

I couldn't hear them. I slowly, quietly unlatched the window and eased it open.

"He had a gun," Ursula said. "He threatened to shoot me if I didn't tell him everything I knew about Armand." Just as she finished the sentence, she came into view, walking across the grass with Stephanie beside her, followed by the tattooed man and a frail-looking blond man I hadn't seen before. They walked toward the professor.

"Have you ever seen this man before?" Frail asked. He had a German accent, and his voice was high. Ursula shook her head. "Think carefully. You may have seen him in town or while running errands. Could he be a local?"

"No, he—" Ursula began, but Stephanie interrupted.

"Where are the goddamn guards? I hired a security team to protect the grounds. Where are they?"

"Ms. Wilbur," Solorov said. "Shut up. We have questions to ask."

"Don't you tell me to shut up! I *paid* them. Now I find that they all ran home to their mommies! I'm going to sue them for so much money—"

"Shut up, Ms. Wilbur, or I will have you shot," Solorov said. Stephanie gaped at her.

I heard an old man's wheezing laughter. They stopped and glanced back as he shambled into view. He wore a bulky black coat and a black fur cap with the earflaps down, and he leaned on a gnarled black cane that had been heavily carved. A pair of black bird-watching binoculars hung around his neck. Frail rushed to him and gently took a black leather satchel from his hand.

I realized I was staring, just as the others were. There was something arresting about him, although he appeared completely ordinary in every way.

Frail walked beside the old man as though he was ready to catch him, but he continued his questioning. "Please, explain why you are so sure he is not a local."

"It was the way he spoke," Ursula said. Her tone was flat. "Some things he said. He said Mr. Yin didn't have Armand anymore. He said that Armand had escaped."

"That's a lie," Stephanie blurted out, apparently forgetting the professor's threat. "I just spoke with Mr. Yin ten minutes ago, and they are en route without incident. He must have been trying to trick you." The contempt she held for Ursula was clear.

"What did he look like?" Frail asked.

"He was a little over six feet tall. Slender and handsome with a knife scar on his cheek. He was wearing a stolen servant's uniform. And he had tattoos on the backs of his hands."

The old man spoke up, his voice raw and low. "What sort of tattoos?"

"Like his." Ursula pointed at Tattoo.

They fell silent.

"What?" Stephanie asked. "What does that mean?"

The old man turned toward Frail and spoke in a soft grumble of German. Frail rushed away on an errand, then exchanged a meaningful look with Tattoo. "Professor Solorov," the old man called. "Bring your people back to the house, please. This is something I will have to take care of, I think."

I heard a cellphone being dialed. "Come back to the house" was all she said. I heard the phone snap shut.

Then I heard her say in a low voice: "Tell me why those tattoos might be important."

The voice that answered was Kripke's. "I thought you people knew—"

"I do know, Mr. Kripke. Now you have to impress me with what you know."

"Well, the tattoos are spells. The part that shows, anyway. Most are probably protection spells."

"So far you haven't impressed me."

"For instance," Kripke continued, emphasizing the

words to show his annoyance at being interrupted. "That one there, on the German muscle's forehead, that's the guiding hand. It's supposed to make others feel something, depending on the little variations. A really common version makes people attracted to you. Sexually, I mean. His is a little different, but judging by how I feel every time I look at him, I suspect it's supposed to intimidate people."

There was a brief pause. Finally, Solorov spoke in a low, urgent, dangerous voice. "You will turn over your spell book to me, along with all copies, or I—"

"I don't have a spell book," Kripke snapped.

"—or I will kill you and everyone in your family. I'll burn their houses down while they sleep at night. Do you understand me?" Her voice was urgent and, unlike the others in her group, completely free of *oh boy I get to be naughty* breathlessness. She was fierce and cold and sharp.

"I don't have a spell book," Kripke said. "I really don't. If I did, I'd be a badass like them. I wouldn't be letting you hold a gun on me."

"Then where did you get this level of information? Or are you fabricating it?"

Kripke sighed. "A guy dropped by the server uninvited. He baited his way in, but before we could ban him, he offered up good information—very good."

"What good information did he give you?"

"It's too complicated to go into it now. Honest. We can review that later, if you want, but one of the things he gave us was a write-up of a couple of dozen spells and the outward glyphs that go with them. Mostly, they were protection spells like golem flesh and iron gate, but he also included odd things like the twisted path and the second word. No summoning spells. He listed the things the spells could do when they were fresh and when they weren't."

"I want to see that."

"Okay."

"And everything else you have."

Kripke sighed again. "Okay. It goes against our TOA, but okay. Another thing: I know where the security guards went. I saw Mr. Yin approach the one at the front door, the lead. Yin flashed ID and ordered them to leave. The guard called someone, and after a couple of seconds, he shrugged and ordered all his men into their Expeditions."

"The harpy hired one of Mr. Yin's companies to provide security?" Solorov sounded amused.

"More likely Yin found out who she hired and bought them out. He's really, really rich."

The old man's assistant returned. Everyone stopped talking. He handed a metal bar to the old man, who shuffled out onto the lawn.

I wondered who had given Kripke his information. I knew the society would be interested in that. I also wondered what he'd meant when he said spells could be fresh. Until Ursula shook off the effects of my ghost knife, it hadn't occurred to me that it might have an expiration date.

I couldn't help but think of my boss, Annalise. She wouldn't have hidden in a dark basement, eavesdropping. She would have bashed heads together.

Would she have killed Kripke and the professor? The Twenty Palace Society killed people who used magic. Did they kill people who were just searching for it, too?

Not that it mattered right now. I wasn't going to kill anyone I didn't have to, and not just on Catherine's say-so. I did need to grab hold of Kripke, though. Like the professor, I wanted information from him.

Tattoo returned with the sour-faced old housekeeper. He held her hand as they walked across the grass. Her scowl had been replaced by an empty, dreamy smile. Someone needed to give her a coat.

Tattoo steered her onto the lawn. The old man waited at the bottom of the slope, twisted iron bar in his hand. I had a bad feeling about that damn bar. I took out my ghost knife.

The old man was about fifty feet from me. I could have thrown my ghost knife and hit him easily. It goes where I want it to go—I don't even really need to Frisbee it, although it moves faster that way. Still, the Fellows had shotguns. And I would have bet every penny I had that the old man was a sorcerer. My little ghost knife couldn't take out all of them, but maybe I could disrupt things and get away.

Assuming it worked on him better than it had on Ursula.

Men crowded around Solorov to ask her questions, and their legs completely blocked my view. I could hear them muttering to one another, half excited and half envious. I needed to get to another window to see what the old man was going to do. I couldn't throw my spell without aiming it, and if I was going to stop him, I'd need to hit the bar—and him—with my first shot.

The window to my left was blocked with garden tools. The window to my right was blocked by an old couch on its end. I leaned back to see if there was a better option farther down the room.

"Christ!" one of the men outside shouted.

I turned back to the window. The men had stepped to the side, clearing my line of sight.

The old woman lay on her back in the grass. The old man had just stabbed the metal bar through her chest into the ground. He stared at a carving on the top of the bar.

"He did that right out in the open," one of the Fellows said. "Right in front of us."

"Be quiet," Solorov said.

I had expected him to consult a spell book, say a few words, maybe draw a circle. Something. But he hadn't, and I had missed my chance. I should have just cut my way through to him, and to hell with what came of it.

Frail ran toward the house, putting a lot of distance between himself and the body. The old man only stepped back a few feet. He looked to the sky, but I couldn't see anything up there besides night clouds and stars.

The metal bar wobbled. It was adorned with a variety of shapes, but at this distance I could only make out the one on top, a large eye.

There was a sudden flash of light. The Fellows leaped back against the building wall. A bolt of lightning had flashed out of the clear night sky and struck the trembling bar—a lightning rod, that's what it was—engulfing the old woman in crackling light.

Her body lifted off the ground as the power poured out of the sky. The lightning—tinged with red now as though stained with blood—curled around her, shaping itself into a ball. The Fellows cursed in fear. A woman screamed—it sounded like Stephanie. I felt like screaming myself. Then the light became too bright to look at.

After a couple of seconds, the light faded enough for me to squint at it again. It had formed a sphere about three feet across. It rose into the air, drawing itself off the lightning rod as if unimpaling itself. The old woman had been reduced to blackened bones. The grass where she had lain was not even singed, although the lightning rod glowed white hot.

The churning ball of burning gas and lightning hovered above the old man.

"Sweet Jesus," someone said. "What did he do?"

I knew the answer already. He'd summoned a predator right in front of me.

I looked at my ghost knife. My spell was written on

laminated paper. Even if it could kill that creature—and that was a big if—I was sure the heat and power of the thing would destroy my spell.

I wasn't ready to do that. It was my only weapon, the only spell I'd created myself, and I didn't have the spell book anymore.

The old man shouted something at the predator in German. "He's telling it to search the woods around the house," one of the Fellows said. "He's telling it to kill everyone it finds between the house and the iron fence."

"But what the hell is it?" Russian Accent asked.

It was Kripke who answered. "I think it's a floating storm."

The predator floated toward the cottage. The old man shouted at it, then shouted again, his voice more insistent and aggravated.

"He's telling it to hunt," Kripke said, volunteering information like a good little employee.

The floating storm did not change direction. It hovered above the spot where the thick black power cable connected to the guesthouse. Blue arcs jumped from the wires into its body. The old man shouted at it again, sounding like a grandfather trying to control a toddler from the comfort of his easy chair. The predator ignored him.

The porch light suddenly went out, and the blue arcs stopped. A couple of flickering tongues of flame appeared on the cottage roof.

Once the power was off, the floating storm glided toward the woods. The old man scowled at Tattoo, who responded in German. The old man shrugged. They both laughed and shook their heads like boys who had launched a firework in the wrong direction. The predator was out of their control, and they thought it was funny.

Tattoo walked up to the lightning rod, which had cooled to merely red hot, and grabbed it with his bare hand. Both men started toward the house.

The predator floated over the bare trees, making shadows sweep across the grass. "Professor," one of the Fellows said, "I think we should be getting inside."

She didn't move. "It's beautiful, isn't it?"

"Um, can we go now?" Kripke said. "It's not safe to be out here." No one moved. "Please?"

Professor Solorov sighed. "Let's go inside and find some candles. We may be here awhile."

They stepped back, leaving me a clear view of the predator as it moved away from the house. Had it sensed Catherine and the gunmen searching the grounds of the estate? It didn't even have any eyes.

Catherine needed to know this thing was hunting her. She had a cell, but I didn't know her number. I had to risk going into the woods to warn her, and I didn't have much time.

I pushed the window closed. I heard a muffled "Hey!" Footsteps came toward me. Damn.

I backed off the steamer trunks and crouched behind a little round table that smelled of mold. A man knelt by the window and shined a flashlight inside. The light was too dim to illuminate the pitch-blackness of the basement, but it didn't matter. I'd been spotted.

A second man knelt by the window. I heard one of them tell the other that he'd seen the window close. While I silently cursed my stupidity and impatience, they yelled for more people. I couldn't keep hiding here. If I was going to warn Catherine, I'd have to move before they got organized.

I pivoted away from the window and bumped into something sharp and metallic. It clattered to the floor, then a stack of somethings crashed in the darkness. Not that it mattered now.

I reached the window I'd cut open and pulled it from the frame. The way looked clear. I climbed up, sticking my head and neck through.

A foot squelched in the mud nearby and I threw myself backward. A shotgun blast tore through the window frame, spraying wood splinters like shrapnel.

I fell back onto the legs of a chair, rolled to the side, and ducked behind a stack of copper pots.

Fat Guy knelt beside the open window and peered in, shotgun in hand. "I saw him," he said to someone over his shoulder. "I didn't get him, though."

I had the sudden urge to leap forward and punch him in the face with every bit of strength I could muster. The son of a bitch had shot at me. I clenched my hands into fists to calm my trembling and hung back in the darkness like a coward.

Whoever he was talking to grabbed his shoulder and tried to pull him back. "The fat lady said he had a gun."

Fat Guy shrugged the hand away. "I saw his hands. He didn't have no gun. Get inside and get down there."

I threw my ghost knife at him.

He must have seen movement because he threw himself back. The ghost knife struck the shotgun, shearing off the front of the barrel and the pump, too. The cut part of the weapon fell through the window into the basement.

I *called* the ghost knife and it zipped through the open window into my hand. It still worked on *dead things*, at least.

Fat Guy held up half of his weapon. "Well, I'll be damned."

"What could have done that?"

"I don't know, but I will soon. Gimme your shotgun."

The other Fellow didn't like that suggestion, and both men moved away from the window to talk about it. The other man eventually agreed to stand guard.

I inched forward, peering around the edge of the window jamb. The Fellow stood about ten feet away, the shotgun against his shoulder as though he was about to shoot skeet. He was the one dressed in biking clothes.

"Hey in there!" he yelled. "Come out with your hands up, and I won't shoot."

He snapped the barrel of the gun to the right, then left, looking very trigger-happy. I didn't want to throw my ghost knife directly into the path of a blast of buckshot. I moved toward the front of the house. The garage offered more cover, but it was too far away. Had they posted a new guard at the front door? I'd have to risk it.

Heavy footsteps clomped overhead. The Fellows were coming—with guns—and I didn't have time to wait around. My only real hope was that they were all coming after me, leaving the area outside unguarded.

I banged my head against something that made a solid wooden *thunk*. I laid my hands on it—it was smooth and curved, but I had no idea what it was. What I could tell was that it completely blocked the path. I had to turn back.

Footsteps stumbled down the stairs somewhere to my left. By the echo, I judged they were coming from the center of the room.

I crept back the way I'd come, keeping low so they wouldn't spot my silhouette against a window.

One of them said something in another language. Russian, maybe. Another answered: "Just one, I think. A guy." The Russian-speaker answered. He didn't sound confident. Someone flicked a light switch several times. Nothing happened.

Damn. I wished I could pinpoint where they were.

"I don't like it down here," another one said. The Russian-speaker said something that seemed like agreement. "I mean, what was that thing outside? We didn't try to buy something like *that*, did we?"

"Shut up, Gregor," another said. I recognized his voice.

It was Fat Guy. "You're gonna talk yourself out of the Fellowship."

"I'm just saying," Gregor continued, ignoring the other man's advice. "You saw that old woman die. You saw her spirit, or whatever that was, float away into the woods. What if it comes for us? Are we supposed to use shotguns against it?"

"Then let's find this guy," a new voice said, "so we can go home."

They were spooked. I just wished they'd been spooked by me. I sure as hell didn't want to fight all of these guys. One at a time, without guns, was bad enough, but like this it was too chancy.

Then I had an idea. I threw the ghost knife into the darkness.

I waited, feeling it move away from me. No effect. The Russian-speaker was talking, and the others were listening quietly. I *called* it back and threw it again in a slightly different direction.

This time I was rewarded by a loud crash across the room. The spell had cut part of an unsteady stack somewhere.

"Christ!" Gregor shouted. There was a barrage of gunfire. I dropped to the ground, but I was pretty sure it wasn't aimed at me. After a few seconds, the shooting stopped. I *called* my ghost knife back, my ears still ringing.

"Goddammit!" Fat Guy yelled. "I'm standing right here!"

The trigger-happy one was breathing hard. So was I. The ghost knife settled into my hand.

"Reload that weapon," Fat Guy said. "And if you shoot one of us, I'm going to kill you and your mother, too. Get me?"

"Sorry," Gregor mumbled.

I slowly got to my knees. My shoe scuffed against the floor, but the Fellows were breathing too hard to hear it.

"We should fan out," Russian Accent said.

"We're not fucking fanning out. Not with this crew. I'd prolly bump an old mirror, and Gregor here would empty a clip of soft-points into me. Stick together and cover each other."

One of them flicked on a flashlight, and I knew just where they were. I sidestepped to get a clear shot.

"What do you think is down here?" Gregor asked.

I threw the ghost knife at them. Please work. Please.

One of the men screamed. It gave me chills—he sounded like I'd cut off a body part. I heard someone fall and a clatter of breaking glass. The flashlight beam swerved around and pointed at the floor. Shapes moved in the light.

"It touched me!" Gregor screamed, his voice stripped of all courage and dignity. "It touched my soul! Don't let it happen again! Please, God, don't let it happen again."

I felt a tremendous relief. My ghost knife still worked. I wondered if Ursula had some sort of special protection against it.

"What happened?" the new voice said. He sounded spooked. The Russian-speaker answered him in the same confused, frightened tone.

I *called* the ghost knife to me. One of the men screamed, "Look out!" then the spell returned to my hand.

"It came from over there!" Fat Guy said, and then a volley of gunshots rang out, all facing away from me. I dropped low anyway. The floor was concrete and the walls were cinder block; I didn't want to be killed by a ricochet.

The shooting stopped after a couple of seconds. One of them let out a high, quavering whine, like a fan belt about to give. "Dammit," Fat Guy said. "Gimme a clip. Somebody gimme a clip."

But it was too late for that. Their morale had been

broken. There was a cascade of stomping footsteps as they fought one another up the stairs. No one wanted to be the last to get out of the darkness.

I crouched in the dark, listening. The basement was quiet, but I could hear footsteps above me, shuffling around. I felt a little smug. Those guys had been afraid of me—well, they'd been afraid of what they'd imagined was in the darkness.

There was probably a lesson in that, but whatever. Someone was moving toward the front of the house, so I headed toward the garage. I still needed to find Catherine. I held my hands in front of me as I went. Although I had to backtrack out of a couple of dead ends, I didn't run into anything dangerous.

The windows on the garage side of the house were about fifteen feet away when a metal shelving unit toppled onto me.

I raised my arm to shield my face, feeling for a moment that the whole building was falling onto me. Something slid off the shelf, bounced off my forehead, and shattered at my feet. I fell back against a second metal shelf, and the two frames closed on my head. I cried out as I scraped myself free.

"Got you!" someone said. It was Fat Guy again.

The shelves struck something and stopped falling. I slid close to the floor where the gap between them was widest.

A sharp pain in my knee froze me in place as a huge shadow moved toward me, black against not-quite-as-black. I'd knelt on something, but I'd worry about that later.

I could hear him breathing through his mouth. He had emptied his gun and asked for a clip. Had he gotten one before his buddies ran upstairs? I lunged for him, hoping to end this quickly. Trickery wasn't going to help me now.

I threw a punch at the general area where his head should have been, holding back a bit in case I missed and struck a piece of furniture. I connected. Lucky.

He took the blow in stride and grabbed my collar. Like a lot of big, slow, tough guys, he wanted to grapple. My shirt rippled. He'd hit me on the protective tattoos on my chest where I couldn't feel it.

Now I knew exactly where he was. I hit him with a right to the side of his jaw and, when he staggered, a left to his temple.

My left hand—which had never fully recovered from an old gunshot injury—throbbed, but the strength went out of Fat Guy. He rolled and fell flat on his back. I heard flimsy metal clatter around him in the dark.

I knelt and patted him down. He carried his wallet in his breast pocket. I took it. I also took his handgun from his shoulder holster and, after checking that the slide was back, pitched it into the darkness.

It only took another minute or so to reach the windows on the garage side of the building. I peeked outside. No one in sight.

By the light of the window, I searched Fat Guy's wallet. He was from Chicago and had two hundred dollars in twenties. How considerate of him. I took the cash and tossed his wallet into the clutter.

I cut a window out of the frame and pulled it free as quietly as I could. Cold, clean air rushed in. I boosted myself up and squeezed my shoulders through the gap.

A familiar voice said something in German. Tattoo was standing by the corner where he could watch this side of the house and the front. He began to stroll casually toward me.

I squirmed through the window and scrambled to my feet. He was smiling and his limbs swung loose. He said something else, sounding almost friendly, and gave a pointed glance at my stomach.

I absentmindedly wiped my hand down the front of my shirt. There was a long slash in the cloth, starting beside my solar plexus and going down and to the left.

Damn. Fat Guy hadn't punched me in the gut. He'd had a knife and I never knew it. The Fellows had been frightened of what they couldn't see, but I'd nearly been killed by the same thing.

Tattoo was just a few paces away from me now. He was smiling like a guy who was going to walk all over me and enjoy the hell out of it.

CHAPTER FIVE

The ghost knife was still in my pocket. I left it there. Tattoo made me nervous and I needed to keep something in reserve. The marks on his body could mean all sorts of things. Maybe he could breathe fire. Maybe he could shoot tear gas out of his armpits. I wanted him to play his hand before I played mine.

Also, I didn't want to go for my weapon right away. I hate to show my fear.

I started toward the garage, but he stepped lightly into my way. His smile grew wide and he clucked his tongue. That wasn't allowed. Hell, if he was going to *tsk tsk* me, he was going to get the fight he wanted. We moved toward each other.

He was fast. When he threw the first punch, I almost didn't see it coming and barely got out of the way, staggering back. He looked surprised that I'd avoided his jab but not particularly worried.

I leaned into him, moving my head to the side while throwing a jab of my own. I hit him full on his tattooed nose while his counterpunch went just wide.

Now it was his turn to stagger back. He kept his balance and his smile. *"Gut, gut!"* he said, as though advising me to try body blows. My left hand stung from the shot I'd landed, but his nose didn't look damaged at all. Damn. His tattoos seemed to be the same as mine, more or less, and he was completely covered by them—even his face. Probably even his scalp. This guy was better protected than my boss.

He came at me again. I went on the defensive, blocking and weaving. I'm pretty quick—I was a promising baseball player once, and I've always had a sharp eye and fast hands.

Tattoo was fast too, but he wasn't unnaturally fast. He wasn't superstrong, either. I wondered just how complete his protection was. He threw a low right hand that I let hit my ribs while I extended my left, fingers out, toward his eyes.

He dodged sideways, almost losing his balance in his haste. In that moment, I landed a solid kick to his crotch.

We backed away from each other. My lunge at his eyes had wiped the smile from his face, but the kick had brought it back. It'd had no effect on him.

"Oh, hell no," I said. "Your johnson, too? That's just not right."

His smile turned sour. Whether he spoke my language or not, he understood what I was saying. Suddenly he wasn't having quite so much fun.

I kept backing away from him, my left hand still aching. I wasn't focused on the fight the way I needed to be. If my head was in the right place, I wouldn't feel my hand until after. My adrenaline was trailing away—I'd wasted it in the basement and I needed it now.

He caught up to me, feinted low, and hit me on the side of my jaw.

I managed to roll with it at the last moment, but the world still blinked dark. I felt something cold against the side of my face—mud? It felt solid. I pushed away and crumpled into the mud for real. As I fell, Tattoo's fist hit the side of the house where my head had been.

I tried to shake my mind clear, but I was still feeling

fuzzy. My ass was wet. My hands were muddy and leaching heat, but that soothed the pain in my left.

Tattoo was talking again. Someone who didn't know about my protective tattoos would have kicked me in the ribs, but he circled behind me. The idea that he might return the favor of a kick to the nuts gave me a much-needed burst of adrenaline.

I rolled onto my hip and held out my forearm. That punch to the face frightened the hell out of me. If he did it again, I might never wake up. His kick struck my wrist. In a desperate grapple, I grabbed his right foot and twisted it with both hands. He yelped in surprise and pain, rolling against the steps Catherine and I had used to enter the house and falling into the mud to avoid a dislocated knee. His other boot scraped painfully across my scalp, but there was no power behind it. He got his arms under him. I didn't have much time. I jammed his foot behind the other knee, then folded his leg over it.

I remembered that sour-faced housekeeper. The old man had sacrificed her without a second thought, and Tattoo had laughed about it.

I rolled over his ankle and broke it.

He screamed. It was a high, girl-in-a-horror-movie scream, full of fear and unaccustomed to pain.

He reached back for me. I twisted his thumb too far, and he screamed again. I loved that sound. It was like a church choir to me. This bastard was faster than me and he hit harder, but the tattoos that protected him from cutting and impacts didn't protect against twisting.

And I couldn't leave him alive. He'd come after me again someday, and I didn't think I could take him a second time.

He swung with his good arm, stinging my ear. I let the momentum of his swing carry him onto his back, but I stayed close. I shifted my weight onto my feet, grabbed his wrists, and stood, lifting him off the ground with his head hanging down.

The stairs were made of stone. That should do. I waddled over there, pinning him with a bear hug. He struggled, but I could hold him long enough to break his neck.

Something came at me from the top of the stairs and slammed into me. The sudden impact broke Tattoo from my grip, and I wanted to cry out like a terrified child. I smelled a lemon aftershave as I sprawled in the mud.

It was the old man's assistant, Frail. I flipped him up and off me, letting our momentum roll me clear of Tattoo. He scuttled off, his hands over his head. Tattoo crawled away from me, dragging his crooked ankle behind him.

I heard shouting and footsteps through the open kitchen door. Tattoo's screams had brought help. My head still hadn't cleared—all I could think about was guns. I turned and ran around the garage into the woods.

I fled blindly, pushing through a break in the blackberry bramble and dodging through the trees so they wouldn't have a clear shot. It wasn't until I tripped at the bottom of a steep slope that I realized they weren't chasing me.

I leaned against a tree, fighting to catch my breath. Why hadn't they come after me with their shotguns? I rubbed my aching hands and face. My head began to clear.

And I remembered the floating storm.

Damn. I scanned the woods around me. I didn't see any floating balls of light, but my visibility was pretty limited. Damn and damn again. I'd planned to steal a car and drive to Catherine's. We could have gotten off the property in a few minutes.

I looked back up the slope. The cars were still there, of course. I could try to sneak back.

No. They knew I was out here. And even if they weren't going to chase me, they were probably watching from the windows. It's what I would have done.

I really wished I'd killed that tattooed bastard.

I jogged along the base of the slope, watching the tree-tops for any trace of the reddish light I'd seen the floating storm give off. The ground was covered with moss, fallen branches, and a few scattered ferns. I made a lot of noise, but it was better than pushing through brambles. After a few minutes, my head had cleared. There was still no sign of the creature.

Predator, I reminded myself. That old man had summoned a predator out of the Empty Spaces. And the Twenty Palace Society existed to kill people like him.

I had bought into that mission. Not an hour ago, I had wondered if I could bring myself to kill again. Now I had a list.

I thought about the people caught up in this mess: Regina and her staff, the Fellows, the old man and his dangerous little crew, and the well-dressed Chinese gunmen. The society was just another gang after the same prize, and Catherine and I were the only ones here to represent. Maybe that should have bothered me, but it didn't. I had bought in. I knew what predators could do, and I was ready to do whatever it took to destroy them.

And God! This was what I'd missed since Hammer Bay. I'd thought it had been the excitement and the danger, but it was really *this* feeling. I had a clear purpose. I had important work. I would do whatever I had to do to stop these people.

But no. That wasn't true. If I'd done to Ursula what Annalise would have done—if I'd killed her—I wouldn't have been trapped in the basement and I wouldn't have fought Tattoo. Hell, the old man wouldn't have summoned the floating storm. That maid's death was partly my fault. Annalise was ruthless but she wouldn't have gotten herself into this situation. It was something to think about.

The wind had picked up, and my wet pants and sleeves were leaching body heat. I wished I'd kept my jacket. I moved forward, scrambling over uneven ground and fallen wood, hoping I was headed toward the long asphalt drive.

I came across a trail of footprints in the mud and stopped. Was someone out here hunting me? I couldn't see anyone. There were actually three pairs of footprints. Two headed toward the house, and the third went back the other way.

They were mine, Catherine's, and Catherine's again. Perfect. At least I was on her trail. I followed the footprints to the long drive and then down the hill.

A thunderclap echoed from somewhere up ahead. Had I failed Catherine already? Had the floating storm killed her? I kept running. I wasn't going to give up on her until I saw her corpse.

That little thought prompted a quick series of ugly mental images that didn't do anything but slow me down.

I reached a steep part of the hill and crouched at the base of a tree. The crashed truck lay on the road below. The Acura was close, and I couldn't see anyone.

I fell once going down the slope. My pants were already as wet as they were going to get. No one shouted or shot at me. A few minutes later, I came to the stand of trees where Catherine's car was hidden.

It was still there. I approached cautiously. Catherine wasn't around. Damn. I peered inside. Nothing.

I circled the car, hoping to find a second trail of footprints to follow. Something moved out from behind a tree. I jumped and cursed before I realized it was Catherine.

"Sshh!" she hissed. "There are still men out here, hunting around. I saw you coming but couldn't tell who you were. So I hid. I sent the license plate photos already, and I've been waiting for you. What did you find out?"

"Stuff," I answered. "But the most important thing is that one of the bidders in that house summoned a predator."

"What?"

"They stuck a lightning rod through an old woman's heart and there was this flash of light and . . . the old man sent it out to kill everyone on the property."

"Well, let's get out of here then."

She unlocked the car and we climbed in. My flannel jacket was lying on the front passenger seat. I put it on, getting mud on the lining; my shoes and pants smeared mud on the car seat. "I'm sorry," I said.

She clipped her seat belt and turned the key. "You're wearing wet clothes on a winter night? Not smart. You'd last longer with nothing on."

I imagined myself lying out in the bramble, shot to death and wearing only smears of mud and underwear. To hell with that. I'd rather freeze.

She backed toward the road, taillights glowing. When all this was over, maybe I'd install a kill switch on her lights so they wouldn't light up the mountainside.

At the driveway she turned toward the gate and hit the gas.

We came around a twist in the road and saw two men blocking our way. Both were Asian, dressed in dark, expensive suits, and held pistols. Yin must be desperate, if he was having his men search every vehicle leaving the estate.

The taller one had no hat; maybe he didn't want to muss his high, moussed-up hair. He held out his hand like a traffic cop, expecting the weapons to make us obey.

Catherine gunned the engine and flicked on her headlights. The men scurried aside. The taller one shouted something to the other and fired two quick shots into the grille.

"Shit!" Catherine shouted. "Those bastards shot me!"

They didn't fire again. It took a moment to realize Catherine hadn't really been hit, just her car. The engine rattled. We began to slow down. I glanced back and saw that the two gunmen were following us, but they didn't appear to be in a hurry. "We were lucky," I said.

"Lucky? I love my car and those bastards killed it."

"We weren't going all that fast," I said. "They could have shot us both in the head. Easily. We're lucky they still haven't found the predator."

We crested the top of a hill and started down. The engine suddenly made a loud grinding noise. The car was dying.

Catherine put the car in neutral so we could drift to the bottom of the hill. "Shit!" she said again. She sounded close to tears. "Those assholes shot at us! Should I have stopped for them and let them search the car?" For the first time, I heard uncertainty in her voice.

"No," I told her. "After they searched, they would have held on to us, and I don't think we would have liked it."

She took a deep breath. "Right. Of course. I knew that." The Acura reached the bottom of the slope and lost momentum against the next rise. Catherine twisted the wheel so it blocked the road. "I'm sorry. The gunfire has me a little rattled. We run for the gate, don't we?"

"I think so. Those guys will be coming up behind us, and the old man ordered the floating storm to kill everyone it found between the house and the fence. Although . . ."

"Although what?"

"He didn't seem to have complete control over it."

She sighed again. "Let me get my jump bag." She grabbed a small, stuffed duffel bag from the floor behind her and got out of the car. Then she began jogging up the road. I followed her but spared a glance behind us. The two gunmen hadn't made it over the hill yet. We didn't sprint because we weren't sure how far we had to go, but we did hustle.

"Ray," she said. She was not breathing hard, but she didn't look comfortable. "I'm sorry for what I said. You've been a solid guy. You didn't have to come out here to warn me, but if you hadn't . . ."

"Thanks," I said, feeling a tremendous sense of relief that I couldn't really explain. It was hard to admit how much I wanted her acceptance, and through her the acceptance of the society as a whole.

And that hadn't been easy for her to say.

"Too bad you're a wooden man."

"Let's save our breath, okay?" But I knew what she meant. A wooden man didn't come with a long life expectancy.

The treetops cast long shadows across the road. The woods around me seemed to become more clear. My eyes were adjusting, I thought, but something didn't seem right. The shadows were too sharp. I grabbed Catherine's sleeve and pulled her to a stop. She cringed just a little, and I let go of her.

The long, crooked shadows of the trees were slowly moving toward us. I glanced up. Ahead and to the left there was a light in the sky. It was dimmer and smaller than a full moon, but it was growing brighter.

"Lord above," Catherine said. "It's coming right toward us."

I heard hissing, like water drops boiling in a skillet. It was, in fact, coming right toward us.

Catherine bolted for the downhill slope at the edge of the road. The bramble was thick there and the ground uneven. "No!" I shouted. "This way!" I ran back up the road.

I glanced back once to see that she had followed and that she could keep up. The floating storm passed over the trees onto the road. We ran around the Acura and up the hill.

"Where are we going?" Catherine called.

I slowed down to let her get next to me. An old joke popped into my head about running away from a bear, but I didn't think she'd find it funny. Catherine's mouth was set in a determined frown, and her forehead was a mass of wrinkles. She already had streaks of sweat down the side of her face.

Ahead of us, the two gunmen had reached the top of the slope. They had already seen the floating storm, of course. The tall one with the elaborate hair was talking very excitedly on his cell. His partner was short and round, with a Moe Howard haircut that made him seem like comic relief. He didn't have a fearful expression; he looked like he was seeing the awful end he'd always expected.

I risked one glance back at the creature behind me. It was traveling along the road now, but I couldn't tell if it was gaining or not.

The gunmen glanced at Catherine and me. I could see their indecision.

"Run for your lives!" I screamed at them, letting my face show some of the terror I was feeling. They shrank away from me, understanding the tone of my voice if not the words. Fear is contagious. The men in the basement had proved that.

They turned their attention back to the predator. Haircut pulled his cellphone away from his ear and winced as though it had stung him.

We were fewer than ten yards from them now. I grabbed Catherine's elbow and shoved her toward a deer path on the side of the road.

It was a steep drop-off. We hopped partway down the

hill until I slipped in the mud and fell, body-sledding into the back of Catherine's legs and knocking her on top of me.

We struck a tree trunk at the bottom of a shallow ravine and tumbled into the mud. I jumped up, pulled Catherine to her feet, and followed her up the slope ahead.

Gunshots. We both stopped at the top of the little slope and looked up at the road.

The two gunmen were holding their ground, standing in two-handed firing stances: shoulders squared, legs spread, one hand supporting the other. The shots went quickly, *popopopop*—it takes surprisingly little time to empty a handgun.

The floating storm was about fifteen yards off the ground and nearly above them. Moe Howard dropped the magazine out of his pistol and slapped in a new one with well-practiced speed. He started shooting again, and I knew he was hitting his target even though I couldn't see any effect. Haircut didn't bother to reload. He began to back away.

Beside me, Catherine said, "Oh, God. No."

The floating storm was above Moe now. There was a tremendous flash of reddish light and a thunderclap louder than anything I'd ever heard in my life. A blast of air staggered me. Haircut was close enough to be knocked down. When I blinked away the lights in my eyes, I saw him struggling to his feet, still half stunned.

The floating storm moved straight toward Haircut. He didn't have a chance.

I turned to run and saw Catherine giving me a withering stare of raw hatred. I was startled, but when she took off downhill, I followed.

We ran, aiming mostly northward because it was downhill. Where the ground was rough, we angled toward one side of the path or the other, trying to keep to flat ground. We also kept to the trees, hoping they would force the predator to stay high and out of range. And the ground was clearest where the trees were thickest. Where they were thin, the way was choked by vines and bramble.

It stayed on our tail, never getting too close and never falling far behind. Would a ball of churning gas and electricity toy with its prey? I figured not.

So we ran. The light from the predator cast long shadows ahead of us. Whip-thin tree branches, nearly invisible in the dim electric light, stung my face, neck, and arms. As we topped a ridge and slid down the other side, the light the predator gave off was suddenly blocked. We had to pick our way through the moss-covered branches by touch until the floating storm came close enough to light the way again.

We were never going to survive this way.

We came to a little stream—not deep, but the banks on both sides were pretty near vertical and too far to jump. Catherine bolted to the right, running along the gap until she came to a place where the bank on the far side was more gentle.

She jumped, hitting the ground with a loud *whuff*. I landed beside her and a little farther up. I grabbed her jacket to help her up the hill, but she shook me off angrily and ran by me. Her breath was coming in labored heaves.

I glanced down at my shadow and realized how short it had become. I sprinted after Catherine, trying to keep close without passing her.

I watched her. It was obvious that she was tired, but she never let up the pace. She ran on willpower, hurdling broken branches and exposed roots. It was barely running—more like hopping through an obstacle course. I didn't think either of us had the stamina to outrun the predator. I glanced back at it again. If it was becoming tired, I didn't know how I'd tell. At least we were putting a little more distance between it and us.

Catherine suddenly angled to the right, and I followed. She'd found a footpath that was clear of broken branches, although the moss was still slippery. The wind chilled the sweat on my face. We made better time on the footpath, and the forest grew darker around us.

"The town is down there," Catherine wheezed. I looked in the direction she pointed. Through the trees, I could see a cluster of faint, distant lights.

We could never run that far. We kept running anyway.

Then we came to the thing I was most afraid of—the ground dropped away in front of us. We had reached the edge of a fifty-foot cliff.

At the bottom was a little pine forest, all laid out in perfect rows. A Christmas-tree farm.

"Shit," Catherine said. "I can't run any more. Boy, you said you had a weapon that could kill a predator."

"I said *maybe*. And it won't work on this one. My spell is made of paper, and that thing is made of lightning. My spell would just burn up."

"Are you sure? You won't even try?"

Of course I would try—as a last resort. To the left of us, there was a section of cliff that had collapsed, making a very slight slope. A couple of trees grew nearly sideways out of the dirt. "Can you climb down this cliff?"

The electric hum of the predator was growing louder, and the woods were growing brighter. "Not fast enough," she answered.

"I'll give you time. Get down to the farm. Find something to kill an electricity monster. I'll lead it to you."

She ran to the left. "What if it catches you?"

I almost answered: *Then when it comes for you, I won't be leading it,* but the predator was close and it was time to run.

I followed the path along the top of the cliff, lengthening my stride to stretch out my legs. I'd already run a couple hundred yards over rough ground, and I didn't have a lot of gas left in my tank. The predator fell behind, but at least it was chasing me, not Catherine.

The woods to my right became steeper, sloping higher and higher until it was a wall of ferns and mud above me. If this trail dead-ended, I would be dead-ended, too. I was too damn tired to run uphill.

A couple of the trees ahead looked strange—too regular, and stripped of their branches. As the floating storm lit the woods around me, I realized they were power poles.

I picked up the pace. The power line came up the cliff below at a slant, ran along the trail for a few hundred feet, and then continued uphill to the right at a rocky point. The nearest pole on the trail was just ahead. The cliff drop to the left was still steep but looked manageable if I had a little time to work at it. I stepped around the pole and backed away from it, gasping to catch my breath.

As I'd hoped, the floating storm went for the power line. It moved carefully through the trees, avoiding branches when it could, setting them alight when it couldn't go around them. It reached the top of the pole and began to draw power slowly, sipping instead of gulping. Blue arcs flashed out of the top of the pole to the predator.

At the edge of the cliff, the muddy ground beneath me shifted. I fell, sliding with the mud down the slope. I had a sudden image of myself lying at the base of the cliff with a broken back while the predator moved toward me.

I managed to grab hold of a cluster of woody brush and stop my slide. I struggled to my knees, but the angle of the slope was too steep for me to hold myself in place, so I let go and stretched out flat. I slid slowly down the hill, finding one foothold after another in tree roots, trunks, and clumps of bushes. There were a couple of sketchy moments, but I survived.

At the bottom of the hill, I scrambled to my feet. The wind was gentle, but it still chilled me. Maybe Catherine was right, but I left my shirt on. I didn't like throwing away resources.

I crossed under the power line. The predator was still up there at the top of the cliff, still feeding. It had apparently learned that it could trip the breaker by feeding too fast. I didn't like that. I wanted it to be like a shark—dangerous but basically stupid. The smarter it was, the harder it would be to kill.

It looked like it was growing larger. Would it stop hunting me if it fed enough from the power pole? I didn't know what to do, so I jumped up and down and swung my arms, trying to keep my muscles warm for the next leg of the chase. All I was sure of was that I was giving Catherine extra time to prepare.

Then I imagined the predator growing large enough to split in two like a dividing cell. That thought scared the hell out of me.

Five quick cuts with the ghost knife on the nearest power pole made it topple—away from me, thank God— and snapped the power line. The blue arcs stopped popping under the predator. Dinner was over.

The floating storm didn't move for a couple of seconds. It bobbed up and down as if it was trying to puzzle out why the juice had stopped. I picked up a rotten hunk of branch and threw it.

The predator was too far away for me to hit it. The branch landed in the bushes near the base of the electric pole, and a sudden crack of red lightning blasted the ground at that spot. The sound startled and frightened me, and clumps of dirt and burning wood chips showered down over me.

The floating storm started in my direction. I turned and ran like hell toward the tree farm. The chase was back on.

CHAPTER SIX

There were no trees here, and the landscape between me and the tree farm was a wall of bramble and bush. I sprinted around the edges, hopping over downed trees in some places and pushing blindly through tall grass in others. My shadow began to shorten. Then I hit a rocky little stream and ran along it, picking up speed. I knew it was stupid to have my feet in water, but it was the only place I could run.

The stream disappeared into a drainage pipe. I scrambled up a dirt slope and ran straight into a chain-link fence.

With my ghost knife, I cut a hole in the chain link and pushed through. My shadow was short—too short. Behind me the creature was humming like a transformer, and I expected to feel lightning any moment. I sprinted out into the neat rows of trees. Flat ground. Hallelujah.

The old man had ordered the predator to patrol within the iron fence, but the chain link was made of steel. Obviously, he didn't know that the black iron fence along the road didn't ring the property. Or he didn't care. I had a moment's hope that the floating storm would turn back at the fence anyway, but that didn't happen. Damn. I kept running.

The trees themselves were just over two feet tall and offered no cover at all. I was glad. I needed to see.

My shadow slowly stretched out before me. I saw a small cluster of buildings way off to my right and angled toward them. There was a figure waving a long cloth back and forth over its head. Catherine.

I tried to put on extra speed, but I didn't have it. I didn't look back at the predator. I didn't need to. I could feel it back there like a high-tension wire, and I was flagging.

There were three buildings: One was a yellow farmhouse well off to the left. The others were a pair of big wooden barns, both painted red.

Catherine stopped waving her jacket at me, backed toward the red buildings, and ducked between them, making sure I'd seen where she'd gone. I was not far behind her.

"Through here!" Her voice came from the darkened doorway on the right. I staggered toward it just as the shadow of the other building swept over me. The floating storm was close behind.

I rushed into the darkness, barking my shin against something low and wooden. I tumbled onto my face, and the pain in my leg made me curse a blue streak. Something wet sloshed onto my leg.

The ground was packed earth and smelled of pine needles. I scrambled away from the doorway until I struck my head against something metal.

The barn lit up with a flickering electric red light.

I turned around. The floating storm had followed me to the doorway but had stopped at the entrance. It bobbed up and down, as though it didn't want to enter an enclosed space.

I glanced around, trying to see what Catherine had planned aside from the water-filled trough across the entrance, but the predator was too bright. I couldn't see into the shadows cast by the doorway.

I had not been this close to the floating storm before. It seemed to be swirling and churning from inside, like a sped-up lava lamp. The outside was a bluish-white cloud of brilliant light, but in the spaces where the swirling gases were thin or parted from one another, I could see a dark red color that swirled like blood in oil. In the center of that was a white-hot fire.

I laid my hand on an old, rusting truck. Would grounding myself lure it inside? Apparently not. To my left I saw a small pile of wooden disks. I grabbed one. It had been cut from the base of a pine trunk and was still sticky. I threw it at the floating storm like a discus. It struck almost dead center, but nothing came out the other side but a little burp of flames. So much for using my ghost knife.

"What are you waiting for?" I yelled. "Didn't the old man order you to kill me? You want to pose for a picture first?"

There was no way to tell whether it understood. I kept throwing hunks of wood at it. One grazed the bottom edge and landed, burning, on the ground outside. The others never made it all the way through.

After the sixth piece of wood, it ducked under the lintel and floated into the room. It must have decided I didn't have anything more dangerous than slices of Christmas trees.

I took the ghost knife from my pocket.

The shadows receded as the floating storm entered. Tucked back into the corner on the right, I saw Catherine against the wall. She had a long wooden pole in her hands.

As the predator moved by her, she dropped the pole and something heavy swung out of the ceiling—chains, it was chains. They fell against the floating storm's body and splashed into the water.

What happened next happened without a scream or a moan or any of the sounds you would expect from a living creature. It seemed to bleed light and heat into the hanging chains. The water below boiled. That lasted a few seconds until the creature's core had deformed into a teardrop shape as the power flowed out of it.

The glowing chains melted apart and dropped into the boiling trough below.

The predator flew erratically for a few seconds, seemingly disoriented. It was very much reduced in size, but for a split second I was sure that Catherine's trap would have killed it if I hadn't let it drink so much power from the electric lines. *My fault,* I thought. *All my fault.*

Then the water sprinklers turned on.

Steam blasted off it. The floating storm sank toward the ground and passed near the door on the left side. Sparks shot out of its body onto every metal object within ten feet—door handle, hinges, nails in the wood, even the still-glowing chains.

A wave of flame billowed up the wall. The predator struck a pair of metal trash barrels, releasing the last of its life and energy in one sudden blast. I was knocked flat near the rear wall, my ears ringing. Aside from the flickering firelight of the burning doorway, the room was dark.

The predator was dead.

Flames climbed the walls on either side of the door, and even the trough was on fire. I wouldn't be getting out that way. I couldn't see Catherine anywhere.

I hopped up onto a table saw and cut a circular slash in the wall above it with my ghost knife. The flames had already covered both side walls and had spread to the loose pine needles and sticky pitch on the ground. The sprinklers were not going to stop this fire.

I pushed the cut section and jumped out, running far away from the building. My scalded skin cooled quickly in the night air, and I knew that soon my wet clothes would be stealing body heat.

But I was alive. A predator had chased me halfway down a mountain, and I had survived.

Catherine came around the edge of the building, giving it a wide berth. We jogged toward each other.

"Thank you!" I said.

"No one has come out of the farmhouse," she said, ignoring me. Her expression was blank, but her hands were trembling. "Either they're really deep sleepers or there's no one home. Normally, I'd suggest we knock and ask for help, but since we just burned down their barn, I think we should get the hell out of here." She was still all business.

"Fine." About fifty yards away, I could see a line of streetlights. We headed for it. She took out her cellphone, scowled at it, and put it away. No reception.

"It looked bigger," she said.

"It was," I said. "While I was leading it away, I came to a power line—one that led to the mansion up on the hill, I think. It fed from that before I could stop it."

She didn't respond. The closer we got to the road, the stronger the wind became. I began to shiver.

"We need to get out of this wind," I said.

"Good idea," she snapped. "Let's chop down some trees and build a log cabin."

We didn't say anything else for a while.

On the road, we came to a sign that read WASHAWAY 2 MILES. We headed in that direction, jogging along the shoulder. The wind was strong at my back.

The road narrowed ahead, and the wide, gently sloping area where the trees had been planted gave way to steeper ground. People lived here, although we could only see their mailboxes and driveways.

A pair of headlights came up behind us. Catherine moved to wave the car down, but I grabbed her elbow and pulled her to the drainage ditch. We crouched behind a tree, watching.

Two black Yukons passed. Both had red-and-white cards in the front window. They were bidders, but which ones?

"Don't grab at me again," she hissed.

We kept going, moving more carefully now. We stayed

off the road when we could and hid whenever we saw a pair of headlights. After about ten minutes, a fire truck came toward us from town, lights flashing. We ducked behind a thicket of blackberries just as it rounded the curve and drove by.

We started walking again. I was shivering and my legs were chafed from the drying mud on my pants. My ears were burning cold, and I squeezed my hands in my armpits to keep them warm. Still, I felt elated. I'd faced a predator and survived. Again.

I wanted to thank Catherine in a way that broke through her anger, but I couldn't see a way to do it. She made a point of staying several paces ahead of me, and she didn't want to chat. It was too bad, but it was her choice.

Still, there were things we *had* to talk about. "Hey," I called. "We need to get our story straight."

She was so used to working alone that it hadn't even occurred to her. We settled on a rough carjacking narrative. The barn fire would be a problem; there was no way to deny that we'd passed the building at the time it burned, but what should we say? Catherine wanted to claim we hadn't seen anything, but I'd never met a cop who would be satisfied with *I don't know a thing about it*.

In the end, I convinced her to say it had been fine when we passed it, but we'd looked back and seen the flames from down the road.

Traffic began to flow out of town toward us. Morning was coming. My elation over our victory began to wear thin, and my morale dropped. Catherine and I stopped hiding from traffic, and eventually a battered pickup pulled up beside us.

"What brings you folks out here?" the driver asked as she rolled down her window. She was in her sixties, with a thick head of wavy gray hair and a deep, no-nonsense voice.

"My car was stolen," Catherine said in a high, helpless voice. She had a personality for every occasion.

"Out here?" She sounded skeptical. "What'd they look like?"

"Like Chinese fellas," Catherine answered.

"If that don't beat . . . Hold on. Lemme give you a ride into town."

She climbed out of the truck and grabbed a blue plastic tarp from the back. Catherine thanked her and said of course she wasn't offended to be asked to sit on the tarp, considering how muddy she was, of course not. The driver asked me to hop in back with Chuckles, a sleepy Rottweiler. I looked Chuckles over carefully first; he wasn't made of a blue streak and he wasn't even a little beautiful. I decided he wasn't Armand with a fake ID.

The driver introduced herself as Karlene, then climbed behind the wheel and did a U-turn.

Chuckles and I weren't all that interested in each other. I watched the houses go by—big farmhouses with crooked foundations and peeling paint. We crossed a bridge over a narrow river, and the lots became smaller. More of the houses were decorated with Christmas lights and lawn displays. I slumped down out of the wind. Chuckles leaned against me.

Eventually, we did another U-turn and stopped at the edge of a gravel path. Catherine opened her door, so I hopped out of the bed.

"Chuckles keep you warm?" Karlene asked.

"Other way around, I think."

"Hah! You have to watch out for him. There's a motel way other side of town, but these people are nicer. You can shower and call the sheriff here. And I'm in a hurry, so tell them—wait a minute." She glanced at a pickup driving down the street. "What's Phil doing driving back into town so early? With an empty load? Anyway"—she turned back to us—"you folks take care." She sped off.

At the top of the path was a huge rambling farmhouse on a tiny lot. "One moment," Catherine said. She took out her phone again and pressed the dial button. Then she held up a hand and moved far enough away that I couldn't hear what she said. She spoke a few words, then shut the phone. I might have thought she was bad-mouthing me to the society, but her message wasn't long enough.

We walked onto the porch. The sign by the door said this was the SUNRISE BED AND BREAKFAST. Catherine rang the bell, and a slender woman of about fifty let us in. The warm, dry air burned my face and ears.

The woman led us into a living room with a fire crackling in the fireplace and twinkly white lights on the mantel. Catherine told her we'd been carjacked.

She sized up the situation quickly. "We've only got one room left."

"We'll share, if we have to," Catherine said with the brisk efficiency of an executive.

"And no luggage, right?"

"Not anymore, except for my bag."

"Would you like to borrow some things to wear until the stores open?"

Catherine shook her head and looked at me. I almost said no out of habit. Then I looked down at my clothes. I wasn't in Chino anymore. I could accept an offer of help. I said: "Yes, thank you," but it was hard.

She seemed to understand. "Don't fret, hon. Everyone needs help now and then." She went through a door behind the counter, leaving us alone.

Catherine turned to me. "We're going to hole up here for a little while, but you'll have to pay for it. They have my car, which means they know who I am and could trace my credit cards. They don't know you, do they?"

I took my MasterCard out of my wallet and handed it to her. My dirty hands made it sticky. "No, they don't."

The owner returned from the back room with two short stacks of folded laundry. I held up my hands when she tried to give one to me. "Huh," she said, then led me into the back.

She explained that these were her private rooms and I wasn't to come back here without her say-so. I told her that was fine with me, and she passed me off to a tall, heavy man with dull gray hair and a heavily weathered face. He was big enough to be a pro wrestler, if he had been thirty-five years younger and dosed with steroids.

She left, shutting the door behind her. The man examined the side of my face for a moment, then began to unbutton my jacket. I tried to help, but my hands stuck to the fabric. They were still covered with pine pitch.

"We'll get them clean in a second." He sounded like someone's grandfather. He got my jacket off and I lathered up my hands. The mud rinsed right off but not the pitch. "It's all right," he said. He splashed a little bath oil on my hands, and that worked.

I looked at my face in the mirror. "Shit," I said. "He hit me pretty hard, didn't he?"

"I guess so," Wrestler said. "But it's no excuse for that kind of language."

"Sorry."

"You can take a shower in your room. Take the clothes—heck, you can keep them. They don't fit me anymore." He led me back into the living room.

The woman returned with a receipt on a little black tray. I signed it and kept my copy. The place cost less than I had expected but more than I wanted to give up.

Wrestler handed us keys. "Your room is upstairs on the right. Breakfast is served until eleven. Checkout's eleven, too. If you need anything, just ask Nadia or me."

"Thanks."

He left. Catherine suggested I get a shower first, then come back down to meet her. I accepted.

The room was pretty, with floral prints on the bedcovers and little wooden picture frames on the night table. The lampshades were edged with lace and the floor covered by a throw rug woven out of rags. Nadia and Pro Wrestler took pride in this place, but I would never feel comfortable here.

My shower was quick and hot. Pro Wrestler's clothes were a little too roomy, but the pants had a belt, so I was fine with it. There was even a cotton sweater in the stack. I wouldn't have to put on my muddy flannel jacket again. After I rubbed the pitch off them, I transferred my wallet, keys, and ghost knife to the new clothes. Unfortunately, in all the excitement I'd lost my toothbrush.

When I returned to the living room, Catherine was sitting by the fire, a little plate with a half-eaten bagel beside her. "All yours," I said.

"Ray," she said. "Give me your key."

Was she kicking me out in the street? "Why?"

"Because I'm going to take a shower and change. I can't do that knowing you have a key."

I nodded and gave her the key. She took it carefully so our fingers wouldn't touch.

"Thank you. Don't come upstairs."

I took her spot by the fire. It felt nice to sit. I'd been up for nearly twenty-four hours, and the last few had been way too exciting.

The next thing I knew, someone was gently pushing my shoulder to wake me. I didn't even realize I'd fallen asleep.

"Hey there, son," he said. "I'm sorry to disturb you, but I need to talk to you about last night."

I sat up straight and rubbed the sleep from my eyes. "How long have I been out?"

"I'm told it's been about three hours." I rubbed at my eyes again and got a good look at him.

He was wearing a wool cap and a red plaid hunter's

jacket. He was small, a little older than Pro Wrestler, and he had a genial face that seemed used to smiling.

"Are you a cop?"

"No," he said and laughed a little. "Washaway is too small to have a police force, and the county sheriff has his hands full, apparently. My name is Steve Cardinal. I'm part of the neighborhood watch around here."

"What do you want from me?"

"Not idle gossip," he said, holding his hands up. "If there's a criminal loose in town, we have an email list we need to notify so what happened to you won't happen to anyone else. I'm not an officer of the court, just a citizen, but anything you tell us could be helpful."

What the hell. I told him the story Catherine and I had cooked up: We came upon a big BMW by the side of the road. When we slowed to ask if they needed help, they pointed guns at us and ordered us out of the car. One of them slugged me.

While the two men were arguing in a foreign language, Catherine and I ran for it. They didn't shoot at us or anything. We ran through a big iron gate, hoping to find a house. Instead, we saw another BMW and more men. We couldn't go back, so we went cross-country.

We followed a trail to a tree farm. No one answered at the house, so we went to the road and walked into town.

It sounded fishy to me, but I told it straight, my voice flat from exhaustion. Cardinal asked what the men looked like, but he didn't ask any cop questions, like *Did anyone see you?* or *What time was that?*

Then he asked me why we were hiding along the side of the road when cars passed. I guessed we'd been seen sooner than I'd thought. I told him that we were afraid the guys in the BMWs would come back. In fact, one of the first cars we hid from was a BMW headed toward town.

He didn't like that, but he forced himself to smile. I

gave him a description of the car. He said he'd ask folks to keep their eyes open.

I wanted to ask about the fire, but curiosity is dangerous. Instead, I told him I was glad and let my eyelids sag. He took the hint.

On his way to the door, I heard Nadia speak to him in a low, urgent tone. I couldn't make out what she said, but he did his best to reassure her before he left.

Nadia had a note for me from Catherine. She was going to sleep until at least eleven, and I shouldn't bother her until then. The clock said it was only 10:45, which meant there would still be breakfast. I piled three scones and a mealy apple onto a tiny plate and carried a full coffee back to my chair by the fire.

Once my belly was full, I got restless. I couldn't stop thinking one thing: Where was the sapphire dog?

We had taken on the floating storm, and now I was ready for the main event. I also needed to figure out what, if anything, to do about Tattoo, Frail, and the Old Man. They had killed someone to summon a predator, and that memory brought back clean, welcome anger. Someone needed to do something about that group, and I wanted it to be me.

I did my best not to think about Regina, Ursula, Biker, and Kripke. They complicated things and I wanted simplicity. I grabbed another coffee and went to wake Catherine. We needed a strategy session.

She answered the door on the second knock. She had changed into a pair of dark jeans and a black sweatshirt, which fit too well to be charity like mine. Her eyes were red. She'd been asleep, too.

I felt awkward. "Can we talk about what we do next?"

She stepped back to let me in.

Catherine walked to the far side of the bed and started stuffing things into her bag. Her head hung down to hide her face, and her shoulders were hunched. She zipped the bag closed with a sudden, angry swipe of her arm. Then she wiped her face with her hand and sat by the window. She wouldn't look at me.

I guessed we weren't going to jump into bed and celebrate last night's victory.

"I'm leaving now," she said.

I sat across from her. "We haven't found the predator yet."

"I don't find predators. I don't kill them, either. I don't fight sorcerers and I don't face down gunmen. I'm an investigator. My job is to confirm that something bad is going on, then contact the society. I give them enough information to get started, and I get out of their way. I shouldn't even have gotten this damn job."

"You already sent the photos of the license plates?"

"Yes. Even though most of those cars were rented, they'll still be able to trace them. Pictures of the people would have been better, but that didn't happen. Now we have a predator on the loose and a sorcerer summoning more. We need a peer to handle this. Maybe more than one."

My heart skipped a beat. Annalise was a peer. "Is Annalise coming?"

Catherine gave me a careful look. "I don't know who they'll send."

My whole body grew warm. I wanted Annalise here with me. I needed her. She had power and she didn't falter. Everything was simple for her. She would have dummyslapped Ursula into next week, and I would have never even heard of a floating storm.

Catherine said: "You should leave, too."

"What? Why?"

"For a lot of reasons. You're not trained for this. You have that one spell in your pocket and whatever is all over those tattoos of yours, but that's it. Hell, we don't even know what we're facing."

"Regina Wilbur said it was a sapphire dog."

"She did?" Catherine seemed startled. "Why didn't you tell me before?"

"Because a predator was trying to kill us," I answered, which didn't make a damn bit of sense. I should have told her everything in case she made it but I didn't.

Damn. She had asked me what I'd found out, and I'd answered *Stuff*. She was right. I wasn't trained for this. "I should have, though. I'm sorry."

"Anything else?"

I took a deep breath and told her everything that happened after we'd split up. When I finished, I asked her: "What's a sapphire dog?"

"I heard about one once. A . . . friend of mine said it was a beautiful creature that destroyed anyone who saw it. That's all I know."

"Isn't there a book or website or something? Shouldn't there be a database or an encyclopedia with pictures and—"

"No," she answered. "There isn't one and there never will be one, for good reason. The society doesn't share information."

"We could do our job a whole lot better if they did."

"Information shared is information leaked. Any secrets the society shares with the rest of us would eventually be sold, or be scammed or tortured out of us."

"Tortured?"

She sighed heavily. I was annoying her and she wanted me to know it. "This isn't a low-stakes game we're playing, Ray. Anyone who finds out what we are will want to know everything we know. Everything. And they won't be gentle about it, either. The more people hear about sapphire dogs and floating storms, the more they'll want one. That's when they start searching for spell books."

I didn't answer right away. Of course she was right.

I'd already heard Professor Solorov and Kripke say that very thing.

And it wasn't as though this was my first encounter with magic. Both previous times had been bloody and awful. Catherine had a point.

"You said I should leave town for a lot of reasons," I said. "And you've been angry with me since we faced the floating storm. What happened? Should I have used my ghost knife against it?"

She let out an exasperated laugh that turned into another sigh. "I'm not angry with you, Ray. Okay, I was, but not anymore. You mean well. It's this Annalise that pisses me off. She's the one who put those spells on you, am I right? And she has you thinking she's such hot shit that you're practically creaming in your pants over her."

I suddenly felt very still. "Watch it," I said.

"Or what?" she snapped, straining to keep her voice low. "What are you going to do? Feed me to a predator?"

"What the hell are you talking about?"

"See? This is what I'm talking about. This! When this Annalise brought you into this life, what did she tell you about the predators?"

"They love to be summoned but hate to be held in place," I said. There was some other stuff she'd explained, but I didn't think Catherine was pissed off about where they came from or whether they were angels, devils, or, as Annalise said, neither.

"And that's it?"

I didn't like the way this was going. It was one thing to have her angry with me, but this was worse. She was treating me like a fish just arrived on the cellblock.

It made me want to lose my cool with her to make her back down, but part of me knew her anger was justified. I didn't know why, but I trusted her enough to assume it. "And we have to destroy them. Kill them," I added, because she was being honest with me, and I wanted to be honest in return.

"That's what I thought. What about feeding them? What about serving them a late-night snack?"

I felt my face flush. I'd let the floating storm feed from the power lines for too long, and she knew about it. "I'm sorry," I said. "I cut the power pole as soon as I realized, but—"

"Power pole? I don't care about a power pole. I'm talking about people."

I stared at her, trying to figure out what she meant. "Do you mean the two assholes who shot at us?"

"Of course I do, Ray. You led the predator to them and let it feed."

"It zapped them with lightning. Red lightning. It didn't *feed*."

"Predators feed in all sorts of ways. . . . Okay. Listen up. When I first signed on to this damn job so-and-so years ago, I was investigating a string of overeating suicides. People were eating and eating and they could not stop themselves. Eventually, they ruptured their guts and died in agony, but if anyone tried to restrain them, they howled like starving dogs. Nobody could figure out what the hell was going on, but I did. It turned out that it was a tiny little predator that looked like a songbird, sort of. People were killing themselves because they heard this birdsong, and somehow this predator was feeding off of that."

"What happened to it?" I asked.

"I don't know. I sent my report and skipped town before it noticed me and sang outside my window. No one ever tells investigators how it turns out. We're not secure."

"You think the floating storm fed on them, somehow?" I asked, still doubtful.

"I don't know how it works," she said. "They're not like us. There's a different physics where they come from.

A different reality. All I know is that they don't kill for fun, and they don't waste their time."

I looked down at the woven rug. The weave was complex, all twisted around itself and bound tight. I wondered what I would have to know to be able to make a rug like that and how much it paid, because I wasn't as ready for this life as I thought.

And while Annalise had been shockingly ruthless sometimes, she had never allowed a predator to kill anyone.

Catherine stood and straightened her sweater. "Don't be too hard on yourself. You screwed up in a big way, but you didn't know any better and we fixed it. And I wouldn't have survived the night if not for you. Besides, when I said I didn't want to see people killed, I was including you. None of this will be in my full report."

"Don't lie for me," I said.

"Okay then." She took out her cellphone and dialed a number. "Catherine Little, supplemental report," she said. Then she repeated what I'd told her but much simpler and faster than I had. She'd had practice, I guess.

She also told them the floating storm had taken two victims at my instigation because I had an "all enemies" outlook.

She paused to listen to their response. She looked at me and said, "Absolutely not. He just needs someone willing to explain how all this works."

That gave me a chill. I was grateful to her for having this conversation where I could hear.

Catherine explained that she was leaving the site and hung up. She went into the bathroom and returned with a couple of small bottles, which she jammed into her jump bag. "Ready to go?"

"I want that phone number."

She smiled at me. There was a trace of kindness in it. "So many do. If they want you to have it, they'll give it to you."

We went downstairs. Catherine suggested I check out, but I surprised us both when I said I wouldn't. She studied my face for a moment, but nothing needed to be said.

On the street, the air was brisk and damp, and I thought we'd have rain soon. There was no sidewalk and we had no car. We walked along the shoulder of the road, watching for careless drivers and Yukons, BMWs, and Mercedes.

A couple of pickup trucks drove by, and a man with a thick, dreadlocked ponytail pedaled by us in a recumbent bike decorated to look like Santa's sleigh.

Catherine seemed to know where we were going. She led me through an intersection with a four-way stop, then turned left at the next. At that, we'd entered the business district, such as it was.

The first building we passed was a visitor's center, which was closed, then a bagel shop and a general store. After that, we passed a bar, a bank, and a beauty shop, all decorated with tasteful white lights. There was a single sporting goods store behind the beauty shop. I noted the location in case I needed another change of clothes.

A banner strung above the street announced the upcoming Christmas festival.

Just beyond a pizza place, the neighborhood turned residential again. The road twisted and turned up ahead, with a steep hill behind the homes on one side and a long drop behind the homes on the other. Washaway was laid out in the flattish spaces that followed the twists of the ravines and gullies.

We turned the corner and approached an auto mechanic shop. The building was painted nausea green, and the sign above the door was obviously old but kept in meticulous condition. The front door was open despite the time of year. It looked like any other garage I'd ever seen, maybe cleaner.

There was only one person there: a short guy in green

overalls working under the hood of a Dodge Aries. I scuffed my feet so he wouldn't be surprised by our approach, and he stood up. He was Asian, and for a stupid moment I thought he was one of Yin's men, waiting to ambush us.

He had a broad, tranquil face that showed the ravages of teen acne. His hair was cut into a buzz, and there was a smear of black grease on his nose. He picked up a rag and began wiping his hands, presumably so we wouldn't offer to shake his hand. "Hey, now," he said, his voice surprisingly deep. "How you folks doin'?"

His name was Hondo, like the movie, not the motorcycle, he said. With the flat, clipped tone of the executive again, Catherine asked if he had cars for rent, and he answered yes. He put his tools away carefully and led us around back, explaining that he did a decent side business renting to folks while he worked on their cars.

There were three to choose from. Catherine went with an Acura again. I nixed a Corolla hatchback and picked a Dodge Neon. I'd have preferred something bulkier, just in case, but those were the choices.

We went into the office, which wasn't as clean as the rest of the garage. We filled out the forms, and he ran my credit card through his little machine to put down a deposit. He told Catherine how to get to the train station and offered to pick up the car there for an extra charge. I bought all the insurance he offered, which made him nervous.

Catherine and I went out front while Hondo brought the cars around. "You should change your mind," she said.

"I can't." A Volvo station wagon puttered down the street. There was a Christmas tree stuffed in the back. "What's an 'all enemies' outlook?"

She looked at me evenly. "*All enemies are equal.* It's someone who thinks serial killers, business competitors, pedophiles, or abusive fathers-in-law are just as bad as the predators from the Empty Spaces. To the society, there's only one true enemy, along with the humans who summoned them. No feeding the monsters, no matter whose head you put on the platter."

I nodded. She presented so many different faces to so many people, I couldn't help but wonder whether she was acting for me, too. Normally, I wouldn't care—if she acted roles, she had a reason for it. It wasn't up to me to peel back that disguise.

But we'd killed a predator together. We'd been a team. I was grateful to her, but even though she was right beside me, she was still remote. I was afraid that my gratitude wasn't getting through the defenses she kept.

Maybe it was selfish of me and unfair to her, but I wanted a glimpse of the real Catherine Little before she drove out of my life forever, so I said: "How did it feel to kill that predator?"

Her expression softened and became thoughtful. A smile turned up the corner of her mouth.

The Acura arrived. She tossed her bag into the backseat. "See you again sometime, Ray." She was still smiling as she got into the car.

I watched her pull away. Part of me thought I should have gone with her. Neither of us was qualified to face a predator. She was doing the smart thing. A peer was coming, after all. This job was best left to them.

Except I had no idea how long that would take. It was one thing if a bidder captured the sapphire dog and got away. They could be tracked down. But what if none of them captured it?

And really, what did I have to do that was more important than this? Stock shelves at the supermarket?

Hondo gave me the keys to the Neon, and I got behind the wheel. If I was going to run back to the straight life I'd once wanted so badly, now was the time.

I couldn't do it. I couldn't go back to facing cereal

boxes while a predator was on the loose. The idea was absurd.

Besides, Annalise might show up at any time.

I pulled out of the lot with no destination in mind. Maybe the sapphire dog would run into the street and under my tires. Maybe I would come up with a real plan. Each possibility seemed as likely as the other.

There was a gunshot from somewhere nearby. I stopped in the middle of the intersection and rolled down my window. There were two more shots. The echo seemed to come from the center of town, so I did a U-turn and drove into the residential area.

There was some other traffic, but I didn't see anything unusual. I didn't hear any more shots.

Then I saw a house with the side door standing open. I parked and got out of the car.

The house was white with black trim. Above the third-floor window, someone had painted a black-and-white checkerboard. The front door was shut and the drapes drawn tight.

I went around the side of the house, my shoes sloshing through the mud. There was no one at the windows. For a moment, I thought I had come to the wrong place. Then I reached the open door and peered in.

It was a kitchen, also done in a black-and-white checkerboard. On the floor, a woman lay stretched out, a pool of bright red blood spreading around her.

CHAPTER SEVEN

I drew my ghost knife and stepped inside. If a phone was handy, I'd call 911 for her, but I didn't think it would do much good. Her belly had been cut wide open.

The kitchen was a mess. Loose mail and newspapers were stacked on the counters, and the table was dusted with crumbs and splotches of purple jelly. I spotted the phone on the wall beside the fridge and started toward it.

"Clara!" someone called from outside. It was an old man's voice. I put my ghost knife into my back pocket. "Clara!" he called again and stepped into the doorway. "Oh my Lord!" He moved toward the body, splashing the toe of one rubber boot in her blood. He had a double-barreled shotgun in his hands. Then he saw me.

"Hands in the air!" he shouted. I complied. "What the hell did you do here, huh? What did you do?" His voice trembled with rage, and I thought he might twitch hard enough to shoot me accidentally.

"Don't pull that trigger." I kept my voice calm. "The police will be here soon if we call 911."

"I already have, smart-ass." He smirked at me fiercely. He straightened his shoulders and brushed back his wispy white hair. He was posing like a hero. "Don't wet your panties. I'll just hold you here until the sheriff comes. Unless you try something stupid. Get me?"

"Got you," I answered. He didn't like my tone. He wanted me afraid, but I wasn't going to give him the satisfaction.

"Why shoot you when you can get the needle, eh? I hear that's real painful, like burning to death on the inside. A man who murders a woman don't deserve no better than that."

He was a terrible bluffer, and I wasn't spooked. He decided to drop it. We both looked at the woman on the floor. She was wearing a fleece pullover decorated with poinsettias. There was a little Santa pin on her collar.

She also had a white mark on her face, just like the well-ventilated gunman on the Wilbur estate. Because she was on her back, I could see the whole thing; it started near the point of her chin, ran across her lips, up her cheek, and onto her forehead. It was about the width of the pad of my thumb, and it looked very much like a bleach stain on cloth.

I had no idea what it meant, but I was pretty sure it hadn't killed her. If it had, she wouldn't have needed so many stab wounds.

Still, where had it come from? It could have been a birthmark or an old scar, I guessed, although the odds that a woman in a small town in the American Northwest would have the same mark as a hired thug from Hong Kong weren't worth taking seriously.

Then I noticed the revolver in her left hand. It was big, clunky, and black, the sort of gut blaster home owners prefer—no concealment necessary.

There was a china plate on the floor by my foot. A raw porterhouse had been placed on it, but it was untouched.

So, the woman and the gunman were both armed when they were killed. The plate on the floor suggested a dog, and the expensive, untouched steak suggested even more.

My arms were getting tired, but I had no intention of asking permission to put them down. After a few minutes, Steve Cardinal stepped into the doorway. "My God," he said when he saw the body on the floor. "Isabelle! What happened?"

"About time someone got here," the old man said. He sagged, letting his shotgun droop, and slumped into a dining room chair. It hadn't occurred to me that he would be getting tired, too. "I caught the feller. He was still standing over the body. Almost shot him, too."

Cardinal looked down at the body, then at me. "Oh, Preston, he's not the killer. Isabelle has been stabbed, and he doesn't have a drop on him."

"What?"

"Unless you found a spear in his back pocket. But thank you for calling me. One moment." He took out his cell and went outside. It was only a minute before he came back in. "Bill and Sue are on their way." Cardinal looked at me. "You can put your arms down, son. What are you doing here?"

Now he was ready to play the cop. "I heard gunshots and came out this way. I saw the open door and found her on the floor."

Cardinal turned toward Preston and laid a friendly hand on his shoulder. He managed a smile, but it was strained and his face looked pale. They were two old men trying to find the strength to do an unpleasant job. "Preston, I need to ask you a favor. Go out to the street and look for the ambulance. If Stookie is driving, we'll have to send up a flare to get him to the right address."

Preston took a little white pill from a pill bottle and put it under his tongue. "I can do that." He shuffled out the door.

Before Cardinal could start questioning me again, I asked: "She doesn't live here, does she?"

Cardinal put his hand in his pocket. "Now, how did you know that?"

"When Preston came in, he was calling 'Clara,' not 'Isabelle.' She lives nearby, though? Lived, I mean."

"I'm the one with questions that need answering, son. Having you pass the Breakley place just as it burned down—and that's the only way you could have gotten into town from the estate—was quite a coincidence. This is too much."

"You know something of my history, don't you?"

"I can Google," he said. "I know about the arrest in Los Angeles and the time you served. I know about the incident in Seattle last year, although some of the details don't make much sense. Drugs, wasn't it? Some kind of designer drug made a friend of yours go on a killing spree."

He wasn't even close to right, except about the killing spree. I felt a flush of shame at the memory, though. Not only had Jon killed people, he'd eaten them, too. I was grateful Cardinal hadn't mentioned that, because if he'd read news reports on the story, he knew about it.

Still, "drug-induced psychosis" was the official explanation for the events of the previous fall when I tried to save my oldest friend from the Twenty Palace Society—and from himself—and ended up killing him instead. But that official explanation could be useful.

"That's pretty much it," I said.

"Well, what's happened here doesn't have anything to do with that, does it?" A siren grew louder.

I hesitated before I answered. "I don't know."

He sighed and drew a small revolver from his pocket. "If you won't talk to me honestly, son, I'm going to have to do things neither one of us likes." He took a pair of handcuffs from his back pocket. "I'm going to make a citizen's arrest. I'm not going to have trouble with you, am I?" The siren was close.

"Me? I'm Mr. Cooperation. You don't have to cuff me."

"I'm afraid I do. I have to look around now. I'll be back in a few to let you loose, but I can't rightly take any chances. Not with what's been going on today. Hold your wrist next to the handle there."

He pointed at the oven door. It was an old-fashioned black iron handle and attached pretty solidly. I put my wrist beside it so he could cuff me easily.

If Cardinal was nervous about me, he didn't show it. I didn't let my nervousness show, either. I doubted he'd be convicted if he "accidentally" shot me. Hell, he probably wouldn't even be arrested. I was an ex-con from L.A. Who cared about me?

And he hadn't said a word about the things I did in Hammer Bay.

The siren fell silent. Cardinal went outside and waved to someone, then returned to the house and walked through the other rooms.

The first paramedic was a black woman about my age with unruly hair pulled into a ponytail. She was squat like a fireplug and had broad, strong hands. The man who followed her through the door was a six-foot-four white guy with a wool-lined hunter's cap and a bushy gray beard. They carried a gurney.

"Holy . . ." The woman let her voice trail off.

"That's Isabelle, all right," Bushy Beard said. "What a fucking day."

Ponytail stepped up to the body. I could hear her shoe splash in the blood. "Damn."

Bushy Beard had a clipboard in his hands, but he wasn't writing anything down. Instead, he was looking at me. "I knew her."

"I'm sorry for your loss," I said. That made his eye twitch. "I'm the one who found her."

"Yeah, right," Ponytail said. "That's why you're in cuffs. This woman went to grade school with my mother. She drove our whole family to my grandfather's funeral."

They were angry and trying to talk themselves into letting it go. It wasn't a sudden anger, though. They seemed more tired than shocked. I wondered what else had happened that day. Had they been to the Wilbur estate? Had someone been hurt at the burning barn?

"You shouldn't have done this," Bushy Beard said.

"Shouldn't have done what? Find a body?" I was getting annoyed. Everyone was so sure I was guilty just because they didn't recognize my face.

"Yeah," Ponytail said. "Right."

"What did you want?" Bushy asked. "Money?"

I took a deep calming breath and tried to shrug it off. These people had just lost a friend, I told myself. There was nothing to be gained by losing my temper.

But he wasn't done. "How did it feel? Did you get off on it?"

That was my limit. "Go fuck yourself," I said. "You think I'd come to fucking *Washaway* if I wanted money? Or to get off?"

That was what he wanted. He moved toward me. "It must have been something else, then."

"Kick his ass, Bill," Ponytail said.

I had the ghost knife in my pocket but no way to use it without both of them seeing. I was glad that I'd offered my left to Cardinal. If I was going to fight one-handed, I wanted to use my right.

He lumbered toward me. I threw a right jab at his chin. He was expecting it and caught my arm. Grappling, we fell against the stovetop, his massive weight bearing down on me. I wriggled my right arm, trying to get it in a position to gouge at his face, but he was too heavy and too close. His breath smelled of cheap teriyaki and expensive mints.

He hit the side of my face with a huge, heavy left. It hurt, but I'd been hit harder in the previous twenty-four hours.

The punch loosened things up between us. Before Bushy Bill could close in again, I drove my knee into his crotch. He hissed, doubled over, and staggered back a couple of steps. I threw a right elbow toward his face, but he felt it coming and leaned away from it. He threw a wide, swinging right at me. I couldn't block it with my left, so I ducked and caught it on the crown of my head. It hurt, but I knew it hurt him more.

"For goodness sakes!" a thin voice yelled. "What's going on here?"

Cardinal stood in the kitchen doorway with a swaddled baby in his arms. He had a diaper bag over his shoulder and an unhappy look on his face.

Bill shuffled to the opposite counter and stared at the floor, looking as if he would back all the way through the wall and out of town if he could.

Cardinal marched up to him and laid the baby in his arms. I caught a glimpse of its tiny, perfect little face. Cardinal folded the blanket over its eyes to block the light. "Don't wake that baby, Bill. Take him out to the ambulance and check him over, you hear me? Check him over good. Now."

Bill waddled to the door. Cardinal turned to Ponytail. "For goodness sakes, Sue! Don't you know any better?"

"We saw him handcuffed next to Isabelle's body, and we thought—"

"No, you didn't think! Gosh darn it!" Cardinal's voice was high and thin, more of a whine than a shout. Sue looked ashamed. "You'll be lucky to just be suspended. This man could press charges against you."

"Him?" She sounded startled and outraged. She glanced back at the cuffs. "But Isabelle and the Breakleys—"

"He's an innocent man, Sue. Innocent. Can I tell you how I know that? Because no one has proved him guilty yet. Even that befuddled old Lutheran from the public defender's office could get him sprung now. When the sheriff comes, he may have to arrest *you*. Do you understand why we can't have this sort of malarkey?"

"I'm sorry, Steve."

"Have you pronounced yet?"

"Yeah."

"Good. Go out to the ambulance and try to figure out where we're going to find two paramedics to replace you."

Sue went outside. Cardinal took a deep breath and took out his handcuff keys. "Mr. Lilly, I'd like to apologize for myself as a man and as a citizen of the town of Washaway. I expect better from our people, and I certainly don't want you to think I put handcuffs on you so Bill could . . . do what he did. I'm truly sorry." He opened the cuffs and put them away.

"I know you didn't," I said.

"Will you press charges?" he asked reluctantly, as though he would have to do the paperwork.

"I don't know yet," I said. I didn't have any interest in suing the town, but the threat was leverage I wasn't prepared to give up. "What did she say about the Breakleys? Did the fire spread to their house?"

"No." I was tremendously relieved. "The whole family is dead, though. A seven- and a nine-year-old girl, both parents, and the girls' grandmother. Sue and Stookie just came from the scene," he added, trying to get a little sympathy for them.

"What happened?"

"I can't really talk about that. Did you or your lady friend know them?"

"No, not at all." I shut my mouth, hoping Cardinal would fill the silence.

He didn't oblige. "What did you see on their farm, Mr. Lilly? Why did you rush toward the sound of gunshots? Does it have something to do with what happened to your friend?"

"Can I call you Steve? Because my name is Ray."

"Sure, Ray."

"Shouldn't the cops be asking these questions, Steve?"

He took a deep, weary breath. "They should, if they would answer our calls for help. The fire truck came for the Breakley fire, but the sheriff hasn't showed up yet. Maybe he had a car accident or something. But yes, it should be the police asking these questions. We're going to have to make do. Does this have anything to do with what happened to your friend?"

"Maybe," I said. "Did the Breakleys look like they'd been eaten?"

Steve looked back at Isabelle and the untouched porterhouse on the floor. "No, they didn't. Now tell me why you ask."

I knew I should keep my mouth shut, but I talked anyway. "Last night, while those guys were carjacking us, I got a weird vibe off them. Something about them reminded me of that friend of mine who died last year."

"What was it, specifically?"

"I don't know," I said. "Something about the way they talked and acted. Something about the look in their eyes. Maybe it doesn't make sense, but I thought they were high in the same way that Jon—that my friend was."

Steve took that in with a thoughtful nod. I could see that he still didn't like my story, but he believed it. His cell rang. He answered, listened for a moment, and said, "I'll get out there right away."

He turned to me. "Ray, we seem to be having quite a busy day today. I think you and your lady friend should stay in town for a while. When he does finally get here, the sheriff will want to talk to you. I'll contact you later at the Sunrise."

Obviously, he was used to throwing his weight around town. I nodded and he rushed outside. I followed.

Bill and Sue gave me a sullen glare as I passed their ambulance, but Preston was gone. Good riddance to him and his shotgun, I thought. Steve climbed into his car, an old Crown Vic, and started the engine. I lagged behind, acting as if I was in no rush.

He pulled into the road. I followed him as he drove into a less populated area. Traffic was sparse, so I let him pull way ahead. Eventually, he stopped by the side of the road behind a charcoal-colored Honda Element. By the time I pulled in behind him, Steve was standing by the Honda's driver door, talking into his cell. There was an Escort parked on the other side of the road.

Steve didn't look pleased to see me. A woman came toward me as I climbed out of the rental. She was about thirty-five, with a pixie cut and a runner's physique. She wore wool pants and a pink jacket, and she looked pissed. "Keep your distance," she said as I approached. "This is a crime scene."

"You're not a cop," I said as I walked by her. "I think I know what I'm going to see here, but I have to see it for myself."

I stepped up to the window. A woman of about Isabelle's age was slumped in the driver's seat. She had dyed red-gold curls that looked like they cost a lot of money. A long white mark ran up her cheek and across her nose. Her lap was drenched in blood. She had been gut shot. A bloody butcher knife was in her hand, and there was an off-color circle on the passenger door.

It was feeding, I suddenly realized. Whatever the sapphire dog was doing to these people to make them kill one another was how it fed itself.

And it had just spent more than two decades in a plastic cage. I bet it was *starving*.

"I can't understand it," Steve said, ending his call. "The hospital is back the other way."

"This is Clara, isn't it?" I asked as I went around the front of the car. The engine was still running.

"Yes," Steve said. "Why did she leave her grandson? Why didn't she call 911?"

"What's out on that road?" I asked.

The runner stepped into my field of vision. "Who are you?"

"I'm Ray Lilly. Who are you?"

"Justy Pivens. I'm part of the neighborhood watch. What do you know about this?"

"I know people in your town are starting to kill one another. What's out at the end of this road?"

Steve was too shaken to play cop for a moment. "Nothing. The camp and fairgrounds, and a feeder road that connects to I-5, eventually, but there's nothing out there for a woman with a bullet in her. Not for miles."

I went around the car. There was another discolored circle on the outside of the passenger door. Steve and Justy hadn't noticed it, so I didn't point it out. There was another line of soup-can footprints in the mud leading away from the car.

"What are you looking at?" Steve asked. He came around the car. "What the heavens could those be?"

Justy frowned at the prints. "They aren't animal tracks," she said. "They look like stilts. Four-legged stilts?"

The tracks went up a bare hillside toward a lonely farmhouse.

"Is your gun loaded?" I asked.

Steve hesitated before he answered. "Yes, it is. I loaded it this morning."

"What about you, Justy?"

"In the car."

"Get it and follow us, if you want."

We went up the hill, following the footprints in the mud.

"Ray, I need you to tell me what's going on. I can't just

go on this way without knowing what to expect. And we've had more deaths in town today than we've had in the last three years. Gosh darn it, don't keep me in the dad-blamed dark!"

He was whining again. I wondered what it would take to drag a little profanity out of him. "I'll be honest with you," I said. Justy had followed us, and I made sure to address her as well. "I don't know. Let's go up to the house and see if anyone is still alive."

It was only about twenty yards to the front porch, but Steve was an old guy. I tamped down a tangle of scraggly bushes and steadied him over an old log. He was slowing me down, but he and Justy were locals. I wanted them with me.

The porch was made of unpainted cedar, weathered until it was as gray as Steve's hair. A small stack of fertilizer in plastic bags gave off an unpleasant farm stink. The strings of lights around the porch were dark. The boards creaked loudly under our weight.

Steve walked up to the front door and slammed the knocker three times. I was a bit surprised at that; I'd been peeking in windows and breaking into houses since last night. Actually knocking on a door seemed quaint.

Heavy boots clumped toward us, then the door was yanked inward and a woman leaned out. She was in her mid-thirties, plain-faced, and had what looked to be permanent bedhead. She was dressed head to toe in fleece sweats. A set of keys jangled in her hand.

A long white streak ran from her jawline over her ear and up into her hair.

"Penny, have . . . are you okay?"

"I'm fine, Steve," she answered. "What do you want?"

"There's been some trouble in town." Steve's tone was cautious. "It led us out front."

Justy said: "What's that on your face?"

Penny shifted from one foot to the other, obviously

anxious to get back to whatever she was doing. "Nothing's on my face. And there's no trouble here. Okay? Gotta go."

She glanced at me without interest and started to close the door. Steve blocked it with his foot. "I'm sorry, Penny, but you do have a white something on the side of your face. Where did you get it?"

"I was baking earlier," she said, her voice flat and unpleasant. "It's flour."

"Is Little Mark here? I'd like to come in to talk some more. To both of you."

"It's a bad time, Steve."

"Please, Penny?" he persisted. "Folks have died."

That didn't interest her at all. "It's a bad time for me. Maybe tomorrow."

"Now, Penny, I'm afraid I have to insist."

She sighed again. "Fine. Give me a moment." She glared at his foot until Steve drew it back, then she closed the door.

Damn. This wasn't right. She wasn't curious about me, the trouble in front of her property, or the deaths in town. Something was very wrong.

"It's okay," Steve said, maybe sensing my unease. "Penny's my cousin and we get along very well." He wrung his hands nervously, looking from me to Justy and back again. Justy looked pinched and skittish. She stayed close to the top of the stairs.

In the window behind the fertilizer, I saw a curtain move. It was a boy, maybe fifteen years old, with brown hair in a ragged bowl cut. His eyes were big and brown and empty. He had a white mark on his face, too.

The door swung open suddenly. I heard a low growl and lunged forward.

Penny heaved herself through the doorway, swinging something over her shoulder at Steve. I caught hold of it even as I realized it was an axe and pushed. The blade passed over Steve's skull and thunked against the door-frame.

Steve cried out in a high voice. Footsteps thumped on the wooden stairs, leading away.

Penny jabbed the butt end of the axe at me. I ducked. The handle whiffed by my jaw. I put my shoulder against her hip, wrapped my arms around her knees, and upended her onto the floor.

The axe flew out of her hands and bounced across a dingy throw rug. She reached for me, hands curled like claws, but I caught her wrist and pulled her onto her stomach, then planted a knee in her back.

Steve was still standing in the doorway, his mouth hanging open. Justy was nowhere in sight.

"Bring your cuffs in here before someone gets killed!"

That jolted him into action. He fumbled at his back pocket.

I took my ghost knife from my pocket and slipped it through the back of her head. It passed through without leaving a mark the way it always does with living people. It didn't even cut her hair.

But it didn't stop her thrashing. It didn't cut away her anger and hostility the way it had for Horace. Damn. She was immune, just like Ursula. Was it something to do with the stain on her face, which Ursula didn't have? I didn't know, but I was pretty sure it wasn't my spell.

I glanced around, worried that the boy would come at me with a kitchen knife, but I couldn't see him.

Penny tried to wrench her arm out of my grip. I didn't want to hurt her, but I wasn't going to be able to hold her for long if I didn't do something drastic.

Which was the same choice I'd faced with Ursula. People had died and I'd nearly gotten myself killed because I couldn't be ruthless with a woman who wanted to murder me.

I leaned my body weight onto her, pinning her arms to

her back. I could have broken them, hit her behind the ear, or stomped on her, but I held back, and my refusal to make that choice became my choice. If that made things difficult later on, so be it.

Steve knelt beside her but didn't cuff her. He pleaded for her understanding, apologized for what he had to do, and generally irritated me by trying to be reasonable with a person who had lost all reason. "Just snap them on!" I barked. I bent her arms behind her back, and he did it.

We heard a car engine rev outside.

"No!" Penny screamed. "Don't take him from me! You can't take him away from me!"

I sprinted through the door and across the porch. A dirty white pickup roared across the yard, heading downhill toward the street. It lurched and swerved in the mud. I raced after it.

The truck skidded on a steep part of the yard and slammed against a tree.

I ran around a thicket toward the truck, ghost knife in hand. Maybe the spell was useless against these people, but it made me feel better to hold it. The truck bed was empty, so I circled toward the driver's side. There was a strange sound, like a high-pitched keen mixed with a metallic scrape. I had never heard anything like it; I figured it was a damaged fan belt.

I reached the driver's window. The brown-eyed kid was behind the wheel, holding his bloody forehead—the pickup was too old to have air bags.

"Sit still," I said. "We're going to have someone take a look at that head."

He looked at me, his expression still empty. "I'll kill you," he said. "If you try to take him from me, I'll kill you."

I glanced over at the passenger seat. It was empty. The plastic lining on the passenger door had a discolored patch.

Goose bumps ran the length of my body. The sapphire dog was very close.

I stepped back and looked around. I couldn't see anything but trees, leafless bushes, and mud. Justy laid rubber peeling away down the street. Steve was running toward me as fast as he could, which wasn't fast at all. He had almost reached the back fender when he looked toward the passenger side of the truck.

And stopped. He gaped at something on the other side of the truck that I couldn't see.

I walked toward him. My guts were in knots, but I refused to be afraid. I had come here for exactly this moment.

You're not trained for this, Catherine had said. *It destroys anyone who sees it.*

Steve stood and gaped as I came around the back of the truck and saw the sapphire dog.

CHAPTER EIGHT

It was walking away from us, and I didn't think it looked like a dog at all. It didn't have fur, and its skin was a brilliant electric blue. Its body swayed as it moved, as though it was part cougar and part python. Its four legs extended and retracted in a disturbing, boneless motion, like a set of tentacles or springs. It didn't have wings, but it did have two rows of dark spots running down its back. A second glance showed that they weren't spots at all but actually faceted blue crystals embedded in its flesh. Its long, slender, whiplike tail snapped and wavered the way a stream of water might move as it flowed over a pane of dirty glass.

Then it reached a patch of grass about a dozen feet away from us, turned, and sat on its haunches. Suddenly, it looked very much like a dog. Its broad, oversized head tapered at the front to a snout that had no opening. There were more blue crystals on its forehead and around its impossibly narrow neck. Its ears were long and floppy, almost long enough to be rabbit ears. And its eyes . . .

Its eyes were huge, as large as a cartoon animal's. Its pupils were shaped like eight-pointed stars, and there were five of them in each eye, all shining gold and arranged in a circle.

It stared at us with an unfathomable expression while its pupils slowly rotated. The effect was hypnotic.

The sapphire dog was beautiful. That's a simple word I've used to describe anything from a new car to a moment of karmic payback, but it could never capture the impact the sapphire dog had on me. Framed in bare trees and mud, the otherworldly beauty of it hit me like a punch in the gut. It didn't look solid. It didn't look real. I thought I might be having a vision.

"Lord, thank you for this day," Steve said. He was a few paces to my right. It took an effort to look away from the animal, but Steve was just as stunned as I was. He stepped toward it, and so did I. I didn't want him to be closer to it than I was. I didn't want to share.

The sapphire dog looked at Steve, and I felt a twinge of jealousy—I wanted it to look at me. I wanted to punch the old man in the back of his head and knock him cold, so the sapphire dog would want me and only me.

There was a familiar pressure against a spot below my right collarbone. It meant something, but I couldn't quite remember what it was.

The tip of the sapphire dog's snout began to recede, the way a person might suck at their cheeks to make them hollow. The snout changed color—first to a dark purple, then to shit brown. A nasty, puckered opening appeared—round, wrinkled, and toothless like a shit-hole.

We were in danger. I remembered that the twinge under my collarbone was a warning that I was under attack. There was a tiny feeling of unease deep inside me, but thoughts of the sapphire dog had crowded it out.

This wasn't right. I knew it wasn't right, and if I didn't wake up, I was going to be dead.

It lifted its snout toward Steve. I bolted toward him and knocked him into the mud just as the sapphire dog's long, bone-white tongue snaked out at him.

The tongue passed over us, swiping through the air near my shoulder. I felt Steve hit the ground hard, the air *whuff*ing out of him.

A second wave of love-struck longing washed over me, but this time I recognized the twinge under my right collarbone. My iron gate, one of the protective sigils on my chest, was trying to block a magical attack.

These weren't my feelings. I had to focus on that. The animal—no, the *predator*—across from me was trying to control how I felt.

It turned its attention on me. I rolled to my knees in the freezing mud and cocked my arm to throw the ghost knife. Its eyes widened.

I threw the spell.

The sapphire dog seemed to move in three directions at once. It slid to the left and right at the same moment, and shot straight up from the ground. It was almost as if it was a still image that had split apart.

The three afterimages vanished. The ghost knife passed through empty air.

I jumped to my feet, stepped between Steve and the ghost knife, and *called* it back. Hopefully, he wouldn't see.

The sapphire dog was gone. Although it had split into separate still images before it vanished, there were footprints in the mud heading to the left and right for a few feet. Damn. At least it wasn't cloning itself.

I scanned the area around the house. The predator was nowhere in sight. I ran around to the other side of the truck, but it wasn't there, either.

I laid my face against the cold metal cab. I felt empty. I had a raw, hollow space inside where my adoration for the sapphire dog had been. I knew those feelings weren't mine. I knew they'd been forced on me, but I still felt their absence as a terrible ache. And I knew that, because of them, I'd missed my chance to kill a predator.

Steve was still on his back in the mud. He stared up at the overcast sky and muttered to himself.

A few seconds ago, I'd been about to put his lights out, and I'd been partly protected by the iron gate Annalise had given me. How much worse had it been for him?

I heard a crash from inside the house. The front door was still standing open, but I couldn't see Penny. Damn. Of course she couldn't just wait quietly to be taken to prison.

I kicked the bottom of Steve's shoe. "Get up," I said, my voice more harsh than I'd intended. "You have to call those ambulance assholes for the kid in the truck. You have to take your cousin to jail, too."

I jogged toward the house. The predator might have hidden inside. I didn't think it was likely, but I had to check. It's what I was there to do, after all.

Penny was not in the living room, but the axe still lay where she'd dropped it. I stepped carefully inside. I couldn't see anyone, but I did hear the far-off rasping of metal on metal.

I walked toward the sounds. The throw rug in the middle of the floor and the dingy brown sofa were coated with a fine layer of white cat hairs. Beside the sofa was one of those structures built of flimsy wood and cheap gray carpeting that are supposed to be fun for cats. This one was four and a half feet tall and three feet around.

A dead cat lay on the floor beside it. It had been stomped on, probably by someone with a heavy boot. Someone like Penny.

The kitchen was also coated with cat hairs. The smeary fridge had book reports and pop quizzes held on with magnets. The kid out front was a straight-A student— exactly the sort I used to beat up in my own school days.

Maybe, just maybe, the white stain on his face was temporary.

On the far side of the fridge was a set of stairs leading down to the basement. The sound of metal-on-metal sawing was coming from there.

The wooden stairs creaked under my weight. "Get out!" Penny screamed. "Get out of my house!"

The basement had a concrete floor and a low ceiling. There was a long workbench at one end and a stretching mat at the other. The mat had been repaired many times with duct tape.

Penny was beside the workbench. She'd managed to clamp a hacksaw into a vise and was rubbing the chain of the cuffs up and down the blade.

"Your son is outside," I said. I had a pretty good idea how she would react, but I had to be sure. "He's hit his head and is bleeding pretty badly."

"Get out!" she screamed again.

"An ambulance is on the way to pick him up."

"Get out of here before I kill you!"

Just as I'd thought. When she'd screamed not to take "him" away, she was talking about the sapphire dog, not her own son. It had touched her face and made her fall in love with it. It had fed on her.

She fumbled for a screwdriver on the bench. Her hands were still pinned behind her, and her charge was awkward and slow.

I yanked the screwdriver out of her hand and kicked her behind the knee. She fell onto the padded mat. I took a claw hammer off a hook on the wall. "That was a pretty little animal, wasn't it?"

"Are you a fucking moron? It was the most beautiful thing I've ever seen. If you try to keep me from it, I'll chop you into tiny pieces."

"Yeah, sure. It needs a ride out of town, right? I'll bet it wants to go to a city. Right?" She didn't answer, but the hateful look in her eyes was all the confirmation I needed. "Now listen to this: I'm going to put you in the back of Steve's car. If you fight me"—she began cursing at me, so I raised my voice—"if you fight me, I'll break both your legs."

I slammed the hammer on the concrete floor. She stopped shouting.

"Then," I continued, "you won't be able to take anyone anywhere, and the sapphire dog will find someone else to be with. Get me?"

She glared at me, her breath coming in harsh gasps. Just the idea of losing her precious pet made her eyes brim with tears. "Bide your time," I told her, "or you'll lose any chance you might have had."

Penny let me lead her out of the house to Steve's car. He told her an ambulance was on the way to check her son over, but she didn't even look at him. She didn't care. She sat in the back and I closed the door.

Steve rubbed his face. "We have a jail cell in the basement of the town hall. Sheriff uses it sometimes. The mayor's on her way here with the key."

"Good." As long as she hadn't picked up the predator's knack for walking through solid objects, Penny would be out of the way for a while.

"Now. What in the Sam Hill was that thing?"

Before I could answer, the ambulance arrived. Steve waved Bushy Bill and Sue toward the crashed truck.

"That's the first I saw of it," I said.

"It . . . it was beautiful. And it vanished into thin air, didn't it? I felt . . ."

"You loved it," I said. "You loved it and you wanted it all to yourself."

He squinted up at me. He'd come into contact with the world behind the world, and he didn't even know what questions he should ask.

Information shared is information leaked. But he'd seen the predator, so he already had the most damning information. And I knew he would talk to Penny soon enough; I didn't want her version of the sapphire dog to be the only one he heard. I had enough enemies as it was.

I said: "This is how it started last year with my friend.

Understand? There was a creature that could make certain things happen. In my friend's case, it healed his back and let him walk." There was no need to mention Hammer Bay, so I didn't. "This is something else, though."

"I loved that animal."

"It's not an animal," I told him. "It's smart. It may be smarter than us."

"By golly," Steve said. He rubbed his neatly shaved chin. "Today I don't think that would be too hard."

"Not any day for me," I said. "I've never been smart. But that doesn't matter. What matters is that we have to kill it."

"Can't we just capture it?" I could see the *wanting* in his expression.

"For Christ's sake," I said. Steve winced at my language, and I was glad I hadn't said what I'd originally meant to say. "Look at your cousin. Was she a bad mother before today? Did she hate her son?"

"No," he said. "She loves that boy."

"*Yesterday* she loved that boy. Today all she can think about is that damn sapphire dog." That seemed to stagger him, but I wasn't finished. "And you already know that Clara and Isabelle killed each other over it, don't you?"

Steve stepped away from me, his shoulders slumping forward as if he suddenly bore a heavy weight. "Oh my heavens."

"Maybe it's temporary," I said. He shot a look at me; he hadn't even considered how long it would last. Of course, I'd seen predators at work before, and when they destroyed people, they didn't do it on a temporary basis. "But our first job has to be to find that thing and kill it."

"You made it vanish," he said. "What did you throw at it?"

Now he *was* asking for too much information. "A credit card." I pulled my MasterCard out of my pocket and showed it to him. "I scared it off. I don't think it knows very much about this world."

"Who brought this devil into our world?"

We were getting close to another subject I wanted to avoid. If Steve started talking about Jesus, I wouldn't be able to turn him away from it, and judging by the way he talked to the paramedics, he had a lot of authority in this town.

Annalise had explained that predators and magic had nothing to do with God or hell, angels or demons. Magic was a way of controlling reality, and predators were just what the name suggested—hungry things from a place *outside*, sometimes called the Empty Spaces and sometimes called the Deeps.

If Steve started telling the people of Washaway that they were facing a devil, they might try to protect themselves with prayer and crosses, which was as effective as stopping a sniper's bullet with a hopeful thought.

"It's not a demon," I told him. "It's an alien."

"Oh."

"It didn't come here in a ship. It's just here. And it's been here a long time."

"It has? Where?"

"In Regina Wilbur's house."

"Regina? Why, she . . ."

His voice trailed off. I could see him reconsidering everything he knew about her in light of what he'd seen today. "But she doesn't have a mark on her face."

"No," I said. "She's kept it prisoner. It's been hidden on her estate for all this time. But it can affect us at a distance. I think it did exactly that to her for decades. And I think it's getting stronger."

"What do we do?"

The paramedics were loading the boy into the ambulance. Sue had a bandage on her wrist; from the way the kid was lunging and snapping at them, I guessed he must have bitten her.

"How many roads lead out of town?"

"Just two," he said. "This one, which leads to I-5, and Littlemont Road, which goes past the Breakleys' to the pass."

"We need to block them off. The predator is trying to get to a heavily populated area. Can you block the roads without causing too much suspicion?"

"No," he said, "but the state police can. I'll tell the mayor to call. Heck, considering everything that's happened, it would be suspicious if we didn't block them. But we're going to do more than that, aren't we?" He looked stricken and miserable. I couldn't help feeling sorry for him.

"We'll try," I said. "And help is coming."

"I'll take your word for it. Just tell me one thing, son. You didn't cause this, did you? You didn't let this thing loose on my town?"

The question startled me, although it shouldn't have. "No."

He sighed in relief. He believed me, although I had no idea why. "I'll take Penny . . ." He trailed off as a battered yellow pickup screeched to a halt at the edge of the road. "Looks like you're going to meet the mayor," Steve said.

The driver's door opened and a burly, gray-haired woman bowled out. She wore a Santa cap and a red-and-green coat covered with snowmen. She bustled up the hill toward us.

Steve turned to me. "What should I tell her?"

"You know her. I don't. Would she believe the truth?"

He sighed. "Not a chance on God's green earth."

"Like I said: you know her. Tell her what you have to."

"Good Lord, Steve, what's going on?" she said when she was a few paces away.

"People are going crazy, Pippa, and the crazy is spreading."

I kept my mouth shut, letting Steve take the lead. She stopped next to us, breathing hard. "Explain. No, wait. First, who are you?"

She stepped close to me. She may have been past sixty and barely five feet tall, but she looked at me with the same bullish challenge I'd gotten from cops and prison-yard toughs.

I didn't answer. "Ray Lilly," Steve said, "this is Pippa Wolfowitz, mayor of Washaway."

"Nice shiner you got there. You're the fellow who got himself carjacked last night."

"I am."

"Funny how all this happened just as you came to town."

I was about to tell her it wasn't funny at all, but I didn't. For all I knew, one of the bodies I'd found today was a member of her family. She was entitled to be a little testy.

"Pippa, Ray here saved my life. Penny tried to chop me down like a tree, but he stopped her."

"Big Penny?" Pippa looked at the back of Steve's car. "What's she got against you?"

"Not a thing as far as I know. It's like I said: everyone is going crazy. It started at the Breakley place, then somehow got to Isabelle's house. Isabelle brought it here, and it got to Penny and Little Mark."

"It? What *it* got to all those people?"

Steve looked at me, his mouth working. "We don't exactly know yet."

"Don't play games with me, Steve Cardinal. I'm too old for that stuff."

"Sheriff get here?"

"No, and don't change the subject."

"It's all the same subject. You need to call the state police and have them block the roads. We can't let this spread."

"Block the . . . ? The festival is tomorrow! People here *need* this festival. They have bills to pay!"

"Pippa—"

"Is this about November, Steve?"

"For goodness sakes, would you listen to me?" His voice got high and whiny when he was angry. "This has nothing to do with the election."

He was losing her, and the more I thought about it, the less it seemed to matter. What could she do, anyway? Organize a posse? Warn people to stay indoors? I wasn't even sure how useful a roadblock would be.

What I did know was this: I was wasting time listening to these people. I backed away from them and looked up at Penny's house. It was dark and quiet.

I went inside and took out my ghost knife.

I searched the house from basement to attic but didn't find anything out of the ordinary. The sapphire dog certainly wasn't hidden there, and Penny didn't have any spell books I could find. The only things I found were a pair of tabby cats cowering under the bed and an old police-band scanner in the kitchen.

When I went back outside, Pippa and Steve were standing at the back of Steve's car, talking to Penny.

I walked toward the Neon. Pippa heard me coming and held up her index finger, signaling me to wait. I ignored her and kept walking to my car.

Pippa frowned and followed me. "So, this is your dog?"

"Nope."

"But you know about it," she said. "What's wrong with it? Rabies? Why is it blue?"

"Steve and Penny both saw it. Why not ask them?"

She stepped too close to me again. I'd have suspected she was clueless about personal space if it hadn't been for the look on her face. "I have. Now I'm asking you."

Steve had felt the effects of the sapphire dog. I'd talked to him because he already knew enough to get killed. With Pippa, things were different.

And I didn't like or trust her.

The ambulance siren chirped as it pulled out.

"Come on, Pippa," Steve said. "He saved my life and he's trying to help."

She ignored him. "I don't trust you. When the sheriff gets here, I'm going to have you locked up until the real truth comes out."

"Well, you should call him, then."

"I think I will."

She walked away, putting her cellphone to her ear. Steve came close. His expression betrayed his embarrassment, but he didn't apologize.

"Once Penny's locked up," he said, "we'll talk again. Go back to the Sunset, okay? You look like you could use some sleep anyway."

"You'll block those roads, right?"

"Right," he said. "Pippa will order it. I'll make sure."

He started toward his car, but I wasn't finished. "Steve, what happened to the Breakleys?"

He glanced around to make sure Pippa was still on her cell. "They were home when the fire broke out," he said. "The fire chief said he saw them in the basement window while the crews were dousing the barn. They wouldn't come out, though. A couple of hours later, I went back to check on them.

"There was a hole in the stone foundation of the house, like someone had tunneled through. They were all dead. They'd killed each other, starting with the little ones."

"Any white marks?"

"The parents each had one, and the grandmother."

"But not the kids?"

Steve shook his head, got into his car, and did a U-turn to head back to town.

Parents killing their own children. I tried not to think about that. The sapphire dog hadn't touched the two little girls. Maybe it hadn't gotten the chance, or maybe they were too young. Steve had said the girls were seven and nine, and while Little Mark had a white stain, he was at least fourteen or fifteen. The baby Steve had given to the paramedics hadn't been marked, either. Maybe the predator needed its food to be ripe.

After a quick circuit of the rental car to make sure the predator hadn't materialized in the backseat, I drove farther out on the road. There were no more houses or buildings out this way. I passed several signs telling me the highway turnoff was coming up, and I saw a couple of scattered businesses, a campground, and a turnoff for the church and fairgrounds. Another banner told me the Christmas festival was taking place at the fairgrounds, and a little sign below told me the church was having a benefit lunch . . . well, it was happening right then, as it turned out.

I drove by, passed the school grounds, and entered the town from the other side. I hadn't seen the turnoff for the highway. I did a U-turn and drove back. I missed it a second time. Maybe some joker had moved the signs.

This time I pulled into the fairgrounds. The church was off to the right on a low hill; it looked like exactly the sort of church I'd expect in a little town: small with a peaked roof and a steeple. I parked below the church in the fairgrounds parking lot, a wide asphalt patch that overlooked the fairgrounds below. The grounds were slightly larger than a football field, which I thought surprisingly small until I realized that level ground must be a pretty scarce commodity around here.

I shut the engine off and sat in the car. The sapphire dog had not come this way by accident. It was possible that Clara had chosen the route, but I didn't believe it. Little Mark had tried to chauffeur the predator, too, and I remembered the way it felt to be near that thing. Whatever it would have wanted, I would have wanted, too. The sapphire dog was the one in control.

But why this way? Maybe it wanted to go camping. Maybe it wanted to go to church. Maybe it wanted to get on the feeder road—which I couldn't find—to the highway and then hit the big city, where there were hundreds of thousands of people to make crazy. But it had failed.

Now I was looking across the fairgrounds at a cinderblock building. The door kept swinging open as people went in and out. Why go all the way to Seattle to feed when it could stop off right here?

I climbed from the car and walked along the parking lot. I passed an old fire engine; the firefighters had probably stopped off for lunch after the Breakley fire.

To catch this predator, I'd have to figure out what it wanted. *Eat and reproduce* was the simple answer, but Catherine and her songbird story had made me realize that this wasn't as simple as it seemed.

Maybe it just wanted its freedom. Maybe the most important thing to it right now was not to be captured and starved in a cage again. Then, once it was far away, it would do its thing. Maybe it would call more of its kind here. Or start a cult. Maybe it would create an army and install itself as Pet Emperor.

Unless I destroyed it first.

The cinder-block building was painted white, and I walked inside feeling like a man with a bomb strapped to his chest. I had come eagerly to this little town to kill and possibly be killed, and none of the old ladies smiling at me as I dropped fifteen dollars of Fat Guy's money into the food-bank kitty had any idea how dangerous I felt. There was a second door right in front of me, and behind the welcome table on the right was a long hall filled with lawn equipment.

I accepted a tray in exchange for my donation and went into a much larger room. As I moved down the line at the kitchen windows, a heap of mac and cheese, a pair of chicken drumsticks, succotash, home-baked rolls, and broccoli-cheddar bake were put on my plate. I said thank you. No one had white marks on their faces, and no one seemed likely to go on a murder spree.

The sapphire dog hadn't come here. Not yet.

As I stepped away from the serving line, I scanned the room. There were a dozen round tables set up and ten chairs at each table. Most of the seats were full. At the center table, a half dozen firemen were holding court. They were tall, well-muscled men ranging from their mid-twenties to mid-fifties. Several women—two dozen or so in all—sat at their table or chatted with them from an adjacent table. I wondered if I could sit close enough to hear what they knew about the Breakleys.

"Oh, please join us," a gray-haired woman said from the table nearest me, at the edge of the room. She was sitting with three people: an Asian woman who looked just a few years younger; a brown-eyed toddler wearing tiny earrings; and a woman I assumed was the toddler's mom, plump, with dark hair and a lot of eyeliner.

The gray-haired woman, who had the whitest skin I'd ever seen, introduced herself as Francine, then went around the table and introduced Mai, Estrella, and Graciela. I told them my name was Ray, and Mai immediately asked me if I was the one who had his car stolen. I retold that story, because it would have seemed odd to refuse. The women clucked their tongues and made a fuss over my black eye. Then conversation turned to the Christmas festival.

Just as I was about to steer the topic toward the Breakley fire, another woman stopped by the table. The others called her Catty, which startled me. For a moment, I thought they had copied my habit of giving descriptive names to people, but no, it was just an unfortunate nickname. They traded forced pleasantries until Catty left, then Graciela admitted that she felt obligated to buy some of Catty's jewelry at the festival because Catty had helped her out so often.

Mai kindly told me that Graciela's husband was serving overseas, and while the whole town was happy to help her out, only Catty hinted that she deserved some sort of repayment. Graciela listened to this without looking up from her plate.

They chatted about the display Catty would have and how much Graciela should spend. I wasn't a part of the conversation, but it was too late to move to another table. I was not getting any closer to finding the predator.

I had looked into the sapphire dog's eyes only an hour before. After I'd seen something so alien and beautiful, the everyday chatter around me made me feel utterly out of place.

Then Hondo stopped by. He greeted everyone enthusiastically, especially little Estrella. Turning to me, he said: "I take it your lady friend decided not to leave after all."

Someone on the other side of the room laughed uproariously. People were having fun. "What do you mean?" I said.

He was a little surprised by my tone. "Your friend. She paid me a pickup fee for the train station, but it only takes a half hour to drive out there. I'm still waiting for her call."

Francine noticed the look on my face. "Maybe she has a problem with her phone," she said in a soothing tone.

Now Hondo was looking concerned, too. "I don't

think so. Arliss at the station knows my cars. He says it's not there."

Catherine didn't arrive at her destination. I dropped my napkin onto my plate. "Excuse me."

"Hey, man," Hondo said, "do you need help?" Everyone at the table looked ready to jump up and join the search.

"Thanks, but no. I'm sure she's fine. I just need to make certain for my peace of mind."

I pushed my way toward the door. As I passed the firefighters, I heard one of them say he had to get back to his family for Christmas, then they stood, too.

I made my way back to my car. It was nearly three-thirty, and Catherine had left around noon. I had to find out what had happened to her.

CHAPTER NINE

I parked across the street from the B and B. Two people on stilts came down the shoulder of the road. They were dressed in silver costumes, with white masks over the top half of their faces and delicate dragonfly wings on their backs. The costumes were decorated with snowflakes and reflective tape. The rented Acura was nowhere in sight.

I went into the Sunset, still feeling like a bomb ready to explode.

Pro Wrestler was sitting at the little desk in the living room entering figures into a computer. He hunched over the keyboard, carefully tapping the keys with thick fingers, and I felt a startling yearning to be like him. To hell with feeling like a bomb. I'd rather be a human being. I walked up to him and extended my hand. "Thank you for your help this morning," I said. "I'm grateful. My name is Ray."

He already knew my name from my credit card, of course, but he took the hint. "I'm Nicholas. Those clothes look a little loose on you."

We were smiling. "Yeah, but they're warm."

"Good to hear. Staying for the festival?" He looked around the little lobby. I did, too. A man in a long tan coat and a wide-brimmed tan hat sat by the fire. Nicholas's expression was slightly disappointed. Obviously, he'd hoped for a bigger crowd. "Sure," I said, because why not? "Sounds like fun."

I was about to ask if he'd heard from Catherine when Nicholas said: "I almost forgot." He took a manila envelope from the bottom drawer of his desk and handed it to me. My name was written on it in sweeping lines of delicate brown ink. The envelope held something bulky and small.

"Where did this come from?" I asked.

"Nadia found it on the front porch."

I tore open the envelope. It was a cellphone wrapped in a sheet of notepaper. It was Catherine's, but I turned to Nicholas and said: "Someone found it. That was nice of them."

"Does it say who?"

I said the note was unsigned, thanked him, then went to my room. Once the door was locked, I sat on the corner of the bed and opened the slip of paper. It read PRESS REDIAL in the same sweeping hand.

What the hell. I'm good at following directions. The phone rang twice. "Hello?" It was Well-Spoken Woman, and she had me on speakerphone.

"Thanks for the phone," I said. "I have a pal in Tokyo I'd like to call."

"We know your name, Mr. Lilly, and we know why you are here. If you would like your friend to live through the night, come to the Grable Motel. It's out past the Breakley farm. Come right away."

"Give me an hour or so to wrap up."

"Unacceptable."

"I have to wash the blood off," I said testily. If they really did know why I was here, they would believe that.

"All right then." She sounded hesitant, which was what I wanted. We hung up.

The bed smelled like laundry soap, and the plug-in pine scent made the air close. God, how good it would have felt to lie back and close my eyes . . .

There was a knock on the door. I opened it, figuring Nicholas must have another envelope for me.

It was the man in the tan coat. He was a little shorter than me, even with his hat still on, and his skin and hair were the color of sand. "You're Raymond Lilly, aren't you?"

I didn't like the way he was smirking at me. "Yeah. Who are you?"

"I'm Talcott Arnold Pratt. The society sent me here to clean up this mess."

His coat was open, presumably to give me a glimpse at the sigils burned into the lining. A peer! An honest-to-God peer had finally come.

I must have let my relief show. He gave me a sour, condescending smile and pushed into the room. "Shut the door," he said. I did.

Everything about the guy gave off contempt, but I was glad he was there. A peer in the Twenty Palace Society ought to have the power to take out the sapphire dog, not to mention the bidders.

"The investigator who brought me here is—"

"I know who she is. I've read her report and don't need to talk to her."

"You don't understand. She's been kidnapped. I need your help to get her back."

"I don't rescue people. I kill predators."

Of course not. I hated this guy already, but there were bigger things at stake than my feelings. "Okay. What can I do—"

"I don't answer questions from wooden men. Are we clear?"

I felt the skin on the back of my neck prickle. Was I going to have to throw down with this guy right here? "We're clear."

"Has anything happened since the last supplemental report?"

"I don't know when Catherine made the last supplemental report," I answered. I kept my tone neutral.

"It was this morning."

"Then yes."

Pratt was getting annoyed, too. "Yes, what?"

"Yes, something more has happened since the last report."

He glowered, then looked away and laughed a little, shaking his head. He loosened his coat, probably to give me another look at his sigils. "Has she told you what's at stake here?"

"Wait . . . let me guess. End of everything that matters to us, right?"

"That's right. Creatures from the Empty Spaces are terribly inefficient predators. They invade a habitat and hunt it to destruction. They don't have any balance about them."

"The sapphire dog isn't killing anyone—just making them crazy."

He continued as if I hadn't spoken. "But you want to put your pride above all of that, don't you? You want *respect*." He gave me a thin smile. I'd seen that look before. It was a cop's expression—a look of superiority so complete he would never think to question it.

"Sure, sure," I said. "The stakes are so high you get to do whatever you want and I have to take it. Let me give you an update so you can make your big exit."

I gave him a quick rundown of everything that had happened since Catherine and I rented the cars. I described the predator, the way the victims had looked, and how it seemed to split apart when threatened. He asked what I had threatened it with, and I told him Steve's gun; I wasn't going to tell this jerk about my ghost knife.

When I started telling him about the cellphone and the kidnapping call, he lost interest. When I got to ". . . then

I opened the door and was insulted by you," he was already walking out.

He stopped in the hall and smirked. "You're done. Run along home now, if you can." He left.

There was a moment when I could have booted him in the ass, but I let it pass. If Pratt was anything like my boss, he could have pinched my head off with one hand. Peers were strong and tough—they had to be to face predators. And the guy killed for a living.

I checked my pockets to make sure I still had everything, then went outside to the Neon. I didn't know the names of any of the streets in Washaway, but I knew how to get in and out. I followed the road to the bridge, drove by the burned-out Breakley farm, then kept going. I passed the Wilburs' black iron gate and finally reached a shopping center. A road sign promised to connect me with a state route just down the hill, but I didn't see the road.

The Grable was set in the back corner of the shopping center. All that was visible of it was a cinder-block wall painted the same color as the field house and an entry arch with a sign at the top. The NO VACANCY sign was lit.

As I cruised by, I saw an open courtyard/parking lot with just enough space for cars to drive down the center and angle park in front of the units on either side. In fact, there were three BMW X6's in there now, all parked in front of units at the far end of the lot. The Maybach was in the last slot.

There was no possibility of getting in the front way without being exposed to every unit. I drove across the lot.

The shopping center was laid out in the shape of a U. At one end was a drugstore. At the other was a supermarket. In between was a variety of little shops and storefronts—a small bookstore, a pitch-dark bar, a dentist, a drive-up burger joint, a teriyaki restaurant, a Subway, and several darkened windows with FOR LEASE signs in them. All were one story tall, except the drugstore and supermarket, which had peaked roofs. The Grable sat in the back corner of the U.

All the windows were papered with sale prices, garlands, and religious displays. There was a huge inflatable Santa and reindeer on the roof.

Santa gave me an idea. I parked beside the drugstore and went inside. I bought a newspaper, a lighter, and a votive candle with Fat Guy's money, then went around the back of the building.

The alley was strewn with trash and smelled like old piss. It was wide enough for a trash truck to squeeze through. The paint on the buildings was peeling, while the guardrail on the other side of the alley, where the ground dropped away to a nettle-ridden slope, was dented and rusty.

At the far end of the alley, I came to more white cinder block. I'd found the edge of the Grable. I stepped onto the guardrail but couldn't see over the wall. I could see the broken glass cemented into the top, however. The Grable had been built for privacy.

Turning around, I saw a young woman in the doorway, puffing on a cigarette and watching me. Her hair was a dull, fake black that she brushed into her raccoon-dark eyes. She was positioned beside the Dumpster, and I'd been so intent on the motel grounds that I hadn't noticed her.

"Uh . . . ," I said, trying to think up a plausible lie. She rolled her eyes, stubbed out her cigarette on the scarred edge of the Dumpster, and turned her back on me. She couldn't have cared less.

After she went inside, I laid a wooden pallet against the building and, with a running start, used it to jump up and get a grip on the edge of the roof. Thankfully, there was no broken glass here.

I pulled myself up and lay across the tarred paper. If I made too much noise, stood too high, or walked onto a section that couldn't support me, I was going to spend the night in jail. At best. I kept low, crawling on my hands and knees toward the edge of the building and the white wall of the motel.

I wondered how Catherine had been caught. They probably staked out the only place where we could have rented replacement cars. I should have tried to look more interesting; maybe they would have taken me instead.

The top of the motel wall was even with the drugstore roof. I swept the ghost knife through the glass shards, slid belly-down over the wall, and dropped between it and the nearest unit. There wasn't even enough space for me to turn all the way around. I edged toward the back of the building.

Each unit had a small window at the back that would have shown nothing but wall. Maybe it had once offered a view of the forest. I knew that peeking in a window with a big white background was a good way to be spotted. I peeked anyway.

The walls inside the unit were yellow and the bed-sheets a slightly darker yellow. It looked like an invalid's room. At the far end, a slender, dark-haired man in a black suit sat in a chair. He hunched forward to peer through a crack in the curtains into the courtyard. He had a Glock in his hand.

I ducked down and hurried to the next room. This one was empty. There were two more units in the row, but only the end unit was occupied.

I went back to the first empty room, cut the window out of the wall, and climbed through.

I took a towel from the bathroom and set it on the bed with the candle, newspaper, and lighter. One of the things people don't realize about prison is that it's vo-tech for criminals. The trick I was about to set up had been taught to me by a college kid who liked fire a little too much. I'd never tried it myself, but I remembered his instructions. At least, I hoped I did.

I set things up and climbed out the window, then used the narrow space between the end unit and the wall to scramble back over to the drugstore roof. Night was falling.

My hour was up. I lowered myself into the Dumpster alley and hustled around the buildings. The cellphone in my pocket vibrated. I didn't answer. The motel entrance was just ahead of me, and they could talk to me in person in a minute.

I paused at the arched entrance and slid my ghost knife into the stone. The only evidence that it was there was a paper-thin slot in the cinder block. No one would find it, and maybe it would be close enough for me to *call* if I needed it.

In the front office, the clerk looked up at me in surprise. He looked like he would appear surprised by the arrival of lunchtime.

"Which room is Mr. Yin's?" I asked.

A newspaper rustled behind me. A short, athletic Chinese man stood, stepped toward me, and dropped a comics section onto the floor. He didn't pull out a gun, but he did gesture toward the door with a slight bow and a polite smile.

We walked through the courtyard. Mr. Yin, of course, was staying in the room farthest from the entrance. It was a well-defended spot, but it didn't leave him an escape route—not unless he had a pogo stick that could bounce him over a ten-foot wall.

Drivers inside the BMWs and the Maybach started the engines and drove out of the lot.

My guide knocked on the door and led me inside. This one had a genuine painting on the wall. It showed a man in robes sitting on a hill between some twisted trees. It had been painted on something thinner than canvas, but I didn't know enough to identify it. The painting obviously didn't come with the room.

"Ah!" a middle-aged man said. He stood at the far end of the room, six bodyguards standing near him. This had to be Mr. Yin. He had a thick neck, a black suit, a placid smile, and a gold ring on every finger. His eyes were wide, almost bulging out of his head, as though he was studying everything around him. This was a billionaire?

A dark-skinned woman in a gray suit stood beside him. By the way she had wrapped up her hair in a bun, I figured she was Well-Spoken Woman.

I glanced over at the painting again. Maybe he took it with him everywhere. "You have an eye for quality!" Yin said. "Your attention goes directly to the most arresting object in the room. Excellent."

His English was better than mine. "Where's Catherine?"

"Close by," Mr. Yin said, "but not so close that you could kill us all and take her away unharmed." He was smiling at me. What the hell was he talking about?

He turned to the woman beside him. "Well?"

She was staring at the backs of my hands where my tattoos were most visible. Her eyes were shining, and she looked like a pirate who'd found buried treasure. "*Mowbray Book of Oceans,* I'd say. I'd need to see more to be certain."

This was not going as I'd expected. These were the nicest kidnappers I'd ever met. And that remark about killing them all . . .

Of course.

I sighed and chuckled, mostly to buy myself time to reset my body language and tone. "I'm not here to play games," I said. "And I'm sure as hell not here to strip for you. I have a predator to kill. Give me my investigator, and I'll let you all get into your cars and drive away."

One of the gunmen drew his pistol and aimed it at me. It gave me goose bumps, but I kept my smile in place. Mr. Yin said something to him in Chinese. I couldn't understand the words, but the tone said *Don't bother.*

Yin thought I was a peer, which meant he also thought I was damn near bulletproof. I'd hate for his bodyguard to prove him wrong all over the cheap carpet.

"You must understand," Mr. Yin said. "I spent a hundred twenty-eight million dollars last night for the rights to that unusual creature. Then someone shot at us, allowing it to escape. I can't allow you to kill my dog, Mr. Lilly."

"You know it's making people murder each other. Parents have killed their own children. Do you really want to bring that thing into your house?"

"Ah, but *these* people are *bumpkins,* and Americans, too. I will exert more control."

His body language was still utterly self-assured, although he was wary of me, too. I knew my body language wasn't as confident as his, and I knew he'd noticed that.

I looked over at the man who had drawn his gun. He hadn't put it away. "What do you want for Catherine?"

The gunman and I looked at each other. He wasn't impressed with me, and I wanted to punch him right in his stupid smirk. I hate to be afraid.

"I propose a trade," Mr. Yin said. "I will return to you the woman, unharmed, if you will give me everything you brought with you for this mission: your computer, your files, your research books, and any enchanted artifacts you have on you."

He wanted my ghost knife. "You have to be kidding me."

"I also want safe passage out of the country and your personal assurance that you will not try to kill me or any of my descendants, ever."

"Do you want my left foot, too?"

"If your left foot is of value, then yes, I want it. I want everything a man can want."

He smiled, waiting for my answer. I didn't have any research books, of course. I didn't own a computer and I didn't have any files.

And my ghost knife was a part of me. I *couldn't* give it up, not even for Catherine.

Mr. Yin fussed with the lapel of his jacket. "You appear distressed," he said.

"Because you're wasting my time with this MBA negotiating crap. This isn't a boardroom where you ask for a long list of things you know you're not going to get so we can whittle all the way down to what you actually want. You're not getting away with the sapphire dog. The mayor has already asked the state police to block off the only two roads out of town."

Two of the gunmen seemed nervous about that—he had only brought two English-speakers. Yin wasn't nervous at all. "Another thing," I said. "You're not the only one out there looking for it. While we're chitchatting, one of the other bidders could be capturing it right now."

Suddenly Yin didn't seem so smug. "The sapphire dog is mine. I paid for it."

I rolled my eyes. "Keep telling yourself that, because I'm sure if one of the others had won the auction and then let the creature get away, you'd totally return it to them. Let's cut the crap and get to what you really want for my friend."

Yin smiled again. His contentment was like a suit of armor. "Your computer, your files, your research materials, your enchanted artifacts, your assurance of safety for my descendants and for me."

Annalise would have already started killing. "Here's my counteroffer: your life, and the lives of all your people, for as long as it takes me to have a turkey and ham at the Subway. I'm in the mood for pepperoncini. No guarantees after that."

He turned his lapel over. There was a patch of white fabric pinned to the other side, and it had a sigil on it.

I blinked. For some reason I was staring at the carpet from just a foot away. My iron gate felt as though someone was pushing a needle through it.

I was on my knees. Yin had hit me with a spell, and like an idiot, I had fallen for it.

I felt hands patting me down. They were searching me very thoroughly. Two men grabbed my wrists and cuffed my hands behind my back. I was too woozy to resist.

"You are not a peer," Yin said. His voice had a little twist of contempt. "At best, you are an apprentice, hm?" He kicked me in the shoulder, but my tattoos blunted the impact. "You dare try to bluff me? I admire your courage, but it will cost you your life."

"Okay," I said. "Okay." I tried to lift my head, but any movement at all made me dizzy. Instead, I pressed my forehead against the carpet and dragged my knees under me. With my hands cuffed, it was a struggle to keep from falling over. Still, I managed it.

It was the perfect position for one of these assholes to put a bullet in the back of my head. Just the thought made my guts watery. "Okay," I said again, looking up at Yin. "A sandwich and some chips. That's my final offer."

Instead of ordering his men to shoot me, he laughed. He said something in Chinese, and I was hauled into the bathroom.

Someone was already in there, sitting on the toilet. It was one of his own men, bound and gagged. Thank God his pants were up.

They spun me around and shoved me into the tub. They made a special effort to tear Nicholas's shirt.

I tripped over the rim and toppled back, smacking my head against the tile. I saw stars and the pain made tears well up. Damn, those tears made me furious. I was not going to let these bastards think—

"Mr. Lilly," Yin said. "See? This is the spot where your friend would be, if I actually had her. It seems we were both bluffing!" He laughed with a high, girlish giggle.

I blinked the tears away. Yin was waiting for a response. "You're full of shit," I said. "You had her phone. Where did you hide her?"

"I do have her phone, but not her. She is a clever woman. Your society has more wit left to it than I'd heard." He kicked the bottom of my foot. "Not in you, though. This fellow here"—he gestured to the man on the toilet—"is the one who let her escape, so he has taken her place.

"In many ways," Yin continued, "I am an innocent in this world. I'm merely a financier with a mania for collecting. Without my collection, I would have no use for my money or these good, brave men. And I would have no use for torture."

His tone was still calm and friendly. Nothing worried him at the moment. "Still," he continued, "we can hardly employ such methods here. But I have other options." He leaned close, wide-eyed and smiling. "I brought some of my collection with me."

He turned toward the door. Well-Spoken handed him something wrapped in a black cloth. It was smaller than a T-ball bat. He unwrapped it with reverence.

It was a long knife, or maybe a short sword. I don't know the difference and I don't care. The scabbard was black and gleaming like polished stone. Yin drew it with a sudden motion, then held it up to admire it. The blade was straight, and as wide as two thumb widths. It had been honed and polished, and it looked like an antique. Yin held it up to the light as though he was about to discuss its history, then he turned and stabbed the bound man through the throat.

I shouted something inane like "Hey!" Bound didn't have time to gasp. He froze, a grimace on his face. He looked around the room, finally stopping on me, and I thought how brutally unfair it was that I would be the last thing this stupid bastard ever saw.

Yin pushed the sword downward through his breastbone and stomach all the way to his belly button. He had to put his weight behind it, but it was not as difficult to cut through the bones as it should have been. Then he pulled the sword free. There was no blood, no cut, no wound at all. I stared at Bound, waiting for the blood.

Yin yanked off the man's gag. Bound looked up meekly and said something in Chinese. Yin seemed amused. "He has just apologized to me."

It's an illusion, I thought. Yin had a trick sword, and Bound was playing along.

But I had no idea why they would bother; I was already in cuffs and at their mercy. I looked back at Bound and realized I needed to change his nickname. The ropes he'd been tied with were lying on the floor in pieces. His clothes were cut open, too. I'd been so focused on looking for blood that I hadn't even noticed.

Bound slid down to his knees and hung his head.

"Do you see?" Yin asked, showing me the blade. There was a small sigil engraved near the hilt. "This mark is from the *Ketrivisky Book of Oceans.* This is a soul sword. It does not leave a mark on his flesh, but his will now belongs to me."

The bastard had a ghost knife of his own.

CHAPTER TEN

Yin studied the sword. "It is not as powerful as it was in the hands of the man who sold it to me. I'm sure you know what happens to magic each time it changes hands." He pointed it at me. "I wonder how many of the spells on your body I could cut before it shattered?"

Now was the time. "I don't have files," I said, not bothering to hide my hatred of him or my fear of that damn blade. "I don't have any authority to guarantee your safety or the safety of your children. I only have one thing to offer: I can give you a spell of your own."

Yin's eyes narrowed on me and the sword lowered. "A spell?"

Bingo. "It's the only one I know. Give me a big sheet of paper and a pen and I'll draw out both parts for you. Then you let me go and leave us alone. We pretend this meeting never happened. I can't offer more than that."

He smiled at me. He was terribly smug. "I agree. Understand, though, Mr. Lilly. If you betray me, I will make sure others hear about our deal. I know how your superiors respond to trading spells."

Two of his guys pulled me upright and unlocked my cuffs.

"Remember," Yin said, "do not—"

"Just give me the paper and pen so we can be done with it."

Well-Spoken brought them to me. I laid the paper on

the bottom of the tub and wrote "for the mind" in the upper left and "for the hand" in the upper right. I'd only cast a couple of spells in my life, including the ghost knife, and while I couldn't have re-created them from memory, this was how they had been drawn in the spell book.

On the left side of the page, I drew a couple of squiggles that might have been a hole in the ground and maybe an eyeball. On the right, I drew a couple of short lines that suggested a campfire. I have never been much of an artist, but considering what real sigils look like, that worked in my favor.

I handed them the paper. They cuffed me again.

Yin laid his hand over the drawing on the left. He knew enough to recognize the danger in looking at that part of a spell before he'd learned the right-hand drawing.

"What does it do?" Well-Spoken hurried toward him and peered at it over his shoulder.

I glared at Yin. "Wait for it," I said.

It took less than a minute, but eventually the fire alarm clanged. His gunmen looked nervous, but Yin was greedily delighted. "An arson spell?"

"I don't recognize it, sir." Well-Spoken had to shout over the alarm. "I don't even recognize the style."

"Is it . . ." He searched my expression. When he strained his voice, his pitch went quite high. "I have heard that the *Book of Grooves* is in this part of the world. Is this from the lost *Book of Grooves*?"

I looked him straight in the eye. "I have no idea what you're talking about," I said truthfully.

He looked flustered for a moment, then his smug expression returned. "Of course. I forgot to bargain for its provenance. Have no fear, Mr. Lilly. My people are very good at their jobs. I'll have my answers soon enough." He waved his men out of the room and backed away.

"Of course, you forgot to bargain for the keys to those handcuffs!" It was his parting shot, and I let him have it. I kicked the door shut.

Bound was still kneeling on the floor. Yin had abandoned him, but I couldn't bring myself to care. I bent low, passing the cuffs under my feet so my hands were in front of me, then peeked into the living room. No one put a bullet in my head. They were gone. Through the front window I could see black smoke pouring from one of the units across the way.

I was suddenly very tired. I glanced at my watch and saw that it was dinnertime. I needed sleep, and while I wasn't desperate enough to lie down here, it would have to be soon.

Bound was still crouching there. The fire across the lot was growing strong. I dragged him to his feet. Together, we hustled out the door.

We hurried toward the arched exit, keeping as far from the fire as possible. Glass shattered somewhere behind me. I shielded my face and dragged Bound past the office.

The fire engine screeched to a stop at the entrance to the motel, while the clerk waved at them with a windmilling arm. I pulled Bound through the arch and off to the side, but we'd been spotted. A firefighter jumped from the back of the engine and ran toward us.

"You two!" he shouted. "Get to a safe distance, but don't leave the area. We're going to have some questions . . ."

He noticed the handcuffs and stopped talking. Then he looked again at Bound's torn clothes and hunched, face-to-the-ground body language. He didn't know what to say.

"What?" I said. "We're consenting adults."

He frowned, then pointed to a place well away from the

fire. "Go there. Stay." Then he turned and ran through the arch.

"How did you get here so fast?" I called, but he was already gone.

I laid my hand against the stone arch and *called* my ghost knife. I held it close and said, "Come on." Bound followed me.

We went farther than the fireman wanted, hurrying by the people filing out of the bar to watch the flames.

With the ghost knife, I cut the cuffs off—carefully. I didn't know what effect the spell would have on me, and now was not the time to experiment.

I dropped the cuffs into a planter. People were coming out of the stores, and I didn't want any more attention than necessary. Then I saw Yin step into the Maybach. His driver closed the door for him and got behind the wheel.

Movement off to my right caught my attention. It was Tattoo sitting on a Megamoto. I felt the sudden flush of fear that comes from finding myself too close to a guy who wants to kill me, but he was watching Yin. He hadn't even noticed me.

As the trio of BMWs rolled out of the parking lot, Tattoo stuck a piece of toast in his mouth and pulled his helmet on. He didn't have a cast over his thumb or ankle, and I was sure I'd broken both. Damn. All that work and nothing to show for it. He started his bike and followed Yin's people.

Without thinking about it, I bolted away from Bound and ran toward Tattoo, ghost knife in hand. Yin was a bastard, but Tattoo was worse.

It was no use. The cars were out of the lot and Tattoo was only fifty feet behind them, too far away for me to use my ghost knife.

Bound was standing where I'd left him. I pushed him

against the wall and patted him down. His gun was gone. He let me take his passport and billfold. He had credit cards, foreign cash, even a notepad and pen. None of it interested me, and none of it was worth taking.

"Hey," I said. He wouldn't look me in the face. "Hey. Where's Catherine? Your boss said you had her, but she got away. Where did she escape? What did you do to her, you asshole?"

He said something I didn't understand. He repeated it again, and I realized he was saying: "Help me." Apparently, that was the only English he knew.

"Sure thing, buddy. Sure thing." I smiled and laid a reassuring hand on his shoulder. Yin's ghost knife didn't leave him enough vigor to smile in response, but he did look relieved.

I took the notepad and pen out of his billfold and wrote: *I don't speak English but I do like to start fires. Please arrest me.* Then I tucked the billfold back into his pocket, gently put the note in his hand, and gestured toward the men by the bar. He started walking meekly toward them, note held in front of him.

I didn't stick around to see how that would turn out.

As I approached the Neon, I passed a pair of old hippies watching the fire. It was still going strong. One of them turned toward me. "What happened, dude?" I couldn't see his mouth moving underneath his wiry gray beard.

I shrugged. "I just got here. Is there another motel in town?"

"Naw, just the Sunset, but that's a really nice place."

I smiled while he gave me directions, then thanked him and climbed into the car. I couldn't go back to the Sunset. Yin knew about it.

I pulled out of the lot and headed away from town. I would have to sneak around the roadblock and find a room at the next exit, whatever it was, and come back for my car when I'd gotten some sleep and food.

A green pickup drove toward me. Hadn't the road-block been put up yet? Had the mayor decided not to call it in because of the festival?

The car in front of me was a Volvo station wagon packed to the windows with loose laundry. It was about a hundred feet ahead when its brake lights came on. I slowed down, too. My iron gate twinged, but that seemed unimportant.

The Volvo stopped. I slowed to parking-lot speed, the twinge in my shoulder growing stronger. After a couple of seconds, the Volvo did a three-point turn and drove back toward me.

I braked and took out my ghost knife. The driver was a bird-faced old woman who didn't glance at me once. She simply drove past me toward town with a pained expression on her face.

Weird. I took my foot off the brake and started toward the highway again. The first flare of a headache started, and I slowed again. I couldn't remember why I was driving out of town. It didn't make sense. Washaway was where I needed to be.

I stopped in the road. There was a reason I needed to leave, but I couldn't remember what it was. A beer truck came up the road toward me, but it stopped about a hundred and fifty feet away and turned around. I watched it drive away.

I touched my iron gate. It was throbbing, but there was no one else around, not even other cars.

I saw a blue tarp on the side of the road. I got out of the car, leaving the engine running, and walked into the weeds. There were actually several tarps. The closest was the smallest, and I knelt beside it, my headache growing stronger. The edges were tucked underneath the object it was covering. I took out my ghost knife to slit open the top, then thought better of it and just pulled it back.

It was a little girl. I won't describe her in detail, but

she'd been beaten and strangled to death many hours before. She did not have a white mark on her face. I tucked the tarp under her again.

When I pulled back the tarp on the next one, I found Clara's red-gold curls. I didn't need to see more.

I stood and backed away, my head pounding. The other tarps were probably Isabelle and the rest of the Breakley family. I could have pulled them all back to see if Biker was there, or if the gunmen had been brought down from the Wilbur estate, but I didn't. I didn't want to look at more dead faces.

Sue and Big Bill had obviously brought the bodies out here and laid them by the side of the road. That seemed perfectly logical to me. The tarps would protect them from animals, and while it didn't make sense to take them out of Washaway, they had to be put *somewhere*.

I headed back to the car, instinctively understanding that I would feel better if I went back to town. I did a three-point turn and drove back toward the fire and the trucks. My headache eased and my iron gate stopped aching.

But I still didn't have anywhere to go. It wasn't safe to stay at the B and B, and the motel was gone. There were empty houses I could break into, but they were all crime scenes. Besides, I didn't really want to sleep in the Breakleys' bedroom tonight, knowing what had happened there.

If I couldn't sleep, I needed to find the predator quickly. I needed a plan.

I drove through town and pulled up in front of Penny's house. The pickup was still against the tree, but her front door was closed. Both had been surrounded with yellow tape. At first I thought the mysterious sheriff had finally arrived, but when I got closer I saw it was caution tape, not police tape.

I went inside. The house was dark, but the entry to the

kitchen was lit by a nightlight. The police scanner was still there. I turned it on to make sure it worked, then pulled the plug and tucked it under my arm.

Something rustled behind me. I took out my ghost knife and crept into the living room, hoping I was about to catch the sapphire dog by surprise and not Penny's cats.

It was neither. Little Mark lay on the couch, sleeping peacefully. His head was covered in a big white bandage.

It looked like the same bandage the paramedics had put on him. Obviously, they hadn't taken him to the hospital. I could have taken him myself, but that didn't make sense; I couldn't leave Washaway. I needed to stay, and Mark probably did, too.

I left by the front door without waking him.

I needed to find a place where I could work on the scanner and connect it to the Neon's electrical system. Something private and well lit.

As I drove through town, Steve's Crown Vic came toward me in the opposite lane. He pulled left, blocking the road but giving me enough room to brake. A second car, a rusted Forester, stopped beside his.

He climbed out and came toward me. I could see he was angry. "I thought I asked you to stay at the Sunset."

God, I hated that whining voice. "I didn't have a choice. Can we leave it at that?"

The Forester's driver door opened and a short, plump woman climbed out. At first I thought it was Pippa, but as she stepped into my headlights, I saw that she was a black woman with Coke-bottle-thick glasses and a long, quilted yellow jacket. I guessed she was yet another member of the neighborhood watch. A man climbed out of the Forester behind her. He was a fat little cowboy with a Wilford Brimley mustache.

"No," Steve said. "Things have been happening pretty fast around here. Look at this." He took a sheet of paper from his pocket and held it up. It was already too dark to read it. "I'm the new chief of police in Washaway—temporary emergency position only. Pippa saw to it."

"The sheriff hasn't come yet?"

"No," Steve said, "and I've called him eight times today. But I was a patrol officer in Wenatchee for a few years, so Pippa figured I'm the best candidate for the job. Now, tell me where you've been, or I'm going to arrest you."

"At Penny's. Did you know that Mark is there right now? Sleeping?"

"With a head wound? Is anyone with him?"

"Nope."

He turned to the others. "We can't leave that boy alone with a head injury. Sherisse, Ford, would you go and collect him, please?"

They hustled back to their car. Steve turned to me. "You haven't been at Penny's this whole time, though, right?"

"No."

Steve sighed in irritation. "What about the other strangers in town? They're looking for this thing too, right?"

"Yes, and we can't talk about this here."

"Well, we *could* have talked at the Sunset, if you'd done like I asked, but *no*—"

"Oh, for . . . They found me there, okay? They know I want to kill it, and I'm not safe there anymore. I need a new place to crash." I rubbed my eyes. "I'm pretty much running on fumes."

"Okay." Steve rubbed the faint stubble on his chin. "Let's go."

I followed him through town, turning off Littlemont Road onto a winding asphalt street barely wide enough for two cars. He stopped in front of a clapboard, two-story house with a long garage, walked up the front lawn, and opened the garage door. I pulled inside.

"This is my house, if you haven't guessed." The walls were covered with tools on pegboards. There was a thick layer of dust on them. If Steve had been handy at one point in his life, it was long ago.

I followed him through a mudroom into a little kitchen, then a living room. Everything was perfectly clean and neatly arranged, but it was a depressing little house. It seemed to absorb light, but every scuff of our feet echoed as if we were in a drum. He led me to a threadbare couch and offered me tea and sandwiches. I said yes, thank you, and he went into the kitchen.

A four-foot tree stood in the corner. It was undecorated.

Steve returned and set a foldout table in front of me. There were two little plates on it, each with a white-bread sandwich and a handful of corn chips. Beside them were thick white mugs with steaming tea.

I thanked him again and took a bite of the sandwich. It was yellow cheese with mayo and iceberg lettuce. I was hungry enough to enjoy it.

Steve took a bite of his sandwich, more out of politeness than hunger, I could see. When he swallowed, he set it down and settled back in his armchair. It looked too big for him. "I think it's past time you give me the *full* rundown."

"Okay," I said. I set down my own sandwich and sipped some tea, just to buy time. "Regina Wilbur had this sapphire dog in the little cottage behind her house for decades. It was trapped in there, and she kept it all for herself."

He nodded. We both remembered how the sapphire dog had made us feel. "You said it was a gift?"

"That's what she told me. She was grateful for it, but I don't think the gift giver was doing her any favors."

Steve opened his mouth to respond, then paused. He knew the history of this town and the Wilbur family.

"When she was younger, Regina Wilbur was a terror in this part of the county. She had very definite ideas about what had to be done and who should be allowed to do it. Then she simply stopped coming to planning meetings and became a hermit. Lots of folks were relieved."

"But something changed recently, right?"

"Well, her niece had her declared incompetent. There was a videotape of Regina pitching a fit in her drawing room, claiming that they were keeping her dog from her. A dog that died twenty-five years ago."

"Named Armand, right?" Steve nodded. "I thought so. She gave that name to the sapphire dog, too. You can imagine how she'd behave if they kept her from visiting it."

"The niece . . . Does she know?"

"She held an auction last night. She sold the sapphire dog to a Chinese guy for nearly a hundred thirty million dollars." It was hard to believe that all this trouble had taken place in less than twenty-four hours.

"Lord help us. I know about the men, of course. Washaway has been full of rumors that he was looking to invest nearby and had come to see the festival. But they were here for this auction?"

"Yeah, but the creature escaped. Now the Chinese guy—and the others who lost the auction—are looking for it. They all have guns, and they aren't squeamish about using them."

Steve winced. I described the groups who had been at the estate in a general way, leaving out the summoning of the floating storm and the spells on Tattoo's body.

"What about you? Did you come for the auction, too?"

"No," I answered. "With me, it's . . ." What the hell could I say? I couldn't tell him about the society. ". . . just bad luck."

He didn't look impressed with that answer. "And what does this have to do with what happened to you in Seattle?"

"Near as I can tell, nothing. It was similar to this, though—weird creature, people going nuts."

"You did solve that problem, though?"

I kept my face carefully neutral. "I did."

"How?"

I thought back to the last moments of that ordeal, when my best and oldest friend had pleaded for me to spare his life. The smells of spoiled blood and field turf came back to me, and so did his voice. The old injury on my left hand throbbed.

I opened my mouth to answer, but the words wouldn't come. I'd only talked about it to one other person, a peer in the society I had never seen before or since. At the time, I was still in shock and I'd expected him to kill me. Since then, I hadn't said a word about it.

And I wasn't going to start with a cop, even a temp cop, no matter how politely he asked.

"Never mind," Steve said with a wave of his hand. "I understand."

We didn't say anything for a while, and my eyelids began to droop. He noticed. "Let me set you up for some shut-eye. Any fool can see you need it, even this one."

The pillows and blankets he brought were pink and flowery. I stretched out on the couch, feeling awkward and vulnerable, but when I closed my eyes, I dropped into a deep, dreamless sleep.

"Get up."

I came awake suddenly, thinking that Yin's men had found me again, but it was Catherine.

"I mean it," she said again. Her tone was sharp. "Nap time is over."

I sat up and rubbed the bleariness out of my eyes. The VCR clock said it was almost ten, but was that the evening of the same day, or had I slept all the way into the morning? "It's nice to see you, too. Is it early or late?"

"It's still the same day, if that's what you mean. And I'm hungry again. Those bastards took my emergency food with the jump bag. Come on! Up!"

As a rule, I don't like being snapped at, but I was too damn tired to care. Maybe I was just glad to see that she was okay. "Don't talk to me that way," I said out of habit. "How did you find me?"

"Goddammit, Ray." She sat down on the edge of the couch and folded her arms across her breasts. "I *saw* you go into the motel to meet Yin. What kind of game are you playing?"

"I'm not playing any kind of game. Do you think he turned me? Do you think he bought me off?"

"It wouldn't be the first time."

"That's bullshit," I said with more anger than I'd expected. "He sent me your cellphone and told me he'd kidnapped you. I went there to free you."

She sighed and set her hands on her knees. "And I watched you go in, thinking you were collecting a payoff."

"He nearly killed me, but the fire made him back off."

"That was lucky."

"Not really."

She smiled and I smiled back. We had a moment. Then she looked away and her smile vanished. She held up her hands. They trembled slightly.

"I'm forty-five years old, you know. I'll be forty-six in August, if I live that long. This job isn't as exciting as it was when I was twenty-five. I'm better at it now, but . . ." She rubbed her hands together and leaned back. "They did get me, you know. They stopped my car and dragged me out onto the asphalt. It seemed like a dozen of them, all smiling shit-eating smiles and holding their guns against my body. All over my body."

She was silent for a moment. I waited for her, and eventually she said: "They couldn't keep me, though. They underestimated me, and when I saw my chance I took it."

"I'm glad." It was a stupid thing to say, but I couldn't think of anything better.

Catherine just nodded. "How did you get into this? How did you get sucked into this life?"

Maybe she didn't know my history. Or maybe she was testing me to see if I shared information. I didn't care. "My best friend . . . my best friend had a predator in him. Annalise was there to kill him, but I tried to save him. I took his side against her, but he was past saving."

She nodded. "With me it was my nephew. He was a little wild and very funny, but one summer day he could suddenly *do things*. When the society came hunting for him, the whole family hid him away. They protected him. Except me. I knew he was killing people, and I decided to turn him in. I had to do the right damn thing, no matter what it cost. My family . . . isn't my family anymore. I'm married now, with two girls, but they've never met my mother or sisters. I don't want them to hear the things my family says to me—what they call me now. I got this damn job out of it, though."

I couldn't imagine how hard it was to do society work as a parent, and I said so.

She pulled away from me and let her body language become neutral. "I have ways of dealing. There are ways of doing this job that help keep a little distance. I don't do any of the violence, and I'm never around when it happens. There's no need for me to see that and carry it around with me, bring it home to my family. Not after what happened to my nephew. I take care of my own people and let these people take care of themselves."

That last bit was a little cold. *I don't rescue people.*

I kill predators. But I did my best not to react. People have to cope the best they can.

She continued. "But . . . maybe it's just that I know more now. Maybe I just know more about the danger and the . . . the suddenness. It can be so quick. One minute everything is just fine, and the next you've lost all power and control. They only had me for about twenty minutes, okay? That's how long it took me to get away, but . . . When they have you, they can do anything to you. Kill you, rape you, torture you . . ." She paused while she ran through the possibilities in her mind.

I couldn't ask what Yin had done. I didn't have any real need to know except self-indulgent curiosity. What I needed to do was make her feel better. "Want to go kill them?" I asked.

"Yes!" she answered, but she didn't jump up and rush for the door. "But I'm not the type. And it wouldn't get me anything. I'm going to have nightmares about this, I think. I'm going to have nightmares for a long time about this. Christ, I'm collecting them like scars." After a moment, she added: "Do you really think we should kill Mr. Yin?"

I spread my hands. "Catherine, I bought him off with a fake spell. *Someone* is going to have to kill him."

We had a little discussion about that, where I explained what I did and how I did it. Catherine didn't like the idea on general principle but couldn't think of a specific reason to object. She even admitted that the society publishes fake spell books to discourage wannabes. Then she explained that Steve Cardinal had told her where to find me. It seemed that most of the town was looking for us, with instructions to call him if we were spotted.

"He seems to know more than he should," she said. She watched my response carefully, as if trying to decide whether I was sharing information I should have kept to myself.

"He saw the sapphire dog," I said. "In fact, it nearly fed on him. So yeah, he knows more than he should." I told her about the predator, how it looked and what it could do. She was motionless while I spoke, staring at me intently.

Then I told her about my visit with Pratt. She seemed to recognize the name.

"Did he give you his number?" she asked.

"He wasn't that into me. Actually, he was a complete asshole. He told me to go home, and he wouldn't help deal with Yin."

Wouldn't help rescue you was what I should have said. Catherine seemed to understand anyway.

She rubbed her face. "Well, we can't leave," she said. "It wouldn't make sense to leave Washaway now."

My head felt foggy and sore for a moment, probably from the effects of sleep. "Right, that doesn't make sense."

After that, she set up the police scanner. Steve was out, so I went into his kitchen. I couldn't find any coffee. We had to settle for black tea and sugar. His fridge contained nothing but condiments, Wonder bread, white cheese, and hamburger buns, and his freezer was packed with microwavable meat patties. I felt a little awkward raiding the man's kitchen, and the dismal selection made it easy to leave it all untouched. Maybe we should order out.

We listened to the scanner for the better part of an hour. It was extremely dull, but Catherine had an amazing capacity to focus on something that might become useful at any moment. I got up and moved around the room, swinging my arms and trying to keep loose. My face felt stiff, and when I checked a mirror I saw that my eye was not swollen anymore but was an ugly dark color. The spot where Bushy Bill had hit me was slightly red but not too bad. No wonder the women in Washaway weren't tearing their clothes off when I walked into the room.

There was squawking on the scanner when I came back. It barely sounded like human speech. "Do you understand any of that?"

"Fire at the motel is out," she said. "The whole thing is a loss. The neighborhood watch is supposed to find locals who can put the firefighters up for the night."

I wasn't sure why they weren't going home, but that didn't seem important. What was important was Steve's house; I didn't want to be there when he got home. I didn't like that clean, quiet, depressing little place.

"I want to get out of here," I said. "Do you want to stay and man the scanner?"

"No," she said quickly. "I'll come along."

That surprised me. "Are you sure?" I didn't say *This is a safe place* or *We might run into bad guys*. I didn't have to.

"They know about me, so there really isn't a safe place anymore. And I'm not the stay-at-home type."

She took the keys to the Neon and carried the scanner into the garage. While she fiddled with the wires under the dash, I went into the kitchen, boiled water, and poured it into a thermos. Then I added a tea bag and the last of Steve's sugar.

Back in the garage, I found Catherine sitting behind the wheel, the engine running and the scanner hissing. I opened the garage door and she pulled out. I closed the door and climbed inside.

The scanner sat on the floor mat beside my feet. I didn't dare move for fear of pulling out a wire. "I'm the one who rented this car, you know."

"Maybe, but I'm a better driver."

Fair enough. We drove back and forth through town, waiting for something to happen. At one point, a black Yukon passed us going the other way. The bidders had the same idea. After almost an hour, a thin fog billowed in, but nothing else came up. Finally, Catherine said what I'd been afraid to say. "Could it already be gone? Things wouldn't be this quiet if it was still in town, right?"

"Maybe," I said. "Except that the Breakleys were only discovered because we burned down their barn. Maybe it's holed up somewhere, feeding and biding its time."

"I don't know about that," she said. "The cage was surrounded by lights, remember? What if it only wanted a ride because it needed to avoid daylight? What if it set out cross-country once night fell?"

"Fuck." That hadn't occurred to me. The predator hadn't walked like a creature that could cover a lot of ground, but I wouldn't have guessed it could move through walls, either.

"Driving around is a waste of time," I said.

"I agree completely." Catherine did a U-turn in the middle of the street and headed back toward the shopping center on Littlemont.

The Grable was sealed off with more yellow caution tape. The arch was blackened on one side, and the building was a shell. I didn't like looking at it.

Catherine parked in front of the bar. "I'm going to socialize," she said. "You're designated driver, so you can have Pepsi. After I get inside, count to five hundred and come in. This works better if people think I'm alone."

She went inside. I sat and counted slowly. There was a Fleetwood parked a couple of dozen yards away. It took a moment for me to remember where I'd seen it before. I got out of the Neon.

I approached from an angle that would keep me out of the side and rearview mirrors, but I didn't need to bother. The driver was alone and asleep. It was Regina Wilbur.

She was wrapped in an expensive cashmere coat, and she'd managed to clean herself up. Her hair had been washed, at least. She had a duck hunter's shotgun in her lap.

The button for the door lock was up, so I yanked the door open and snatched the shotgun away from her as quickly as I could. She woke instantly. If I'd been any slower, I'd have been staring down the barrel. I was glad I hadn't underestimated her.

"Hello, Regina," I said. "It's kind of a chilly night to be sleeping in your car, isn't it?"

"Oh," she said. "It's you." If she had bothered to remember my name, she wasn't going to say it. "I know why you're in Washaway. If I get my hands on that shotgun again, I'll use it to part your miserable skull."

"You don't know as much about me as you think," I said.

That got a rise out of her, as I'd hoped it would. "That little German bastard told me everything I need to know. He says you want to kill Armand."

"And you believed him? You can't trust that guy. He murdered a member of your own staff in cold blood."

"Pfah!" She waved a liver-spotted hand at me. "Why should he lie to me? I'm just a helpless old woman!"

I almost laughed in her face. But that "little German bastard" wouldn't have been fooled by her any more than I was. "And I'll bet he offered to capture Armand for you."

"Not just for me," she said, sounding as if I'd insulted her intelligence. "He wants to bring in a team to study Armand, and he thinks the home I built for him would be the best place to do it."

"So he wants to share the sapphire dog with you? Like the poetry professor?"

"Yes!" she drew out the hiss at the end of that word with malicious joy. "He and I will share the same way I shared with the poetry professor, as soon as he catches Armand in one of those big, black Yukons of his."

I couldn't resist correcting her. "The Yukons with the red-and-white cards on the dash? Those aren't his. That's a different bidder entirely."

She smiled like a snake, and I realized I'd made a mistake. She started the engine and backed out of her parking slot. I had to jump out of the way of the open door. She gave me one last sneer before she pulled out, leaving me holding her shotgun.

Damn. I had underestimated her after all, but what should I do about it? I could have tried to call the new emergency chief of police, if I had his number, which I didn't. And if I followed her, I would be separating from Catherine again.

That hadn't worked well the last time, and I wasn't going to do it again. I tossed Regina's shotgun onto the roof of the teriyaki place. Maybe she had another gun, but I think she would have tried to shoot me if she had. And while she could certainly afford a new one, she'd have to wait until the stores opened. I had time. I hoped.

I decided that I'd waited at least a five-hundred count and went inside.

Catherine was sitting at the bar, chatting amiably with the bartender. She had a glass of white wine in front of her. Her body language was different from what I'd seen before—yet another personality. I wonder how she chose them, or if she went by instinct. I took note of where the bathroom was and picked a spot where I'd have to walk by her to get to it.

Two stools over from me was a guy of about

twenty-five. He was slumped over a beer, reading the label as if it might make him happy.

In the corner was an older couple sipping from tall drinks with a careful, trembling elegance. They both looked shriveled and wasted on the top half of their bodies and thick with flab on the bottom half. They seemed like people who had once had much better uses for their time but would have been offended at the label "barfly."

A pair of young guys shot pool in the corner. They didn't talk, but I couldn't tell if that was because they didn't like each other or they were just intent on their game.

The last person in the bar was Pratt. There was an empty bowl and crumpled napkin in front of him—he'd come here for his dinner. I wondered if, like us, he was here to find information or if he was slacking off from his job. Which wasn't fair, but to hell with him. I didn't like him.

The bartender tore himself away from Catherine long enough to take my order. He was a middle-aged guy with a slouching belly and no ring on his left hand. His face had started to go pouchy, but his hair was thick and combed straight back as though he was proud of it. I asked for a root beer and a menu. He dropped them off and wandered back to Catherine.

I could overhear a little of their conversation: she was complimenting the town in ways that prompted the bartender to brag a little. He described the Christmas festival that would happen tomorrow, explained the history of it, and flirted with her shamelessly. She didn't encourage him, but she didn't back away, either.

Depressed Guy tapped his empty bottle on the bar and the bartender brought him a new one. He took my order, too. I went for the grilled cheese, figuring it was cheap and too easy for him to screw up.

Catherine went back to doing her thing. I couldn't hear everything she was saying, but it sounded like small talk. Whatever information she was getting was coming at a leisurely pace, and she didn't seem interested in speeding up the process. My grilled cheese arrived; I'd never had a better sandwich in my life.

Depressed Guy muttered something to himself. I glanced over at him. He said: "Ever love someone or something so much you can't live without them?"

I remembered the way the sapphire dog had made me feel. Depressed Guy suddenly had my full attention. "Yeah, man. I think I have."

Encouraged, he turned toward me. His eyes looked a little bleary and he had trouble focusing, but he could talk without slurring. "It hits so hard at first. It's like . . . all the love in your life is *ripped* away from you all of a sudden. All you have left is this, like, little tattered shred of something in your hand, because you tried to hold on too tight. Ya know whutamean? You think I tried to hold on too tight?"

Catherine did this for a living, I thought. She drew people out, listened to their stories, and found the information she needed. Not me. Everything I'd ever learned about investigations had come from being on the other side. I couldn't play this game her way; I had to do it mine.

"I don't know, man. Who did you lose?"

"My wife." I immediately lost interest. Still, he kept talking. I glanced away and saw that one of the pool players had joined Catherine's conversation. Whatever they were talking about, she seemed interested. Was she a good actress, or did she enjoy this? "She dumped me over the phone. Can you believe that? After ten and a half months of marriage."

I glanced around the room. Pratt was looking straight at me. I looked back, and he didn't look away. In some places, that would have been an invitation to brawl, but I haven't had much luck with bar fights.

Depressed Guy wasn't finished. "Almost eleven months! I thought we were in love."

"That's rough," I said.

He went back to his beer. "I'm keeping the damn fish tank, you can believe that."

I imagined a tank full of dead fish, and it suddenly occurred to me that Pratt might have completed his job already. Maybe this was his victory meal, as pathetic as that sounded.

I slid off my stool and crossed to his booth. He was dipping his spoon into a bowl of grayish chowder when I sat across from him. Before he could tell me to get lost, I said, "Well?"

"Well, what?"

I met his stare. Apparently, he wanted me to talk out loud in front of all these people. "Well, have you taken care of that dog?"

"I don't report to you." Which was true, but he struck me as the boasting type, so I figured the job wasn't done.

"Fair enough. How about another supplemental report?"

"You don't file reports," he said. "I get those from the smoke."

For a moment I thought he was talking about smoke signals, or visions in magic smoke or something. Then I realized—duh—he meant Catherine. "You're a real charmer."

He stirred his soup. "Get out of here," he said without looking at me, "before I break both of your legs."

So much for warning him about Yin's ghost knife. I glanced back at Catherine. She was looking at me, and her expression was difficult to read. I stood and went to the men's room, washed my hands in the dirty sink, and walked toward my original spot. As I passed Catherine's stool, the bartender said, "Hey, man. Are you Clay Lilly?"

I stopped. "My name's Ray Lilly."

"Well, I'll be," Catherine said, her voice lilting. "I knew that was you. How is your mother?" She slid off her stool. "Excuse me, Rich," she said to the bartender.

I heard the bartender curse under his breath, but it was too late. Tonight's entertainment had walked off with another guy. I led her to the table and picked up my soda. "Did—"

She interrupted me right away. "Is your mother still working at that law firm?" We had a conversation about a woman I hadn't seen for years. While we were talking, Pratt laid a couple of bills on the table and walked out.

Eventually, I said I had my mother's phone number out in the car, and Catherine smiled as though I was learning the game. I paid for my food, and while we were waiting for the slip to sign, Depressed Guy looked blearily over at us.

Catherine couldn't resist. "How are you, honey?" Her tone was maternal.

"Alone," he said. "My wife just left me."

"I'm sorry to hear that. What happened?" If she was pretending to be interested, she was damn good at it.

"Thass the thing. I don't even know! This afternoon everything was great between us. An hour later, she called me and said that she didn't love me anymore. She said she'd found someone else. Someone with stars in his eyes."

Catherine looked at me. I looked at her. I fought down the urge to grab the guy and shake him until he told me more.

"That's terrible," Catherine said. Her voice was shaky and she'd lost her grip on the kind, maternal, cry-on-my-shoulder character she was playing. "Where did she call from?"

It was a crazy transition, but Depressed Guy was drunk enough to take it in stride. "She rides out at the stables three nights a week." He took a pull off his beer. "He's prolly a cowboy or something."

The credit card slip came. I signed it. Catherine and I walked calmly and slowly toward the door.

Once through it, we ran to the car. We had our lead.

CHAPTER ELEVEN

I scanned the parking lot. Pratt was already gone, dammit. "Do you know where the stable is?" I asked.

"I know how to find it." She took out a cellphone, dialed 411, and got the address from the operator. "There's only one in the area," she said. "Shit. I wish they hadn't stolen my cell."

"What's that in your hand?"

"The bartender's. He loaned it to me, without realizing he was loaning it to me. But I can't use it to file a supplemental report. The number would turn up on his phone bill."

I was feeling keyed up. "I'm sorry," I said. "The answer we needed was sitting right next to me, and I didn't realize it."

"Don't worry about it. That's my job, not yours. Not that I found out a damn thing. All those boys wanted to talk about was the festival tomorrow. They're worried that it may be canceled after 'what happened today.' I wasn't sure how much they really knew, but they were being careful."

I wondered what the festival would be like. If we destroyed the predator tonight—and did it quickly and cleanly—the town could have Christmas in peace: no more killings, no more people going crazy, no more burning buildings. Maybe there would be something nice I could pick up for Aunt Theresa and Uncle Karl. And maybe I could find a gift for Catherine, if—

"God, I hope we can finish this tonight," she said. "I want to spend Christmas with my family. Was that man in the tan coat who I think?"

"That's Pratt. He didn't want to talk to you at all."

She seemed to understand right away. "They're like that. A lot of them. They live a couple of hundred years, and everything they knew about the world gets turned on its head. They see a black woman alone at a bar, talking to men she doesn't know, and they immediately think *prostitute*. They're old-fashioned, squared. Some of them even talk about the good old days before the Terror."

I didn't know what "the Terror" was, but I got the point. "Do you know anything about him?"

"One of the other investigators said Pratt likes killing people, which doesn't exactly set him apart from the crowd. He should have talked to me. Now I can't even get a new report to him." She sighed. "So, we're going to check out the stables, right?"

"Oh, yeah."

She started the car and we rode through the dark town. I wondered how late the stables would be open, and if we'd have to break in.

We headed toward the fairgrounds but reached the turnoff well before the festival banner appeared. There was a split-rail fence, a gate, and a sign that said CONNER STABLES. The gate was bolted and padlocked. I cut the padlock, opened the gate, let Catherine drive through, and closed it again.

She drove down the long path with the headlights off. Our plan was simple: Sneak in as close as we could without being spotted, just like the Wilbur estate. Locate the sapphire dog. Use the ghost knife on it, preferably from ambush.

Catherine wondered if we could use bright light to trap or stun it, but I didn't trust that idea. Sunlight hadn't bothered it at all, as far as I could tell. I suggested that its cage might have had special bulbs in it, and we agreed that we should have stolen a couple when we had the chance.

"Are you sure you want to come with me for this?" I asked. She gave me a look.

There were no turnoffs from the main drive where we could stash the car, so Catherine pulled all the way into the stable's parking lot and backed into a spot. There were three other cars already there.

I was getting a lot of practice closing car doors quietly. We walked toward the gate as if we belonged there. I was keyed up and jittery, and Catherine seemed to feel the same.

The muddy lot was ringed with trees and heavy scrub. Ahead was a wooden rail that looked just like the one at the edge of the property. It could have been part of a set in a cowboy movie except that the gate attached to it was made of welded aluminum pipes and locked with another Yale padlock.

There were two fenced-in areas for the horses to ride in; one was a muddy circle about twenty-five feet wide with a tall fence made of more welded aluminum. A second, larger area was bordered with low wooden rails to make an oval about seventy-five feet long. Cedar chips had been spread over the ground, and obstacles—long window planters without plants and uprights with cross-bars that formed an X—had been left out. There was a Porta Potti and an overturned wheelbarrow to the left, but they couldn't have been the only source of the odor that made us wrinkle our noses. This place must have been stink heaven on hot summer afternoons.

Farther left there was a cluster of big, windowless wooden buildings decorated with pennants. I guessed those must be the stables.

I hopped the fence. Catherine climbed over it more

slowly, but that was what I wanted. I had the tattoos and should be in the lead. I made my way toward the nearest stable. No one shouted a challenge at us. No waving flashlights came out of the darkness, no little squares of window light appeared in the distance. No one knew we were there.

There was a low, echoing rumble of thunder from somewhere nearby. It seemed to rebound against the mountains around us, coming from every direction and muffled by all the trees and brush nearby. Rain was coming.

I walked along the building. A lamp was shining on the other side of the stables, and we made our way by indirect light. The wind hissed through the branches, but aside from our footsteps, there was no other sound.

At the corner of the building I peeked out. There were three more buildings, all four set two by two facing an open area about thirty feet wide. A single light glowed above the open door across the way. I peered into the darkness, searching for a human silhouette. I didn't see anything.

I stepped out of hiding. All four of the stable doors were open. Was that normal on a chilly winter night? I had no idea.

Catherine followed me into the yard as the mist thickened into a light drizzle. The stable beside us was dark and quiet. Then we heard steps from the stable across the yard. A horse slowly stepped out of the darkness.

I grabbed Catherine's arm. "It has a white mark on its face."

"Lots of horses have that."

This mark was completely off center, starting on the left side of its nose and passing under its left eye. "But can they be all crooked like that?"

"Maybe it's a paint," she said, which I didn't understand.

It stared at us. God, it was big. I heard Catherine back away. I was about to ask if we should just walk by it when she said: "Is it bleeding?"

I looked again; its ear was ragged and its mouth was bloody. It also had open wounds on its shoulder.

It lowered its head.

Catherine's voice was a low whisper in my ear. "Is that mud on its hoof?"

The horse stamped its foot. *Something* coated the hoof, but it looked too red to be mud. I raised my hands to clap. "Horses run from danger, right?"

Then it charged at us.

Catherine cursed and fled into the open stable behind us. I backpedaled after her, keeping the protected part of my chest toward the horse.

Christ, it was fast. Catherine yelped in pain and fear, but I couldn't turn to see why because the animal was already next to me.

It tried to bite me but missed. Even its mouth seemed huge. I ducked to the side, raising my arms to protect my face. My heel struck something and I nearly fell; in that same moment, the horse reared and kicked.

It caught me full in the chest. Already off balance, I tumbled back, feet flying over my head. I landed on my shoulder in the corner, my legs hitting the wall above me. The shin I'd bashed against the water trough flared with pain again. I fell with dirty straw in my face and long-handled wooden tools clattering around me.

I was exposed. A kick would cave in my skull, and—

Catherine screamed.

I rolled to my knees, shrugging off whatever had fallen on me. The stench of horse shit filled my nose, but I'd worry about that later. My hand fell on a thick wooden handle, and I grabbed at it like a lifeline.

The horse snorted and stamped. I jumped to my feet and raised my hands. I was holding a push broom.

That wasn't going to do me any good. Catherine cried out again, a sound more of fright than pain. I threw the broom underhand, hard, like I was throwing a shovel into the back of a truck. It struck the horse's hind legs, startling it. The horse jumped and kicked a little, turning its huge body toward me.

I reached back down into the straw, unwilling to look away from the animal. My hand fell on something thin and metal, and I dragged it out of the straw. It was a pitchfork.

The horse moved toward me. I backed toward the corner. There was a narrow pen in front of me to the right, and a second at my right elbow. Close on my left was the wall, and there was no back door. I was trapped.

I held the pitchfork high so the light would fall on it. Could the horse see what I was holding? I could. Would it understand and back away?

Apparently not, because it kept coming toward me, stamping its feet and snorting angrily. I yelled "Yah!" at it, just like a movie cowboy. It didn't have any effect. I pretended to jab at it, shouting "Hah!" each time.

I really, truly did not want to stab this animal. The thought of this dirty metal entering its flesh made me nauseous.

But it wouldn't back away. It was coming more slowly, more cautiously, but it wouldn't stop coming and I was running out of space. Soon it would have me pinned against the wall, the pitchfork would be useless, and it could kick my skull in.

"Yah!" I shouted again, half hoping that, even if the horse wouldn't back off, someone who worked here would suddenly show up and take control of the animal. There wasn't time for that, though. The horse reared back and kicked with its right hoof. I tried to pull the sharp tines away, but it struck the side of the fork and I nearly dropped it.

My nausea knotted into naked fear. To hell with this. I wasn't going to be killed just because I wasn't willing to defend myself. I jabbed with the pitchfork, just barely striking the horse's shoulder as I yelled "Back!" It wasn't enough to do real damage, I hoped, but it would break the skin and sting a little. Whether the horse could see well in the dark or not, it knew what I was holding now.

It suddenly made a high, hair-raising shriek and lunged at me, kicking with both front hooves. I jumped back and felt the pitchfork wrench upward, shivering, as a hoof nearly knocked it out of my hands. God, the *sound* the horse was making . . .

I tossed the pitchfork high, making the animal flinch and step back. I lunged to the right, into the pen. Running away from a horse was a lunatic idea, but if I stood my ground, I was going to have to kill it.

The horse followed—I could hear and feel it just behind me. I leaped up, grabbing the top of the wall between the enclosures. Adrenaline gave me the strength and speed I needed to practically throw myself into the next pen. I felt something snag my pants cuff—was the horse trying to bite me again?—but my momentum pulled it free.

The room suddenly darkened—not completely, but something big moved to block the light from across the yard.

I got my feet under me just in time, then jumped for the wall of this second pen. I didn't have the same quickness that comes from having a huge, hostile animal at my back, but I still had plenty of fear.

And I could hear the horse backing out. It didn't have room to turn around quickly, but I still didn't have a lot of time.

I dropped down on the other side of the wall, my weight pitching forward and my hands landing on something huge, soft, and cool right in front of me. It was another horse, this one dead and lying almost against the wall.

One of the front doors had been closed, and the other was scraping shut, cutting off my light and means of escape. I stumbled over the dead horse, half running, half falling toward the exit. I didn't look back. If those hooves were coming toward me, I didn't want to see it. I slipped through the doorway and sprawled in the mud just as Catherine slammed it shut.

The doors banged and jolted as the horse tried to kick them open. Catherine was knocked several inches away from them, then threw her shoulder against them again.

"Get something!" she yelled at me, and I jumped to my feet.

There was no way I could see to lock both doors—no bolt, no bar, no padlock. There was only a wooden catch, which I closed, but it was worn and fragile. It might not have held up in a strong windstorm, let alone a couple more kicks.

I turned, scanning the yard. What I needed was a truck or tractor I could drive up to the doors and block them with, but there wasn't one nearby, and I couldn't have gotten any of the cars in the lot through the fence.

Instead, I ran to the aluminum pen and cut off two lengths of pipe. As I ran back to Catherine, I shaved one end of each into a point, then staked them into the ground at the base of the doors.

Catherine stepped back carefully, ready to throw her body against the doors again if the stakes didn't hold. I stood next to her with the same thought.

The stakes held, but the doors still wobbled with every kick. And damn, it was loud.

"That's not secure enough," Catherine said, and I agreed.

I cut and shaved two more stakes from the aluminum fence. I had a twinge of guilt at destroying someone else's property, but I figured it was minor compared with what had happened to their two horses. I tossed them both to Catherine.

The doorway across the yard was built the same way, with two doors on two hinges each. With my ghost knife, I cut through the hinges on one of them and let it fall across my shoulders. I carried it across the mud, dropped it on its side, and tipped it against the staked door. Catherine drove the two stakes into the mud at its base, bracing it in place.

The *thump* of the doors slamming together must have startled the horse inside, because the steady *bang bang bang* of its kicks halted. We stepped back and surveyed our work again. Catherine turned to me. "Better," she said. She lifted her forearm and tenderly laid her hand against it. Was she injured?

"I'm sorry," I said. "I had a pitchfork in my hand, and maybe I could have stopped that horse without—"

"Ray, forget that shit. If you think I wanted you to kill that animal, you haven't been paying attention."

"No, I know that," I said. "We would have been safer, though, if I'd been willing to go all out. If I hadn't held back."

"I'd rather be good than safe."

With that, the conversation was over.

I crossed the yard and went into the stable the horse had come from. There was a trough filled with hay and two more dead animals. Both had their skulls crushed.

"A horse wouldn't . . ." Catherine's voice sounded tiny.

"Both of these have white marks, too."

So, the sapphire dog fed on animals as well as people. Hopefully, no one kept any lions around.

We searched the other stables. We found three more dead horses and a dead woman. She was dressed in dirty coveralls, but she'd applied her makeup with extraordinary care. She'd even plucked her eyebrows and drawn them back on. Her neck was crooked—broken by a horse's kick, maybe. And she had a white streak over her left ear.

Catherine searched her and produced a driver's license. She was Lois Conner, just like the name above the entrance. She was forty-nine, and like me, she carried a single credit card. I stood watch in the doorway while Catherine finished. I didn't have the stomach for another corpse. Instead, I stared at the braced stable door, watching it shudder under the trapped animal's kicks. They were slowing and growing weaker as it tired.

"She's been dead for hours," Catherine said. Apparently, there was nothing else about her that mattered to us.

Beyond the last stable was a bungalow with an OFFICE sign over the door. Behind that was a house that looked like an uneven stack of wooden boxes. The office was locked up and dark. A single light shone in the house.

We searched the office first, just in case. I held my ghost knife ready, but we didn't find anything.

The front door to the house was standing open. I entered first. We walked through the living room into a quiet little den with a sunken floor. The rooms were nicely furnished but filled with clutter: stacks of papers, pretty seashells, two dozen books all lying open and facedown on counters and coffee tables. Everything looked like it had been set in a random but convenient place and then forgotten.

Catherine got ahead of me and peeked into the hall. A light shone from a room at the far end, illuminating a body lying curled in the corner of the corridor floor. I caught her elbow and pulled her back. I was the one who was a little bit bulletproof. For once, she didn't cringe at my touch.

I turned the body over. He had long, graying hair like a hippie cowboy. He'd been shot in the chest and had fallen with his face to the wall and died. If he had a white mark, I couldn't see it.

"It isn't a very efficient predator, is it?" Catherine asked.

Pratt had said something similar. "What do you mean?"

"Well, its prey drives off or kills other prey. It's one thing if a cougar catches a sheep and the bleating frightens the rest of the herd, but in this case the sheep sticks around after it's been eaten, driving away other potential meals. I don't know why this thing hasn't gone extinct yet."

I remembered my idea that the sapphire dog might become Pet Emperor. "Maybe it's starving. It's been trapped for a couple of decades. Maybe it's feeding hard."

"Sure. Maybe."

We stood. I led the way around the corner into the lighted room. It was the kitchen. A huge refrigerator was lying on its side, and a little old gray-haired lady was trapped beneath it.

But I didn't notice that at first, because the little old lady was holding a big damn revolver, and I was looking right down the barrel. She had one eye squinted shut as she squeezed the trigger.

Click. It was empty. I stood in the doorway like a paper target at a pistol range. She let the end of the barrel fall onto the dirty tile floor.

"Damn," she said. "Wasted too many shots."

Catherine tried to step around me, but I held her back. I wasn't convinced it was safe yet. "What did you waste them on?" I asked, hoping she would say "A blue dog."

"Them," she said, and coughed blood onto her chin.

There were two more dead bodies by the stove: both young, tall, and slim, with long dark hair and short, upturned noses. Each woman had been shot multiple times. They looked enough alike to be sisters. Was one of them Depressed Guy's wife? I honestly didn't want to know.

The old woman reached for a box of ammunition on the floor beneath a kitchen chair, but it was out of reach.

"Would you hand that to me, sonny?"

I stepped into the room, allowing Catherine to follow. "I don't think so," I said quietly.

"Well, fuck you then. Get out of my house! You can't have him."

Catherine walked around the old woman, taking in the scene without expression. I wished there was a mirror nearby so I could see if I had the same composure. I didn't think I did.

The old woman looked very slender and frail, and her face was terribly pale. She had a streak across her forehead.

I felt very tired. "We should call an ambulance," I said.

"Don't you touch anything, you . . . *burglars*. Not even the phone. I forbid it."

"We will," Catherine said to me, ignoring the woman on the floor. "After we check the rest of the house."

I nodded. There was a set of stairs going up. I led the way, stepping over the two young bodies to get to them.

I wondered how long it would take to get used to seeing corpses. Maybe it was callous of me, but I wanted it to be soon. I wanted to stop feeling sickened by the blood and the slack, empty faces. I wanted to not care about the smell. I wanted . . .

I wanted all sorts of things I wasn't going to get. I took a deep breath and forced myself to focus on the job. The next old woman might not be holding an empty gun.

The upstairs had the same clutter, but there was no sapphire dog. I stopped in the bathroom to look in the mirror. I couldn't see any horse shit on me, which seemed like a minor miracle. Then we checked the back bedroom.

The walls were covered with posters of horses, and there were toy horses everywhere. Some people couldn't get enough, I guessed. Then I heard something scrape against the carpet. It was a tiny sound, but it made the hairs on the back of my neck stand up. I stepped in front of Catherine and held my ghost knife ready.

"Come out!" My voice was harsh and low. I knew it wasn't the sapphire dog—it had always fled, never hidden. "Come out right now!"

I heard a tiny, frightened gasp, then a little voice said: "I'm sorry!" The voice was choked with tears. "I'm sorry for hiding!" Behind me, Catherine gasped.

A girl slowly crawled from under the far side of the bed. She was about ten, thin as a rail, and she tried to make herself as small as possible. She also wouldn't look at us, letting her hair cover her tear-streaked face. I couldn't tell if she had a white mark.

"Are you alone?" I asked, but Catherine pushed by me before the kid could answer.

"Oh, honey," she said, "what happened here?" Catherine went around the bed and took hold of the girl's hands.

"My granma tried to kill me," she said. I expected more sobs, but her voice seemed to hollow out and become steady. "That *thing* licked her and she went crazy."

"You saw it?" I asked.

"Yeah, it walked right by me. I saw what it did to my mom and gran. Then they turned against me." The girl's voice cracked. "They hated me. I don't know what I did, but they hated me so much. . . ."

"Oh, honey," Catherine said, and gathered the girl into her arms. "You didn't do a single little thing to deserve this. Not a single little thing."

The girl began to cry. Catherine held her close. I stood in the doorway, weapon in hand, feeling useless.

"We have to take her away from here," Catherine said.

"No!" the girl shouted. She broke Catherine's embrace and retreated to the corner. "My granma is still out there, and so is that *thing*. It's out there doing that to other

people, and I don't want to leave here I won't go I won't
do it—"

Catherine pressed her fists against her chest. "It's okay,
honey. It's okay. You don't have to do anything scary."

"We can't bring her anyway," I said. "We're hunting."
I was surprised by the sound of my own voice; it sounded
flat and miserable. *I don't rescue people. I kill predators.*

The girl was willing to tell us her name, Shannon, but
she absolutely refused to leave her room. Catherine
promised to call emergency services for her. Shannon
slid back under the bed, and we went into the hall.

"Oh my God, Ray," Catherine whispered. "That little
girl . . . I wasn't ready for what happened to those horses,
but that girl breaks my heart."

"The sapphire dog didn't feed on her," I said, trying to
think about something, anything else, "but it did feed on
Little Mark. What do you think is the age break where
people become food? Puberty?"

"For Christ's sake, Ray." Her voice was harsh but still
low. "Didn't you notice—"

I hissed at her to cut her off. It didn't matter that she
was right. At that moment, I couldn't bear to be told
that I wasn't feeling enough.

My misery and adrenaline turned to anger. "I may not
be *trained for this*, but I'm trying to focus on the job.
Maybe you . . ." I almost said: *should take care of your
own people and let these people take care of themselves,*
but it would have been too much. I wasn't going to turn
something she'd told me in confidence into a weapon. I
turned away.

"It's okay," she said. "I shouldn't have said that."
Then she patted my hand briefly.

We went down the stairs into the basement. I led the
way again, stepping around stacks of newspapers and
old board games, trays full of glass candleholders, and
other crap.

I switched on the light. The Conners kept their basement relatively clear, compared with the rest of the house. There was a leather saddle up on a stand and leather-working tools laid out on a workbench.

I remembered the rumble of thunder I'd heard outside. I hadn't heard a second one. The thunderclouds might have passed, or maybe I'd heard a rock slide and didn't recognize the sound. Still, something felt off about it.

My iron gate twinged. I knew that feeling, and I could feel where it was coming from. I turned toward the basement window behind me.

The sapphire dog was there, peering through the window at us from outside the house. It was lying on its stomach, its bright eyes almost pressing against the glass. Its star-shaped pupils seemed to be glowing.

CHAPTER TWELVE

Behind me, I heard Catherine say: "My God, it's beautiful."

I could feel those waves of emotion hitting me, but I was ready this time. Palming my ghost knife, I lifted my hands toward my face. Once my arm was curled, I would throw it as hard as I could right between that thing's eyes. If that didn't kill it, I'd fetch that revolver and box of ammo from the kitchen.

From behind me on the left, I heard the distinctive sound of a round being chambered.

I ducked down and to the right just as a gunshot boomed beside my head. I dropped to one knee, spun, and swept my ghost knife upward.

I missed the gun in Catherine's hand but hit her wrist. She gasped and her hand opened. The weapon clattered to the floor. I lunged for the pistol but I didn't need to rush. She didn't do anything but clutch her wrist and say: "I'm sorry." I could barely hear her above the ringing in my left ear.

It was a small stainless steel Smith & Wesson with a plastic handle. Where had she gotten it? I looked back at the window. The sapphire dog was staring at me.

I'd already thrown my ghost knife at it once, when it was much closer to me, and it had vanished. Now that I'd lost the chance to surprise it, I tried something else. I lifted the S&W and emptied the clip into it.

I saw the bullet holes in the glass, so I knew some of

my shots had hit their mark. The sapphire dog didn't re-act at all. It didn't recoil or flinch, and no bullet holes appeared on it. It was like shooting a hallucination.

The old woman in the kitchen above thumped her gun against the floor. I glanced up, then back at the window. The predator was gone.

Catherine stared at me sheepishly. She apologized again. The ghost knife had worked on her, even though she'd been under the sapphire dog's influence.

"Where did you get this?" I asked, holding up the gun. I tried not to shout.

She handed me a spare magazine. "I took it off Lois Conner," she said, and in that adrenaline-fueled mo-ment I had no idea who she was talking about. It didn't matter. The sapphire dog was gone, and I had to go after it.

"Go to the car," I said. She was already nodding obe-diently. "Drive to the fairgrounds and wait for me. Stay away from people, okay? If you can't avoid someone, don't do what they ask you to do. Just do what I told you."

"I will," she said. Her eyes were wide and blank. "What if I see the sapphire dog?"

"You can try to run it down with the car, if you think you can hit it." I ran for the steps, then stopped. She was still staring at me with a passive, helpless expression. "On second thought, don't try to run it down. Don't do anything. Just hide. Hurry."

I ran upstairs. In the drawer by the back door, I found a flashlight. I took the phone off the hook and dialed 911. I felt a stabbing headache so strong that I could barely understand the operator who answered. Could it have been a delayed reaction to the gunshot? I said what I needed to say and hung up. My headache eased up al-most immediately, and I put it out of my mind.

I ran outside. When I reached the bullet-ridden window

my ghost knife was in my hand, but I didn't have a target. The sapphire dog was gone.

The soup-can footprints were right where I expected, running along the edge of the house into the woods. I followed the trail.

Catherine came out of the house and lightly jogged toward the car. I guess that was the best version of *hurry* I could expect after the ghost knife had done its work on her.

She didn't have a white mark, like Penny, but neither had Ursula. So why had my spell worked on Catherine but not Ursula? Maybe the predator had used its influence on her many times over the years. Maybe, after all that time, she had lost her ability to feel anything else, just like the people with the mark.

But this wasn't the time to speculate. The footprints led to a horse trail. I peered into the woods, trying to see if the sapphire dog was hiding in the shadows, but I couldn't see anything. Was it behind a bush or tree, waiting to feed on me when I got close? The thought of that bone-white tongue touching my face made me shiver. Maybe my iron gate would protect me, but I didn't want to bet my life on it.

I turned on the flashlight. Lois Conner's reloaded gun was in my pocket, and my ghost knife was in my right hand. The tracks led straight down the center of the trail—almost as if it was avoiding the greenery. I started after it.

Of course, it wasn't native to this planet. Maybe it was *afraid* of the underbrush and the more mundane predators that it might run into there.

Which made me immediately think of Catherine. I couldn't help but wonder who she might run into. What if she met the bartender again, and he invited her back to his place? Had the ghost knife taken away her ability to say no?

Damn. Maybe I should have asked her to come with me, but after I saw the look on her face, I didn't want her anywhere near the sapphire dog. Catherine was smart and tough when she was herself, but the ghost knife turned people into victims.

The wind rustled the tree branches. I froze in place. Could the sapphire dog climb trees? It didn't have hands or claws, but underestimating it could get me killed.

I had to put Catherine out of my mind for now. If I'd made a mistake in sending her out on her own, it was too late to fix it. I had to focus on the job at hand.

Where the hell was Pratt, anyway?

The flashlight beam could reach about ten feet—a respectable distance but not enough to show me the tops of the trees. I crouched beside a tree trunk and played the light along the path. The weird round footprints continued for as far as the beam could shine.

Of course, I'd seen the sapphire dog's tracks lead in multiple directions—it might have left this trail for me to follow while crouching in the shadows to ambush me. I kept moving forward, putting all my thought, all my attention, into my sight and hearing. I examined every shadow, every rustle. My shoes had soaked through from the mud, and I spared a single, stupid moment envying the Fellows and their hiking boots.

Then I pushed that thought away. I crept forward, thinking about the sapphire dog, its glowing eyes, and its long, floppy ears. I didn't know how fast it could move or how far it could travel without rest. I just kept going, determined to destroy it or be destroyed.

It didn't ambush me, but I didn't catch up to it, either. It was fleeing and I was being careful. I was never going to catch up to it this way. I increased my pace, my feet squishing loudly in the mud.

At the top of a rise, the trees and underbrush suddenly thinned. After fifteen feet of gentle slope, the ground flattened into the fairgrounds. Farther out there was a ring of halogen lights on poles set in a circle, and all the lamps were on. The locals were setting up the fair, although my view of them was obscured by the white-washed buildings and a set of bleachers.

To my left was the high-peaked church. The back door was open, letting yellowish light into the yard. From this angle, I could see a little house behind it.

To the right were more woods, open fields, and darkness.

I shone the flashlight down into the mud. The sapphire dog's trail split into three directions, just like on the Wilbur estate. On the left, the trail led across a muddy patch and then into the high grass beside the church. In front of me it led down the slope, and to the right it went through the bushes.

Crap. I ignored the footprints that led to the right into the underbrush—if the predator had avoided that sort of cover for this long, I doubted it would take it up now.

On impulse, I started down the slope toward the fairgrounds. The footprints were more difficult to find among the tree roots and hard soil of the hill, but they were there. They led straight out into the grass.

Maybe if I'd grown up a hunter, with weekend trips into the woods with deer rifles and orange earflap caps, I could have followed the predator's tracks across the newly mown lawn. But I'd grown up on baseball and video games. I couldn't find the trail or even tell if it ended suddenly like the ones on the Wilbur estate.

I didn't like the way this looked. So far, the sapphire dog had been drawn to people and buildings. It had fled from its captors, sure, but it had gone from one house to another, feeding and controlling the residents.

The only people on the fairgrounds were the ones out in the lights setting up. If the sapphire dog was going to go for them, it would have had to angle more to the left, not straight ahead into the dark open space of the lawn.

I scrambled back up the hill. The left-hand tracks pointed directly toward the church and the open, lighted door. I followed them.

After about fifteen feet, the tracks disappeared. As expected. The grass was unmowed and dripping wet. By the time I was halfway there, my pants were soaked from the knee down.

A pickup truck backed up to the open door, and a short, wiry man began unloading boxes from the bed and carrying them inside. I switched off my flashlight and I walked toward the open door, the ghost knife in my hand and the gun in my pocket. On the near side of the church was a neatly mown lawn. On the far side was a cracked asphalt parking lot.

The night must have been darker than I thought; the man unloading the truck didn't notice me until I was close enough to tap the edge of the truck. I startled him. He was wearing a clerical collar and had the quick, limber movements of a karate teacher.

He looked me up and down. I could see by the light shining from the inside of the church that his expression was carefully neutral. "If you're looking for money," he said, "we don't have any. We're a rural church. If you're hungry, though, you've come to the right place."

I looked into the bed of the truck. It was half full of grocery bags of canned food and boxes of premade stuffing. I glanced down at my clothes. I was still wearing the shirt Yin's men had torn, and I supposed my eye was still ugly.

"I'm not looking for food or money," I said. "I'm looking for a dog." Maybe it would have been better to say it was my dog, but the words wouldn't come out of my mouth. "It has fur that's been dyed blue, and it's sick. Contagious, actually."

"Contagious?" I had his attention. "I haven't seen any dogs running loose, and I've been driving around picking up donations. I can make a couple of calls, though. Help me carry some of this inside, and we'll see what we can do."

He grabbed two grocery bags in each hand and turned his back on me, confident I'd follow. I looked around but didn't see the predator. I picked up a crate filled with boxes of muffin mix and went inside.

It was a wide, shallow room filled with cheap metal shelving. Almost half the shelf space was filled with food donations. There was a second door nestled between the shelves. A dead bolt held it shut. A chipped wooden desk stood in the corner. A cheap portable stereo on the edge of the desk played seventies disco.

Had the sapphire dog come in here? The room was lit well enough that I could see the pastor didn't have a white mark, and there were no discolored circles on the walls.

The pastor reached up and scratched the ear of a pudgy, long-haired cat. "Those muffin mixes go there." He indicated a high shelf.

I set the crate there. "If you see that blue dog, don't go near it. In fact, stay far away. I'd be grateful if you would spread the word."

I started toward the door. One circuit of the church should tell me if the sapphire dog had gotten in through the walls; then I'd check the house. If I didn't find anything, I wasn't sure where I'd go next.

He took out his cell. "Let me make a couple of calls."

I nodded. "Be right back."

Outside, I played the flashlight across the lawn but didn't see anything interesting. I walked around the truck, then the church. There were no openings the predator could have used and no dark circles that indicated it had gone through the wall.

I was on my way to the house when the pastor came out of the church. "Are you Ray?"

"I am," I said, still walking.

"I'm Aaron," he said. It seemed weird to think of him by his first name instead of Reverend Surname, but what did I know? Maybe he'd invite me in to play Guitar Hero. "I spoke with the manager down at the fairgrounds. No one down there has seen your dog, but they'll keep an eye out. Also, Steve Cardinal asked you to wait here for him. He'll be over as soon as he can."

I nodded, but I wasn't about to wait, not if the sapphire dog was as close as I thought. I wished he hadn't said the dog was mine, though.

I walked around the porch, shining the light on the base of the walls. It wasn't until we reached the far back corner of the house that I saw it: a dark circle on the brick beneath a kitchen window.

"Crap."

"What is it?" Aaron knelt beside the mark.

"Don't touch it," I warned him as he reached out. "I need you to get away from here."

"Is it in my house? I have . . . I have family inside. Loved ones." He looked jumpy.

"Leave them to me," I said.

"You said your dog was contagious. Will they have to be quarantined? Does your dog bite?" His voice was going high with stress.

"Aaron, go to your truck and stay there."

He turned and ran back along the house, then vaulted over the porch rail with the ease of a gymnast. I shouted his name, but he was already at the door. I ran after him, but I heard the door close and lock before I could even reach the porch.

I climbed up over the rail after him, but much more slowly. Maybe I should take up parkour, if I survived.

I dropped the flashlight into my pocket and took out the gun. I slid the ghost knife between the door and jamb, then hesitated. The pastor and his family didn't know me; I didn't want to charge into his home with a gun in my hand. I put it back into my pocket and hoped I wouldn't get killed because of it.

I cut through the locks and pulled the door open. The house lights were on but the place was completely quiet.

"Hello!" I shouted. There was no answer. Had Aaron found the sapphire dog already? Maybe not. Maybe he was in his room hiding his porn.

I crept into the living room. The couch was covered with stacks of newspapers and old travel magazines. There was an uncluttered easy chair by the fireplace and an empty office chair beside the desk. The biggest piece of furniture in the room was another four-foot-high cat playground. The room smelled like damp carpet and cat litter. What family did the pastor have in here?

The kitchen was cleaner but didn't smell any better. The trash overflowed with pizza boxes and teriyaki take-out cartons. There were three kitty-litter trays in the corner.

The sapphire dog wasn't in there, either. The back door was locked and the basement door had a discolored circle at the bottom.

I twisted the knob and jiggled the door. The discolored circle collapsed into a billowing cloud of dust. The sapphire dog must have entered the basement and come up through there. I went back into the living room and found a flight of stairs leading to the second floor. I started up, avoiding stacks of cheap paperbacks by the rail.

I heard something slide upstairs and called Aaron's name. Again, no answer. Footsteps sounded above me.

I rushed to the top of the stairs. There were three doors up there, and one was partly open. That was the bathroom, and it was dark. I went through the door on the left.

It was the master bedroom. There were clothes all

over the floor. Below the window was a double bed with piles of dirty laundry on one side. Three big cats stared at me from under a clothes bureau.

Damn. The pastor didn't have a family in this house. He had run toward a predator because of his damn cats.

I raced into the hall, then into the other room. It was storage, with banker's boxes stacked against the walls.

The window was open. I rushed to it. The pastor had climbed down the porch roof and was already on the lawn. He opened the door to his truck, and something low and blue slithered into the passenger seat.

I reached for the gun in my pocket, but it snagged on my jacket and clattered to the floor. I cursed at myself as I picked it up. It was only a second's delay, but it was long enough for Aaron to get into the driver's seat.

I looked down at him. He looked up at me. Just before he closed the door of his truck, I saw by the cab light that he had a single white dot on his forehead.

He started the truck and began to back away. I put two bullets into the grille, then two more into the front driver's corner, where the battery should be. Aaron slammed the truck into reverse and did a one-point U-turn onto the church parking lot. I emptied the gun at his tires, but I've never been what you'd call a crack shot. I was pretty sure I'd missed the battery, too.

The truck labored onto the street. I ran through the house and out the porch door. The pastor's taillights turned onto the road toward town. At least he'd left the fairgrounds. I sprinted across the grass and parking lot. I was never going to catch them on foot, but I hoped the truck would break down before the sapphire dog could reach another victim.

I ran out into the road and jogged after them, but the truck was already out of sight. Headlights appeared behind me and I stepped onto the shoulder of the road. An ambulance screamed by, with Steve Cardinal's car close behind. I waved to him, and he stomped on the brake, screeching to a halt.

Justy was in the passenger seat. She rolled down the window, but it was Steve who spoke. "What in heaven's name have you been doing?"

"I saw it! It just caught a guy in a blue pickup."

"My God. Who?"

"Aaron. The pastor. I don't know his whole name. I damaged his truck. We need to catch him before he finds another ride."

"Well, get in then."

I pulled the back door open and climbed in. He stomped on the gas before I could get fully into his car. I yanked my foot inside just as the car's momentum slammed the door shut. I fussed with the seat belt. Steve was talking. "Reverend Dolan's a good man. He's forthright and strong in his faith. He grew up here. When he was a boy—"

"Don't write his eulogy yet." I didn't say that the pastor wasn't important. It was the sapphire dog that mattered.

"It's not a eulogy. He's a strong man. Maybe he'll resist it." Steve was quiet for a couple of seconds, then said: "I've been to the estate."

"What?"

"I've been to the Wilbur estate. No one was there. Everything was locked up and dark, but I found where they've been holding it all these years. I found the plastic cage with all the lights. Was it the plastic that kept it trapped?"

"No," I said. "It can go through plastic."

"The lights, then. It was the lights that held it all this time?"

"Maybe. There are a couple of things you need to know about, though: there's a girl named Shannon at the Conner house. She's all alone there." Justy took out her phone and began typing out a text message. "The adults are all dead or . . . damaged like Penny. And I saw Regina Wilbur in town. She had a shotgun. You might want to—"

"There!" Justy suddenly shouted. "I saw brake lights." She pointed toward a gravel turnoff on the right.

Steve slammed on the brakes. "Are you sure?"

"Positive."

Steve backed up and turned onto the path. "Where does this lead?" I asked.

"Back to the fairgrounds."

The road curved to the right, then led downhill to connect with the fairgrounds parking lot at the opposite side from the church. Justy finished her text message without glancing down at her phone.

"There's the truck right there," I said, pointing into the lot. The blue pickup was parked crooked beside the cluster of vans, trucks, SUVs, and other vehicles. Steve slowed down, approaching the scene carefully.

Now that I was closer, I saw just how blindingly bright the fairground lights were. The workers—volunteers from town, I assumed—had already constructed two huge tents, not as large as circus tents, but still big enough to house dozens of disaster victims, with two more ready to be erected. The canvases had been painted in different designs: red with white snowflakes, white with green Christmas trees, that sort of thing.

Everyone was working. They were unfolding canvas, connecting pipes, uncoiling electrical cable, whatever it took. No one was standing around watching. No one was fighting. Two people stopped and embraced while a third person rested a hand on their shoulders, but that looked like grieving. The predator wasn't there.

In the far end of the parking lot, half hidden among the trees, was the Neon I'd rented. I hoped Catherine was there and that she was okay. I'd check later, if I had the chance.

I saw a shape move behind a van. "Stop. Stop!" I said, unclicking my seat belt and opening my door.

"Heaven's sake, stay in the car." Steve's voice was tense.

I didn't. He chirped the brakes as I climbed out, nearly dumping me on the ground. I ran around the edge of the parked cars, then dropped low.

Christ, the asphalt was cold. Why hadn't I used my plastic to buy gloves? I peered under the cars, looking for moving feet and, maybe, a glimpse of a blue leg. No luck. I scrambled to my feet and peered through the car windows. Still no luck.

Steve had circled around the cluster of vehicles. He was too close, only ten feet from the pastor's pickup. He should have known better. It occurred to me that I could use him as a distraction, as a wooden man, but I rejected that idea. I wasn't here to sacrifice innocent people. I wanted to save them, not destroy them.

Several of the builders had noticed me creeping around their cars and stopped working. "Hey! Fella!" someone shouted. Six or seven of the workers began walking this way. Crap.

I was about to ask about a dog when Steve's reedy voice cut through. "Have any of you boys seen Pastor Dolan?"

That question stopped them cold. The man in the front, wearing a wool-lined jacket and hunter's cap, waved an arm vaguely behind him. "His truck broke down. Esteban is giving him a ride somewhere."

I looked across the field in the direction Hunting Cap had waved. Midway down the tree line, there was a break in the woods. It was another feeder road.

"You saw that?" Steve asked him. "You saw the pastor get into his truck?"

"Yeah," Hunting Cap said. "He was carrying something in his arms, like a load of laundry or something."

I was already running toward the car when Steve called my name. Justy threw open the back door for me and yelled: "If you see either of them again, keep away! Let everyone know!" I climbed in and slammed the door shut. Steve raced down the slope across the grass toward the second feeder road.

The seat belt was difficult to click with the bumps and jolts of the uneven ground, but I managed it. "What kind of truck does Esteban have?"

"Cube truck," Justy answered. "He's a plumber." Her tone was clipped. Steve hissed as he jounced around behind the wheel.

We reached the feeder road without breaking an axle, and Steve slowed. This road was made of mud and ruts. We had to be careful, or we were going to be stranded.

I wondered whether we'd find Aaron or Esteban in the truck when we caught up with it. So far, none of the people who'd been marked by the sapphire dog had wanted to share.

We hit a deep pothole, and the whole frame jolted. Steve slowed even more, which frustrated me even though I knew it was the smart thing to do. I hoped that whoever was driving the truck was less sensible and had stranded himself.

It didn't happen. We eventually reached a two-lane asphalt road. There were no taillights visible in either direction.

"Town is to the left," Steve said. He turned that way, really giving it gas.

I knew the road to the right also led to town, although it was a longer drive, but fair enough. I sat in my seat, staring ahead. The road twisted and curved, but there were no turnoffs. Eventually, we came to the top of a rise and I could see the lights of Washaway below.

"There he is," Justy said. I saw a pair of taillights speeding toward town. Steve stomped on the gas, and for once

I wished we were in a genuine cop car with lights, sirens, and everything. We zoomed down the hill, taking a long, slow curve at twice the speed the top-heavy truck could manage.

Justy turned around and stared at me blankly. "I'm sorry," she said. "At Big Penny's, I wasn't ready. I ran—"

"Don't worry about it. You didn't do anything wrong." I meant it. She looked grateful, then nodded and turned around.

Within two minutes, we were right behind him, honking our horn. Of course, the truck didn't pull over.

"Dad-blastit," Steve said. We angled across the double yellow line to pull alongside him, but the cube truck swerved, nearly smashing us off the road into the trees. Justy screamed, and Steve slammed on the brakes. I wished I could drag him out of his seat and jump behind the wheel.

"Esteban's not answering his phone," Justy said, snapping her cell shut. "I'm going to try Aaron now."

We hung back from the truck for a few seconds. The gun in my pocket was out of bullets, and I didn't think Steve would loan me his so I could shoot at the truck's tires. Hell, I couldn't hit the pastor's tires when he was pulling out of a parking spot. There was no reason to think I'd do better now.

Of course, I also had my ghost knife. It would hit whatever I wanted it to hit, but it was just a piece of paper. Cutting into the edge of a moving tire would probably tear it apart, and I'd lose the last chance I had for killing the sapphire dog.

Steve gritted his teeth and stepped on the gas again. "Hold on!" he shouted. He rammed the back corner of the truck as we came to a sharp turn.

God, it was loud. We were jolted harder than the truck was, but we were expecting it. The truck driver overcorrected toward the left, swerved into the other lane, then swung back too hard to the right.

Steve slammed on the brakes. The truck struck a fence, then, skidding, hit a tree.

Steve's car fishtailed to a stop. I opened my door and stepped out, ghost knife in hand. No one told me to stop this time.

I crept along the passenger side of the truck, half expecting the sapphire dog to jump on me. Instead, I heard the driver's door open and close. I moved back to the rear of the truck.

Steve opened his door and stood behind it, his little revolver trained on someone I couldn't see on the other side of the truck. "Drop that!" he shouted. "Esteban, you drop that or I will have to fire!" He sounded desperately afraid.

Steve didn't change position. I moved toward the corner of the truck as quietly as possible. Not quietly enough, though. A Hispanic man with a sizable paunch and the biggest monkey wrench I'd ever seen turned toward me. He was smiling.

He had a white circle just below his left eye.

Esteban was a lefty, and when he swung that wrench, it came at me in a high, slow arc like a Frisbee. It was so slow that I actually caught it and tugged him off balance. When he stumbled, I hit him once, quickly, where his jaw met his ear. He dropped to the asphalt.

Steve holstered his weapon. He looked relieved.

I knelt on the plumber's back while Steve handcuffed him. At least it wouldn't have to be a citizen's arrest this time. I jumped up and walked around the truck. There were no signs of activity in the cab and no dark circles on the sides. I hopped up to peek into the window.

Empty. I went around to the back. The latch was padlocked, but Steve had fished a fat, jangly key ring off

Esteban's belt and was fumbling with the keys. I could have cut the padlock off in a second, but I didn't want to use the ghost knife in front of them. Instead, I stood and waited, holding my breath to hide my impatience.

He found a likely key and slid it into the lock. It sprang open. He drew his revolver and waved me back. I reached into my pocket and held on to my ghost knife.

Steve opened the door and shined a flashlight inside. The walls were lined with tools and shelves, and there was no place for the predator to hide.

"Esteban," Steve said. "Where is it?"

The man on the ground had come around enough to laugh at him. He tried to get his knees under him, but he was still unsteady. He fell onto his side and kicked at me, still laughing.

Steve and Justy tried to pressure him into sharing more information, but it wasn't going to happen. He laughed and jeered at everything they said, pleased that he had tricked us into following him.

I knelt beside him and held his face still. The mark was just a spot rather than a streak. The texture of his skin was unchanged—the pores and tiny hairs inside the mark were the same as outside—but the skin itself had become as white as a sheet of paper. I poked at it; it felt normal.

"Why has the sapphire dog decided to stay in Wash-away?" I asked. "Why isn't it trying to leave anymore?" He didn't answer.

"He's not going to help us, is he?" Justy said. She didn't want to get close to him, and I didn't blame her. Esteban cursed at us and laughed again.

Steve sighed. "Help me put him into the back of the car."

I did, slamming the door shut. Esteban didn't fight me and didn't try to break out. He just sat and smiled.

"What do you think?" Steve said.

"Let me check something." I went to the truck and climbed into the cab. Hunting Cap had seen the pastor get into the truck with something in his arms. If Esteban had attacked him, it would have happened in here.

There was no blood. There was no evidence of a fight at all. And I didn't believe for a minute that Esteban could have taken that quick little pastor in a fight. I climbed out of the cab.

"Something's changed," I said. "The sapphire dog's previous victims fought one another over it, but this guy left it with someone else to lead us on a wild-goose chase, and he's *happy about it*."

"And the mark is different," Steve said.

"Either it's learning how to control us better, or it's eating more carefully. Probably the latter. I bet it's still with the pastor."

"But where is he?"

A car whooshed by us. There were two people inside, but they were gone before I could catch a glimpse of them. "Pretty much anyone in town would offer a ride to the pastor, right?"

Steve sighed and rested his hand on the roof of his car. He looked tired. "Yes."

"We should see if he doubled back."

"What if he didn't?" Justy asked.

"Then we'll drive around town, looking for him or anyone else with marks on their faces."

Steve's car rattled and clicked as we drove back to the fairgrounds. He kept looking into the rearview mirror and talking to Esteban, trying to pry cooperation from him with reason and social connection. I watched Esteban's ironclad serenity and knew it was wasted effort. The sapphire dog had taken away the parts of him that Steve could appeal to.

The men and women working at the fairgrounds swore up and down that Pastor Dolan hadn't returned and that none of their cars were missing. They had to shout at us while we talked; a snow-making machine on top of the field house was running, and it was *loud*. We found the church and the house dark. We broke down the doors and searched together. Steve clucked his tongue over the mess in the house, but we didn't find any signs of life. Even the cats were gone.

We walked out into the yard. Steve offered me a ride back into town, but I declined. He drove away.

The Neon was parked in the same spot. Catherine opened the door for me.

"How are you?" I asked.

"I'm fine," she said, to my tremendous relief. "Thank you. I'm sorry I tried to shoot you."

She still had that look. I didn't like it and I had no idea how long it was going to last. She gave me the keys and slid into the passenger seat. She clicked her seat belt in place and folded her hands in her lap.

I started the engine. "Keep an eye out for hitchhikers. And for the predator."

"All right." Her voice sounded dull and thin. All the fire and sharp intelligence were missing. The ghost knife had done just what the sapphire dog did—it took away every part of a person's personality but one. In that way, we were alike.

But who gave a damn about that? The predator was feeding on people, and it was my job to stop it.

I drove toward the campgrounds, the school, and the possibly mythical highway feeder road. My high beams lit the greenery around me, but I didn't see any movement. I saw blackberry vines, ferns, and moss-covered trees, but no people hiding in the greenery. Certainly no pastor.

I rolled down the window. The air was bracing but Catherine didn't complain. I drove quietly, radio off, listening and watching.

Nothing.

After a couple of miles we came to the campground entrance, a wide dirt path leading off the main road. I decided to pull in.

"What's that?" Catherine asked.

The headlights had flashed on something bright red in the bushes. I put the car in park and stepped out. Immediately, I could see that it was a dead man.

CHAPTER THIRTEEN

I leaned close to him. It was Stork Neck. He'd been shot once through the chest and then fallen into the hedge. Had the sapphire dog gotten loose among the Fellows, turning them against one another? Or was something else going on?

I touched his hand. It was cold, but so was mine. I lifted the bottom of his ski jacket to feel his belly. It was still warm.

That was a bad sign. I glanced around quickly but didn't see any other bodies. I had no idea how close the shooter was or whether he was coming back. I should probably have gotten out of there, but I didn't. Instead, I got back into the car.

My headlights shone down the dirt path into the campground. Down the slope, I could see the tops of three motor homes, each with a dark SUV beside it. I'd found the Fellows' camp.

"Stay low," I said. Catherine ducked below the dash. I pulled all the way into the grounds, which seemed like a better option than parking on the shoulder of the road.

There was a second body beside the entrance to the nearest trailer. It was Fat Guy. He was sitting against the trailer wheel, his head slumped down over a bloody red hole in his breastbone. He didn't look so dangerous anymore, but no one did once a bullet or two had run through him. There was a third body, one I didn't recognize, beside the next trailer. Blood spatters from the exit wound had sprayed onto the white siding.

The shooter had fired from somewhere behind me, on the hill across the road. Someone was using a long gun and using it well.

I parked as far from the trailers as I could. Maybe the shooter, if he was still around, would assume I was alone in the car. Of course, the sniper had had plenty of time to take a shot while I'd stood over Stork Neck's body. Maybe he wasn't in position anymore. Maybe he was creeping closer in to inspect his handiwork.

"Stay as low as you can and keep out of sight. You're safest if no one knows you're here."

Catherine nodded and I climbed from the car, walking quickly away from it. I took the ghost knife from my pocket.

The closest trailer was dark and all the curtains were drawn. I didn't get any closer than ten yards as I trotted past. The second trailer was not lined up with the others—someone had hooked it up to a Yukon and tried to pull away. There was a bullet hole in the driver's window and blood on the windshield, but I couldn't see a body. I didn't look for it, either.

I did see the red-and-white card on the dashboard. It was a parking permit for the campgrounds. Damn. I'd told Regina exactly where to find them.

The last of the trailers was parked beneath the trees. It was also dark, but the curtains were open. Everyone still alive must have fled. Then I heard a woman shout a warning, saw movement in a darkened window, and heard the shot.

Strangely, I felt something tear at the front of my shirt before I saw the window burst open. It took a moment to realize I'd been shot in the chest and should play dead. I toppled sideways, letting my right hand fall across my chest to hide the spot where the bullet hole should have been.

I tried to stay completely still, although my heart was racing—in fact, my heart was speeding up as I lay there. Some asshole had just taken a shot at me, and if he'd gone for my head, I'd be as dead as Stork Neck.

It scared me, and being scared pissed me off. The freezing mud soaking into my clothes pissed me off. Somebody was going to have something unpleasant happen because of this.

For now, though, I put that out of my mind. I heard a thin screen door smack shut and the squish of approaching footsteps. I held my breath and kept still. Through my half-closed eyes, I could see the trailer. A figure with a white ski mask and a white sleeve peeked around the front of the RV and aimed a rifle at me. My arm was curled and ready to throw the ghost knife, but the gunman was twenty-five or thirty yards away. By the time the spell reached him, he'd have put two or three bullets into my brain.

After a few seconds, the figure decided I was dead and aimed at the car. I hoped Catherine was still keeping low.

The sniper stepped out from behind the truck. Despite the ski mask, I recognized her. It was Ursula. She was wearing the same clothes she'd had on when she held a gun on me in the guesthouse behind the Wilbur estate. I could even see the cuts the ghost knife had made in her white jacket.

I'd been thinking of the shooter as "he"; I should have learned better by now.

She walked directly toward the car, rifle to her shoulder like a soldier. She stepped around my feet and out of my line of sight. I counted four squishy, muddy steps after she'd passed, then a fifth and a sixth before I decided I was being a coward. I rolled over and threw the ghost knife.

She turned toward me, swinging the rifle around. The ghost knife cut through it, and the weapon came apart in her hands.

She gaped at the broken rifle for a few precious seconds while I rolled to my feet. Then she threw the halves aside and reached into her waistband.

There was no time to be gentle. I charged her and hit her once in the same spot I'd hit Esteban. She staggered but didn't go down. I did it again.

She fell into the mud, arms waving vaguely in the air, still trying to defend herself even though she was out. I pulled her handgun out of her belt and dropped it into my pocket.

She also had a knife, which I threw onto the top of the nearest trailer. Then I took her wallet and keys, just because she was annoying. In her inside jacket pocket, I found three pairs of handcuffs with keys.

I dragged her by the heel to the nearest trailer, wrapped her arms around a tire below the axle, and cuffed her.

I pressed my ear against the wet, freezing shell of the trailer. Someone had shouted a warning to me, and it sure hadn't been Ursula. I didn't hear anything, so I circled around to the door. One of the tires was flat. I knelt and saw a bullet hole in the rim. It was almost the same spot as the one on the tire of the overturned delivery truck on the estate. Ursula was quite a shot.

The trailer door was wide open. I reached in and felt for the light switch, flicked it on, and stepped back.

No gunshots zipped by me. I looked in, leaning farther into the doorway until I saw a woman's fur-trimmed leather boot and the leg that went with it.

I went inside. The boot belonged to Professor Solorov; she was slumped against the wall in the little booth that served as a dining area. Her eyes were half closed and her mouth was hanging open. Blood had soaked through her blouse on the lower left side. She did not look like the same woman who had taken Kripke at gunpoint, or who had threatened to kill his whole family if he didn't turn over his spell book.

The window above her had a bullet hole in it. I was standing where Ursula had stood when she shot at me. Solorov must have shouted the warning, although I doubted she knew who she was shouting at.

She looked at me, blinking sleepily as she tried to focus. "Did you kill her?"

"No. I'm going to call an ambulance, okay? Where's the phone?"

"Right there." She didn't have the energy to point, but I did follow her gaze to the cell on the floor. It had been smashed.

"Hold on," I said. I went outside and knelt beside the nearest corpse. It was Horace Alex; I took his cellphone again. The campground got one bar, but that was enough. I dialed 911. My headache flared and I said what I needed to say. I didn't give my name, but I didn't kid myself that it would be a secret for long. My headache faded as I went back inside. "Someone will be here soon."

"Let me out," a new voice said. "I don't want to be found here." It came from the back of the trailer. Through a tiny hallway I saw Stuart Kripke handcuffed to a narrow bed.

"Yes," Solorov said. "Get out. Both of you get out."

I went into the back. His cuffs matched the ones I'd taken off Ursula. I took the keys from my pocket and freed him. He rolled over onto his wide ass and sat rubbing his wrists. He looked me up and down. "You look like crap."

Charming. I went back into the other room and leaned close to Solorov. She had ordered Biker killed and tried to do the same to me, but I still felt sorry for her. "Is there anything I can do for you?"

"Yes," she answered weakly. "Go fuck yourself. I don't

need your pity. Wait! Wait." She worked her carefully painted mouth, trying to call up enough spit to keep talking. "If you kill that Norwegian cow, I'll pay you ten thousand dollars."

"Why did she do all this?"

"Why do you think? That tattooed bastard told her we had the package. Of course it was a lie, but she didn't want to hear it." Solorov raised her other hand from beneath the table. Her fingers had been smashed crooked. "On second thought, don't kill her. I want to do it myself."

Kripke squeezed through the narrow hall. "I'll pay you five hundred dollars if you can get me out of town before the police arrive." His voice was too loud and too blunt. "Everyone else here is dead."

I didn't have time to deal with him. "Just a minute," I said.

He leaned over Solorov and flipped open her sport jacket. The professor didn't like that but couldn't do anything about it. "You keep your hands off, you fat creep."

"Hey!" His voice was bullish and thick. "You don't get to tell me what to do! Not after all this. You're lucky I don't fuck you right here and now."

I grabbed hold of his shirt. "That's enough out of you! You keep running your mouth and I'm going to cuff you again."

"And give up five hundred bucks?" he said, as if he was calling my bluff. There was something off about the guy, but I didn't know what it was. He seemed like a brainy guy who wasn't very smart. It wasn't until he looked at my face that he backed down, muttering something about *jocks*.

I turned back to the professor. "Where can I find the tattooed man?"

"Forget him," she answered. "He's a big, bad grown-up

and you're just a little boy. And his boss is something else entirely."

"Let me worry about that. Where can I find them?"

"Hah. What's in it for me?"

"She can't tell you," Kripke interrupted. "She won't ever admit that she doesn't know something or that she's in over her head. That's how she ended up like this."

Solorov sighed and closed her eyes. For a moment I thought she'd died, but when she spoke, her voice was whisper quiet. "Get out. Both of you. I don't want you near me. Just go."

I grabbed Kripke's shirt and pulled him out of the trailer. He complained about the cold and the drizzle and the mud on his shoes. The sound of his voice put me on edge, but I didn't tell him to shut up. I wanted him in a talking mood.

Ursula had come around and was working furiously at her cuffs, scraping them back and forth along the bottom of the axle. She was tenacious, if nothing else.

I put Kripke in the backseat of my Neon and climbed behind the wheel. My muddy clothes were cold against my skin. Catherine sat up and looked at me in silence.

"Before the cops get here," Kripke said. "Five hundred bucks. I'm not kidding."

I took Ursula's handgun from my pocket and gave it to Catherine. "If he does anything stupid, shoot him."

"Okay," she answered.

He was silent as I pulled out of the campground. I didn't hear sirens.

I glanced into the rearview mirror at Kripke. He was sulking. I'd interrupted my search for the pastor and the sapphire dog, and he was all I had to show for it. He'd better be worth it.

I drove by the school and beyond that the little houses and cross streets. I looked at Kripke in the mirror again. "Where have you been staying?"

He rolled his eyes. "Nowhere. I came to the auction. I was kidnapped. That's where I've been staying, with my kidnappers."

I wanted to question him, but where? Steve Cardinal might look for me at the Sunset. The Grable was a wreck. It was late enough that the bar would have closed. I wondered how Steve would react if I showed up at his house.

Kripke blew out a long, slow breath. "I shouldn't have come anywhere near this place. I just want to go home and pretend none of this ever happened."

"What about your buddy?"

"Who? Oh. Paulie. We weren't close. Besides, he was *supposed* to be my bodyguard. It's not my fault he blew it. Look, if you can get me out of town, I can get you two hundred dollars right away. That's the ATM limit. I'll send you a check for the rest."

I parked in front of a narrow house with a lopsided porch. A six-foot-long baby Jesus had been mounted on the siding, and it watched us with big blue eyes. I turned off the engine, then turned around, took the gun from Catherine, and dropped it into my pocket. She went back to doing nothing. I wished I had the real Catherine here. This next part needed an investigator.

"I heard you talking to the professor outside the Wilbur house. Right before the floating storm was summoned. How much of that was true?"

He ran his fingers through the hair above his ears, fluffing the frizzy tangle. His motions were sharp and annoyed. "Oh, come on. Really? Are we going to do this here, on a public street? Are you going to threaten to shoot me in your own car? Please."

"You don't have to be impressed. Just answer my questions."

"What if I don't?"

"More people will die."

He snorted. "Oh, noes! More people like the kidnappers who killed my bodyguard! Let's do everything we can to prevent *that*!" His voice was raw with contempt.

I'd had more of him than I could stand. "I don't think you understand the situation you're in."

"You don't scare me any more than Paulie did," he said. "You think this is still high school? You may have been King Dick among the jocks back then, but I have the money, the house, and the job. What do you have except a Walmart name tag?"

For a moment I just stared at him, astonished. If he'd given that little speech to Arne or one of my old crew, he would have gotten a beating so ferocious he would never stand up straight again. He'd lived all his life in the straight world. He had no idea how to behave in mine.

I took the pistol from my pocket and fired off a round. It passed through the back window about a foot from his head, but I'm sure it felt much closer.

Catherine shrieked. Kripke slapped his hand over his face as if he'd been shot. He rubbed at his cheek, then checked his palm for blood. A fleck of gunpowder must have landed on his skin, but he couldn't tell the difference between a burning speck and an entrance wound.

"High school?" I said. "I didn't go to fucking high school. While you were carrying your books in the halls and complaining about homework, I was on the street stealing cars and getting high. I was doing time in juvie for *shooting my best friend*. Don't you brag to me about your money or your house, motherfucker. If I want anything you have, *I take it*. Understand?"

His eyes were wide and blank, but there seemed to be a little spark of understanding in there. "Everything I said to the professor was true, but there was some stuff I left out."

"I'm waiting."

"Okay, um. The guy who baited his way into our

server and gave us all that information? He was logging on from somewhere in Bozeman, Montana. And he called himself TheLastKing."

King? I knew someone named King. I hoped to God it wasn't the same guy. "What was his real name?"

"I don't know. He always logged in from a public wireless network. We could never find out who he was. We were going to ban him, but his first posts were full of great stuff, so we voted against it."

"What did he teach you?"

"Well," Kripke said, and swallowed. He lifted his hand close to his chest and pointed at my gun hand. "That's the closed way on the back of your hand."

I felt goose bumps run down my back. He knew more about the spells Annalise put on me than I did. I scowled to hide my excitement. "He taught you to recognize spells? What did he tell you about the closed way?"

"That it stops physical attacks the way a washed-out road blocks a traveler. That when a primary casts it, the marks are invisible and the skin can feel anything unspelled skin can feel, but as you go down to secondary, tertiary, and so on, the spells become hard to hide and you lose sensation."

I stared at him. Months ago, during our time in Hammer Bay, Annalise had used the word *primary* to refer to a very powerful sorcerer, but at the time I couldn't press her for more information.

I couldn't press Kripke, either. As soon as he realized I wasn't testing him—that he had information I wanted—he'd want me to bargain for it.

"TheLastKing, huh? Did he give any idea who he might be or where he got the information?"

"Well, he had a spell book." Kripke's tone was almost disrespectful.

"Are you playing with me?"

"No," he answered, almost swallowing the word. "He said he had a pair of spell books. He said he stole them, and that if we bought the sapphire dog for him, he'd share six of the spells with us. He didn't say who he'd stolen them from."

"I want to meet him."

"I'll bet, but I'm not going to be able to arrange that. The guys on the server already know I lost the auction. I texted them as soon as the price got out of reach."

"All right," I said. "Then let's narrow it down by which spell books he has. Can you recognize any of these?" I set the gun on the seat and stripped off my jacket and my shirt. My bare skin prickled in the winter air, but I felt warmer with my wet clothes off. After glancing around to make sure there were no cars coming toward us, I turned on the dome light.

Kripke squinted at the spells on my chest. "Iron gate," he said and pointed just below my right collarbone. "It protects against different kinds of mental attacks."

"Is that it?"

He pointed low on my left side, just at the bottom edge of my ribs. "The twisted path. It's a shape-shifting spell for primaries, but as you go down the . . . um . . . chain, it doesn't do much more than alter your fingerprints and the way people remember you. And you can't control it. Um, hey, can you control it?"

This guy was unbelievable. "Still want to know about magic? I guess you haven't been kidnapped and shot at enough. There's a lesson to be learned, if you have the brains for it."

He didn't seem to get my point. "You're part of the society, aren't you? You're the reason TheLastKing couldn't come, because he said you were looking for him. You know who he is, don't you?"

"What about the rest?"

He glanced over my chest and stomach. "I recognize

the closed way around the edges, but the other spells . . . he never went over those. Most of the spells he showed us were for summoning."

"What?" If Kripke knew a summoning spell, I was going to drive him out of town and put a bullet in him immediately. There was no way I'd trust this idiot with that much power.

"Only the written part!" he said quickly. "Only the visible part. He only gave us enough to recognize one. He said that summoning spells don't decay the way other kinds do, so we'd be seeing more of them."

I believed him. He was too brain-damaged to lie this well. I picked up the gun. He winced but stayed silent.

I laid my thumb against the safety. Should I kill him? A single predator loose in the world could call more of its kind and feed on us until there was nothing left. People who summoned them, or just wanted one, were risking everyone on the planet.

And Kripke here had tried to buy a predator.

So. Bullet to the head, right?

He'd failed here in Washaway, but what if he hunted down a new spell, or bought one directly from his anonymous Internet buddy? Kripke was like a guy who'd tried to buy an A-bomb or a vial of anthrax. I couldn't arrest him, but could I let him go?

Annalise had warned me about this. She'd told me that, because I was part of the society, it was my job to make corpses. And yeah, if I'd been ruthless with Ursula, no one would have known I was on the estate and the floating storm wouldn't have been summoned to hunt me down. I didn't like it, but being soft on these people had cost lives.

Kripke cleared his throat. "You're trying to decide whether you should kill me, right? Because I tried to buy the sapphire dog."

"Hell, yeah," I said.

"You don't have to," he said. "I can help you find The-LastKing. I can even connect you to the others in my group. Some of them claim to have a full spell or two."

"You're offering your friends to me to save your life?"

I expected him to make excuses, but all he said was: "Yes." At least he was as blunt with himself as he was with others.

Kripke had given me an excuse to spare him, and I grasped at it. If someone in the society wanted to kill him later, they could do it after they'd collected his buddies' spell books.

"Give me your wallet." He did. I took out his license and made a point of studying the address, then I tossed it back to him. "I'm not going to drive you out of town, and if you offer me money again, I'm going to punch you in the mouth, understand?"

"I do."

After putting my shirt and jacket back on, I drove through the winding streets until I hit one I recognized. From there I made my way to the Sunset B and B. They had a VACANCY sign in the window. Yin might expect me to turn up here, but I doubted they'd be looking for Kripke.

"What's this?" he asked.

"A place to hole up tonight. There's probably a bus in the morning. Ride down to Sea-Tac and catch a flight home. Get a lawyer and tell the cops you came up here because you heard about the festival, but you got robbed. They'll believe it. Just stick to your story."

"On Christmas Eve? I'll never catch a flight!"

"Then stay in Washaway. I don't care. In the airport you'd have to eat overpriced food and wait around a really long time. I'm sure you'd rather be kidnapped again."

"You're right," he said, and for the first time I heard a note of humility in his voice. "Of course you're right. I . . . I just . . ."

"I don't care," I told him. "Get out." He opened the door. "And Stuart? You'll be hearing from me. Do I need to tell you not to mention our deal to anyone?"

"No, sir," he said, which startled the hell out of me. He left the car and walked up the gravel path.

I did a quick U-turn and started back toward town. Did I have enough gas to keep driving around looking for Dolan?

A pickup started its engine and pulled up next to me. I was reaching for my ghost knife when I recognized the driver. It was Ford, Steve's friend with the Wilford Brimley mustache who had gone to check on Little Mark's head injury. "By God, it's about time!" he said. His voice was deep and clear like a country-music singer's.

"What's going on?"

"Chief asked me to fetch you. He said there's some dead Chinese millionaire fellas you need to identify. You want to follow me?"

That changed things. "Give me a minute." I turned to Catherine. She was still staring at me with cow eyes. I couldn't keep dragging her around with me. Ursula could have killed her, and Catherine would have sat there and let it happen. Not to mention what the sapphire dog would do to her.

But if Yin was dead, the Sunset would be safe for her again. "Go up to the room and get some sleep." I gave her my key. I was going to say more, but she opened the door, shut it, and walked up the front path without asking for an explanation. She'd do whatever I asked without question. It was creepy.

Ford had his cellphone to his ear. He held up one fat finger without looking at me. Then he said, "Okay," and switched it off. "Change of plans," he said to me. "Follow behind."

He backed up and did a three-point turn. I followed him around the block, past Hondo's darkened garage to a street I hadn't seen before. There was a shoe store, a gift shop, and what could only be the town hall Steve had mentioned. It was made of red brick, but the window ledges were marble, and at four stories, it towered over the other buildings on the block. Four round steps led up to a pair of unlikely stone columns and a single cramped door.

We parked in the adjoining lot. Ford waddled toward the back of the building and down concrete stairs to a basement door. We were going in the back entrance.

The room we entered had three more chairs and one more desk that it could comfortably hold. Papers were jumbled everywhere, and the corkboard on the wall was six deep with tattered flyers.

As Ford shut the door behind me, a heavy wooden door across the room opened. A black woman with Coke-bottle glasses came in. It was Sherisse again, who had gone with Ford to pick up Little Mark. She was younger than I'd first thought, and she trundled forward to give Ford a quick kiss on the lips. "Thank you for coming," she said in a ragged, whispery voice.

"Of course, sugar kitten. What do you need?"

"I couldn't get through to Steve," she answered. "And I need him to know about this. Come on." She looked at me. "You can come too, if you think you can be useful."

She needed three steps to turn herself around, then she led us through the back door. The next room had a single desk and a huge boiler in the far corner. When Sherisse closed the door, I saw the jail cell.

It was only about seven feet by four feet. Inside was a bare wooden bench that someone had taken from a picnic table. Penny lay on the bench, her face slack. She was dead. One glance told me that.

Little Mark sat slumped in the corner. He was dead, too. Within the confined space of the cell, he was as far from his mother as he could be.

"My God," Ford said. "What happened?"

"I thought they would want to be together, so when I brought Little Mark here, I put him with his mother. He didn't seem to mind, but they didn't even talk to each other. They wouldn't even look at each other."

Ford cleared his throat. "Honey song, how did they die?"

"Well, Penny started yelling at me, but it was all gibberish. Her left arm was hanging at her side like she couldn't move it, her left eye was partly closed, and she started drooling. My Auntie Gertie had a stroke while she was teaching me to make piecrust, so I knew what was happening. I called 911 right away, but it was already too late. They were both . . . like this."

"Strokes?" Ford said. "Well, Little Mark did bump his head. . . ."

"But both at the same time?" Sherisse said.

She was right. That wasn't a coincidence. "Have they had any visitors?" I was suddenly sure that Pratt had killed them both with one of his sigils, just to be careful.

Sherisse seemed surprised by my question. She glanced behind her. There were two doors beside the cell: one had a sign that said RESTROOM hung on it, and the other was unmarked. She had glanced at the unmarked door. "No one that has anything to do with Penny or Little Mark."

"That's good," I said. "Who?"

Ford cleared his throat. "If Sheri says—"

I lunged between them, stepped up onto the chair, and jumped the desk. Neither of them reacted quickly enough to stop me. I rushed to the unmarked door and yanked it open.

The next room was dark, lit only by the glow of a small television. *Fantasia* was playing, and three small children sat in front of it, legs crossed, faces pale and serious.

The sudden light from the opened door made them all turn toward me. "Momma?" the smallest one said, but when he saw it was me, he turned back to the show. The sound was very low, and I realized that there were six or seven more kids bundled up in blankets and sleeping bags on the couch and carpet.

The child who looked oldest said: "It's you!" She jumped to her feet and came toward me. It was Shannon, the girl who had apologized for hiding from us. Staring up at me, her expression hidden in shadow, she grabbed hold of my wrist. "Did you kill it?" she asked. "Did you?"

"I'm sorry, but no. It got away from me. But I haven't given up. I'll keep after it."

"Please," she said. "*Please* kill it. I want my granma back. Please kill it."

"That's enough now," Sherisse said, and pulled me out of the doorway. "Shannon, this is the last video, okay? I need you to be the big girl and get the rest of them to sleep a little. Okay? Will you do that for me?"

"Please," Shannon said to me. "There's no one else I can ask. No one is listening. Please." She looked at Sherisse then, without saying anything else, and went back into the darkened room. Sherisse shut the door.

Ford's phone rang. He answered it, moving away from us.

I lowered my voice so no one but Sherisse could hear. "How many kids are in there? Is Shannon the oldest?"

"She is. There are nine in there right now. Most of them, their parents just vanished. They don't answer their cells, and no one knows where they are."

I was about to tell her to prepare for more when Ford cut in. "All right," he said in a sharper tone than I'd heard before. "That was Steve. You and I have to go right now."

I shrugged and followed him out to the cars.

We drove back toward the fairgrounds yet again, but well before we got there, the pickup turned onto a feeder road. Fallen trees made it looked blocked and abandoned, but Ford led me around a sudden turn and I followed him uphill.

The pickup was big enough that I couldn't see the road ahead, just a high back fender and cargo net. We turned sharply and drove up a switchback trail for another fifty yards or so before pulling into a small field. Steve's Crown Vic was parked at the far end, and there were two burgundy BMWs and the Maybach beside him. Ford pulled in behind Steve, blocking him in, but there weren't many other spaces left. I parked at the entrance, blocking everyone in.

The field wasn't very large, but it was tremendously muddy, even by Washaway's standards. To the left was a large log cabin with a shake roof. I'd have called it rustic if it hadn't been painted fire-engine red. A few dozen yards behind the cabin the mountains rose straight up for several hundred feet.

The front door swung open and Steve strode out. He moved quickly, but he looked tired. I was already walking toward him when he waved me over. As I slipped between the BMWs, I glanced inside. They were empty.

Before he could say anything, I called: "I don't know if they told you, but I found more dead bodies at the campground, and one woman who was near death. I haven't heard an ambulance, so you might want to have it checked out. One of Regina Wilbur's people, a woman named Ursula, shot up the place."

"Thank you for telling me. After we finish here, I'll head over there to look into the mess you . . . found."

For a moment I thought he was going to say *made*. I kept my mouth shut and took a deep, calming breath. "What did you want me to see?"

"Before we get to that: Why were you in the camp-ground?"

"I was looking for the pastor, obviously."

"Who did you take away from the scene?"

Damn. He knew more than he'd let on. Well, to hell with him. "No one. I did have Catherine with me, though. Why?"

Steve turned to Ford. "Did you see a third person in his car?"

Ford's face flushed and he looked at the ground. "Um. I didn't see everything. . . ."

Which meant he'd been waiting for me at the Sunset and had fallen asleep. I sympathized with him. Steve looked even more irritated than he had been. "Ursula said you took a man out of the trailer and drove off with him."

"Maybe she thought Catherine was a dude. She never seemed all that sharp to me. Or maybe she's lying. I did knock her down and cuff her, after all."

He rubbed his chin. "She didn't mind admitting to mass murder. I find it hard to believe she'd lie after being honest about *that*."

I shrugged. "I did . . ." *Hit her pretty hard*, I was about to say. I felt dirty just thinking it.

"What about her gun?" He stared up at me squarely.

"Oh, you mean the handgun I took off her?" I laid my hand against my jacket pocket, then moved it away when I noticed Steve's sudden tension. "Do you want it?"

He held out his hand. "Please."

I had been aware this whole time that Ford was stand-ing somewhere behind me and to the right, but I'd mostly ignored him. I felt his presence keenly as I took Ursula's pistol from my pocket. I handed it over slowly.

Steve accepted it. "This weapon has been fired."

I wouldn't be able to hide the bullet hole in the back of

the Neon. "Yeah. I thought the safety was on." I shrugged again. "I'm not really a gun person."

"What about Ursula's rifle?"

I should have ditched it after I cut it apart. "What about it?"

"Ray, if I find you've been playing games with me—"

"Oh, for fuck's sake!" I shouted, my voice echoing off the mountains around us. Steve flinched, but I couldn't hold it in anymore. "Games? You think I'm having fun here? You think I want to hang around some strange town, tripping over gut-shot people? Over corpses?"

And yet, this *was* what I wanted. This was my part in the society. I'd sought it out and now it made me sick.

"Chief," I said, trying to give Steve a little respect because I wanted him on my side, "when all this happened to me that first time, it ruined my life. I can't sleep right anymore, can't focus at work, can't . . . I sit in my room with a book in my hand and stare out the window for hours. I think about this stuff all the time. I'm constantly on the watch for it, in the faces of people on the street and in the newspaper and . . . and now here I am again. I found it here and I'm trying to stop it, because it absolutely has to be stopped."

"I understand what you're saying, Ray. But that doesn't mean you've told me everything you know, does it?"

I saved you, I wanted to say, but I didn't. I hadn't saved him to earn a marker I could call in. Still, it would have been nice to have a little more trust, even if he was right.

Steve sighed and turned away from me. "I believe you're trying to do what's best, son, but if you hold back on me, I'll see you in jail, you hear?"

I nodded. I'd been in jail before and I'd expected to be back already. It wasn't much of a threat.

Steve led me into the log cabin, and Ford followed.

For a moment I thought they were flanking me, but they were too relaxed for that.

Inside was a store, with racks of skiing, climbing, and camping gear, along with flyers promoting climbing lessons and kiddie camps. Yin's bodyguards lay around the room, handguns in their fists, their guts and brains all over the floor and walls. There'd been a gunfight. They'd lost.

Steve's voice was shaky. "Ford found a .32 slug in the wall, but these fellows are all carrying .45-caliber weapons. They fired them, too. See the casings all over the floor? Doesn't look like they hit what they were aiming at, does it?"

And I'd heard them, too, but I'd thought it was thunder. "What were they aiming at?" I asked, although I was pretty sure I already knew the answer.

"I was hoping you could tell me."

"Sorry. I can't."

"Then come look at this." He led me behind the counter, through the back office, past a very interesting little goosenecked desk lamp and out onto a weatherbeaten wooden deck. There were three more bodies out here. Two were burned and shriveled, lying on scorched sections of the deck. The third was Yin himself. His thick tongue stuck out of his mouth, and his face was purplish. He'd been strangled.

Lying on the deck beside him was his soul sword. It had been broken into three pieces.

The smell of blood and burned flesh became too much. I stepped off the deck and vomited into the bushes, making a mental note not to eat greasy grilled cheese when I was on society business.

When I turned back, Steve and Ford were giving each other a significant look. I wasn't sure what it meant, and I didn't care.

Steve cleared his throat. "Don't feel bad, son. I did the same thing. Just I knew where the bathroom was."

I didn't answer because I didn't feel bad at all. I'd feel bad when a building full of burned and head-shot corpses *didn't* make me puke. I went back onto the deck.

"Do you know him?" Steve asked. It was a simple, dangerous question.

"Not personally," I said. "You know who he is, too."

"Sure, but I want to hear what you have to say."

"I already told you this. His name was Yin, and he was rich. He won the auction but let the sapphire dog get away. The people at the campground were some of the losers."

Steve's mouth was a thin, tense line. "Any other bidders I should know about?"

I sighed. If I really did want him on my side, I couldn't exactly say *no*. "There was a fat guy from California and an old man from, I think, Germany. I don't know whether they left town or are still here hunting for the sapphire dog."

"Any reason you didn't mention them before?" Steve's voice was sharp.

"Because this is what they do to people who know too much about them. And how did you know about the campground? I doubt 911 dispatched you."

"Justy found them. She talked to Ursula, then she called me and I called Bill and Sue direct. Then I called the staties. I gave up on the sheriff hours ago."

I looked at my watch. Steve looked at his. How long until they arrived? He took out his cell. "Let me get an ETA for the state police."

I felt a dull ache in the iron gate on my shoulder. It was a warning that someone was using a spell against me, but it didn't seem important.

"Hi, Marlis," Steve said into his phone. His voice

suddenly sounded vague and dreamy. "Steve Cardinal over in Washaway. How're the kids? That's great news. I'm sorry you'll be working through the festival. We'd have loved to have had you." He paused a moment. I moved closer to listen. "Trouble? No," Steve said, "we're not having any trouble here. Just the usual Christmas spirit."

The ache in my shoulder became very strong, and I closed my eyes against it. I heard a woman's voice at the other end of the phone say: "Lots of you folks down in Washaway have been calling all day to wish me a happy Christmas. It's . . . it's . . ." She sounded a bit confused, as though she was trying to remember something important. "It's very sweet," she said at last.

Steve answered her in the only way that seemed logical to me: "Everything is just fine over here. You be sure to give a Christmas kiss to those kids of yours."

He hung up the phone, and the pain in my shoulder eased. He'd said what he needed to say. He nodded to Ford. "That should get them out here right quick."

I was glad Steve had made that call. I was glad the state cops knew about the trouble we were having.

I rubbed my face. "Where's the woman?"

Steve looked startled by that. He turned to Ford, who didn't have anything to add but a shrug. "Describe her."

"Short black hair and dark skin. She looked like she was from Indonesia or something. She wore dark suits and had her hair up in a bun like a librarian. She was maybe my age, just a little under thirty. She was part of Yin's entourage as some sort of researcher, I'd guess."

"Does she have a name?"

His tone was getting annoying. "Yeah, but I don't know it."

"We searched the whole grounds and didn't find any women. Could he have sent her home before all this?"

Steve was obviously a glass-half-full sort. "It's more

likely that she's been reduced to a pile of greasy dust, or that she's gone to work for the people who won the gun-fight."

Steve nodded. "There's one more thing I want to show you." He led me off the deck and across the muddy field. Ford was still trailing me. Now it did bother me to have him at my back.

I stopped, turned around, and said: "Hi. My name is Ray."

He looked a little surprised, but not much. "I'm Ford."

"Nice to meet you, Ford. This is ugly business, isn't it?"

"That it is," he said. He opened his jacket to show me his holstered gun. "Whoever's responsible for all this shit is going to be shut down." He gave me a hard stare as he said it, as though I was suspect number one and a wrong answer away from a beating.

"I agree completely," I said. Then I turned to follow Steve.

We passed a swing set and an open sandbox. As we walked, Steve spoke to me over his shoulder. "When this Yin character rented the Johnson place over on Outpost Road, Pippa did a little checking. He's so rich I can't even imagine it. Who could have tempted this missing Indonesian woman away from him?"

I remembered the pirate's expression on her face when she'd seen the tattoos on my hands. "Some things are more important than money."

He grunted his agreement.

Steve led me down a trail, which ran alongside the cliff face. The night air was cold enough to sting. After about thirty yards, he stopped.

"Know this fella?"

We were well away from the cabin lights by now, and there were very few stars out. Steve flicked on a heavy flashlight and shone it into the bushes.

At first I couldn't make sense of what I was looking

at—it looked like a jumble of brown clothes. Then Steve played the light across a face.

I recognized the hat and the tan coat. It was Pratt.

Oh, shit.

"Well?" Steve prompted. "Do you know him?"

"Remember when I told you help was coming? Here it is."

CHAPTER FOURTEEN

Pratt looked like someone had laid a burning fern leaf on his face. "What happened?"

"I've seen this before," Ford said in an authoritative voice. "I spent a couple of years doing missionary work in the high places in the Congo. This man was struck by lightning."

That startled the hell out of me. I jumped up and scanned the skies around us. I didn't see any lights, and I didn't hear an electric hum.

Time to get the hell out of there.

"Settle down, son," Steve said. He shone the light in my face, blinding me. "We have a bit more jawing to do. Are you still armed?"

"I already gave you my only gun," I said.

"You'll have to forgive me if I don't take that at face value," he said. "You've been holding out on me from the start, haven't you? Who is this fella, and how was he really killed?"

What I needed was a time-travel spell that could send me back to the moment just before I told Steve help was coming so I could dummy-slap myself into silence. I'd wanted to give him hope, but all I'd done was make him curious.

But I sure as hell couldn't tell him about the Twenty Palace Society. *Information shared is information leaked.* "I can't answer that. I'm sorry."

I heard Ford pull back the hammer on a gun. I turned

and saw that he was pointing a snub-nosed police .38 at me.

Steve rubbed his chin and glared at me. "I'm afraid I'm not giving you any choice, son. I'll admit that I don't know a thing about these people." He waved his arm toward Pratt's corpse and the cabin behind me. "For all I know, they're just a bunch of gangsters and crooks. But Penny is my cousin. Isabelle nursed my wife through the final stages of cancer. I was godfather to the oldest Breakley girl. Do you understand what that means in a town like this?"

I didn't answer. He frowned at me. "Everything. That's what it means. Now, I want to know everything you know, and if I think you're holding back, I'm going to arrest you for murder. I'm sure I can make it stick. Do you want to talk to me here and now, or through the bars of a cell?"

"I'm not the enemy here."

"So you say."

Enough. I liked him, but I didn't have time to play these games. I turned my back on him.

Ford aimed his revolver at my breastbone, the way you're supposed to. But he was too close. "Ford, you realize that if you shoot me, the bullet will pass through and hit Steve, right?"

That startled him. He said: "Uh . . . ," and looked at Steve.

I rushed him, knocking the gun aside. It went off, and the shot echoed against the rocky cliffs around us like the "thunder" I'd heard earlier. I hit him once in the belly. He let out a huge *oof* and fell sideways into the thicket. His gun landed in the mud.

I spun around and saw Steve down on one knee, his left hand over his head like a child about to be beaten, his right fumbling at his holster. I was on him in two steps. I clamped my hand over his, trapping his weapon, and drew back a fist.

Steve flinched and bared his teeth in fear. Damn. I couldn't throw that punch.

After a couple of seconds he realized I wasn't going to hit him. I yanked his pistol out of his hand. He lost his balance and fell back onto the path. I took Ursula's gun from his pocket, then turned to Ford. He was lying in the thicket, moaning and holding his belly. I picked up his gun, too.

"I'm sorry, Steve," I said.

"Son—"

"Don't. I'll leave your weapons on the hood of your car." I wanted to say more—about the risk to him and to all of Washaway if he learned too much about magic— but the words wouldn't come together in my head. I ended up saying nothing.

I jogged back up the path and went around the cabin. There was a brick barbecue pit in the side yard and a stainless steel gas grill. Between them, I saw a tarp lying over something vaguely human-shaped. I knelt beside it and caught a whiff of an outhouse.

I lifted the tarp just enough to see that it was Frail. Blood had trickled from his mouth to his ear; he'd died on his back. On a hunch, I pulled the tarp back farther and saw what I'd expected to see: he'd been stabbed through the heart by something big, like a lightning rod.

"No one else handy, huh?" I asked him.

I left his face uncovered so Steve would notice him, then hustled to the car. I didn't see Well-Spoken, and I didn't see another body under a tarp. I tried to speculate who Frail had been—servant? apprentice? both?—and what he'd done, if anything, to make the old man stab him.

I set Steve's and Ford's weapons on the hood of the Crown Vic but slipped Ursula's gun into my pocket. Right now, Washaway wasn't a place for anyone to go un-armed. Using my taillights to guide me, I backed down the road.

I couldn't return to the Sunset—even if Yin was dead, Steve and Ford knew to look for me there, and they might bring friends. I'd end up in a cell while the sapphire dog ran loose, turning people into its pets.

But at least the cell would have a place to sleep. I blinked until my blurry vision cleared. The short naps I'd been getting weren't enough. I was weary. I'd lost the support of everyone, even Steve and Catherine. I didn't know what to do about the predator or the bidders, but there was one job I could still do.

I drove directly to Steve's house and kicked the back door in. He would be out looking for me, of course, but I didn't think he'd come here first. I pulled the patties out of the freezer, dropped them into a stainless steel mixing bowl, and rushed back to the car. Maybe I should have defrosted them first, but I couldn't imagine myself stand-ing in Steve's kitchen, anxiously waiting for the micro-wave to ding.

I drove back to the cabin. Steve's and Ford's cars were gone. Good. I turned the Neon around so I wouldn't have to back down the feeder road, then carried the bowl of patties into the woods.

If Pratt was anything like Annalise, he could be healed from injury by eating meat. The fresher the better, but these frozen burgers would have to do.

I knelt in the wet moss beside him and cut a thin sliver from the column of meat. It didn't want to go down his throat, but I wiggled it in. Then I did it again and again. I had a hair-raising moment when I imagined Pratt clamp-ing his teeth down on my fingers and swallowing them, but that was all imagination.

It didn't do any good. He didn't come alive. Damn. I'd

seen other peers survive damage worse than this, but maybe there was some sort of magical *oomph* behind the floating storm's red lightning.

And while I didn't like Pratt, I could have used his help.

I left the last three patties defrosting in his mouth and tossed the bowl away. No other cars had come up the road to block the Neon. I drove down the hill and back onto the road.

I was alone again, and now I had no idea what I should do.

The sign for the school appeared in my headlights. On impulse, I pulled in and drove past the tiny playground. I switched off my headlights and parked behind a Dumpster.

I closed my eyes, but as tired as I was, I couldn't sleep. The smell of those dead bodies stuck with me, and my head was churning with thoughts of the sapphire dog. I leaned my head against the window and stared up at the blank night sky.

At first the sapphire dog seemed to want to get out of town, but something had changed. Esteban hadn't tried to drive it away from Washaway; he'd been a distraction. And how many hours had it spent hiding out at the stables? If I was going to figure out where it had gone, I needed to know what had happened.

My biggest problem was that I knew so little about it. It came from another place. I couldn't bring myself to use the word *dimension* or *universe*, even in the privacy of my own head. It was just too dorky.

Still, I'd seen that place—the Empty Spaces, as the society called it, although others called it the Deeps. It was a nothing, a void, but what did I know that could help me understand the sapphire dog?

Steve's Crown Vic drove by and was gone. I assumed he was after me, and I wondered where he would start his search. I didn't know a thing about Washaway except what I'd seen over the past couple of days, but if I'd been local, he would have known where to search for me. He would have gone to my home, my friends, my work, my hangouts. He would've had a place to start.

But I was a stranger. I didn't have any place to go, so I could have gone anywhere.

This was the same problem I had with the sapphire dog. The big difference was that the predator had the pastor to guide him. If I knew what the predator wanted, I could figure out how the pastor would try to give it to him.

But of course I already knew what the sapphire dog wanted. It wanted what every living thing wanted: to eat. And somehow, it fed itself by making people crazy. My ghost knife cut away every part of a personality except compliance. The sapphire dog took everything but love for it.

Until the stroke hit, that is.

The darkness and the cold became too much. I closed my eyes. Just for a moment.

When I opened them again, there was light in the eastern sky. It was Christmas Eve morning.

I rubbed my face, hard, to get the sleep out. Time to move. I climbed from the car and emptied my bladder against the back of the Dumpster. The temperature had dropped below freezing overnight. I was hungry. My back and neck ached. I needed a toothbrush. Worse, the job I had come here to do was not over yet.

I rubbed my arms, trying to make myself feel warm and awake. I was alone here, an ex-con with a couple of spells, trying to find a predator before a full sorcerer did. I was completely outclassed, up to my ass in corpses, and I had no leads at all.

I couldn't even talk to Catherine. Steve would be looking for me, and I had no way to contact her without running into Nadia and Nicholas.

Unless . . .

I climbed behind the wheel and started the engine. I had half a tank left, which was pretty good considering how much driving I'd done already. Then a motorcycle rumbled across the road ahead, headed toward the left. Toward the fairgrounds.

It was Tattoo. He was watching something mounted on his handlebars. If I wanted another shot at him, now was the time. This time I'd twist him until all his bones were broken.

And I just happened to be sitting in a car.

I drove to the mouth of the driveway. I was about to turn to follow him when a line of ten or twelve trucks and vans cruised by.

I cursed at them and wrung the steering wheel. The last pickup went by with a bed full of poinsettias, and I pulled out after it.

To me, the line of cars seemed as slow as a parade. I tried to peer around them, but I couldn't see the front vehicle, let alone Tattoo. Eventually, they all pulled into the fairgrounds. Had Tattoo pulled ahead and vanished around the next turn of the road, or was he in the fairgrounds?

I turned with the other vehicles and followed them in.

They drove to a low corner of the parking lot and onto the field. None got stuck in the mud, but it was a near thing for a couple of them. I parked at the edge of the grass and looked out over the grounds. People rushed around, setting up stalls in the early light. They were already selling things—Christmas ornaments, tiny jars of what looked like preserves, warm clothing, Yule logs, and model train kits.

The pickup with the poinsettias pulled up beside a tent,

and a woman with long gray hair began carrying the plants inside. Three men followed her in with a big gas heater.

The snow machine was silent, and the ground beside the field house was coated with snow. I wondered what would happen if I ran out there and jumped around in it.

The people were smiling. There were no cards, no happy greetings, but I did see them shaking hands and hugging one another. Washaway, their community, had gone through a tough couple of days, but these folks were determined to keep going—to celebrate. If the hugs seemed to be more out of consolation than joy, and if a couple of the people wiped gloved hands across their cheeks while they spoke, that just showed their strength and connection to one another.

And I hadn't gotten inside any of it.

I didn't see Tattoo anywhere nearby, so I didn't belong here. I backed out of my spot and took the side road to the church. It was closed up tight, and the windows in Dolan's house were dark. The upstairs front window was still open. The pastor had not come back here.

I drove toward town. The sky was finally bright enough that I could turn off my headlights. I would be easily recognizable in the Neon, but short of stealing a new car there was nothing I could do about it.

In town no one stopped me, and I didn't come across any roadblocks. I drove by the Sunset B and B and pulled into a little gravel road. There was a space on the far side of a stand of trees, and I parked there. It didn't hide the Neon all that well, but it was better than parking on the street.

I ducked between the trees. The Sunset was encircled by a neatly mowed lawn, but beyond that was a fringe of heavy underbrush. I pushed through it, little chips of ice breaking off the branches and melting against my clothes, until I reached the back of the building. Damn, it was cold.

The closest ground-floor window—in the kitchen—had a light in it, but all the windows in the upper floor were still dark. After a little figuring, I decided my room was the one on the far left. Catherine should be there; I hoped she was.

Movement in the lighted downstairs window made me duck low. Nadia entered the room with a bag of flour in her arms. She looked at the window, and for a moment I thought she was looking straight at me. Then she tucked some stray hairs behind her ears, and I realized that she was looking at her reflection.

She sighed, took a bowl from a high shelf, and moved away.

I breathed a sigh of relief and crept, shivering, along the edge of the property. I couldn't find a stone to throw at the window, but I did find a small piece of bark. That would do.

As I drew my arm back to throw it, the kitchen window darkened. I ducked low again, but it wasn't Nadia blocking the light. It was an irregular spatter of red fluid.

Blood. There was blood on the window.

I threw the wood chip at Catherine's window and ran to the building. I couldn't see into the kitchen, but I could see shadows moving back and forth on the grass. I couldn't tell how many people were making those shapes, but it was more than one.

The upstairs window opened. "Catherine!" I hissed.

She stuck her head out and looked down. "Ray, what the—"

"Enemy in the building," I said. Maybe that wasn't the best way to say it, but her expression showed she understood. She leaned back and, after a few seconds, stuck her head out again.

"Get up here!" She tossed a heavy quilt out the window, letting it hang down to me.

At least the effects of the ghost knife had worn off. Was it because the spell wore off after a while, or did sleeping reset her personality? "Is that a joke? Come down before you get killed."

"Ray," she said, her voice harsh. "Get your skinny ass up here."

Fine. I stepped away from the building, took two running steps, and jumped up. I set my foot against the windowsill and grabbed hold of the quilt.

I knew Catherine hadn't had time to tie it to something solid—and how would you tie off a quilt, anyway?—so I expected it to come loose and drop me back onto the lawn. That didn't happen. I began pulling myself up hand over hand.

Suddenly, the quilt began to draw back through the window as though pulled by a winch. I was so startled I nearly let go. Instead, as I came to the open window, I let go of the cloth and grabbed hold of the sill.

"Christ, what the hell was that?"

Catherine stepped out of the darkness and pulled the sleeve of my jacket. It didn't help, but the thought was nice. I hauled myself through the opening, flopping into the dark room with all the grace of a drunk sneaking into his house.

"Come on," I said, as I got to my feet. "Let's get out of here."

Out of the corner of my eye I saw the quilt flutter onto the bed. I shouted in surprise and spun around. Another figure stood in the darkness well away from the window. A jumble of thoughts rushed through my head. At first I thought Catherine had brought a guy to her room, then, seeing how small the figure was, I assumed it was a boy, which would have been a screwed-up thing to go to jail for, and last night she'd been under the influence of my ghost knife, so that would have been another awful thing I was responsible for.

The figure spoke. "Ray, what the hell have you been doing here?" I knew that high, deadpan voice. The lamp snapped on.

"Boss!" I said, much too loudly. It was Annalise, the peer in the Twenty Palace Society who had bulletproofed my chest and arms, and who had led me through the whole mess in Hammer Bay.

I almost hugged her, but her ribs-backward, shoulders-forward body language made it clear she didn't want to be touched. I stopped myself after an impulsive step forward and let my hands drop to my sides.

"Boss, I've been screwing everything up from moment one."

Catherine started to protest, but then she noticed the ghost of a smile on Annalise's face.

Annalise moved toward the door and listened. She looked just the same as when I'd first met her—her dark red hair was clipped so short you couldn't grab a strand between thumb and forefinger, and she wore a new pair of black, steel-toed boots and a new firefighter's jacket. Her pale face was small and delicate. Black tattooed lines just like mine peeked out from the collar and sleeves of her shirt.

She looked to be about twenty-two years old, but she'd already lived longer than most people do, and the things she'd seen had made her hard and dangerous. One look into her eyes could tell you that.

That absurd little voice of hers sounded loud in the room. "Someone was killed downstairs, you said?" She glanced down at a scrap of lumber in her hand.

"Yeah, Nadia, the owner, I think. I couldn't see how. Just . . . blood. Is that why you guys were sitting in the dark?"

"No," Catherine said. "I was debriefing her, and we

didn't want anyone to know I was up. Don't worry, Ray, you didn't interrupt anything."

I felt my face grow warm, and Catherine smirked at me. I said: "You're pretty comfortable, considering."

"I can't help it. It's a tremendous relief to have a peer right here with us. I feel safe for the first time in days."

Downstairs, something fell over with a muffled thump. "Okay," Annalise said. Her expression was serious. It was always serious. "You don't know who's in the building?"

I didn't answer right away. It could have been Tattoo, but I thought I'd have heard his Megamoto. Then I remembered the missing third Mercedes at the red cabin. "Whoever it is, they're working for the old man. He's the only one left. If I had to guess, I'd say it's the last of Yin's guys with a new boss."

Before the room fell into darkness again, I stepped closer and confirmed what I already expected: the scrap of wood had a spell drawn on it. It was a glyph that wriggled like a nest of snakes when certain kinds of magic were nearby.

It was dead still.

She tossed the scrap of lumber at me. I caught it. The sigil flashed silver as it reacted to the magic Annalise had put on me. On the other side of the door, we could hear the floorboards creaking.

Annalise said: "Look after yourselves." Then she yanked open the door and stepped into the hall.

Immediately, I heard a sound like a series of low sneezes. Something invisible tugged at Annalise's clothes. Someone was using silencers. She raised her arm to cover her eyes and charged forward.

"Stay low," I said to Catherine. "Count to thirty, and then follow Annalise out of the building."

I swung my leg out the window into cold morning air. Then I lowered myself as far as I could and dropped onto the grass. I didn't break my leg, and no one shot me. So far, so good.

I sprinted around the side of the building. The gun in my pocket bounced against my hip; I'd forgotten about it again. I could have used it against the gunmen inside, but Annalise could handle them better than I could. Killing people was her calling in life.

CHAPTER FIFTEEN

I came around the side of the house just as a man in a dark suit fled down the porch steps, firing desperation shots back into the doorway. He didn't see me come at him.

I hit him from behind at full speed, knocking him face-first into the gravel. He didn't make a sound as he scraped across the stones, but I hit him once behind the ear just to be certain.

I heard the *chunk* of a car door closing. Well-Spoken Woman charged out from behind a parked X6 and ran down the street in her expensive shoes.

The gunman's pistol had landed a few feet from me. I snatched it up. The slide was back; it was empty. I tossed it away and took out Ursula's gun, then I ran after Well-Spoken.

It felt good to run. I liked stretching my legs, and she was not fast at all. However, she *was* carrying a shotgun. I held Ursula's gun ready and stepped as quietly as I could.

When I was just five paces behind her, I slipped on a patch of black ice and fell hard on my hip. My whole body jolted under the impact and my gun fired, the round skipping off the asphalt into the air.

It took Well-Spoken seven or eight stutter steps to stop her run, turn, and point the shotgun at me. That was plenty of time for someone as motivated as I was to get to my knees and aim my gun at her.

I didn't shoot and neither did she.

"It appears we have a standoff," she said, trying to sound confident.

"Except only one of us is bulletproof," I answered. I showed her the damage to my jacket and shirt. Her mouth fell open. She didn't have an answer for that. I reached out with my left hand, and she walked toward me and laid the shotgun in my palm.

Thank God. She'd been aiming a little too low to hit my bulletproof parts.

I stood and led her back to the B and B. Catherine and Annalise were standing over the man I'd knocked down. Well-Spoken stumbled and almost fell against me. I took her elbow to support her. "Thank you." She sounded grateful. "My name is Merpati." She looked up at me with wide, innocent eyes.

"I'm Ray. See that woman up ahead? She's a peer." I felt Merpati slow a little, but I urged her forward. "We have another few seconds before we say hi to her, and I want you to think about how you're going to present yourself. Helpful? Snotty? Pretty, wounded girl who needs a big guy to save her?"

She let go of my arm immediately. We walked together up the middle of the street toward the B and B. Townspeople stood in open doorways or in lighted windows, watching us.

We joined the others. Annalise had her foot on the gunman's back, holding him belly-down on the gravel. Catherine was kneeling beside him. He was talking in Chinese.

"I don't understand you, young man. I don't understand."

His wraparound shades had come off, and I was startled to see just how young he was. I didn't think he was old enough to buy a beer.

Merpati said: "He wants to go back to Hong Kong. He has a sister there who needs him."

I looked back at the B and B. A tall, slender young couple stood on the porch. Kripke stood beside them. They had the shell-shocked look of people who'd just been through a disaster. "How many dead bodies inside?"

Catherine stood. "Aside from this guy's friends? Five that I found right away. Nadia is one of them. I didn't see Nicholas, but I didn't search all that hard." She looked down at the kid on the gravel. "I wonder how many of them had sisters who needed them? Or kids?"

"Enough," Annalise said. She slapped the back of the kid's head. It made a sound like a cracking walnut, and he fell still.

Damn. Whether he deserved it or not, I didn't think we were the ones to dish out that sort of punishment.

Catherine gaped at Annalise. She didn't look relieved to have Annalise to keep her safe anymore. Suddenly, she looked afraid. She stepped toward Merpati, clasped her hands in front of her body, and spoke in a low, friendly voice: "Hello, honey. Did you order all this killing?" It was a new role for her.

"No!" Merpati responded. "Never. I was forced to come here by the man who killed my employer. The old man. He ordered this. They were going to leave me at the scene to take the blame."

This was the same voice that had bartered Kripke's murder in the Wilbur kitchen. Of course, now that she'd been caught, she was all shocked innocence.

"Who was the target?" I asked. I shouldn't have butted in on Catherine's shtick, but I was angry and I couldn't keep my mouth shut.

"I don't know," she answered, turning back to Catherine's friendly face. "I wasn't involved in the planning of this terrible, terrible crime."

"For Christ's sake," I said, my voice sharp. Merpati turned toward me quickly. If she was pretending to be afraid of me, she was doing a damn good job of it. I thought I might have been stepping on Catherine's work, but the expression on her face was encouraging. I waved my hand at the dead kid. "This guy spoke German, did he? Or did that tattooed bastard speak Chinese?"

"Cantonese," she corrected, with the habit of someone who corrected other people often.

"Whatever. I'll bet the only way they could have gotten their orders was through you. You're saying the old German guy didn't make you a better offer? You didn't switch teams and bring a couple of dumb young guys with you? You're going to be stuck with that story for a while, so you better be sure."

She turned back to Catherine. "I swear. I am telling the truth. I swear."

Catherine bent low so their faces were close together. "We know that's not true, honey. I don't want them to kill you, but I can't stop them if you don't help me."

Holy crap. I was the bad cop.

Unfortunately, Merpati wasn't sold. "It's the truth," she said. Her voice quavered as she spoke—she was afraid, but she wasn't going to change her story.

"We don't have time for this," Annalise said. She stepped forward.

"Wait!" Catherine snapped. She turned back to Merpati. "Honey, you have to give me something."

Merpati looked at her and shook her head. She had tears on her cheeks. She believed she was about to be killed, and she wasn't going to give us a thing. Whatever the old man had on her, it was strong.

Catherine sighed. "Okay," she said to me. "Go ahead."

I blinked at her. Go ahead and what? I hope she wasn't expecting me to start throwing punches. I had a shotgun in my hand. Was I supposed to use it on her, with little mobs of neighbors gathering down the street to watch us?

"Ray." Catherine sounded annoyed with me. "Quickly, or your *boss* is going to break this woman's neck."

"What?" I was completely at a loss.

"Lord," Catherine said. "You'll use it on me but not her?"

I suddenly understood what she was talking about. I tucked the pistol under my arm and took the ghost knife from my pocket. "I used it on you because you were trying to kill me." I grabbed Merpati's wrist and swept the ghost knife through her little finger. It cut a notch in her braided gold ring, but her flesh was unharmed.

She gasped. Her shoulders slumped and her hands drew up next to her chest in a frightened, defensive posture. "Both of you," she blurted out. "I'm sorry. He sent us to kill both of you, along with Mr. Kripke, if we could find him."

Catherine leaned toward her. "Who sent you to kill us?"

"His name is Zahn." I heard Annalise inhale sharply. That wasn't a good sign. Merpati kept talking. "He's what Mr. Yin has wanted to be his whole life. He's a real sorcerer. When his man approached me and offered to make me an apprentice, I couldn't refuse."

Catherine's voice was quiet. "So you double-crossed your employer for him."

"I . . . yes," Merpati said. "Mr. Yin . . ." Her voice trailed off.

Three of the townspeople, all men, began walking up the street toward us. One carried a rifle. The others were probably armed as well, but no weapons were visible. I lifted my empty hand to tell them to stop, and startled by the gesture, they did.

"Mr. Yin was the forty-sixth richest man in the world. He was ruthless and a little crazy, but he was a good

man, in his way. He loved me. He even asked to marry
me, and my solicitor assured me the terms of the prenup
were excellent. Here I was, just a bank teller's daughter
from Surabaya, and I would have been set to take care
of my parents and siblings for life. And of course my as-
sociation with him would have enabled me to pursue my
only real interest: magic."

She glanced at the marks on the back of my hand. We
were all quiet, waiting for her to continue.

She looked at Catherine again. "When we kidnapped
you, I thought we were going to get everything we would
ever want. But Mr. Yin . . ." She looked at me. "He
wanted that spell you offered him so much that he lost
all caution."

I didn't look at Annalise. I didn't want to see the expression on her face.

"When Herr Zahn approached me, I made the same
mistake. Exactly the same. He promised me the secrets
of the world behind the world, and I threw away everything. I lured Yin to his death. Me. When Zahn ordered
me to take the few men I'd saved for myself and come
after you, I knew he'd used me. He didn't care if I made
it back, and if I had, he would have killed me. I betrayed
a man who would have given me a good life for nothing.
I'm so sorry."

She began to weep. A sorcerer had once promised to
show me the world behind the world, but instead I had
stolen his spell book and created my ghost knife. In the
end, he had seemed like a decent guy—for a sorcerer—
but I saw the world behind the world without his help.
And just like Merpati, I wanted more.

With that thought, I couldn't help but look down at
the dead gunman at my feet.

The townspeople were slowly moving closer to us
again, and this time they had a crowd behind them.

Whatever we were going to do with her, it would have to happen soon.

Annalise stepped over the boy's body and jostled Catherine aside. She laid the scrap of wood against Merpati's shoulder; the sigils didn't react. She wasn't carrying any magic.

Annalise's voice was quiet. "Where can we find Zahn?"

"He's been staying at a cabin near the fairgrounds. It's where he lured Mr. Yin and his men to kill them."

"I was just there last night," I said. "The chief of police discovered Yin's body—and the others—but the sorcerer was long gone."

"No," Merpati said. "He has a way of forcing you to think certain thoughts and turn away from certain places. Sometimes he can make people not see him when he's right there with you. He thinks it's funny."

"Merpati," I said.

"Yes?"

"I want you to tell those people"—I gestured toward the approaching townspeople—"that you came here with these gunmen to kill everyone in the building, and that you did it on Zahn's orders. You can say they forced you or whatever, but don't tell them about the magic. Make up a believable lie. Understand?"

"I will," she said. "Do I have to spend the rest of my life in jail? I'm afraid."

"No," Annalise said. "Someone will be along to debrief you and ease you out of this world. You're done, but if you talk about spells or predators to anyone—*anyone*—I'll personally kill your whole family. I promise."

Merpati's mouth dropped open, then shut. She nodded.

The three locals at the head of the crowd were about ten feet from us by then. "Excuse me," the man with the rifle said. "What's going on here?"

Merpati glanced at Annalise one more time. I knew she would do what I told her until the effects of my spell wore off, but the look she gave Annalise told me that she would stick to that story for as long as she had to.

Then she turned toward the three men. "These others are not involved. I will explain," she said in her perfectly accented English.

Annalise gave me a look. "Let's go." I followed her along the side of the road toward town, away from the throng of people gathering around Merpati.

"Hold it right there," one of the men said, hustling in front of us to block our path. He was a balding guy with a couple more chins than were strictly necessary, but the double-barrel shotgun in his hand was tough enough.

Annalise sighed. "Let me show you my identification," she said. She reached into her jacket.

"Boss—" I was suddenly afraid for Balding's life. But Annalise pulled out a white ribbon and showed him the sigil on the bottom. Balding suddenly closed his eyes and turned his back on us. Then he stretched out on the road and went to sleep.

She frowned up at me. "Did you think I was going to kill him?" We started walking again.

I glanced back at Kripke. He was watching me, his face pale and sweaty in the chilly morning air. He turned around and went back inside.

Catherine started to follow us.

"What did I hear about a spell?" Annalise asked. All trace of the tiny smile she'd greeted me with was gone. "You didn't ransom that investigator—"

"No," I said. "No way. I know better. I gave him a fake." I explained how I set up the arson, then got Yin to believe me when it came time to give him the spell.

Annalise nodded but still didn't smile. "That's all right, for this time. But don't do it again. People do crazy things for spells, Ray. If word started to spread that someone bartered with you for a spell, it could cause trouble for you."

I could imagine. "Gotcha. Can I ask a question?"

Information shared is information leaked. But Annalise turned to me and said: "You've earned it. Go ahead."

"Is Zahn a primary, whatever that is? Are you?"

"That's more than one question, but okay. No, Zahn isn't a primary. He's a quaternary, at best, but probably isn't even that high. And before you ask, I'm a senary. Now I'm guessing you want to know what that means."

"Pretty much, yeah."

"There are only three real spell books in the world. They're the source of all the magic on the planet, but they don't have any actual spells in them. They're also not really books, but never mind that. When you read one, you have visions. Dreams."

She fell silent for a moment. "After the visions are over," she continued, "the primary writes them down as clearly as possible, and that becomes what most of these idiots think of as a spell book."

We turned the corner. Annalise's battered Dodge Sprinter stood on the shoulder of the road. I was glad to see it again. I said: "So, if the primary passes the written-out spell book—one named after him, like, *Mowbray Book of Oceans,* to an apprentice, that apprentice becomes a secondary."

"Right."

"And the secondary casts the same spells, but they're weaker. Because, I guess, you can't pass on a vision to another person without having it change a little."

This time Annalise did smile, just a bit. "Very good."

"And the Twenty Palace Society doesn't have those

three original spell books anymore, so you've been slowly losing power."

"We had two, but that's right. Several centuries ago, they were stolen. It's an ugly part of our history."

We reached the van. Annalise gave me the keys, and I got behind the wheel. It was just like old times.

Except I wasn't thrilled the way I had been when Catherine picked me up. It wasn't an adventure anymore. It was a job. An ugly job. I couldn't understand how I'd been so excited to come back to it a few days ago. "Are more peers coming?" I asked.

"No. Why would they?"

"First Pratt, then you—"

"Pratt was assigned by the peers. He won't be replaced until his death is confirmed."

"Then why did you come, boss?"

"Because I'm checking on you, Ray. You're my wooden man. You belong to me."

Catherine pulled the driver's door open. "Are you going to leave me behind?"

"Yes," Annalise answered.

"You can't. Not after all this."

"Hey," I said, "what happened to *this is not part of my job*?"

"I can't walk away from all this," she said. "Not now. All these years that I've been snooping around, making a phone call and then bugging out. I've been hiding, making the easy choice. . . . Last night, with the horses and that little girl . . . and I was watching those people set up for their festival, but I couldn't feel anything at all because of the ghost knife. They were working so hard in the dark and the cold—sometimes stopping to hold someone while they cried.

"But I couldn't feel anything, not until I woke up this morning when the effect had worn off. I haven't . . . God, that little girl *apologized for hiding*. I can't walk away from that. I need to do the right damn thing. Again."

Annalise leaned across the center of the van toward Catherine. "Will you be my wooden man?"

I mouthed *No!* "You're already an investigator. A good one."

Catherine frowned at me. "Pratt was a quinary, wasn't he? And Zahn killed him."

"Pratt was an arrogant ass," Annalise said. "He thought everyone would tremble at the sight of his big hat and long coat. I'm not as precious. And I have help."

"I want to help, too. I won't be a wooden man, but I'll do what you ask me to do."

"Get in," Annalise said.

I unbuckled and slid out of the driver's seat to let Catherine sit there. I gave her the keys. While she started the engine, I sat on the deck. The van was cold and my clothes were still wet.

"Ray, you've been to the cabin before?" Catherine asked. I gave her directions, and in a few moments we were on our way.

Annalise said: "Zahn isn't the only dangerous one here. Issler is trouble, too."

"Who's Issler?" I asked.

"Zahn's tattooed bodyguard. He's good. Three years ago, he took a hand off a full peer."

"A peer?" Catherine said. "Wow."

No one spoke again for a while. I thought about how close I'd come to killing him on the steps outside the Wilbur house. Things might have been simpler if I had succeeded. Or maybe not. At least I was going to get another chance.

I looked out the back window and saw a boy standing in the open doorway of a house. He was looking up and down the street, and I was pretty sure I knew what he was searching for. I hoped someone would call Sherisse about him soon.

"Is there a plan, boss?"

"Yes," Annalise said. "Catherine is going to drop us off at the entrance to the property, then drive into town to look for the predator."

Catherine stared at her. "Is that really what you want me to do?"

Annalise grunted. "When I brought Ray in, I had hours to put spells on him and prepare him to face a full sorcerer. With you, I have five minutes. You're not ready. You're still as soft as Jell-O."

Annalise looked back at me. "Here's our part of the plan. We sneak up on the cabin and kill Zahn and his people."

"I'm not sure I can remember all the steps," I said. "You know what would be useful? An Apache helicopter."

"Some peers use military equipment overseas. It draws too much attention in the U.S."

We were at the turnoff. Catherine slowed to a stop, and Annalise and I piled out.

"My cell is off," Annalise said. "If you find the predator, leave me a message. Use the one in the glove compartment."

Catherine opened the glove compartment, took a slender cellphone out, and dropped it into her pocket. "Can I try to kill it?" she asked.

"Sure, after you've left the message. Try not to get killed unless you can make it count."

I stepped back into the doorway and set the sawed-off shotgun on the passenger seat for her. Just in case. I closed the door and she drove off.

"What if Zahn already has the sapphire dog? What if both of them are up there?"

"What do you think?"

"Kill them both. I get it. But what if I have to choose?"

She stopped and stared at me. "Nervous, Ray? Asking questions you already know the answer to isn't going to make this easier. Now shut up. I don't know if Zahn has extra-sensitive hearing or not."

We started up the muddy drive. Of course I knew the answer to my own question: the sorcerer summoned predators, so he was top of the hit list. At least, that's how I saw it.

I was surprised that no one had strung police tape across the drive. I'd heard Steve call the state cops, although I was a little fuzzy on what he'd said. Still, considering what had happened, the National Guard should have been marching through.

Instead, there was only us.

I didn't care about Yin or his people. They were assholes. I did care about that housekeeper. She'd been murdered right in front of my eyes, and there was no one but me to make that right.

But this was a problem. I was the one who needed to believe the person I was going after was a murderer or worse. I was the one who needed more than "knows magic" as a reason to kill someone.

That wasn't the job I had come here to do. I wasn't here to kill a murderer; I was here to kill a sorcerer. Knowing he had killed, too, made this one job easier for me. But the next time—

"Your mind is clear, right?" Annalise asked.

"Absolutely." I forced myself to imagine the cabin and the land around it. I still wasn't sure Merpati was being straight with us about Zahn staying there. Somehow, I didn't think he was bedding down in the ski aisle.

I walked along the center of the path where the ground was relatively dry. All I could hear was the sound of my breathing, the wind rustling the trees, and our squelching footsteps. We were almost at the top of the drive when fat, wet snowflakes began to fall.

The BMWs and the Maybach were still in place. I kept low while I headed toward Yin's cars, leaving Annalise to slip into the underbrush.

The snowflakes melted on contact with the cabin windows, distorting the view inside, but I wasn't interested in the cabin. The second car had a strip of gray cloth hanging out of the trunk. I was certain it hadn't been there when I'd passed through last night.

The key for this car was probably on one of the dead gunmen. Assuming they were still inside, there was no way I was going to search them all unless I had to. And I didn't. I slid the ghost knife back and forth until it cut the latch. The trunk opened.

I loved my little spell.

Inside, I found empty halogen floodlight packages along with a car battery wired to an AC adapter and a three-pronged plug.

It had to be part of a carrier for the sapphire dog. The real question was simple: Where was the cage itself? I hoped Steve didn't have it. He'd be tempted to use it, and nothing good would come of that.

Or did Issler—I had to get used to thinking of Tattoo by that name—and Zahn have it? More important, were they still here, and could we kill them in their sleep?

I backed away from the trunk. It couldn't be closed again, so I left it up. That was a good thing, though. I was the wooden man. It was my job to draw attention to myself so Annalise could attack from behind.

I strolled back to the cars and the front of the cabin, doing my best to fake a casual calm I didn't feel. Issler might be aiming a gun at me from one of those darkened windows, or Zahn might have sent him to fetch the lightning rod.

Or maybe they were sitting in the back office playing cards. Why didn't I ever imagine good things?

I stepped up onto the wooden porch and tried the doorknob. The door wasn't locked. It swung inward, letting sunlight into the darkened store.

CHAPTER SIXTEEN

The smell had gotten worse—the door and windows had been shut for hours, letting the stink of blood, shit, and spoiling meat seep into everything. I flicked on the light switch by the door and saw that the bodies were still there. Steve had pulled camping blankets off the shelves to cover them, but no one had come to take them away.

What the hell did it take to get help in this town?

I looked around. Zahn and Issler were not napping among the dead. I went into the office. The interesting goosenecked lamp was on, which was strange, but there was no one there. I went out the back door and flicked on the porch light. Yin was covered with a heavy tarp weighted down at the edges with skis.

I shooed away the crows that were trying to get under there, and if the squawking they gave me didn't draw enemy fire, there was no fire to be drawn.

Annalise came out of the underbrush. "Nothing?"

"Nothing," I answered.

She stepped up onto the porch. "You came through the building pretty quickly. You checked the second floor, too?"

"There is no second floor," I said.

She gave me a funny look and went into the office. "What do you call that?" She pointed at the wall.

"A wall." If it had been anyone else, I would have thought she was joking. She gave me a funny look again, then her brow smoothed as if she'd had an idea. She went to the wall.

Whatever. The light over the desk was still on, which I still thought was strange. Something about the light was—

Wood cracked and splintered. I spun around, startled, feeling as if a huge weight had been lifted off me.

Annalise was standing beside a flight of wooden stairs. She pointed at the broken bottom step. Black steam fizzed out of it. "See that sigil?" I looked at it, although every time I did, I felt an unbearable urge to look away. The urge grew less and less powerful as the magic drained out of it, and I felt much less fascinated by the very ordinary desk lamp across the room. My iron gate ached.

"Oh, crap." I rubbed my face. Issler could have shot me from that step, and I wouldn't have seen it coming.

"These are on the roads in and out of town," Annalise said. "No one leaves and no one comes in, and they all think it's their own idea. Let's go."

I followed her up the creaking steps. She reached under her jacket and took out a green ribbon.

There was a yellow door at the top of the stairs. She pushed it open and went inside.

I followed her into a small living space. To the right was a kitchen that was little more than a dent in the wall and an open door that led to a bathroom. To the left was a chair and three mattresses on the floor. Blankets were bunched in the corner, but there were no suitcases or clothes nearby. A threadbare couch sat beneath the far window.

"Pretty spartan," Annalise said.

"Boss, could they still be here? Could they be watching us from a corner where we can't see them?"

"Yes," she answered. Then she sighed. "I think they're gone. There's no luggage, no vehicle out front. They might come back, but—"

"What's that?" I led her toward the kitchen. Beside the sink was a heavy tarp wrapped around something big. I peeled it back, expecting to find another body. It was just an oven.

Someone had bent the seal on the metal door so it would close over a thick black electrical cable. Light shone out through the dirty window on the oven door. An electric hum made the floorboards vibrate.

"What the hell have they done here?" Annalise asked. With one hand, she shifted the fridge to the side. It was unplugged; the heavy black cable had been plugged into that socket. Someone had put a powerful light—or several powerful lights—into the oven. I peered through the oven window, trying to see inside. It was no use. Then I remembered the halogen-lamp packages out in the car.

"The cage the sapphire dog was kept in for all those years was ringed with lights," I said.

She knelt and peered at the gaps in the door. She didn't have to ask the next question: *Was the sapphire dog in there right now?* She set her scrap lumber on the stovetop. The sigil on it twisted and writhed like an orgy of snakes. Whatever was inside, it was magic.

"Take the handle," Annalise said. "Don't open it until I say go."

I stepped around her and stood by the stove but kept my hands at my sides. She reached under her jacket and took out two more green ribbons. She closed her eyes.

I wondered if Catherine had told her everything about the sapphire dog, and whether I had told Catherine everything. Did she know it could pass through solid objects? Did she know about its tongue?

Annalise opened her eyes and nodded to me. I laid my hand on the handle. It was warm to the touch, but—

"Go!"

I yanked the door open and jumped back. The electric hum immediately stopped. The connection had been broken, but the light from inside didn't shut off. There were no halogen lights, but the oven seemed to be full of light anyway. At the bottom, I saw the blackened silhouette of a tiny rib cage and a human skull.

This wasn't the sapphire dog at all.

The churning light floated toward me just as Annalise threw her three green ribbons. The ribbons burst into flame—the same weird green hissing fire that I had seen her use to burn people down to their bones. I was already backing away.

The floating storm emerged from the wall of green fire, gases trailing behind it. Annalise said something, a curse, I think, and began throwing more ribbons.

Another billow of green flame struck the predator, then a brown ribbon flashed and the white-hot churning core of gasses I thought of as its face suddenly pointed the other way, moving toward the kitchen. Beams of blue light burst from a handful of thrown ribbons, some of them impaling the creature, all linking together to form a lattice. But the floating storm moved right through them, turning back to us.

Annalise's face was grim as she reached under her vest for another ribbon. The predator was closing in on her.

The stairs were right behind me. I could have sprinted down to the back door and been out on the road in three minutes. I knew the predator couldn't catch me out on the asphalt. But I couldn't leave Annalise. I was her wooden man, and this predator needed to be destroyed.

The pipes leading through the roof down to the sink told me where the water tank was. But I'd missed my chance. The predator was already too far away from it to replay the water-sprinkler trick.

An old set of skis and poles stood in the corner. The poles were pitted and crooked, but they were made of aluminum. I grabbed one and ran across the room.

Annalise had stopped throwing spells at the creature. She grabbed a mattress off the floor and heaved it. The fabric was already burning when it struck the floating storm, but it had no more effect than it would on a column of smoke. Pieces of mattress fell into the corner and set fire to the wall.

I threw the aluminum pole like a spear. It flew crookedly, striking the predator at an angle. That weird red lightning played along the pole's length as it passed through. Arcs jumped to other objects nearby, including the metal nails in the couch. The couch started burning.

The ski pole hit the floor, still sparking. The floating storm turned toward me. I backpedaled, drawing it away from Annalise as I went for the other ski pole.

Annalise picked up the burning couch and threw it. I think she was trying to kill the predator by breaking up the swirl of gases at its center, but all she managed to do was fan them out, set a new fire, and delay the thing for the few seconds it needed to pull itself back together.

I grabbed the other ski pole off the floor and, with two cuts from my ghost knife, shaved the end to a sharp point.

It was nearly on me. "Take this!" I shouted, and threw the pole through the predator. It sparked just like the other one did, shrinking the floating storm slightly. But not enough to kill it.

I backed toward the steps, the predator moving closer to me. Swirls of orange, yellow, and red curled around one another in sudden spirals and breaking wave fronts. It was like watching a half dozen small hurricanes collide in slow motion. In its own way, this thing was beautiful, too.

It passed over the burning couch, and now there was nothing between it and me. I backed down the stairs, well aware of what would happen if it got above me.

I hoped Annalise understood what I was doing.

Just as the predator moved into the stairwell, the ski pole shot through it and wedged into the wood paneling.

The floating storm froze in place. Red lightning flashed off it, draining into the wall studs. The paneling caught fire.

I bounded down the steps. The wall beside me groaned and the glass in the back door shattered. I turned away from the door and ran to the main part of the store.

There was a sudden, deafening blast from above. Hot air struck me from behind, followed a bare instant later by pieces of broken wood. I sprawled forward onto the trembling floor, feeling something huge and heavy land on my back. For a moment, I thought the terrible pressure of it wouldn't stop until my back was broken.

For once, I wasn't afraid. I pulled my knees under me and struggled to my feet, gratified that I still could. Firelight shone from behind me. I staggered toward the door but tripped over one of Yin's men.

My balance was shot and my ears were ringing. I stood anyway and looked back at the office. A section of the wall was missing, and everything was on fire. I could see fire upstairs through holes in the floor. I stripped off my jacket, but it wasn't burning.

The floating storm did not come through the doorway after me. I breathed a heavy sigh and leaned against a rack of winter coats. I needed to get out of this building, but for the moment, I didn't trust myself to cross the room without help. My head was still swimming and my skin felt scalded. I tried moving my arms and back—my ribs hurt, but I didn't think anything had been broken. Lucky.

Another explosion shattered the windows. This one sounded different from the one in the stairwell, but my ears were still ringing. I saw a sudden flare of light and stumbled toward the office.

I couldn't enter, but I could see into the backyard through a gap in the wall. Annalise was out there, and she was on fire. Another explosion struck the ground at her feet, and she was thrown back into the bushes. The cabin rattled with the blast.

The floating storm didn't attack like that. I ran to a side window.

Issler stood in the falling snowflakes. He held something that looked like a massive, two-handed revolver. As I reached for my ghost knife I heard him shoot it—*foof!*—and another blast of firelight erupted from the back of the house. He was smiling.

He didn't see me as he started toward the backyard. I threw my ghost knife at him.

The spell didn't go where I wanted it to go. It had never missed before, but it turned away from him just as I had turned away from the stairs in the office.

At the last moment, I willed it toward his weapon instead.

The ghost knife cut through the top of the barrel just before he squeezed the trigger. The gun burst apart in his hands, fire flashing over his face and neck. He screamed.

I turned and staggered toward the front door. Firelight shone down at me from the ceiling. The cabin groaned as if it was about to collapse. I yanked the door inward, feeling it scrape against the floor, and sprinted into the yard. The men inside would be getting a Viking funeral soon.

I *reached* for my ghost knife again. It was almost too far, but it came.

I held it ready to throw as I came around the barbecue pit, but it wasn't necessary. About fifteen feet away, Issler was kneeling in the dirt, squealing and grunting from the pain. With one hand he smeared mud into his left eye, and with his other he dug inside his mouth. I could hear meat sizzling.

I wondered if the ghost knife could hit him if I held it in my hand rather than throwing it. There was only one way to find out. I started toward him.

Suddenly, the shadows around us slid across the ground. The floating storm came over the top of the cabin and moved down toward Issler. It was small—no larger than a cantaloupe—but if it fed, it would get bigger.

I still had the gun in my pocket, but it was useless. I pressed my ghost knife to my lips. I didn't know what would happen to me if it was destroyed inside the floating storm, but I might have to chance it.

The only thing nearby was the barbecue pit and the stainless steel gas grill. I cut through the gas hose and dragged the tank out of the bottom. I couldn't tell if it was full or empty, and at the moment I didn't care. It was metal and it was handy.

But I was too slow. The floating storm was already directly above Issler and moving downward.

The tank snagged on something. I tugged and twisted it, trying to tear it free. It wouldn't come.

The floating storm was close enough to Issler that he could have reached up and touched it.

Red lightning never struck. The predator floated above him, swaying back and forth as though trying to find a way in. Maybe it was having the same trouble my ghost knife had had.

I shook the tank, making a horrendously loud noise but finally freeing it. The predator floated toward me.

I swung the tank once in a wide-armed circle and heaved it. It struck the floating storm dead center. I wished the propane had blown up like a bomb, but that didn't happen. I had to be satisfied with a couple of sparks and a slight delay in the chase.

Damn. Annalise was nowhere in sight, and I had no one to help me. For all I knew, she was dead in the bushes back there.

But that didn't mean I was out of ideas. Getting inside one of the cars out front would protect me from real lightning, and now seemed like a good time to try it against magic. I didn't know what I'd do after that, but maybe I'd have a chance for my head to stop spinning.

I ran to the front of the building. The firelight was bright and the heat was raw against the side of my face. Wood cracked and crashed somewhere nearby, followed by a roar of flame. The front wall of the cabin trembled and leaned toward me.

"Ray!"

That was Annalise's voice. I stopped and looked for her, letting the predator get uncomfortably close. I saw her silhouette waving at me from the far side of the cabin.

I angled back toward her and the heat. The little floating storm followed at about shoulder height. I could have sworn that it was having trouble staying in the air.

The wind changed, choking me with a gust of black smoke. I gave a wide berth to the porch, even though the fire hadn't reached there. The flames were flickering along the outside of the wall, slowly spreading downward.

I rounded the corner with tears streaming down my face and nearly ran headlong into Annalise. I dodged to the side as she stepped forward, and I could only catch a glimpse of the thing she was holding over her head as she tipped it over and slammed it onto the ground.

It was the water tank from the roof. She'd dumped it over the floating storm.

Scalding hot mud shot out from under the lip of the tank. It scalded me through my pants, and I dropped to my knees in the freezing mud to leach away the heat.

"Where did Issler go?" Annalise asked. Her clothes were in tatters, exposing pale skin from her chin to her ankles. She was completely covered with protective tattoos, as I had always suspected, but what I hadn't expected was how she looked. She always wore clothes that were large and loose, but I never expected to see all her ribs, her bony hips sticking out through her skin . . . I wasn't prepared for how *starved* she looked.

Then I saw that the sides and top of her head were burned nearly black. There was a section of undamaged skin on her face about the size of both her hands, but the flesh around it was actually smoking.

"Jesus Christ, boss," I said, with more fear in my voice than I'd intended. I jumped up and slipped out of my jacket. She let me wrap it around her shoulders. Her usual expression of stony anger turned a little sour, but she didn't shake it off. It looked as big as a quilt on her. The smell of her burns made my stomach twist into knots. "Is there something I can . . . Does that hurt?"

She pulled the jacket closed. "I hate it when they burn my clothes."

"Issler is on the other side of the building. He was still alive when I left him."

"I can fix that," she said, and started walking in that direction. "Get away from the building."

I sprinted for the line of cars and crouched behind the trunk of one of the BMWs. A few moments later, Annalise walked around the pit with Issler dragging behind her. His head hung at an awkward angle. Dead.

She lifted Issler's corpse in front of her like a shield and kicked the front door of the cabin open. Flames roared out. She threw him inside, then trotted toward me. My jacket was smoking, too.

"Well," she said when she reached me, "that was annoying."

As we walked down the switchback trail, Annalise

stayed a few paces behind me. I didn't know whether she was sparing me the sight of her burned flesh, using me as a lookout so that no one would question her injuries, or using me as her wooden man again. It didn't matter. We walked in silence, and when I glanced back to see if she was about to go into shock or something, she glared at me.

Back at the road, Catherine was waiting for us in the van. She slid open the back door to let us climb in. I stepped aside to let Annalise get in first.

"I thought I told you to find the sapphire dog," Annalise snapped.

Catherine glanced at her, gasped, and shouted: "Oh my God!" She shoved her door open and fled into the road, running to the opposite shoulder to retch into the dirt.

Annalise knelt at a big plastic cooler behind the driver's seat. She took out a Tupperware tub and peeled off the lid. It was filled with little cubes of uncooked red meat. She popped one into her mouth.

That was it for me. I slid back out of the van and walked a few paces away, grateful for the clean, cold breeze.

Catherine had finished, but she stayed on the far side of the street. She looked spooked, so I moved toward her.

"What's she doing in there?" she asked.

"Healing her burns," I answered. "She has a spell that protects her, and when she needs to recover from an injury, she eats meat."

"She's . . . *eating*?" The look on her face showed that she was close to losing control again.

Raw and fresh, I almost said, but I didn't want to make either of us queasier than we already were. Instead, I went with: "Glamorous, isn't it? Don't worry, she'll be back to normal soon."

"What happened up there?"

That was a good question. Issler and Zahn had left a booby trap for us, and it had nearly worked. A normal gangster would have just left a bomb in that oven. It would have killed me in a blink. It wouldn't have killed Annalise, though, or any of the other peers I'd met. Zahn and Issler had gone to a lot of trouble to set up that disaster, and when I thought about the tiny bones in the bottom of that oven, I wanted to kill Issler all over again.

Not that it would be enough. Nothing would ever be enough to set right all the things that had happened in Washaway.

"Issler is dead," I told her. "We aren't." Then I remembered telling her *Stuff*. I gave her a quick rundown, making sure to mention what had happened to Penny and her son.

I shivered in the cold but didn't head for the van. I didn't care how warm it was, I didn't want to see Annalise's body—not the injured parts, not the uninjured parts.

The driver's door suddenly swung open. "Let's go!" Annalise called out. Her little voice had a nasty sharpness to it.

Catherine and I crossed back to the van. "I'm still driving," Catherine said. I laughed and went around to the side door.

Annalise had changed into heavy canvas pants and a heavy canvas jacket. Her head was pale and healthy and completely bald. She pulled a knit cap on, then opened her jacket and began alligator-clipping ribbons to the inside lining.

I knelt between the two seats. "You okay, boss?"

She tossed my jacket at me. I pulled it on. It stank of smoke and other things I didn't want to think about, but I was too cold to be fussy. "Except for all the spells I wasted, yes. Now, did you find the sapphire dog?"

Catherine started the engine. She wouldn't turn her head to look at Annalise. "I left you a message, but I guess you've been too busy to get it. I didn't get close enough to see it, but I'm pretty sure I know where it is."

"Then go."

Fat, damp snowflakes that wouldn't stick were still falling. Catherine pressed the gas and we pulled onto the road. I knelt on the metal deck and watched where we were heading. I didn't need to. I already knew.

We had to take the long way to the fairgrounds. The feeder road we had used to chase the plumber's truck was blocked by two pickup trucks and three men with deer rifles. We drove around the property into the main parking lot. There were men here, too, but they didn't display their weapons. I was sure they were close at hand, though.

Catherine stopped when one of the men raised a hand. She rolled down the window and said: "Is there a problem?"

"Not here," the man said. He wore a big, beautiful cowboy hat with a plastic rain cover. There was no white mark on his face. "But we've had some disturbances nearby."

"I've heard about that," Catherine said. "What's been going on?"

"Don't know," Waterproof Cowboy answered. "Outsiders have been causing trouble, and some of our own folks have suffered for it. We're being careful this year."

"Good Lord," Catherine said. "I wish people had the decency to keep their messes in their own yards."

"Me, too. Most of the outsiders have left Washaway, though. We're not seeing as many shoppers as we used to."

"Well, I hope you're not going to send me away without a poinsettia. And I have some last-minute gifts to buy."

Waterproof looked us over and nodded. "Be sure to try the sugar cookies. The proceeds help the food bank." He stepped back and we drove in.

We pulled ahead and parked. There were a lot of open spaces. Once Catherine had slipped the shotgun under her jacket, we climbed out of the van and started down the slope. The snow-making machine was off, and there was a quiet chill in the air. Catherine and Annalise spoke in low voices, pointing out toward the tents. I was about to join the discussion when movement off to the side caught my attention.

Six men marched toward Waterproof Cowboy and his pals. They carried hunting rifles, and one had a banana-clipped assault rifle. They spoke for a few minutes in a way that wasn't friendly or unfriendly. Waterproof tilted his head as though something puzzled him, but the new-comers stood in neutral positions with very little body language.

Finally, Waterproof shrugged and led his buddies toward the tents. The replacements took up their positions.

I jogged to catch up with Annalise and Catherine.

"This is a waste of time," Annalise said. "There's no evidence the predator is here. Just her guesses." She held out her hand.

Catherine sighed and gave her the van keys. "It wants victims. This is where the town is going to gather. Isn't it—"

"I'll go to a hotel until you have something solid."

"Boss, there *is* something weird going on here. Look."

The nearest tent was twenty yards away. A pair of heavyset women were beckoning for another to come out from behind her glasswares stall. Their persistence wore the other woman down. She followed them toward the cinder-block field house.

Annalise didn't respond, but Catherine said: "I'm guessing that's where we need to go."

We walked toward the field house. The stalls we passed were all set up but completely abandoned.

Finally, just a few dozen yards from the entrance to the field house, we came to an occupied stall. A little old gray-haired lady in a parka with a fur-lined hood stood in front of a huge display of gift chocolates and candies. ALL HOMEMADE, the sign said; she'd obviously spent a lot of time getting ready for this day.

She smiled pleasantly at us as we approached. "Excuse me—" Catherine said, but the woman interrupted.

"You should get out of here right now." She didn't let her smile falter, but the look in her eyes was fierce. "Right now. You're in terrible danger here. Go quickly."

"We're here to help," I said.

The woman glanced to the side, and her smile turned bitter. "Behind the table," she said. "Get in and get down. Quickly!"

Catherine rushed around the edge of the table and crouched behind the white tarp that covered it. I followed, herding Annalise in front of me. We hid.

"Why are we hiding?" Annalise asked. She sounded annoyed. "We should find the most heavily defended spot and attack."

I wanted to kill the sapphire dog with as little collateral damage as possible, but Annalise had other priorities. "The sapphire dog is fast," I said. "We have to sneak up on it, or it'll get away again."

The woman in the parka kicked me and said, "Hello, Rich. Back again so soon?"

"Come with me, Livia," a man's voice said.

"I'm not here to go to your town meeting, Rich. Whatever you have there, I'm not interested. I'm here to sell, not buy."

"I'm sorry to hear that." I heard his footsteps squish in the mud as he came around the stall. Then I saw his legs. He was wearing puffy snowsuit pants—the kind you'd see on a toddler. They were bright red with little candy canes on them.

I surged upward at him, but Catherine was faster. She slammed into his legs, knocking him to the mud. He fell facedown and was still. Weird. I grabbed the shoulder of his candy-cane jacket and rolled him over.

It was the bartender from the night before. He'd been holding a syringe and had fallen on it. The needle stuck out of his shoulder. I had no idea what was in it, but he was out cold.

I turned to Catherine. "Don't use up our good luck on mooks."

She was about to laugh when Livia hissed at us. "Get back under there and don't do that again! More are coming!"

She started pushing me down to the ground. I didn't want to fight her, so I got down on my knees and hid under the table.

"I've been hearing gunshots and explosions all morning," Livia said. "I think they've already killed a number of us. I can't get to my car, and I certainly can't walk out, not with my heart. But maybe I can distract them long enough for—well, if you're really here to help, maybe long enough for you to help."

I knelt in the mud and kept quiet. Annalise and Catherine did the same. If we raised a commotion here at Livia's stall, we'd draw every armed citizen in the fairgrounds. The sapphire dog would run, and we'd have to hunt it down all over again.

Besides, I wasn't keen on killing the sapphire dog's victims. I was hoping that, once the predator was dead, the townspeople would return to normal. Hey, it could happen.

There was a supermarket milk crate on the ground beside me. I looked inside and saw candies. My mouth watered and I wished I'd stolen a little time for breakfast.

More footsteps approached.

"Livia," a woman said. "Everyone is waiting. Join us."

"Thank you, Constance," Livia said, "but no."

"No one is coming today," Constance said. I wished I could see her face. "There's no one to sell to. You know I'm right."

"I'm still staying put."

"The pastor is asking for you."

"If he wants to buy some truffles, send him over."

Catherine was kneeling beside another of the plastic milk crates. She looked inside.

"I'm already here," a new voice said. It was Pastor Dolan.

From where we were hiding, I could see back to the church and the pastor's house. There was a sudden flash of reflected sunlight in an upstairs window. I tapped Annalise's shoulder and nodded toward the house. The flash came back, and she saw it. Someone was watching from there.

Livia's voice was strained but still pleasant. "Come to buy some chocolate-covered almonds, Pastor?"

I heard the distinctive double click of a revolver being cocked. "Livia," the pastor said, "if you don't come out right now, I'm going to shoot you in the stomach. Then we'll drag you back to join the others. You won't live long, just long enough. Now come on."

That was it. Whether we had to sneak up on the sapphire dog or not, I couldn't just cower here while this woman was led away at gunpoint. My ghost knife would be useless against them, but I still had the gun. And since they couldn't feel fear anymore, I couldn't control them at gunpoint. I'd have to shoot them.

I started to move out from under the table. Livia held her hand in front of my face. It wasn't visible to the people she was talking to, but she was telling me to stop.

God help me, I did.

Livia sighed. "I guess I don't have a choice." She walked around the edge of the stall.

"What about the strangers?" Dolan asked. "Rich said you were talking to them."

"I told them to get out of town." Livia sounded just as pleasant, but I couldn't see her face. I assumed she wasn't smiling anymore. "I warned them off, and they ran that way. They're out of your clutches, you self-righteous little fucker."

"Get her inside," the pastor said. Squelching footsteps receded.

"We don't have enough guns," Constance said. "You shouldn't have sent so many men into town."

"We need to gather everyone. He's hungry."

"*She* needs to be protected more than she needs to be fed," Constance responded. I guess they didn't like to call the sapphire dog *it,* or look under its tail.

"When the next missionary group returns, we'll keep them here. Better to be safe, I guess, until the outsiders are caught."

"I'll get some people together to search," Constance said, her voice flat.

More footsteps receded. Catherine turned toward me and said in a low voice: "We can't stay here. As soon as Livia is turned, she'll tell them everything."

"I'm leaving," Annalise said.

"What?" Catherine's voice was too loud.

I held up my hand to Catherine, and she calmed down. It had worked for Livia, and it worked for me. "Boss, do you want to go after Zahn right now?"

"I do. He's a slippery bastard, and I don't want to let

him run back to whatever hole he hides in. What he did at the cabin is SOP for that fucker. It's not enough to keep the sapphire dog from him; he needs to be dead, and the society has been hunting him for fifty years. Besides, I bet he didn't bring any predators with him. We may not get a better shot."

"What about the sapphire dog?"

"I'm leaving that for you two."

It was my turn to be shocked. "What? You're going to face him without me? Boss . . ."

There really wasn't a delicate way for me to ask if she could take him in a fight. She was powerful, but she wasn't the *most* powerful. Besides, she'd used up a lot of her spells on the floating storm. She needed me.

She narrowed her eyes at me. As it turned out, I didn't have to ask that delicate question. She understood exactly what I was going to say. "Yeah, he's dangerous, Ray, but you know what? If he can be killed, I can kill him."

"Okay, boss."

Annalise turned to Catherine. "You follow his lead in this. You're good at what you do, but he knows this."

Catherine nodded and looked at her shoes. Annalise turned to me. "You just worry about taking care of that predator."

"Okay," I said. I didn't like it, but I didn't have much choice. Annalise rushed out of the booth and slipped into the tree line.

"What's the plan?" Catherine gave me a steady look.

I pulled the ghost knife from my pocket, then stuffed it down the front of my pants. I had an absurd moment when I worried it might slice off something I wanted to keep, but of course it didn't. It didn't cut through the bottom of my pocket, after all. "I'm going to get myself captured. I'll make a big enough distraction that you should be able to get to the parking lot and steal a car. Can you steal a car?"

"Yes, but Annalise—"

"Annalise told you to do what I say. The best way to get through all these people is to let them bring me to the sapphire dog. If I can kill it without hurting them, maybe they'll get better." I tried to say it with conviction, but I didn't have any. I'd never had much luck curing the victims of a predator. I didn't expect it to work, and I didn't expect to get out of there alive. But there was no need to say that aloud. "But you're an investigator. You got us where we need to be." I was tempted to say *You don't have to die, too.* "You have kids."

"A lot of these people here have kids. Somebody needs to stand up for them. Somebody has to be ready to pay the price, Ray, and I'd rather be good than safe."

It seemed the definition of *good* was more fluid than I thought. "I'm not doing this to save your life," I said. "Well, not only to save your life. Washaway is full of these bastards. Someone ought to report this—" I stopped talking for a moment as a sudden migraine overtook me. Catherine winced, too. *Don't think that thought.* Instead, I said: "I might be the one who makes it, not you."

Catherine sighed. "If we both survive, I'll buy you a beer. If you survive and I . . ." She took a deep breath. "I have two daughters, Ray. If something happens to me, I want you to stay away from them. You and the whole society. There's nothing you can tell them about me that they don't already know. Okay?"

"Absolutely. Here." I offered her Ursula's gun. "They'd take this off me anyway."

She took it. "Ray, I'm going to say this quickly and get out of here. You're a decent guy, but you'd better *do what you have to do.* You're sending me away, so I'm relying on you. Whatever it takes. Okay?" I wasn't sure if she was telling me to kill or be killed, and I don't think she knew, either. She turned and scrambled into the woods.

I took a candy out of the crate beside me. It was delicious. Then I stepped out from under the table and vaulted into the open.

CHAPTER SEVENTEEN

I sprinted through the stalls, dodging between the tents and hopping over cables. Someone shouted, "Hey!" and I turned at a right angle and ducked under a sign that said SNOWMAN CONTEST HERE!, then ran around a tarp covered with melting, machine-made snow into the open field. I heard shouts behind me and, because I wasn't really trying to get away, glanced back.

Men, women, and children raced across the field after me. They were slow, even the teenagers, and for a few moments I worried that they wouldn't be able to catch me. Then I saw a pickup bounce across the field in my direction. It was the guards who had replaced Waterproof.

I ran faster, knowing I would only reach the safety of the trees if the truck bottomed out or wrecked.

For a moment I thought they might try to run me down. I prepared to veer off to the side, but the driver slammed on the brakes a dozen yards away and the men in the back aimed their weapons at me. I stopped and raised my hands. "Don't move!" one of them shouted.

"What are you guys doing?" I shouted back, letting my voice crack with fear. Staring down the barrels of their guns, I didn't have to put much effort into acting. "I just want to leave!" I hate to be afraid, but they'd be suspicious if I didn't show some fear, and I hated them for it.

The driver climbed from the truck. Three dozen people were running toward me.

As I expected, they were complete amateurs—they stepped into the gunmen's line of fire and generally milled around me. When they patted me down, they missed the ghost knife.

One boy of about fourteen, sweat running from under his knit cap, took up a position behind me, knife in hand. I told them I would go peacefully, but they didn't care. They made me walk with them toward the field house and continued milling as we trudged through the mud. The smallest of them, a handful of kids that barely came up to my armpits, had enough energy to run wide, looping circles around me. A couple of them had guns, but most had knives, hammers, shovels, and other household tools.

I wanted to look over at the pastor's house, but I didn't. If Zahn was watching, and I suspected he was, I didn't want to give anything away.

Hondo was right beside me, a smear of auto grease on his forehead, and once I'd seen one familiar face, I saw more: one of the stilt walkers, Sue the paramedic, Justy Pivens. None had a white mark that I could see, but they all had the single-minded glare of the sapphire dog's pets.

One of the men walking beside me was a tall guy with a jaw like a train cowcatcher and sullen eyes. He stumbled slightly, then turned toward me, his left eye closing in a slow-motion wink. He said: "Buh buh guh glerr," then his mouth and left arm sagged and he fell onto the grass.

I lunged at him and turned him over. His hat fell off and a thick strand of drool hung from his lip. He was dying right in front of me—dying of a stroke just like Penny and Little Mark in their cells—and there was nothing I could do about it except watch.

I rubbed at the stubble of hair on the top of his head. It only took a moment to find a patch of white skin beneath his hair. The sapphire dog had learned to hide its mark.

The pets moved closer to me, and I held up my hands again. Seven or eight of them fell on me, pressing me down onto the wet grass. They bent my arms behind my back. I cursed at them and tried to struggle free, so they leaned on my arms until I thought my shoulder would pop. I stopped struggling and let them cuff me and pull me upright. Damn. The only way I could get to my ghost knife now would be to *call* it through my own body. No one tried to help Sullen Eyes.

Across the field, I saw a gray Volvo creep out of the parking lot. No one else seemed to notice. Go, Catherine, go.

They shoved me along. As we came near the field house, I saw Preston among the folks still standing guard. He was still holding his double-barreled shotgun, but he didn't seem interested in scaring me anymore.

Behind Preston I saw Pippa Wolfowitz and Graciela. I looked for Graciela's toddler with her tiny earrings, but I didn't see her nearby. Pippa was still wearing the same Santa cap and bulldog expression she'd worn outside Big Penny's house, but underneath her jacket she wore pajamas. She looked up at the sky as though she wanted to study the clouds, then fell over backward and was still. No one moved to help her.

Damn. They were dying all around me.

Pastor Dolan pushed through the crowd. "Where are the two women who were with you?"

The stone-cold way he looked at me gave me a chill, so I smirked at him. "They escaped while you dipshits were chasing me."

He wasn't insulted. Maybe he didn't know how to be insulted anymore. "You'll tell us more soon enough."

"Yeah, sure I will," I said. "Take me to your pet."

Everyone stopped and turned toward me. They looked

to be a half second from stomping the life out of me. I felt a sudden nervous tingle on the back of my neck.

"He isn't a *pet*," the pastor said in a low voice. "Do you hear me? Don't use that word again."

"Sure, sure. But next time you threaten someone, stand on a box first."

He didn't react, just turned away. Hondo grabbed my right arm, and a man I didn't recognize grabbed my left. This was it. I wished my hands were free so I could grab my ghost knife. The entrance to the field house was just ten yards away.

A green light lit the sky on the right. Everyone turned toward it, and I stepped back to get a clear view through the tops of the festival tents.

Green fire had blasted a hole in the roof of the pastor's house. There was a loud boom, then a series of sharp cracks. It sounded almost like fireworks.

A nest of blue lights came through the wall. The whole house appeared to buckle, a piece of roof blasted upward, and we heard the explosion a second or two later.

There was another sudden flare of green flame. "Go, boss," I said under my breath. "Kick his ass."

A section of the downstairs wall suddenly blinked out of existence. The building sagged in on itself. There was a high-pitched sound almost like a scream. The walls shuddered and a column of white flame tore through the entire roof.

Burning wood rained down on the nearby lawn. I had a sick feeling in my gut. I'd never seen Annalise use white fire; maybe it was a spell she kept in reserve.

The walls twisted and collapsed into rubble. I stood in the crowd, watching the pieces of broken shingle and siding burn in the mud. I looked for a figure moving amid the wreckage, a glimpse of a dark coat, but I couldn't see anything.

Boss, please still be alive.

The pastor turned toward Waterproof. "Get together a dozen men and check that out." He glanced back at his house, his expression showing as much concern as he'd show for a toppled Porta Potti. "Actually, bring twenty. With guns. Kill anyone you find over there. We don't want to take any chances with his safety."

Waterproof took about a third of the crowd with him, maybe two dozen people, but these guys weren't operating under military discipline. They marched across the open field in a mob with their mismatched weapons.

I was hustled toward the open door. People stepped over Pippa's body as if she was a rotted log. "I'm cooperating," I snapped. "You don't have to hold my hand. I'm cooperating!"

They didn't let go. My stomach knotted up as I thought about being dragged in front of a predator with my arms pinned. Damn, did I feel stupid.

We went inside, passing a halogen floodlight set on a stand in the back corner. This was the same white room where I'd eaten the church lunch. The tables, chairs, and steam trays had been removed, and the room was flooded with light. I counted four halogens, each set into a corner and each shining onto a pedestal near the far wall. I nearly tripped over the fat black power cables that ran along the base of three of the walls.

And there on the pedestal was the sapphire dog, sitting on a big satin pillow like pampered royalty. Its tail wavered, sometimes weaving slowly and sometimes snapping from one position to the next too quickly for the eye to see.

Its back looked different than I remembered. The last time I'd seen it, it had been smooth like a snake, but now I saw a row of polyps.

It turned its weird, rotating eyes toward me.

My God.

I shut my eyes, trying to think. The floodlights didn't make sense. Regina and Yin had used lights to trap the thing, but the people it fed on—its pets—had never done that. At first they'd tried to get it out of town, then they'd kept it safe. But they'd never kept it *prisoner*. So maybe it wasn't a prisoner right now.

I felt a sudden rush of affection for it. It was trying to control me again. I shut my eyes and focused on the pain in my iron gate, but I couldn't keep them closed. I had to *look*.

"I love you!" I shouted, fear and hatred giving power to my voice. I lunged forward, breaking the grip Hondo and his buddy had on me, then pretending to fall onto the stone floor. I took most of the impact on my shoulder and a little on my forehead. The pain was sharp, but it reminded me why I was there.

Was I in range of the sapphire dog's tongue? The space where its mouth would be was still smooth and unmarked; it wasn't opening its "jaw." I had moved my my cuffed hands behind my knees when Hondo and his buddy caught my arms again.

There was a gunshot outside. Then more shots followed in a sudden rush, including the harsh pecking sound of automatic fire. It faded away, then surged again as people reloaded. I closed my eyes and refused to think about who they might be shooting.

There was a quick double honk of a car horn from outside. After a few seconds, I heard Steve's high, strained voice. "What the heavens is going on here? Who are those men shooting at?" He was trying to push into the room with his gun drawn. No one seemed afraid of it. He started calling people by name.

Of course. No one here had a visible white mark. Steve didn't know everyone had been turned into pets.

I heard him shout, then his gun went off. He cried out "Kerry!" in horror and was shoved into the room, unarmed. "What are you people *doing*?" He looked terrible, pale and drooping, with dark pouches under his eyes. He obviously hadn't even gotten the meager sleep I had. He scanned the room, then gasped when he noticed the sapphire dog. "Oh," he said quietly. "The lights. Good work, everyone."

They stared at him. I passed the cuffs under my feet, then rolled to my knees. I pulled the ghost knife out of the front of my pants and palmed it as best I could.

As soon as my hand touched the spell, the sapphire dog turned toward me. I had its full attention.

"I love you!" I shouted and lunged forward.

The sapphire dog jumped off the pedestal immediately. It knew.

Hondo and the other man pounced on me. I didn't even have time to throw the spell before they pinned me.

I cut a slot in the concrete and dropped the ghost knife into it. The pets would need a jackhammer to get it now.

The sapphire dog hurried toward the wall on its awkward, crumpled-leg gait. Steve had just come in through the door on that side, and he shuffled to intercept it. Neither were quick, but Steve managed to step into its path. He crouched low and held out his arms as though about to catch a running child.

None of the pets tried to stop him, and I knew something was wrong. I remembered the way the sapphire dog found us at the stables, and the way the pastor had immediately run from me when he had no way to know I was planning to kill it, and the way Hondo and his buddy had just pounced on me before they had any way of seeing my ghost knife—the sapphire dog was in their heads.

Not in the heads of the people it had controlled at a distance, like Regina and Ursula, but the heads of people it had fed on and marked.

And there was no way it would let them trap it here, no matter how much they loved it.

I shouted: "Get out of the way!" Steve looked at me in surprise, but it was too late.

The sapphire dog leaped up as if it was jumping into his arms. Its head struck Steve low on his torso and then *sank into him*. Its legs, body, and tail pulled back into a thin column behind that oversized head, like the tentacles of a jellyfish, and it slowly, excruciatingly, passed through Steve's body and the wall behind him.

It couldn't have taken longer than five or six seconds, but it seemed much longer. As it happened, Steve's mouth fell open and a sorrowful expression came over his face. He looked as though he realized he'd done a terrible wrong to someone he cared about.

Then the predator was through and gone. Steve's face went slack and he fell onto the floor in a sloppy mess.

I laid my forehead onto the freezing concrete floor and let out a long string of curses. The predator had not recognized me, or it would have had me shot out in the field. It had seen the ghost knife as soon as I touched it, though, and it had fled. Steve was dead because of me. The sapphire dog had not even bothered to feed on him.

I had failed.

Hondo and his pal still held on to me. I struggled, but they were using all of their weight. I was sure the next thing I was going to feel was a bullet punching through my skull.

"Move aside," someone said. The speaker's voice was low and gravelly and heavily accented. "You will move aside! I have only come to talk." He pronounced *will* as "vill" and *have* as "haf" like a cartoon villain.

They moved aside and Zahn limped in, the right side of his head scorched black and his right arm withered to the bone. His clothes were in tatters, and his left leg was a mess of raw meat. Annalise had hit him hard, and I was glad she'd gotten her licks in. Still, just seeing him walk in here instead of her filled me with an empty, grieving rage.

Zahn didn't act like a man with critical injuries, though. He didn't even walk like a scrawny old man. "Is it not here?" he shouted, his voice raw. "I will speak to it immediately!"

The sapphire dog's pets stared at him with the same inscrutable gaze the predator had given me.

"Very well," Zahn said. "I will speak to underlings." He walked up to a young woman in a long red coat, seemingly chosen at random. "I have sealed this town off from the rest of the world. Unless I lift this seal, no one will ever come here again, and no one but me will ever leave. You will be trapped—and starving—on a world teeming with food. Again."

From somewhere behind me, Pastor Dolan said: "What do you want?"

Zahn turned toward Dolan. "I will take you from this place," he said. "As my captive."

Everyone who had a gun raised it in unison and began shooting at Zahn. The old man's skull split open as a shotgun blast tore through it. He staggered, and bits of blood and flesh splashed off his body under the barrage. God, the sound was deafening.

Bullets ricocheted around us. One skipped off the floor near my hand, and Hondo collapsed heavily across my neck and shoulders.

The firing stopped after a few seconds. I glanced around the room. Six people lay dead or dying on the floor, and eight others were pressing their hands against bloody wounds. The nearest corpse had her face toward me. It was Karlene.

I had a sudden vision of her dog Chuckles, sitting on a

blue tarp in the back of her truck. Was he still alive? If so, I hoped he'd find someone to care for him.

Someone behind me threw an empty nine-mil on the concrete floor. Preston's shotgun and a pair of rifles were discarded, too. Obviously, they hadn't brought enough spare ammunition.

The old man had fallen on his back into the corner. He raised his left arm and made a horrible choking sound. The woman in the long red coat lay on the floor beside him, a bright spray of arterial blood pulsing out of her thigh onto the wall. I shrugged Hondo's body off me and got to my knees. Zahn was still making that *hrk hrk hrk* noise.

Then I realized he was laughing.

He sat up. Most of his head and face were gone, and his body was riddled with bloody exit and entrance wounds. His only good eye rolled in his head as he looked around the room.

He saw the bleeding woman beside him and lunged at her wound, ruined mouth gaping.

I shut my eyes. My stomach felt sour, and my skin crawled. I wanted to run for the door, but I could hear a couple of the pets nearby reloading. The sounds the old man was making were revolting. They weren't the wet slurping noises you hear in a horror movie. They were the moans a connoisseur makes during a fine meal.

I couldn't help myself. I looked at him again.

As he gulped down the blood, his wounds were healing, even the ones Annalise had given him. *Raw and fresh,* I wanted to say again, but the thought made my stomach twist. Annalise used that same spell to heal herself, but at least she limited herself to meat bought at the supermarket.

The woman died before Zahn finished healing, so he started eating the meat.

"I don't understand," Pastor Dolan said, his voice flat and toneless. "Why didn't you die?"

"Of course you don't understand," the old man said between bites. "This world is full of things you and your food do not understand. Chief among them is me. You can't kill me with those guns, but they do hurt. If you hurt me again, I will leave you here to starve."

"I don't want to be captured again," Dolan said. I didn't want to look at him. I didn't want to see the expression on his face. I also didn't want to turn my back on Zahn.

"The people who held you captive before didn't understand what you are. They would have fed you if they knew how, but they didn't. I know more about you, and I can guarantee that you—and your new selves—will never starve again."

New selves? That didn't sound good.

"I don't want to be captured again. I nearly starved to death the last time." Pastor Dolan's singsong voice sounded a little closer to me.

"You have been captured already," Zahn said. "You and your food."

"I know this. I tried to escape many times."

"If you come away with me, I will see that you are fed. I don't want to destroy you, like this one does." He pointed at me. "I want to grow in power with you. Or you can starve here. The choice is yours."

"I don't really have a choice," Pastor Dolan said. "Isn't that right?"

The sapphire dog poked its head though the hole in the cinder block. Zahn looked at it and smiled. "It is right," he said as he tore a long muscle out of the runner's thigh. "You have belonged to me all along." He stuffed the meat into his mouth, opening his jaws unnaturally wide to make it fit.

The sapphire dog stepped through the opening in the

wall and curled up on the floor. Four of the uninjured townspeople moved in front of it, blocking my view. Damn. I was probably too far to use my ghost knife anyway.

Then Zahn turned his bloody face to me. He smiled in a way I didn't like. "And now for you."

CHAPTER EIGHTEEN

Without Hondo, the man holding me couldn't keep me on the floor. He was strong, but I thrashed desperately. I knocked him down and moved away from the old man.

Unfortunately, the sapphire dog's pets had clustered in front of the exit, blocking it with their bodies. If I ran that way, they could simply grab me and hold me for Zahn.

So I moved away from him in a direct line. I only managed a few steps before three or four others took hold of me. I struggled but couldn't break free. My legs were kicked out from under me, and I fell to my knees again.

Someone stepped on my calf, pinning it to the stone floor. The pain in my kneecap was intense. I tried to glance back to see who it was, but I didn't have that much freedom of motion.

Zahn stood, took a linen napkin from his pocket, and delicately wiped the blood off his face. He began to resemble the little old man I'd seen on the Wilburs' back lawn.

"Damn," I said, trying to keep tremors of fear out of my voice. "You carry a napkin around? I guess cannibals never know when they'll need to freshen up."

"That word holds no revulsion for me. I have done many, many things that you would consider a horror, but to me they are the price of power and extended life. I do not even think of this"—he held up the bloody cloth—"as distasteful anymore, unless they soil themselves in fear.

"But you find many things to be a horror, yes?" He began walking toward me. I tried to move my pinned leg, but I didn't have the leverage. "I enjoy killing your people, Mr. Twenty Palace Society. I enjoy seeing your numbers dwindle. You were so close to winning, not so many decades ago, yes? Or maybe you don't know that. You were very close to making yourselves kings of the world."

He stopped in place and held his arms out as though a crowd was cheering for him. "But there were always some, like me, who refused to play by your rules. Individualists. Rebels. And how many palaces do you have left now? Eleven? Ten? Six, perhaps? And you have no more dreamers, yes? Soon your kind will be gone from the world, and free men will be free."

He started toward me again, taking his time. I didn't like seeing him so confident and relaxed. I wanted to shake him up. "Free to bring predators here to feed on other people . . ." Maybe he no longer thought of himself as human, but I pressed on. "And feeding on them yourself, too. The world would be better off without you."

Zahn smiled. He should have packed some floss along with his linen napkin. "What would the world be without magic?"

Then, finally, he stepped on the slot I'd cut in the floor.

I said: "What would this town be without magic?" I closed my eyes and *called* my ghost knife.

It cut through Zahn's foot and flew into my open hand. The old man gasped as a jet of black steam shot out of the top of his black leather shoe. I ducked low, letting it blast over me.

The people holding me cried out in shock and pain as the steam struck them, and I broke free. I kicked the leg

of whoever was standing on me, knocking him into a
pile, then dropped to the floor and rolled away from the
scalding blast. With a twist of my wrist, I slid the ghost
knife through the handcuff chain.

I scrambled to my feet as Zahn fell to one knee. He
clasped his hands over the energy blasting out of his foot.
I charged at him, grabbed him by his scrawny neck, and
scraped the ghost knife down his spine.

Another, larger blast of black steam roared out of him.
I gripped my spell in my teeth, grabbed Zahn's leather
belt, and lifted his tiny, withered body off the ground.

I held him in front of me and ran at the human shield
around the sapphire dog. The steam made the pets fall
back, covering their faces and shrieking. They didn't
break and run, but they did fall.

I spun Zahn behind me, dropping him to the floor in
case more pets came at me from behind. He caught hold
of the lapel of my jacket as I let him go, and I wasted precious seconds slipping out of it. Then the sapphire dog
was right in front of me. I grabbed the ghost knife out of
my teeth.

The predator split into three and vanished.

I wanted to roar in frustration, but I didn't have the
time. The pets were all around me. I dropped to the floor
next to Steve's legs. My hand fell on a gun lying against
the wall, and I grabbed it, then scrambled through the
hole the sapphire dog had made.

I heard shouting and commotion behind me. A hand
grabbed at my pant leg, but I fought free. The second hole
to the outside was just a couple of feet away. I scrambled
through.

Then I was outside. I ran, holding the found gun by
the barrel.

I heard two quick gunshots, but I had no idea if the
shooter was aiming at me. I ran through the tents to
make myself a more difficult target. I felt faster without

my jacket, but that wasn't going to last. I was cold, wet, and hungry. The only real weapon I had was my ghost knife, which was useless against the pets. If the old man summoned another floating storm, I was dead.

I stole a cinnamon bun out of a booth and, still running, took a bite. It was sweet and sticky and exactly the fuel I needed.

There was movement ahead. A teenage boy stepped out from behind a plastic tent. He raised an old revolver, but I was too fast for him. I hit him hard and ripped the gun out of his hand as he fell.

I passed the last of the stalls and hit open ground. There were no more pets in front of me, but there were plenty behind. I could hear them yelling instructions to one another. I would have guessed that, with the predator in their heads, they wouldn't need to talk to one another, but that wasn't the way it worked, apparently.

I had five options: the two feeder roads across the open field; the parking-lot exit; the horse trail that connected the fairgrounds with the stables; and finally the pastor's church and ruined house. The feeder roads and parking lot pretty much guaranteed I'd be shot. The horse trail was the safest in the short term, but the locals knew the landscape and would run me to ground eventually.

The last choice had something the others didn't— Annalise. Even if she couldn't help me—and I hoped she was still alive and dangerous, even if only barely—I couldn't leave her behind. Besides, I hoped she would have something I needed.

So I ran toward the rubble of the pastor's house, swerving erratically in case someone took another shot.

At the edge of the field, I scrambled up the small hill bordering the church property. A bullet smacked into the dirt beside me, and goose bumps ran down my back. When I made it to the top of the hill, I looked back. The people of Washaway, teen to senior citizen, ran toward me in a straggling mob, weaving between the stalls. A few carried guns, but most had other weapons.

I turned back toward the church. Waterproof Cowboy and his crew lay scattered across the grass. All of their guns were slag, and all of their heads were missing.

I ran toward the rubble of the pastor's collapsed house. I remembered the way parts of the building seemed to vanish and hoped Annalise hadn't vanished with it.

There. Annalise lay motionless beneath a pile of scorched wood. I stuffed both guns into the back of my waistband and hauled her out by the wrist. She was even smaller than Zahn, but the wood was heavy and the nails snagged on her clothes. It took three tries to heave her into my arms. She wasn't missing any limbs and I couldn't see any blood, but she looked like just another corpse.

Damn. Annalise couldn't help. The pets were nearly at the bottom of the hill.

The back door to the church was only a few yards away. I ran for it, cradling Annalise in my arms. "Wakey, boss." I lifted her onto my shoulder. "Now would be a good time to wake up."

The fastest of the pets had reached the bottom of the hill. I had the ghost knife in hand, ready to cut through the lock, but the door swung inward when I turned the knob. Thank God for country churches.

I rushed into the food bank and set Annalise on the floor, then I slammed the door and flipped the dead bolt lever to lock it.

The room was dark. I switched on the light. Hands jiggled the knob and fists pounded at the main door behind us. I put my shoulder against one of the metal shelves and tipped it against the door, pinning it shut.

I ran back across the room into the church. There was a dead bolt on the main door and I threw it closed, but the bright, beautiful stained-glass windows in here weren't going to keep anyone out.

I rushed back into the food bank and locked the door. After I wedged a high-backed wooden chair under the doorknob, I knelt by Annalise.

A gunshot blasted through the back door. I tipped over another shelf and wedged it against the upper part of the doorway.

Bullets pinged around me. The tilted shelf had spilled seven or eight fifty-pound bags of flour onto the floor, and I sprawled behind them. I kicked the pastor's desk against the wall to make room. Bags of dirt would have protected me better, but this was the best I could do.

I grabbed Annalise and dragged her across the floor toward my meager shelter. I had missed my chance to kill the sapphire dog, but I wasn't ready to give up. Unfortunately, I wasn't going to get at the predator until I'd gotten through its pets first. The two guns jabbing into my hip bones might have helped me with that, but I didn't want to start gunning down innocent people who couldn't control themselves because I couldn't do my fucking job. I didn't care what the sapphire dog had done to them, I didn't want to fight *them*.

What I wanted was the white ribbon Annalise had used to make that man outside the Sunset fall unconscious.

I searched through her jacket, remembering Penny and Little Mark lying dead on the floor of a tiny jail cell, and Pippa falling onto her back. Maybe if I killed the sapphire dog, the pets really could go back to being themselves again. Maybe, just maybe, they wouldn't fall over dead. But I had to be quick, because I didn't know how much time the pets had left, and bullets were still coming through the door.

Annalise looked uninjured, but she was completely still. I couldn't even tell if she was breathing or not. It was as if Zahn had switched her off.

The white ribbon wasn't there. I searched again. She only had two ribbons left. Both were green. I knew what they could do, and it was most definitely lethal.

I spit out a string of curses. The sounds of breaking glass came from the church, then a series of gunshots blew through the door. I knew they would be in the room in a minute or two, and I knew what that would mean.

I stuffed the green ribbons into my pocket. I wouldn't use them—I knew I wouldn't—but I wanted to have them just in case.

The gunshots stopped and the kicking began. The mob was trying to bash their way in—even the dead-bolted door that led into the church rattled under the assault. They were coming from all sides. I scrambled to my feet and shoved over the last of the shelves, tipping it against the interior church door just as it began to swing open. I ducked back under cover.

I took the guns out of the back of my pants, then laid Annalise on top of the bags of flour. Her tattoos made her bulletproof; the same spells that had protected her from Merpati's gunmen would protect her from the pets' guns—and they'd protect me, too, if I stayed low enough. That was as much barricade as I was likely to get.

I aimed the old revolver at the door. Damn. Was I really going to do this?

Do what you have to do, Catherine had said. *Whatever it takes*. I remembered little Shannon Conner looking up at me, pleading with me to kill the sapphire dog and give her grandmother back to her.

When was I going to stop holding back?

I squeezed off four shots. A return volley immediately blasted through the door and wall. The bullets poured through like hail, a terrifying mix of rifle and handgun and shotgun blasts.

My skin prickled as I lay flat. I'd never heard such a

deafening wall of gunfire, and I thought the incredible, oppressive sound of it alone might kill me.

The volley ended quickly. My ears were ringing, but I could still hear the clicking of empty weapons.

Morning sunlight shone through the holes in the walls like a rack of spears, illuminating the floating plaster dust. I lifted both guns and squeezed the triggers until they were empty.

A second volley came through, but the gunfire was thinner and more scattered. A ricochet tugged at the heel of my shoe, but it didn't touch me. Finally, the shots petered out and all I could hear was the clicking of empty guns.

The pets began to smash through the walls with rifle butts, expanding the openings. I lifted Annalise onto the desk, taking care not to kick the cord of the portable stereo. The ceiling was unfinished, and I could see water pipes and BX cable running between the rafters. I jumped onto the desk and stood over her. With my ghost knife, I cut a two-and-a-half-foot length out of the water pipe. Water gushed freely onto the tile floor as I hefted it. It was heavy, but it would have to do.

More arms and legs were pushing through the growing gaps in the wall. The pets who had been smashing against the interior church door had quit, probably to come around the building. They kicked and bashed at the wall and door, then started trying to squirm through. All I could do was wait.

I reached down and pressed Play on Dolan's portable stereo. It was the old-fashioned kind that played CDs. After a couple of seconds, a Spanish guitar version of "Rudolph the Red-Nosed Reindeer" began to play. Holiday music? It was one more reason to hate the world. I watched the pets breaking in.

The waiting was miserable, and my helplessness and fear made me want to scream. I didn't. I stayed silent and still, and I funneled everything I had into a furious red rage.

If only I had Zahn in front of me, or Stroud, the man who gave the predator to Regina so many years ago. Whether I was a match for them or not, they were the ones I wanted to face. Because of them, the sapphire dog was here and alive, and maybe it would get free again and do this over and over all around the world. All this death and misery was the reason the society fought and killed. Because of this. *This.*

But I couldn't vent my rage at Zahn or Stroud because I didn't have them here; I only had the crazed, ruined people of Washaway. I knew the pets weren't in control of themselves. I knew the sapphire dog was really to blame for the death of Little Mark and so many others. But my anger wasn't logical, and it was so terribly, terribly strong.

Someone wrenched the bullet-ridden door open, shattering the hinges and opening a space big enough for a person to enter. It was Bushy Bill Stookie, and I was almost grateful to him that the fight would finally start.

He laid his meaty hands on the metal shelving and pushed at it, scraping it across the wet tile floor. Others pushed at him to get by, and by then one of the holes in the wall was large enough for more people to squeeze through.

They were all men in this first wave—all strong and heavy, with baseball bats and rifle butts and iron mallets. They sloshed through the water, climbing over the toppled metal shelves toward me. Someone outside let out a trilling, alien war cry, and everyone took it up. They howled as they came at me.

I kicked the portable stereo off the desk. It landed in the water still pouring out of the overhead pipe and splashed onto the tile floor.

Nine men froze in place, muscles twitching. I made

sure to count them carefully, so I wouldn't forget. A big, brawny woman pushed through the crowd and stepped into the water. She grimaced and jolted up straight. Ten.

Then the room went dark and silent. Everyone collapsed over the metal shelves, and the woman fell backward through the doorway, bowling through the crowd behind her. So much for saving them from the sapphire dog.

The only light I had left was the daylight shining through the door and the damaged walls. The people pushing their way into the room now were little more than backlit silhouettes. At least I wouldn't have to see their faces.

They were coming with knives, woodworking tools, axe handles, and empty guns. I lifted the iron pipe high and held my left arm low. I didn't have a shield; the tattoos on my forearm would have to do. I put the ghost knife between my teeth. They let out another war scream—a piercing animalistic keening—and I felt like screaming right back at them, but I kept it inside instead, channeling that raw energy to my arms and eyes.

The first guy to get close tripped over Big Bill and fell to his knee in front of me, so I smashed the pipe against his shoulder, knocking him against the one behind him, then I hit the next one hard on the edge of the wrist, sending his hammer bounding off the wall just as two more came close, keeping their balance better this time, and I smashed elbow and shoulder as fast and as hard as I could, blocking a sharpened hoe with my protected arm, but now the pets were crowding in, stumbling sometimes but not enough for me to keep ahead of every swing, of every hand reaching for me, of every sound they made, because I wasn't even looking at their faces anymore, I didn't have time to guess the attack they'd make based on their eyes or body position, they were just a mass of bodies rushing at me, and I laid out with my pipe, swinging everywhere with all my strength against people I'd told Catherine I didn't want to hurt but here I was, breaking arms and collarbones, and the first time a bat struck the bony point of my hip, the pain frightened and enraged me so much that I smashed the man wielding it right on the side of his head, and then every dark shape seemed to be tinged with red as I slapped away attacks with my forearm and crushed bones with the pipe even though many of them didn't even have weapons, just hands that reached to pull me down, so I smashed those, too, watching for knives and swings for my head, and I smashed wrists and elbows and collarbones and fragile, fragile skulls as the pets kept coming for me, climbing over the ones I broke, stumbling, slipping in water and blood and tripping over fallen bodies, then I felt a sudden sharp pain in my calf and looked down to see a girl no older than thirteen stabbing a long knife into my leg, and my fury and adrenaline and hatred and rage made it so easy—so easy!—to slam that iron pipe across both her little arms and I know she screamed even though I couldn't hear it over the noise the other pets were making but *God* I saw her expression and the whole world should have stopped right at that moment but they kept coming and I kept fighting and I knew right then that it didn't matter whether I lived through this, in fact better if I didn't because I was becoming everything that was raw and evil in this world and I didn't deserve to be in it anymore, so I screamed, finally, letting out all my anger and hatred at predators and peers and most of all myself for what I was doing, because I was not going to stop, not ever, until I had done this damn job, and the ghost knife that fell out of my mouth began to zip around the room with the speed of a sparrow, circling me like a rock on a string, and I just kept hitting and hitting, because I wasn't tired at all, evil men never tire of doing evil.

Then one of them—Ponytail Sue—finally got the idea to kick the desk I was standing on. It skidded to the side and I overbalanced, falling into the pets. They were crammed together as tightly as kids at the front of a rock concert. I swung at the nearest one, but three or four people caught my arm and the pipe was yanked out of my grip.

They grabbed me, hands everywhere, pulling my clothes, my hair, my skin, scratching me, screaming at me, bearing me to the floor. Two inches of water splashed up my nose and down my throat. With my free left hand, I reached into my pocket and pulled out one of Annalise's green ribbons, and as I sloshed on the floor, I looked up and saw two kids, neither older than sixteen, lunging for me with knives in their hands and cold, raging murder in their eyes. I slapped the ribbon onto the top of someone's red rubber boot, and I saw the green firelight shine on them.

I closed my eyes. What happened next was something I could not watch.

CHAPTER NINETEEN

When the sound of the fire and the throbbing of the protective spells on my chest finally died away, I opened my eyes again. The room was full of bones. The water sloshed back and forth, and soot and ash made a greasy film on top.

Some of those bones were small. Very small.

Annalise was still lying on top of the desk, and as I expected, she wasn't even singed. I kept looking at her, so small and frail-seeming, but so filled with power, because I didn't want to look at what I'd done.

A shadow moved on the wall. I turned back and saw another person at the door. There were two more behind him and who knows how many I couldn't see.

My dirty work wasn't finished. I moved my foot through the murky water until I found my length of pipe, then I pulled it out of a pile of bones. They came at me.

"They" were a skinny boy of about fourteen, a middle-aged woman with the hunched back of a vulture, and an old man with too much belly and too little biceps. They were all holding hatchets. I could see by their expressions that they weren't going to back down. I didn't need them to. I had my pipe.

It took less than half a minute for me to put all three on the ground. I left them alive because I could, but they wouldn't be bothering anyone for a while.

They screamed curses at me. I was the one who wanted to kill their beloved sapphire dog, and they were sure I deserved to die. I didn't bother to disagree. I felt my ghost knife nearby and *called* it to me. For once, it didn't feel good to have it back. I dragged the last three pets outside.

I carried Annalise to her van and laid her in the back. Then I found a tow truck near the edge of the parking lot with a full ashtray and a pile of fast-food wrappers on the floor. I cracked the ignition and backed it into the corner of the church, smashing through the wood frame and breaking partway inside.

Then I cut my way into the building with the ghost knife and made a slit in the truck's gas tank. I used a book of matches to set a grease-stained brown paper bag alight and let the flames spread. The pews were already engulfed when I ran back to the van.

Someone was going to investigate the deaths in Washaway. Someday. The fire was clumsy, but it would at least explain away the charred bones I'd left behind, as long as no one thought too hard about it.

I had Annalise and I had the van. Leaving town didn't make sense, but I could certainly hide inside Steve's house until another peer arrived. How long could that be? I'd failed to kill the sapphire dog more than once, and now it was with Zahn, a sorcerer strong enough to take out my boss. Sure, I'd surprised him once with a sucker punch, but he'd be ready for me next time. It wasn't as if I had a big bag of tricks.

I had every reason to run. I didn't even know where Zahn had gone, and I certainly wasn't going to drive around looking for his Mercedes with more pets on the loose.

But then I realized there was only one way to transport the sapphire dog.

I turned the key in the ignition and pulled into the road.

My calf started to ache. I looked down and saw blood

on my pants. I'd been stabbed. I was also wet, jacketless, and a fucking child-killer. I began to shiver and had to pull to the shoulder of the road until the feeling passed.

I turned the heat on and held my fingers in front of the vent. Then I found a first-aid kit behind the seat and taped a wad of gauze over the stab wound. It wasn't a large cut, certainly not large enough to kill over. I rubbed my hands together to warm them. I'd think about those people tomorrow. Not today. Today I would think about the ones who still needed killing.

I drove past the Breakleys' home and up the long hill toward the Wilbur estate. The gate was wide open. I drove up the long empty driveway and parked just out of sight of the house.

"Don't go anywhere, boss."

I climbed from the van and closed the door as quietly as I could. There was no sound other than the wind through the trees. I jogged uphill toward the house, keeping low.

Beside the house, at the edge of the asphalt parking lot, I found Esteban's plumbing truck. I went around to the other side and found a half dozen corpses. They were pets, and they had been beaten to death. The nearest one was the pastor—he had a dent in the side of his head about the size of Zahn's fist.

I couldn't beat Zahn in a fair fight, and I didn't see any reason to try. I ran to the corner of the building, squeezed between it and two well-trimmed bushes. The unlit woven Christmas lights snagged at my shirt. I peeked into the nearest window. The room had stacks of fabric and a little sewing machine set where it would catch the sun. No people, though.

I heard broken glass from the backyard. I hoped it was Zahn.

I was only going to get one chance. Jumping out of the bushes wasn't good enough. I needed to hit him before he knew he was being hit.

I cut the lock on the front door, then rushed into the entrance hall. The house was dark, quiet, and smelled like spoiled pork. I rushed to the nearest door on the left and pushed it open. The stink of rotting flesh washed over me. Stephanie Wilbur lay on the floor, still in her green-and-gold outfit, and it was clear she'd been there awhile. Someone had shot her in the chest and closed the door on her.

I hurried to the windows. There were three of them, each twice as tall as me and arched at the top, but made of individual squares of glass no larger than my hand. They gave me a good view of the open back of the truck. I crouched low and pressed my face against the glass, looking toward the backyard. I couldn't see far.

I heard them before I saw them. I stepped away from the window and curled my arm against my chest, ghost knife ready. They were talking very loudly, very excitedly. Or one of them was. Zahn spoke German in a low, somewhat bemused voice, while the other voice was loud but halting, as though the speaker was struggling with the language.

Then they came into view. Zahn was carrying the Plexiglas cage from the cottage, and Ursula was carrying a car battery. The sapphire dog lounged on the bottom of the pen, brightly lit by the floodlights at the corners. It was facing away from me. Ursula babbled enthusiastically.

They did not look up at the house and did not suspect I was watching. When they came about even with me, I threw the ghost knife.

There was only one target that made sense. Ursula wasn't important, and Zahn was too powerful for me to take on. Any fight between us would just set the predator free again and get me killed.

So I aimed straight for the back of the sapphire dog's neck. This time, the creature was facing away from me and trapped inside Zahn's cage. This time it couldn't get away. The ghost knife sliced through the window pane with only a slight *tik*, and then it was through the Plexi and the predator.

I immediately *called* it back. It zipped through the sapphire dog's neck a second time. The creature's head tipped forward and rolled free in the bottom of the cage.

The ghost knife landed in my hand at the same moment that Zahn reacted. He said: "Ah!" and gaped at the predator.

Both of them looked up at me. Ursula glanced at the predator, threw the car battery onto the wet lawn, and turned back at me, her face wild with hate. Then she took off toward the front of the building.

Zahn dropped the now-dark Plexiglas cage. *"Scheiss doch!"* he said, his voice seeming to come from everywhere at once. He raised his arm toward me and opened his palm.

Six shining, buzzing objects came at me, wavering like guided missiles and leaving glowing silver contrails behind them.

Time to go.

I ran for the door, hopping over Stephanie's corpse. The missiles punched through the window glass, and I saw they weren't missiles at all—they were some sort of worm as long and as thick as my thumb, and the little round opening at the front was ringed with tiny, jagged teeth.

Damn. Annalise was wrong. Zahn had brought predators with him.

I rushed into the main hall just as Ursula burst through the front door. She raised a rock the size of a woman's shoe above her head and charged at me, screaming. Guess she'd run out of guns.

I ran at her because I refused to run away. Two of the worms punched through the wall on the right, then two more came a moment behind. Three turned toward me, but the farthest one began to arc toward Ursula.

Damn. As they came close to me, I juked to the left. The worms zipped by, and just being near them made my skin feel sticky and hot. Ursula kept running straight at me—either she didn't notice the predator flying at her, or she didn't care.

I threw my ghost knife. It zipped across the room with astonishing speed and sliced through the worm as it came within inches of her flank. The worm disappeared and reappeared at the spot where it had punched through the wall. It went after her again, and since she was coming at me, it was flying at both of us.

I *reached* for my ghost knife again but didn't watch for it to come into my hand. I had predators on both sides of me and Ursula, too. Not good. And where were the other two worms?

There were stairs at the far side of the room, but I wasn't going to get to them without a fight. Ursula swung the rock in a vicious downward hammer swing, but she'd telegraphed it from ten feet away. I slipped it, grabbed hold of the collar of her ski jacket, and tugged her off course. She stumbled into the sewing room door, smashing through it and sprawling on the floor.

Right beside Stephanie's body. And there, sticking out of Stephanie's corpse, were the tail ends of two shiny worms, wriggling like they were burrowing into an apple. Just as I'd hoped.

I charged into the room and hauled Stephanie's body off the ground. It felt sluggish and heavy, and the room filled with a nasty wet odor. I forced myself to ignore all that and rushed toward the door, getting between Ursula and Zahn's predators.

All four worms zipped straight into the dead body, attracted to whatever meat they could find. And while I knew the society didn't want me to use them against a human enemy like Ursula, I didn't think they'd mind if I used a corpse as a shield.

Then Stephanie's head jerked up. She opened her rotted eyes and looked directly at me.

I screamed something unintelligible and shoved her, stumbling, into the main room. I heard Ursula getting to her feet behind me, and I ducked through the door. I didn't want my enemies on both sides of me.

Stephanie wobbled, barely able to keep her balance, as the worms disappeared under her stained clothes. Ursula had found a pair of scissors somewhere and was cursing at me in her native language, whatever it was, as she stumbled through the door. I backed away from them both, wondering how I would get to the hall, then the kitchen, and finally the back door, because I expected Zahn to step through the open front door at any moment. And I knew I'd be a dead man if he found me here.

A blast of white fire tore through the wall near the front door. The flames looked like they were roaring through an invisible hose four feet thick, and the spell came from the same spot where Zahn had been standing when I hit the sapphire dog. Maybe he wasn't coming through the front door after all.

The white fire began to sweep slowly across the room like a flashlight beam, incinerating doors, walls, and support posts. I heard, again, the sound of screaming that I'd heard when the pastor's house had been destroyed, but because I was close to the spell, I could tell that it wasn't just one scream but dozens, maybe hundreds of voices—as if the fire still held the deaths of all the lives it had taken.

I jumped back, hitting the edge of the stairs, then vaulted up onto them. Ursula threw herself to the floor as the beam of fire reached her, and Stephanie—or the creatures inside her—didn't have the same control. It seemed to suddenly lose all strength and collapsed to the floor.

The fire churned through the opposite wall, then dipped down through the floor. I retreated upstairs, watching the bottom of the staircase burn to ashes.

Then the fire stopped. The scorched edges of the wooden floor and walls sputtered with pale flames for a moment but quickly went out. A loud crash from the left drew my attention, and I saw the wall buckle.

Ursula stared up at me from the floor. Her face was pale and her eyes wide with shock. Death had come awfully close to her. She turned and scrambled on her hands and knees toward the front door. Stephanie was nowhere in sight. Hopefully, she'd burned to cinders.

I glanced to my right and looked through the hole that blast of fire had bored through the house. There was Zahn, still standing just where I'd left him, Plexi cage on the ground at his side. The cage looked different—rounder—but I didn't have the time to study it. Zahn smiled, drew his arm back, and made a throwing motion. A chunk of the wall disappeared at the edge of the fire-blasted hole, then another, larger piece of the wall between the sewing room and the room I was in popped out of existence.

Whatever it was, it was coming right at me.

I sprinted up the stairs and leaped to the left. The invisible thing he'd thrown passed behind me, erasing the steps and wiping away part of the upstairs floor. And it had grown larger, too. I looked through the hole it left at the open mountainside and wondered just how far it would go before the spell stopped turning something into nothing.

Just ahead was the servants' stairs leading down to the back door. I ran to the top as another jet of white fire swept through the floor below, destroying the lower flight and wall beyond the way a lazy hand might clear fog off a misty window.

I turned and ran back the other way, leaping over the gap in the floor. The whole building shifted and jolted, and I fell to the threadbare carpet. Somewhere close, lumber cracked and splintered, making noises as loud as gunshots. I needed to get out of this house and out of Zahn's sights as fast as I could, and the most direct way was through the big arching front windows.

The room with the white sheets over the furniture was just ahead. I lunged upward and threw my shoulder against the door. It didn't open—it broke into pieces, already cracked from the collapsing jamb above it.

Once through, I fell to the floor, sliding on my knees along the sloping floorboards. The room was collapsing toward a huge hole in the center, and I could see the piles of basement clutter all the way down at the bottom.

The whole house shuddered. A wardrobe tilted away from the wall and slammed to the floor. I struggled to my feet as it slid at me, and I tried to jump up and run along the flat back of it but ended up clumsily stumbling across it instead.

I sprawled on the floor again as the entire house lurched. Plaster dust fell onto the back of my neck, and I managed to stand. I did not want to die in here. Not like this. Another blast of white fire sliced upward through the floor, cutting the wall with the tall front windows from the rest of the house.

Everything *leaned* toward the front, and I thought the whole building might fold up right then, pinching me into jelly. There was no way to get out by the front—the gaps were too iffy to jump, and I couldn't trust the floor to hold me even if I made it across. I had to try the back of the house.

The floor dropped beneath me—just a foot—but it

was enough to slam me to my knees again. I imagined myself falling backward onto all that clutter below: the overturned chairs, furniture corners, everything. At this height I'd be lucky to only break my back. Goose bumps ran down my back and arms, and I scrambled on my hands and knees toward the door.

Stephanie came toward me.

God, the smell was awful. I struggled to my feet, determined not to die on my knees. She was standing on a cloud of silver smoke a foot or two off the buckled floorboards. Where her eyes should have been, two worms wagged back and forth, their mouths gaping wide enough to show little teeth.

The wall behind her suddenly vanished, and I knew another spell was coming. I lunged at her just as she reached me, but I was faster. Her ankle squished like a bag of jelly when I grabbed it, but I squeezed tight and pulled, tipping her off balance. She fell back as the spell advanced, and I leapt up toward the broken doorway.

Zahn's spell swept over her and erased her from the world. I grabbed the edge of the doorframe and pulled myself through, barely clearing the edge of the spell.

I scurried along the hall toward Regina's room. She had a window in there, even if getting out that way would leave me on the wrong side of the house. The floor was so crooked that I had to run along the corner where it met the wall. The building groaned and shuddered, and something somewhere close snapped. The sound was as loud as a sledgehammer's blow.

Regina's door was already open, although her bed had slid against the crooked frame. I climbed over it, kicking at the covers as they tried to tangle my legs. I tread on Regina's framed photos, smashing the glass.

The exterior wall leaned above me. When I lifted the window, it slid open like a blessing. I caught hold of the bottom of the sill and started to pull myself through just as everything began to come apart with a sound like a series of small explosions. My footing fell away and the wall rushed toward me. In a burst of desperate strength, I pulled myself through the open window, ignoring the sawdust billowing into my face and the shards of glass striking it.

The wall plummeted around me as I lurched through it. I tumbled down the outside of the house, feeling as though I had used the last of my strength and willpower. I fell into the grass, and somehow landed on the side of the house, practically right on the spot where Fat Guy had been crouching when I'd cut his shotgun apart.

I forced myself to sit up. I was exhausted, and when I looked up, I saw Zahn and Ursula standing where I'd left them. Both were staring at me; Ursula looked pale and shell-shocked; Zahn had a grim smile on his face.

I couldn't make myself care anymore. I'd destroyed the sapphire dog, just as I'd said I would, and I didn't have any more willpower left. Not after everything I'd done. I was finished, and they could see it on my face.

The Plexiglas cage behind Ursula and Zahn had somehow shrunk. I looked at it more closely and saw that it wasn't only the cage that had changed shape. Everything—space itself—had bent toward the cut in the sapphire dog's neck. The cage, the battery, and the ground they rested on bowed inward as though the world was being pulled into the predator's body.

But Zahn didn't see it because he was focused on me. He opened his coat and drew a playing card from an inside pocket with well-practiced ease. The warp suddenly expanded, and the edges trembled as though under tremendous strain. I could feel the distortion inside me, like an urge to scream.

Zahn turned toward it, surprised. Ursula gasped. The warp suddenly swelled and both of their bodies twisted as though they had stepped into a funhouse mirror.

Then the warp released in a single overwhelming blast. I remember the light, but I don't think there was any sound. I felt myself silently lifted up and thrown across the grass.

The light was bright and pure. It filled everything, and it seemed to be full of watching eyes.

I woke on the grass at the base of the hill a couple of dozen feet from where I'd been. Nothing seemed to be broken. I snapped my fingers and heard the sound, which was a tremendous relief.

I checked that I still had my ghost knife, then moved toward the house. Ursula and Zahn lay on the lawn. They weren't whole, though. You couldn't have made a whole body out of both of them combined. There was no blood anywhere, just a lack of parts.

Then I saw a flash of blue near the front of the house. I walked around the bodies, trying not to look at them. I felt hollowed out, and I wasn't ready to fill that empty space with the sight of more dead people, even these.

On the front lawn, the two halves of the sapphire dog's body were fading in and out, appearing here and there in a seemingly random way. It wasn't until I realized that the ghost knife had cut through the predator's eyes, blinding it, that I understood that the two parts were trying to find each other.

The hedge closest to the truck had been spared the collapse of the Wilbur house. I quietly took a set of the woven Christmas lights off the top. There was an electric outlet set in the back of the cube truck. I plugged the lights into it, and they lit up dimly.

I clicked my tongue. The ears on the creature's head suddenly turned toward me, then the head vanished and appeared beside me. I draped the lights over it, then folded it twice for good measure. It stopped vanishing and reappearing. I had trapped it. It wasn't the lights—it liked the light—it was the live wires that the predator couldn't cross. The cages had been spiderwebbed with wires, and the pets had been careful to run cables along only three walls in the field house, leaving one open for an escape route.

I held my hand away from my body and snapped my fingers. When the predator shot its tongue toward the sound, I sliced it off with the ghost knife. The severed tongue fell into the mud and shriveled there. Its body staggered, then crumpled to the ground and lay still.

The head could only twitch its ears. I wondered if it could understand me. "Stay away from my world," I whispered to it. The ears twitched back and forth as though it couldn't find the source of my voice. "There are monsters here."

The head shrunk and bowed in on itself. I backpedaled, but there was no second explosion. The head, tongue, and body each seemed to be sucked into a tiny spot, and then they were gone.

There was still another job to do. I walked to the side of the house. All that was left of Ursula was a pair of legs and the hips to hold them together. The rest of her body was simply gone. Even stranger was that there was no gore or exposed organs at the severed part of her torso. That part of her was covered with smooth, unmarked skin, as though she had grown that way naturally.

Zahn was missing his body from the ribs down. He was also missing one arm from just below the shoulder and the other from just below the elbow. When I bent to see if he also had skin over the severed part of his torso, he called me an asshole.

Yeah, I was startled. I knew sorcerers were tough, but this was a bit much.

"Feed me, and I will teach you," he said. His voice

sounded low and strained. "I will show you the world behind the world."

"Pass. I've seen how you treat your people. No loyalty."

"They were simpletons and they failed me. But you are something else, yes? Not even a true sorcerer, and look what you did."

"That's what I do," I told him. My voice sounded flat, and it scared me a little. "I kill."

"I do not believe you. I can see it. You have killed, but you are not a natural killer. You *care* too much for that. The Twenty Palace Society has lied to you, the way they lie to everyone."

"Is this conversation going to take long? Because my socks are wet."

"And you want *power*. For three hundred years I have been looking for someone clever enough to pass my secrets to. I think that could be you. I need meat. Care enough to save my life, and you save three hundred years of history. In return, I will show you real power the *Hosenscheisser* in the society cannot. Come on, boy. Care enough to save one more life."

I couldn't help it. I laughed at him. "You don't get it, do you? I killed kids today because of the deal you made with that predator. *Kids!* If you think I'm going to . . ."

Why was I talking to him?

I dragged the ghost knife through his torso. Black steam blasted out of him. The smooth skin over the bottom of his rib cage where the rest of his body should have been suddenly burst open. He lost blood and magic in a tremendous rush.

I hit him again and again, and it took me a few seconds to realize that he was laughing as well as screaming.

"A ghost knife!" he wheezed. "You are killing me with a ghost knife, and you cast it on a piece of paper!" He screamed, then laughed again, straining every muscle. "I'll bet you do not even realize what you've done!"

I didn't feel like being laughed at just then. I dragged my spell through his face and head, then stuffed Annalise's last green ribbon into his mouth. That was it for him.

Once Zahn was dead, I suddenly thought it might be a good idea to call someone outside Washaway who could help. I took a deep breath and let relief flood through me. The town was no longer sealed. Help would be coming very soon.

I gave his three-hundred-year-old bones a kick for the hell of it.

In the truck I found the lightning rod Zahn had used to summon the floating storms, along with a carpetbag loaded with candles, jars, amulets, and other suspicious crap, all in a mixed-up jumble.

I set all that stuff at the top of the driveway. Then I dragged the bodies into an opening in the side of the house, dropping them into the basement. That was an ugly job, but I didn't have much choice. I wondered whether Regina had gotten away, or was crushed under a beam in the wreckage or rotting in a ditch somewhere, feeding the crows. Maybe I'd never know.

I parked the truck next to the house and lit them both on fire.

It started to rain again as I made my way to the van. The wind was cold. Annalise was as still as before. I loaded the old man's gear into the back of the van and drove away.

EPILOGUE

I hit Redial on Annalise's cell and told the tweedy-sounding guy who answered what was going on. He seemed pissed that I'd called, but to hell with him. After I disconnected the call, I had an itch to call all the hospitals in the area to ask about my mother. It made no sense at all, but the urge was there.

I drove home. It took four hours, but another society investigator was already waiting for me there. I told him and his recorder everything that happened and showed him the stuff I'd taken from Zahn. He seemed impressed for about three seconds, then called up his poker face again.

When I asked about Annalise, he told me not to worry, they had someone who would be able to find her. I was about to tell him to look in the back of the van, because the search was over, but maybe he meant something I didn't understand.

After that, he left. I half expected him to offer me a ride to a safe house or something, but he didn't. I didn't ask.

I didn't deserve to be safe.

I reported my credit cards stolen and called Harvey. I told him I could work my usual shift after the holiday, and he didn't even ask about my mom. Maybe he heard something in my voice and thought better of it.

The fires and violence in Washaway made the national news, of course, but it took a while for the authorities to settle on a story they liked. While they were hashing it out, the remaining pets died. As I'd expected, killing the predator hadn't saved them. Whatever the sapphire dog did to their brains had cut their lives short. None of them survived to the end of the week.

Maybe that should have made me feel better about what I'd done in the food bank, but it didn't.

The state cops, the FBI, Homeland Security, and news crews from every part of the world descended on Washaway. The feds quashed talk of a terrorist attack, but it took a while before they decided to blame it all on international drug violence and the brave local citizens who were killed in the crossfire. Hanging those accusations on Yin and Zahn was a stretch for some folks, but no one had a better explanation. As for Kripke and Solorov, they were inconveniently alive and spent a fortune on lawyers trying to stay out of prison.

Two full shifts of 911 dispatchers lost their jobs for small-talking when they should have been raising alarm bells. Steve Cardinal was singled out for special scorn—they even played a couple of his friendly calls to the state police on the TV. It was unfair to him, but he was past caring.

But I didn't follow any of this from the comfort of my apartment. By Christmas morning, the cops had found my name and brought me in.

I disappeared from the world.

ACKNOWLEDGMENTS

This was not an easy book to write, and I'm tremendously grateful to the people who helped me put it together: Betsy Mitchell, Caitlin Blasdell, Liza Dawson, Beth Pearson, Margaret Wimberger, and many, many others. Thank you all.

Read on for an excerpt from the next
Twenty Palaces novel
by Harry Connolly

COMING SOON
FROM DEL REY BOOKS

It was August in Seattle, when the city enjoyed actual sunshine
and temperatures in the eighties. I'd spent the day working,
which made for a nice change. I'd just finished a forty-hour
temp landscaping job; dirt and dried sweat made my face and
arms itch. I hated the feeling, but even worse was that I didn't
have anything lined up for next week.

As I walked up the alley to home, I passed a pair of older
women standing beside a scraggly vegetable garden. One kept
saying she was sweltering, *sweltering,* but her friend didn't seem
sympathetic. Neither was I. I was used to summers in the desert;
this weather didn't bother me.

When they noticed me, they fell silent. The unsympathetic one
took her friend's hand and led her toward the back door, keeping a wary eye on me. That didn't bother me, either.

I stumped up the stairs to my apartment, above my aunt's
garage. It was too late to call the temp agency tonight; I'd have
to try them early Monday morning. Not that I had much hope.
It was hard for an ex-con to find work, especially an ex-con
with my name.

I'm Raymond Lilly and I've lost track of the number of people
I've killed.

My ancient garage-sale answering machine was blinking. I
played the messages. Two were from reporters, one from a
journalist-blogger, and one from a writer. They offered me the
chance to tell my side of what had happened in Washaway last
Christmas. Except for the writer's, I recognized all the voices—
they'd called many times over the last few weeks, sometimes
several times a day.

I absentmindedly rubbed the tattoos on the backs of my hands.

They looked like artless jailhouse squiggles, but in reality they were magic spells, and I'd be behind bars without them. None of the survivors in Washaway could pick me out of a lineup, and none of the fingerprint or DNA evidence I'd left behind pointed to me anymore. I was on the twisted path.

I erased the messages. There was no point in calling them back. None of them understood the meaning of the words "fuck off."

The sounds of their voices had triggered a low buzzing anger that made me feel slightly out of control. I showered, then dropped my work clothes into the bottom of the tub, scrubbed them clean, and hung them from the curtain rod. I felt much better after that.

I wiped steam from the bathroom window and looked out. My aunt had not hung a paper angel in her kitchen window. That meant I could order in a sandwich for dinner. I put on my sleeping clothes: a T-shirt and a pair of cut-off sweatpants. I could eat alone, in silence, without someone asking how I was sleeping, how I was eating, and wouldn't things be better if I went to talk to someone?

I wouldn't have to say "Thank you, but I can't" a half dozen times. My aunt was right; I'd probably sleep better if I could talk about the nightmares—and what I'd done to bring them on—but I'd be bedding down in a padded room.

I opened my door to dispel the steam, even though an unlocked door felt like a gun at my back. I went to my bathroom mirror and looked carefully. Damn. I was wasting away.

A voice behind me said: "You look like shit."

I yelped and spun around. In an instant, my heart was pounding at my chest as my hand fumbled across the sink looking for something to use as a weapon.

Caramella was standing in the bathroom doorway, and I was so startled to see her that everything went still for a moment. My adrenaline eased and I could hear my harsh breath in the silence. It had been five years or more, and she'd changed quite a bit. Her skin, which had once been so dark, seemed lighter, as though she spent all her time indoors, and while she still straightened her hair, now she had it up in a bun. She wore orange pants with an elastic waistband and a white halter.

She'd gained some weight over the last few years, and she seemed taller somehow.

But she didn't belong here, not in Seattle. She belonged down in L.A., hanging at the Bigfoot Room with Arne, Robbie, and the rest.

I almost asked her what she was doing here, but I didn't want her to think she wasn't welcome. In truth, I didn't know how I felt about her. "Welcome to my bathroom," I said.

"Thanks. I hate it."

I nodded but didn't respond right away. Her hands were empty, although she might have stuffed a gun into the back of her waistband. Not that I could imagine why she'd want to kill me, but that was how my mind worked now.

"I'm guessing you're not here for old times' sake."

"We don't have any old times, Ray." She turned and walked into the other room.

I followed her, noting that she didn't have a weapon under her waistband. "Then why are you here?" I asked. I kept my tone as neutral as I could, although I had less self-control than I used to.

"I'm paying a debt," she said, as though it was the most bitter thing in the world. "I have to deliver a message to you. In person." She stopped beside the efficiency stove.

"Okay. Here I am."

She looked away. Her lip curled and she blinked several times. Christ, she was about to cry. "You killed me, Ray."

I gaped at her, astonished. She turned and slapped me on the shoulder. Then she did it again. That still wasn't enough, and she slapped my face and head four or five times. I didn't try to stop her.

Finally, she stopped on her own. Hitting me wasn't bringing her any satisfaction. "You killed me," she said again. "And you killed Arne, and Lenard, and Ty, and all the others, too. We're all going to die because we knew you."

"Melly, what are you talking about?"

"Sorry," she said with a wet sniffle. I looked for tears on her face, but her cheeks were dry. "That's the message. That's all you get."

She swung at my face again. I flinched away from the blow,

but it never struck. When I opened my eyes a moment later, I was alone in the room.

I had been standing between Caramella and the door; she couldn't have gotten around me and gotten out, not in the time it took me to flinch. I walked around the little studio anyway. She was gone—vanished in the blink of an eye.

Magic. She had magic. Damn.

My cheek and scalp were sticky where she'd slapped me, and the stickiness was starting to burn. I went into the bathroom and washed my face and head. I could feel a smear of acidic goop that was so thin I couldn't even see it. Plain water washed it away completely. When it was gone, my skin was slightly tender, but the pain had eased.

I checked the washrag after, but it didn't have any unusual stains or smells. I hung it over the kitchen faucet.

Back in the living room, I took my ghost knife from its hiding place on my bookshelf. It was only a piece of scrap paper, smaller than the palm of my hand, with a layer of mailing tape over it and some laminate over that. On the paper itself was a sigil I had drawn myself with a ballpoint pen. It felt alive, and it felt like a part of me, too. The other magic I had, the tattoos on my chest, arms, and neck, were protections that had been cast on me by someone else. The ghost knife was my spell, the only one I had.

Then I took my cellphone out of my sock drawer. After the mess in Washaway, an investigator for the Twenty Palace Society had met me on the street and slipped me a phone number. They trusted me enough to give me a way to contact them, which was damned rare and I knew it. If there was ever a time to use that number, this was it.

The society was a group of sorcerers committed to one end: hunting down magic spells and the people who used them, then destroying both. They were especially determined to find summoning spells, which could call strange creatures to our world from a place called, variously, the Empty Spaces or the Deeps. These creatures, called predators, could grant strange powers, if the summoner knew how to properly control them. Too often, the summoner didn't know, and the predator got loose in the world to hunt.

I was a low-level member of that society, but except for my boss, Annalise, who had put the magical tattoos on me, I knew very little about it. How many peers were there? How many investigators? How many wooden men, besides me, did they have? Where were they based? Where did their money come from?

I had no idea and no way to find out. The Twenty Palace Society took their secrecy seriously. I hadn't been invited to secret headquarters, hadn't trained at a secret camp, hadn't been given a secret handbook with an organizational flow chart at the back. When they wanted me to do something, they contacted me, and they told me as little as they could.

What I did know was this: peers lived a very long time—centuries, in some cases—and the magic they used had left them barely human. Oh, they looked human enough, but they had become something else.

And they were bastards, too—ruthless killers who took a scorched-earth policy when it came to predators and enemy sorcerers. As a group, they didn't seem to care much about collateral damage.

They had their reasons. A single predator, let loose in the world, could strip it of life. I'd visited the Empty Spaces once and seen it happen. So maybe the peers were justified in their "kill a hundred to save six billion" attitude, but it was a slim consolation if your loved one was one of the hundred.

Which was why I set the cell back on the bureau. Caramella had vanished right in front of me. It was magic, yeah, but calling the Twenty Palace Society and asking Annalise to meet me in L.A. was as good as taking a hit out on Mella and everyone else I knew. Annalise would kill them all just to be safe, and I would be the one who hung a bull's-eye on their backs.